A Serpent's Tooth

CRAIG JOHNSON

A SERPENT'S TOOTH

VIKING

VIKING
Published by the Penguin Group
Penguin Group (USA) Inc., 375 Hudson Street,
New York, New York 10014, USA

USA | Canada | UK | Ireland | Australia | New Zealand | India | South Africa | China

Penguin Books Ltd, Registered Offices: 80 Strand, London WC2R 0RL, England
For more information about the Penguin Group visit penguin.com

Library of Congress Cataloging-in-Publication Data

Johnson, Craig.
A serpent's tooth / Craig Johnson.
pages cm. — (A Walt Longmire mystery)
ISBN 978-0-670-02645-6
1. Longmire, Walt (Fictitious character)—Fiction.   2. Sheriffs—Fiction.
3. Mothers and sons—Fiction.   4. Missing persons—Fiction.   5. Mormons—Fiction.   I. Title.
PS3610.O325S47 2013b
813'.6—dc23   2013001530

Printed in the United States of America
1   3   5   7   9   10   8   6   4   2

Set in Dante MT Std
Book design by Alissa Amell

For N.B. East (1938–2011),
who taught me how important the words are.

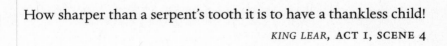

How sharper than a serpent's tooth it is to have a thankless child!

KING LEAR, ACT I, SCENE 4

ACKNOWLEDGMENTS

Every once in a while you've got to step into the epic, even if it means getting your boots a little muddy; what I know about religion, gas, oil, and Hughes drill bits you could put on the head of a Polycrystalline diamond, but I was fortunate enough to get help from the folks down at the Casper office of the Wyoming Oil & Gas Conservation Commission to steer me in the right directions so that I could sip from the Teapot Dome.

Also helpful were Drew Goodman, who helped me with the religious implications of handling the snakes, David Nickerson, who held the medical kit, and Benj Horack for the .410 snake charmer.

The Teapot Dome Oil Field is a wild place and you need snake gaiters on your boots and a trusty shovel, but it's even better to have serpentine guides like my own Gail "Coral Snake" Hochman, and Marianne "Diamondback Rattler" Merola. Winding their way through the editing is Kathryn "King Cobra" Court and Tara "Tiger Snake" Singh, copyeditor Barbara "Black Mamba" Campo and Scott "Desert Horned Viper" Cohen. The open road can also be dangerous but not when you've got a pack of charmers like Carolyn "Copperhead" Coleburn, Maureen "Multibanded Krait" Donnelly, Ben "Puff Adder" Petrone and Angie "Anaconda" Messina.

And, as always, the little Asp I always hold to my breast, Judy.

A Serpent's Tooth

1

I stared at the black-and-orange corsage on Barbara Thomas's lapel so that I wouldn't have to look at anything else.

I don't like funerals, and a while ago I just stopped going to them. I think the ceremony is a form of denial, and when my wife died and my daughter, Cady, informed me that she was unaware of any instance where going to somebody's funeral ever brought them back, I just about gave it up.

Mrs. Thomas had been the homecoming queen when Truman made sure that the buck stopped with him, which explained the somewhat garish ornament pinned on her prim and proper beige suit. Next week was the big game between the Durant Dogies and their archrival, the Worland Warriors, and the whole town was black-and-orange crazy.

The only thing worse than going to the funeral of someone you knew is going to the funeral of a person you didn't; you get to stand there and be told about somebody you had never met, and all I ever feel is that I missed my chance.

I had missed my chance with Dulcie Meriwether, who had been one of Durant's fine and upstanding women—after all, I'm the sheriff of Absaroka County, so the fine and upstanding often live and pass beyond my notice. On a fine October afternoon I leaned against the railing leading to the First Methodist Church, not so much to praise Dulcie Meriwether—or to bury her—but rather to talk about angels.

I reached out and straightened Barbara Thomas's corsage.

One of the jobs of an elected official in Wyoming is to understand one's constituency and listen to people—help them with their problems—even if they're bat-shit crazy. I was listening to Barbara tell me about the angels who were currently assisting her with home repair, which I took as proof that she had passed the entrance exam to that particular belfry.

I glanced at Mike Thomas, who had asked me to bushwhack his aunt on this early high plains afternoon. He wanted me to talk to her and figured the only way he could arrange running into me was by having me stand outside the church and wait for the two of them as they departed for a late lunch after the service.

I was trying not to look at the other person leaning on the railing with me, my undersheriff, Victoria Moretti, who, although she was trying to work off a hangover from too much revelry at the Basque Festival bacchanal the night before, had decided to take advantage of my being in town on a Sunday. The only person left to look at was Barbara, eighty-two years old, platinum hair coiffed to perfection, and, evidently, mad as a hatter.

"So, when did the angels pitch in and start working around your place, Mrs. Thomas?"

"Call me Barbara, Walter." She nodded her head earnestly, as if she didn't want us to think she was crazy.

As Vic would say, "Good luck with that."

"About two weeks ago I made a little list and suddenly the railing on the front porch was fixed." She leveled a malevolent glance at the well-dressed cowboy in the navy blazer and tie to my left, her youngest nephew. "It's difficult to get things done around home since Michael lives so far away."

As near as I could remember, Mike's sculpture studio was

right at the edge of town, and I knew he lived only two miles east, but that was between the two of them. I adjusted the collar of my flannel shirt, enjoying the fact that I wasn't in uniform today, figuring it was going to be the extent of my daily pleasure. "So, the angels came and fixed the railing?"

"Yes."

"Anything else?"

She nodded again, enthusiastically. "Lots of things—they unclogged my gutters, rehung the screen door on the back porch, and fixed the roof on the pump house."

Vic sighed. "Jesus, you wanna send 'em over to my place?"

I ignored my undersheriff, which was difficult to do. She was wearing a summer dress in an attempt to forestall the season, and a marvelous portion of her tanned legs was revealed above her boots and below the hem. "Have you ever actually seen the angels, Mrs. Thomas?"

"Barbara, please." She shook her head, indulging my lack of knowledge of all things celestial. "They don't work that way."

"So, how do they work?"

She placed the palms of her hands together and leaned forward. "I make my little list, and the things just get done. It's a sign of divine providence."

Vic mumbled under her breath. "It's a sign of divine senility."

Barbara Thomas continued without breaking stride. "I have a notebook where I number the things that have to be done in order of importance, then I leave it on the room divider and presto." She leaned back and beamed at me. "He works in mysterious ways." She paused for a moment to glance at the church looming over my shoulder and then altered the subject. "You used to go to services here, didn't you, Walter?"

"Yes, ma'am, I used to accompany my late wife."

"But you haven't been since she passed away?"

I took a deep breath to relieve the tightness in my chest the way I always did when anybody brought up the subject of Martha. "No, ma'am. We had an agreement that she'd take care of the next world if I took care of this one." I glanced at Mike as he smoothed his mustache and tried not to smile. "And there seems to be enough to hold my attention here lately." I turned my eyes back to her. "So you haven't ever seen them?"

"Seen who?"

"The holy handymen, for Christ's sake."

Barbara looked annoyed. "Young lady, you need to watch your language."

I drew Barbara's attention away from a sure-shot, head-on, verbal train wreck. "So you haven't actually seen the angels then?"

"No." She thought about it and stared at the cracks in the sidewalk, the strands of struggling grass having abandoned the hope of pushing through. "They do take some food out of the icebox every now and again."

I kept my eyes on her. "Food?"

"Yes." She thought some more. "And they sometimes take a shower."

"A shower."

She was nodding again. "But they always clean up after themselves; I just notice because the towels are damp or there are a few pieces of fried chicken missing."

I shot Mike a look, but he was studying the banks of Clear Creek on the other side of the gravel walk a little ways away, probably checking for trout and wishing he was somewhere else. My eyes tracked back to the elderly woman. "Fried chicken."

"Yes, it would appear that angels really like Chester's fried chicken."

I leaned back on the railing and watched the dancing pattern of light on the water for a while myself, the scattered golden leaves of the aspens spinning like a lost flotilla. "I see."

"And Oreos; the angels like Double Stuf Oreos, too."

"Anything else?"

"Vernors Diet Ginger Ale."

"You must be running up quite a grocery bill feeding the legions." I smiled and chose my next words carefully. "Barbara, when these things happen . . . I mean, do you make your list and then go to bed and get up and everything is repaired?"

"Oh no, I do my agenda in the morning, then I go out to run my errands or go to my bridge club, and when I get back everything's done."

"In the morning?"

"By the middle of the afternoon, yes."

I pulled out my pocket watch and looked at it, noticing it was ten after one. "So if I were to head over to your place right now, it's likely that I might catch the angels at their labors?"

She looked a little worried. "I suppose."

"What is it you've got them doing today?"

She thought. "There's a leak in the trap under the kitchen sink."

Vic couldn't hold her peace. "Wait, angels work on Sundays?"

I looked at the nice but crazy old lady. "Where do they get parts on a Sunday; Buell Hardware is closed."

Her eyes narrowed. "I get them the supplies, Walter. The Lord provides, but I don't think that extends to plumbing parts."

"Hmm . . ." I stood up, and she looked concerned.

"Where are you going?"

"I think I'll drive by your place while you and Mike have lunch." I shrugged. "Maybe see if we can get Vic here a little divine guidance."

Barbara Thomas folded her hands like broken-winged birds and spoke in a quiet voice. "I'd rather you didn't, Walter."

I waited a moment and then asked, "And why is that?"

She paused, just a little petulant, and then looked up at me with damp eyes. "They do good works, and you shouldn't interrupt good works."

"Do you think there are more crazy people in our county than anywhere else?"

We drove west of town in the direction of Barbara Thomas's house, and I turned down the air in the Bullet so that the fan would not blow Vic's dress any higher on her smooth thighs as she propped her cowboy boots on the escarpment of the dash. "Per capita?"

"In general."

I redirected a vent in the direction of Dog, panting in the backseat. "Well, nature hates a vacuum and strange things are drawn into empty places; sometimes oddities survive where nothing else can." I glanced over at her. "Why?"

"That would include us?"

"Technically."

She glanced out the windshield, her face a little troubled. "I don't want to end up alone in a house making lists for my imaginary friends."

I took a left onto Klondike Drive and thought about how Vic had seemed to be given to philosophical musings as of late. "Somehow, I don't see that happening."

She glanced at me. "I noticed you didn't offer to share your experiences with the spirit world with her."

Vic was referring to the events in the Cloud Peak Wilderness Area that I'd had in the spring, an experience I wasn't sure I'd even fully processed yet. "It didn't seem pertinent."

"Uh-huh."

I gave her a look back and noticed she was massaging one temple with her fingers. "How's your head?"

"Like hell, thanks for asking."

"You mind if I inquire as to what happened at the Basque Festival?"

She adjusted her boots on the dash and confessed. "I was traumatized."

"By what?"

"The running of the sheep."

I thought I must've misheard. "The what?"

"The running of the fucking sheep, which you conveniently missed by taking the day off yesterday."

"The running of the sheep?"

She massaged the bridge of her nose. "You heard me."

"What happened?"

"I don't want to talk about it; you don't want to talk about your imaginary friends, and I don't want to talk about the running of the sheep." She played with the pull strap on her boot. "Suffice to say that I am not working the Basque Festival ever again."

I shrugged as we passed the YMCA and continued down the hill and past Duffy, the vintage locomotive in the park at the children's center. I took a right on Upper Clear Creek Road, then pulled up and parked under the shade of a yellowing cottonwood next to Barbara Thomas's mailbox.

"We're walking?"

"There's shade here, and Dog is hot." I lowered the windows to give him a little extra air. "Besides, I like to sneak up on my angels. How about you?"

She cracked open the passenger-side door and slipped out, pulling her skirt down. Boots and short skirts—a look for which I held a great weakness. "I'm not exactly dressed for a footrace."

I closed the door quietly and moved around to the front of the truck to meet her. "I thought angels flew."

"Yeah, and shit floats."

We walked down the steep gravel driveway that ended in one of those old-time Model T garages and the tiny clapboard house that had been the headquarters for the T Bar T Ranch in years past, before housing developments had chiseled the land away. There was an abundance of raised flower beds and hanging baskets, and I had to admit that whoever the angels were; they were doing a heck of a job, especially this late in the season.

Her tarnished gold eyes flashed. "By the book?"

I looked at her lupine smile and thought about how you could take the patrolman out of South Philadelphia, but you couldn't take the South Philly out of the patrolman. "Look, it's probably some kindhearted neighbor doing the old girl a favor, so let's not scare them to death, okay?"

"Whatever." She started for the porch, and I watched the faded purple dress flounce from her hips as she stalked off, unarmed. "Calling front."

I sighed and started around the back, slipping between the tiny garage and the house. I looked in the kitchen window and paused when I saw a set of legs sticking out from under the open cabinet doors of the sink. Covering the legs were a pair of olive green work pants, the kind custodians wear, and the feet were encased in a pair of heavy brogans without socks.

I shook my head and continued on, wondering which Good Samaritan from the neighborhood this might be. I climbed the concrete stoop that led into the kitchen, pushed the button on the newly rehung screen door, and announced myself. "All right, mysterious home repair, who's . . ."

My voice plugged in my throat when an extremely thin young man catapulted from underneath the sink and braced himself against the side-by-side refrigerator. I had a few seconds to study him—he was an odd bird, looked like a scarecrow with the over-sized pants tied at the waist with a piece of hemp rope and a tan work shirt that also looked to be about two sizes too large. His eyes were the bluest blue I'd ever seen—almost cobalt, wide and deep set. He had a noble prince look about him, but maybe it was the blond, Prince Valiant haircut.

I raised a hand in assurance and unplugged my voice. "Um, howdy."

The assurance was short lived, and he leapt from the room straight into Vic, who was standing in the doorway leading to the living room and front door. He rammed his way past her, but to give her credit, even with a bloodied nose, she clung to his pant leg as he dragged her along with him. "Motherfucker!"

I made the four strides between us just as the pants slipped from his narrow hips. He darted into the living room, bounced off the room divider, and hurtled through the doorway. I watched helplessly as he skimmed off the porch and was gone like a sidewinder.

I didn't even bother pretending to chase him, went back into the kitchen, pulled a dishcloth from the stem of the spigot, and dampened it. I got some ice from the freezer and held it out to my undersheriff as she stood and looked at me. "If I'd had my gun, I would've shot the little asshole."

"Did he hit you?"

"His knee did when he bowled me over."

Tipping her head back, I leaned her against the kitchen counter. "I don't think I've ever seen anybody that scared before in my life."

She held the cloth to her nose, muffling her voice. "Wait'll I get ahold of him again."

I stretched the cord of the rotary phone over to where she stood, called 911, and pulled the cloth away to examine the damage. It was swelling, but it didn't look as if anything was broken. "You're going to have a couple of beauties there."

The phone at my ear suddenly came alive. "Absaroka County Sheriff's Office; you have an emergency?"

"Yep, Vic is going to kill a fifteen-year-old kid."

"Sheriff?"

I listened as Ruby's phone cradle jostled on his shoulder. "Double Tough, is that you?" I never was sure who was scheduled to rotate up from Powder Junction for weekend duty since Santiago Saizarbitoria, one of my other deputies, had run off to visit family in Rawlins for a couple of weeks.

"Yup, what's up?"

"I've got a fugitive on the loose over here on Upper Clear Creek Road, and sure would appreciate it if you caught him before Vic does."

I listened as he scrambled his way around my dispatcher's desk. "What kind of fugitive, Walt?"

"Male Caucasian, approximately fifteen years of age, blond hair, blue eyes with an expression like he's cleared for takeoff—and he was."

I listened as Double Tough started to sign off. "Got it."

"One more thing."

"Yup, Chief?"

I picked up the pair of pants from the edge of the counter where I'd put them. "He's naked from the waist down."

For the first time in the conversation, my deputy was given pause. "Well, that should make things a little easier."

It didn't.

We rummaged the entire neighborhood once and then again but came up with nothing. We were in the office, where Vic sat with a sack of frozen petite peas on her nose and watched me close last year's Durant High School yearbook. "He's not in here."

She looked at me from over the bag of vegetables. "You're sure?"

"Positive."

"You got the age right?"

"I think so." I reached down and ruffled Dog's ears; he liked the relative cool of my abandoned office and the quiet of a Sunday afternoon. "I guess you didn't get a very good look at him."

She stretched her jaw in an attempt to loosen her facial muscles and stared at the escapee's pants on her lap. "You mean did I get the number of the skinny truck that hit me? No."

"Then he's from out of town."

She studied the inside band of the pants. "Maybe." She rested the frozen pouch on the dried bloodstains that were discoloring the neck of her dress. "What?"

"Are you sure you don't want to get your nose X-rayed?"

She dismissed me with a flapping of her hand. "What about the kid?"

"He just seemed odd."

The next statement fairly flooded with sarcasm. "Really?"

I conjured up the brief image of the scared young man and held it there in front of my eyes. "The way he stood there for that moment: flexing his hands repeatedly, no eye contact, on the balls of his feet . . ."

"He's a 'tard?"

I sighed and felt the bridge of my own nose. "Just . . . odd."

"Health Services?"

I dialed the number and listened as it transferred me to the answering machine; Nancy Griffith asked me to record a message. I declined and placed the receiver on the cradle.

I pulled the phone book from the top drawer of my desk and leafed through to the G's. "This stuff is a lot easier when Ruby's around." I pinned Nancy with a forefinger and dialed. On the third ring she answered, and I described a young man she'd never seen. "You're sure?"

"Positive. The description doesn't match up with any of our current clients. Have you tried the Wyoming Boys' School?"

"In Worland?"

"Stranger things have happened." I listened as she chuckled and was reminded that she had sung in the church choir with Martha. "Hey, are you going to the football game on Friday?"

"Why, is there a problem?"

She waited a moment before responding. "Does there always have to be a problem when you're invited somewhere?"

"Generally."

"It's homecoming, and they're retiring your number."

"Oh."

"They're retiring Henry Standing Bear's number, too. Didn't anyone get ahold of you?" There was another pause, but it wasn't long enough for me to come up with an answer or an excuse. "I think everybody up at the high school would appreciate it if the two of you showed up at halftime for the celebration."

"Friday. Um . . . I'll see what I can do. Thanks, Nance."

I hung up the phone and watched as Vic reapplied the now-not-so-frozen peas to her nose. "What was all that about?"

"What?"

"Friday."

"Nothing." I continued to think about the odd young man as I looked at the Durant Dogies annual on my desk. "He's got to live in the neighborhood."

"Was she just asking you out on a date?"

"What?" I glanced back up at her. "No."

Her tone became a little sharper. "Then what's Friday?"

"A football thing; they're going to retire my number."

She looked amused. "You're kidding."

"Nope. Henry's, too."

"I wanna go."

"No."

"C'mon, I never got to do that crap when I was a teenager." She thought about it. "I never dated any football guys in high school."

I was momentarily distracted. "What kind of guys did you date?"

"Thirty-seven-year-olds named Rudy with mustaches and vans—guys that would give my parents heart attacks." She studied me. "I wanna go, and I want a corsage, just like Babs." I didn't respond and slumped in my guest chair. "Please tell me we're not going to canvas the neighborhood in the short bus with have-you-seen-this-half-naked-retard posters?"

"I thought we'd knock on a few doors."

"That or we just bait a few Havahart traps with Double Stuf Oreos." She struggled to her feet. "But I don't think we have to do that here." She reached down and held up the inside band of the pants toward me. It read CITY OF BELLE FOURCHE DEPARTMENT OF SANITATION.

I made a few more phone calls to the services in Butte County, South Dakota, that were open on a Sunday afternoon, but they didn't know anything about a runaway, so we met Double Tough at the gravel turnout above the T Bar T. "Nothing?"

The ex–oil rig jockey was built like a brick pillar. When I first met him he'd been shot, something he'd neglected to mention until later in the conversation; hence, his nickname. "Nope, and I asked at every house within a quarter mile of the place."

"Nobody's seen him or heard of him?"

"Nope."

I glanced down the driveway toward the little white house with the red shutters. "I'll go down and tell Barbara that I'm going to have a look. Why don't you two just hang around up here in the shade and watch Dog?"

As I walked off, I heard Double Tough ask about Vic's nose. Just because he was double tough didn't mean he was double smart. I made my way to the front porch and told Mrs. Thomas about my intentions. "You don't have to do that, Walter."

"I'd feel better if I had a look around. If you don't know this young man or anything about him, it might be best if we at least spoke with him."

She nodded but there wasn't much enthusiasm in it.

As she closed the door, I made my way across the front of the house to the small garage and entered from the side door, which was adjacent to the walkway alongside the house. There was a scary-looking 1969 Mustang convertible with badges on the side that read COBRA JET. It was semihidden underneath a car cover and was a testament to Bill Thomas's last vehicular purchase before his death in '71. The thing probably had a thousand miles on the odometer and was the lust of every driving-age male in the county.

There was a workbench to my right with an assortment of baby food jars filled with screws and nails that probably dated back to Fort Fetterman, but there were a lot of hand tools that looked as though they'd been used recently, as well as spare lumber that had been placed in the rafters, along with a hidden stack of vintage *Playboy* magazines. Other than that, the place looked undisturbed.

I closed the door behind me and remembered something Barbara had said about a pump house. We live in the high desert, and considering that the yard was very green and the flower beds abundant with blooms, I figured the water had to come from somewhere.

Following my boots down a path overgrown with wild morning glories toward the bank of Clear Creek, I veered in the direction of the bridge. I could see the pitched roof of the outbuilding that had had its shingles repaired recently and could even make out the restored patch.

The grass was higher as I cut off from the walkway, and I waded through the stalks to the small pad at the front. There was a clasp screwed into the surface of the door, but the rusted Master Lock was loose, and I unhooked it from the loop and pulled the door open with the wooden handle. It had probably been a smoke house at some point, which would explain the faint odor of charred wood—that and the rusted points in the rafters that were stained from the places where some kind of meat hook had been attached.

There was a small 2.5 horsepower irrigation pump feeding water from the creek to a system with pipes that rose up through the dirt floor and then returned in two-inch diameters. I walked around the pump, placed my hand on the outgoing line, and felt the surge of cold water as it flowed through.

As my eyes settled in the gloom, I could see that there was a steel, fold-up bunk running along the wall on the other side—the kind people used to use for guests. There was an old military blanket on the twin mattress, tucked in so tight you could have bounced a roll of quarters off of it.

When I got to the bed, I heard a different sound under my boots and stepped back, revealing the vague outline of something square buried in the floor. I kneeled down and brushed away some of the dust. There was a small hook on one side, so I moved it and lifted the lid of what appeared to be an old milk jug container buried in the dry dirt. It was dark in the hole, and I wished

I was wearing my duty belt with my trusty Maglite attached, but instead, I just stuck my hand in the submerged box.

The first thing I found was a magazine—*Gun Buyer's Annual*, this year's date. It was an encyclopedic guide to all the weapons available on the private market. The illustrations on the glossy cover, starring a collection of rifles, shotguns, semiautomatics, and radical carbines, had been thumbed away at the center where someone had spent hours studying the thing. I opened the magazine—practically every page was dog-eared.

I set it aside and reached into the hole again, this time coming up with a copy of *Playboy*, January 1972. The magazine was as worn as the gun almanac, and I had to admit that Marilyn Cole, leaning against a bookcase with a novel in her hands and little else, was still looking good considering her photo was over a quarter of a century old and folded into three equal parts.

I rested what hardly seemed to be even mild porn anymore on the stack with the gun porn and reached into the hole again, this time pulling out a moldy-looking tome—threadbare black with gold lettering—the Book of Mormon. When I carefully opened the cover, I noticed that it was published in 1859, and the handwritten inscription on the title page read "For my son Orrin, Man of God, Son of Thunder—your loving mother, Sara."

I tucked the antiquarian book under my arm and stuck my hand back in the container in the floor but couldn't feel anything else. I looked around the place for something, anything, but there was nothing. I returned everything except the book back to the hole, closed the lid, and kicked a little dirt back over it. I stood, keeping the book with me, and walked around the pump to give the dirt-floored room one more going-over. I stepped through the door, closed it, and hooked the clasp of the lock back through the loop, careful to leave it as I'd found it.

When I got back to Barbara Thomas's home, I rapped my knuckles on the screen door and waited until Barbara appeared on the other side of the tiny squares, her image pixelated into a thousand parts. I held up the book and asked, "Who's Orrin?"

She placed a hand against the doorjamb for support and silently put her other hand to her mouth.

"I don't know where he's from."

I watched as Double Tough took another cookie from the plate on the kitchen counter. Barbara, Vic, and I and the Book of Mormon sat at the kitchen table trying to sort things out. "Well, when was the first time you saw him?"

"Like I said, about two weeks ago."

"You also said he was an angel."

She blinked and looked out the kitchen window leading toward Clear Creek and the pump house. "I . . . I might have been confused about that."

Vic had discarded the now-thawed peas for a cold pack, and her voice was thankfully muffled through the dish towel. "Amen, sister."

"Have you spoken with him?"

"No."

"Where did he get the cot and blanket?"

She thought, as she continued to look out the window. "There were things in the garage that I noticed were missing, but I didn't really connect the two." Her eyes came back to me. "Do you really think he's been living in the pump house these last few weeks?"

"I'd say it's a safe assumption; how, exactly, have you been feeding him?"

She looked at Double Tough, still munching on a cookie. "I just leave the food on the counter."

My deputy, feeling a little self-conscious, threw out a review as he chewed. "Oatmeal–Chocolate chip, they're really good."

The older woman's eyes returned to mine. "Can't we just leave him alone?"

I cleared my throat. "Um, no, we can't. . . . He's not a stray cat, Mrs. Thomas; we've got to find out who he is and where he belongs. There might be people out there looking for him. You understand."

"I do."

I picked up the book and opened it to the title page. "A couple of assumptions I'm making are that he's Mormon and that his name is Orrin."

Vic couldn't resist. "Orrin the Mormon?"

I ignored her and continued. "I'm going to place my deputy here in your house this evening, if you don't mind, in hopes that the boy will return."

She nodded, first looking at Vic and then settling on Double Tough. "That'll be fine."

I stood and gave my Powder Junction deputy his command. "I'll come by at around eleven to spell you, if that sounds good."

He picked up another cookie and nodded. "Yup."

"And try not to eat all the cookies."

He didn't answer as he took a seat by the kitchen window, lifted his tactical binoculars to his eyes to view the pump house, and chewed.

Vic fed her uneaten pizza crust to Dog as she picked up a can from my Rainier stash and gulped. "Shit, I just wish someone around here would do decent pizza." She wiped the back of her hand across her mouth and the front on Dog's head. "I checked the National Crime Information Center for info on Orrin the Mormon but so far he's about as available as the Holy Ghost. I left a message at the local Church of Latter-day Saints—who knew there was one here—with Bishop Drew Goodman and even checked with social services over in Utah, but so far nobody's ever heard of the kid."

I sipped my own beer and flipped through the pages of the Mormon Bible. "This thing is probably worth a fortune."

"What about the City of Belle Fourche's traveling pants?"

I set my beer down. "I'll call over to Tim Berg—the sheriff over there—and see if he has any ideas about the pants or the kid."

She held her beer close to her lips and smiled the crocodile smile. "The human pencil holder?"

"Yep." During classes at the National Sheriffs' Association, Tim was famous for placing numerous pens and pencils in his prodigious beard and then forgetting them.

She looked up at the old Seth Thomas hanging on the wall of my office, the hands gesturing toward 10:45 like Carol Merrill from *Let's Make a Deal*. "I was thinking about hanging around and seducing you, but my nose hurts, so I might take it home and go to bed." She took another sip of her beer and then held the cool of the can to the spot between her eyes. "How do I look?"

I studied the two small wings of purple unfurling beneath her lower lids. "Like you coulda been a contendah."

"Yeah, well, if I catch Orrin the Mormon I'm going to pound his head like a friggin' bongo." She stood and stretched, the dress hem riding up her thighs as she sang in a thick Italian accent, à la Rosemary Clooney, "Come on-a my house, my house. I'm-a gonna give you candy."

I smiled up at her. "I thought your nose hurt."

She backed into my office doorway and attempted to draw me

forward by crooking an index finger. "It does, but I just remembered a great way to take my mind off it."

I gathered up the detritus of our impromptu feast, crushed a few of the cans, and tossed them into the empty box—I knew I'd catch hell from Ruby if I left beer cans in the office trash. "I've got to relieve Double Tough in twenty-five minutes."

"We could make it a quickie."

I closed the box, picked it up, and walked around my desk to meet her. "What do you hear from the newlyweds?" Her face darkened beyond the black eyes, and I suddenly realized that clouds were gathering and lightning was flashing in the tarnished gold pupils. "What?"

"I've warned you about that."

"What?"

She leaned against the door frame and downed the last of her beer. "Every time I talk about us, you talk about them." She pushed off the frame and looked up at me, placing the empty can on the flat surface of my box like a smokestack. "I'm not going to get all Freudian and try and figure that out, so just stop. Okay?"

"Okay."

She turned, walked past Ruby's desk, and paused to curtsy, her hair, which she had grown out, striped with highlights. "By the way, you lost your shot at a quickie."

She disappeared down the steps, and I heard the heavy glass doors swing shut as I called after her, "I kind of figured that."

Dog, probably hoping for another crust, appeared at my leg as I took a few steps down the hall toward the holding cells and the back door. "C'mon, you want to go to the Dumpster?" I glanced over my shoulder and noticed he'd sat. "I'll take that as a no?" He didn't move, so I continued on my own. "Well, you're going over to Barbara Thomas's place here in a few minutes whether you like it or not."

I pushed open the heavy metal and carefully nudged the broken portion of concrete block that we all used to prop open the door, which saved the staff the ignominious march around the building to the front entrance that Vic had deemed "the walk of shame and ignorance."

In the distance I could hear my undersheriff ignoring our two red-blinking traffic lights as she sped through town.

Balancing the empty Rainier on the box, I started toward the Dumpster just as a sudden breeze kicked up, which spun the can off the cardboard surface like an aluminum tumbleweed. It skittered across the street toward the fence at Meadowlark Elementary.

"Well, hell."

I continued on my way, slipped the trash under the plastic lid, and then started the trek across the street; I figured that if beer cans weren't allowed in the sheriff's office trash, they probably shouldn't linger next to the elementary school fence either.

The little bugger was continuing to bump against the chain-link, and it took two tries before I got hold of the thing. Feeling the weight of the day, I placed an elbow on the top bar of the fence and stood there enjoying the temperature drop of the evening. It was getting late in the season, and the nights were getting cooler. I thought about what Nancy had said about the weekend, tried to remember what my number had been, and then reminded myself to call the Bear and tell him about the honors that were being bestowed on us Friday night.

I shivered just a little and figured the first frost would be pretty soon and I'd be switching over to my felt hat. I let my mind wander again, this time to what Vic had said, wondering if it was true. Her youngest brother had married my daughter a few months back, and I was hearing from Cady less and less. Delving into a little Freudian slip of my own, I wondered if that anxiety had intertwined with my worries about being even more involved with my undersheriff lately. I didn't consider myself a prude, but the difference in our ages and the fact that I was her boss continued to intrude on my thoughts.

She'd been even a little more volatile as of late, and I wasn't quite sure what that was about.

I allowed my eyes to drift across the freshly mowed east lawn of Meadowlark Elementary when I noticed that somebody was swinging on the playground, his body hurtling into the freshening air, each effort accompanied by the clanking of the chains that supported the swing. He was facing in the other direction, but I could see that he was skinny, startlingly blond—and missing his pants.

2

I had to time it right because I was only going to get one chance.

Keeping behind him, I'd stealthily made my way across the lawn and could only hope that I'd be able to withstand the impact when he swung back. He probably was only a hundred and thirty pounds soaking wet, but he had velocity on his side.

Figuring I'd have only an instant before he sprinted for it again, I'd fastened one side of a pair of handcuffs to my own wrist and was holding the other open and ready to snap closed. By my reckoning, even as fast as he was, Orrin wasn't going to be able to drag my two hundred and fifty pounds very far.

I was maybe ten feet behind his backward arc as he peaked and went forward. I could hear him humming as he skimmed through the air, and I ran forward to position myself a little ahead of the angle of trajectory in hopes of not absorbing the entirety of his velocity, but it didn't really do any good.

I'd been an interior lineman at USC, a Marine investigator in Vietnam, and had taken my share of body blows, but that had been an awfully long time ago, when I had been in better shape and a lot younger. The impact of his bony back into my chest wasn't so bad, but he had curled one of the brogans up under the seat and it planted itself firmly in my crotch.

As luck would have some of it, the cuff had closed around the kid's upper arm, which wasn't as big as the joint at his elbow, and had latched secure. I had fallen backward and pulled him with me, but as soon as we hit the ground, he'd jumped up and, as I'd anticipated, started off. My arm was the only thing he moved, and he yanked himself backward on top of me as he tried the opposite direction, perhaps thinking he would have better luck. My arm crossed my chest after he tromped across me, but at the moment, all I could do was massage my groin and lie there like a ball and chain.

I guess he'd gotten the best of my patience at that point, because I remember curling my bicep and pulling his face in close to mine. "You need to quit that. Now."

He looked terribly scared, but he kicked at me some more, so I finally stood in a hunched fashion and breathed out my final word on the subject. "Stop."

He pulled back from the word, and I was sure he thought I was going to hit him.

I took a deep breath. "Are you all right?"

He fidgeted, flung his loose hand back and forth, and looked at my chest, finally nodding his head. "Yes."

His voice was higher than I would've thought, but I was just glad he could speak. "What's your name?"

He looked around nervously, still looking for an avenue of escape, but seeing none, he kind of collapsed into himself and muttered, "Cord."

I stood fully upright, and the fear played across his face. I was anxious that the populace not be treated to the sight of a grown man massaging his groin, handcuffed to a teenager in nothing but a shirt in the elementary school playground close to midnight. "C'mon Cord, let's go get you some clothes."

When I got him back to the office, I planted him in my guest chair and recuffed him to the arm. Dog watched us from across the room with a great deal of interest. "I'm, um . . . I'm going to go get you some clothes, so just wait here till I get back."

I vaguely remembered Ruby having had a clothing drive for the Methodist Women's League a month back, and that there were still a few bags of assorted clothing downstairs out of which I might find something to fit the young man.

Passing my dispatcher's desk with Dog in tow, I stopped for a moment to phone Double Tough and inform him that the great Mormon manhunt could be called off. As I stood there talking to him, Dog and I both heard some noise from down the hallway and turned to see the boy had fallen in his attempt to drag the chair along with him out the back door.

"I gotta go."

I walked into the hallway, picked him up, and sat him back in the chair, then picked up the chair and walked him back into my office. I set the chair in its original location, called Dog, and told him to sit, which he did. "That is the K-9 unit of the Absaroka County Sheriff's Department, and he's trained to deal with any kind of situation. I can't say what he might do, but I would advise you not to move. Is that clear?"

He nodded. "Yes."

"Good." I glanced at Dog, who I'm sure was wondering what the heck I was talking about. "Stay. And . . . Guard."

He canted his head, looking at me as if I were an idiot, which of course I was.

The kid was looking at Dog as if the beast might go for his throat at any moment, which, of course, he wouldn't, but a nod being as good as a wink in most cases, I turned and went down the steps and rifled through the grocery bags, finally coming up with a Denver Broncos T-shirt and, more important, a pair of gray sweatpants with a hole in only one knee.

I'd started back up the stairs when I heard another commotion.

I got to the first landing at the corner of the building near the front door in time to see Double Tough laying hands on both boy and furniture.

The solid deputy turned with a comical look on his face as he sat the young man in the chair. "I guess you can add theft of municipal property to his list of offenses."

I joined the group—Dog was standing there wagging. "Some guard dog you are."

We carried the prisoner and chair back to my office, where I uncuffed him and led him to the bathroom in the hall, the one without a window, handed him the clothes, and nudged him inside as I closed the door behind him. "Get dressed."

Producing a plastic bag of oatmeal cookies, Double Tough crossed his scuffed ropers, leaned against the wall, and smirked at me. "Have a cookie." I did, as he studied me. "Call up Health Services?"

I thought about it. "Not at midnight. I'll just wait until morning and then give Nancy Griffith another ring."

He waited a moment. "You want, I can stick around up here. There's nothing going on down at the Junction, and Frymire's girlfriend is visiting him."

"I thought he married her."

"Not yet." He chewed his cookie.

"There's no need, I'll just stick around." I noticed the crestfallen look on his face. "Unless you really want to stay up here." I waited for a moment. "Things getting pastoral down there in Powder Junction?"

"Uh-huh, other than some yokels driving around over near the East Spring Draw and being unneighborly." He judged the look on my face. "Nothing big; new owners, and they're a strange bunch—Texans." He glanced behind him at the bathroom. "You gonna put him in the holding cell for the night?"

"Yep."

He stretched and yawned, covering his face with his hand. "You better lock the door."

He stared at the open cell and then up at me, and I was struck by how young the kid looked; I was estimating his age at fifteen, but he might've been younger. "You're not trustworthy, or I'd let you sleep out here on the bench in the waiting room." I gestured for him to go in. "Anyway, the bunks are a lot more comfortable; I should know."

He strung his fingers around the bars of the open door. "What if I promise?"

"Excuse me?"

He stared at my chest. "What if I promise to not run off?"

"Well, considering your track record, I don't know you well enough to trust you."

He thought about it for a second, and then the words poured from him like a teletype machine. " 'Now it is required that those who have been given a trust must prove faithful.' " He glanced up at my face for only a second. "Corinthians four:two."

I stared back at him and nudged him with my hand. "Get in the cell." And then added, "Walt Longmire, quarter past twelve."

He stepped inside but turned as I closed the door. I reassured him: "Don't worry, I'm going to gather up a few blankets and sleep right out here."

"Can I have the Bible? I saw it on your desk."

I thought about arguing religious semantics with him but instead just locked the door; then I retrieved the blankets and his book from my office. I handed it to him through the bars. "Who's Orrin?"

The return words were wooden, just as they'd been when he'd quoted scripture. "The Destroying Angel and Danite: Man of God, Son of Thunder."

"Uh-huh." I nodded and suddenly felt very tired. "Get some sleep."

"I'd rather read."

I felt my shoulders slump but then gathered an old floor lamp that I'd used for just that purpose from the corner of the room and brought it over to the bars, switched it on, and directed the light into the cell. "There."

I flipped off the overhead fluorescents, pulled the mattress off of the bunk in the other cell, dragged it around to the floor, and piled on the blankets and a pillow. I sat on the mattress, pulled off my boots, and covered up. The kid was studying his book and was seated on the far bunk: "Don't worry; we'll get you out of here tomorrow."

He continued to turn pages in the Mormon Bible, his face close to the good book, but I could hear him plainly in that high voice of his: "Actually, I'm okay."

"So this is Orrin the Mormon?"

I spoke from beneath the blanket that covered my head. "He says his name is Cord."

"As in music or firewood?"

"Firewood, I think." I peeled the blanket down from my face and looked up at my undersheriff, now having sprouted two fully blown black-eyed Susans. "Oh my. . . ."

She leaned against the bars and looked in at the kid, the web of her thumb hitched onto the grip of her Glock. "Yeah, I know, I know—it looks like I went all ten rounds at the Blue Horizon."

I looked at her blankly.

"Boxing venue in North Philly." She gestured toward the sleeping young man. "He talks?"

I sat up against the wall. "He does."

"You get anything more out of him other than a first name?"

"Not really."

She gestured toward the book lying next to the boy. "Who's Orrin?"

I repeated Cord's mantra from last night: "The Destroying Angel and Danite: Man of God, Son of Thunder."

Vic shrugged. "Does Orrin have to say that every time he answers the phone?"

"I'm not sure."

"What's he doing with Orrin's book?"

I yawned. "We really didn't get a chance to cover that."

She watched the young man breathe for a few moments, and her face softened just a little. "Nancy is here from Hell's Services; you wanna roust the fool on the hill out for a confab, or what?"

"I'd like to talk to her first."

She pushed off the bars and walked down the hall. "Then get up. I'll get you a cup of coffee, and you can join the in-crowd at Ruby's desk."

When I got to the bench at the reception area, I was still holding a blanket around me as I collapsed against the chief therapist for Health Services and then slid down to rest my head in her comfortable lap. "I'd like to commit myself."

She looked down at me with big, liquid brown eyes. "Commit yourself to what?"

"Getting more sleep, for a start." Nancy had been a good friend of Martha's, and I'd depended on her prowess in dealing with the more delicate aspects of domestic and child-related problems over the years. "We have a little dogie who's been thrown out on the long trail."

She continued to look down at me and started singing:

"Whoopee ti yi yo, git along little dogies
It's your misfortune and none of my own

Whoopee ti yi yo, git along little dogies
You know that Wyoming will be your new home."

Vic stared at the two of us. "What the fuck?"

Nancy smiled. "It's the Durant High School fight song."

Vic nodded. "That's likely to strike fear into the hearts of your opponents."

I interrupted. "I guess he's been living in Barbara Thomas's pump house for the last two weeks."

Nancy nodded. "I wouldn't mind living at Barbara's—it's a nice place."

"His name is Cord, and we can't seem to find anything to indicate that anybody's looking for him. He's carrying the Book of Mormon, and he quotes scripture."

"How old?"

I sat on the ground by Nancy's sensible black flats. "Fifteen, maybe."

She looked up at Ruby and Vic. "There are a lot of LDS splinter sects, fundamentalist polygamy groups that parted ways with the Mormons—Warren Jeffs stuff. There are a bunch in Utah, but there are also a few in southern Colorado, Arizona, Texas, and even one over in South Dakota." She sighed, and her eyes returned to me. "Have you ever heard of the term Lost Boys?"

Vic was the first to answer. "The vampire movie?"

Nancy shook her head. "No."

I ventured an opinion. "Peter Pan?"

She shook her head again. "Mormon castoffs; they're the boys that get kicked out of these groups for what the elders deem inappropriate behavior, but mostly just to make room for the older men so that they can have their pick of the younger women as multiple wives."

"Charming."

"As far as I know the nearest polygamy group is in South Dakota."

"He was wearing a pair of pants that were from the Department of Sanitation in Belle Fourche."

"Probably got them from Goodwill or the Salvation Army." She thought about it. "Is that Butte County?"

"Yep." I waited. "What?"

"I've got a friend over there who works for the school system, and he mentioned something about one of those LDS splinter groups." She thought about it some more. "Something like the Fundamentalist . . . no, the Apostolic Church of the Lamb of God."

Vic sighed. "Oh shit, not more sheep."

I reared up, glancing at Ruby. "See if you can get Tim Berg on the line by the time I get back from the Busy Bee." I looked at Nancy. "It won't do any harm to the boy to get in touch with these people, will it?"

The therapist shook her head. "Chances are they're the ones who tossed him out. I can't see them wanting him back."

"Well, at least we can get some information on the kid." I stood and folded my blanket. "Would you like to make the acquaintance of the Latter-day dogie while I go out and get us all some breakfast?"

"Ready when you are." She stood. "Do I have to do it through bars?"

"The keys are hanging in the holding cell, but I wouldn't turn my back on him for an instant—he's a jackrabbit."

She saluted. "Roger that."

The proprietor of the Busy Bee Café folded her arms and glared at me from the narrow aperture of the partially open door. "We're closed."

I had looked through the windows and noticed that there wasn't anybody else inside. "What do you mean, you're closed. You haven't been closed in thirty years."

"My dishwasher quit again, and I'm tired from working the Basque Festival."

"How about a couple of egg sandwiches?"

"No."

"The usual?"

"No, Walt. I'm pooped." She shut the door in my face.

"Jeez." I turned to Vic. "Dash Inn?"

"Looks like." She turned and started down the sidewalk. "I'm parked on Main."

I caught up with her, and a scorching U-turn and five minutes later we were waiting at the drive-through window at the locally owned fast food restaurant. "Are you going to tell me about the running of the sheep?"

"No."

"Well, who were you drinking with?"

"Why? You jealous?" I didn't rise to the bait, so she answered. "Sancho, Marie, and the Critter." The Critter was the name Vic had given to Antonio, their son.

"I thought Saizarbitoria was in Rawlins."

"They left that lovely town Saturday morning; he said he might take a day or two off." She shrugged. "They're the only Basquos I know, and the Critter is getting kind of cute."

"I didn't know little kids drink Patxaran."

"He should have; it would've kept me from drinking all of it."

The radio on the transmission hump of Vic's twelve-year-old unit sputtered and coughed Ruby's voice, and we both looked at it.

Static. "I've got Sheriff Berg on the landline; do you want me to patch him through?"

I unclipped the mic from the dash and hit the button as Tim's voice sounded through the tinny speakers. Static. "What do you want, redneck?"

I keyed the mic. "Hippie."

He continued unabated. Static. "You got the hot little deputy with you?"

I held the mic out to Vic. "You still got that psychedelic VW bus with the tinted windows you park outside the schools?"

The voice continued. Static. "Only for you, darlin'."

I returned the mic to my own mouth, which was generally a little cleaner. "Hey, Tim, have you got a group in the county called the Apostolic Church of the Lamb of God?"

Static. "Amen, heaven help me."

"What's the story?"

Static. "Oh, they owed about quarter million in property taxes that they suddenly made current here about a month ago. They're putting together a little compound, trying to start a dairy up in the northwest corner of the county and the state. Why?"

"I've got a boy down here; might be one of their castoffs."

Static. "Blond-haired, blue-eyed, slight, and fidgety—about driving age?"

"Yes, he says his name is Cord."

Static. "The mother was in here about three weeks ago asking for him."

"Well, I've got him."

Static. "Hold on to him till I can get hold of her—she's up in that part of the county that's kind of hard to get to."

Vic interrupted as she took our bag of sandwiches through the drive-through window. "Hey, Tim?"

Static. "Yeah?"

She set the bag on the center console and continued. "I heard you got the guy that did that motel arson last week."

Static. "What?"

She started up the engine and pulled the unit down into drive. "I heard you got DNA on the perp and broke open the case."

Static. "I don't know what you're talking about."

"Oh, that's right, genetic evidence isn't permissible in South Dakota—everybody's got the same DNA."

I reattached the mic as his laughter rang through the speakers. Vic turned to look at me. "There, mystery solved."

"I guess."

"What's that supposed to mean?"

"I'm not sure. Anyway, what are we supposed to do with him in the meantime?" I watched the morning traffic, what there was of it, drifting by as a man with very long hair and an extravagant beard stood on the corner and raised his hand to us.

Vic's eyes followed mine as I tipped my hat at the man with the rucksack on his back. "Another friend of yours?"

I slumped in my seat as we rolled past the individual who continued to hold his palm out to us. "Nope, but it's coming up on fall and time for all the hitchers to disappear south."

When we pulled into the parking lot, Dorothy's familiar Subaru was parked in the spot closest to the door, and, when we got inside, there was a large cardboard box full of pastries from Baroja's, the Basque shop, on the dispatcher's desk. The repentant café owner was sipping coffee with the dispatcher herself.

Dorothy turned and looked at me. "I started feeling bad about turning you away, so I went over to Lana's and got some treats." She pointed at the paper bags we carried from one of her competitors. "My being closed doesn't appear to have slowed you down."

I rested the bags on the counter and nudged Dog out of the place where he had put himself in case anybody got careless with the pastries. "A man's got to eat, and I hope you got something more than donuts 'cause you know I don't like them."

"You don't like donuts?" Cord was sitting next to Nancy, a maple cruller in his hand.

I shrugged. "I know it's against type. . . ."

"I don't understand."

My undersheriff gestured to the office at large in an exasperated fashion. "Cops, donuts . . ."

He looked at her questioningly and then back to me. "Is it because you're big?"

Vic snickered, and there was a long silence. Dorothy, in an attempt to deflect, spoke up. "Walt, if you don't have any objections, I've offered the boy a job."

I turned and looked at her. "What?"

She nodded. "Washing dishes."

The incredulity wrote itself on my face. "Dorothy, could I speak with you and Nancy in my office?" I took one of the bags of food with me as I made my way around the dispatcher's desk and gestured from Ruby to the young man so that she knew to keep an eye on him. "Now, if you would."

Vic joined the two women and, sticking her finger in the hole where the doorknob to my office used to be, closed the door behind us. I set my breakfast on my desk and took off my hat, hooking it onto the hammer of my sidearm, crossing my arms over my chest. "What are you two up to?"

Nancy was the first to speak. "Walt, it was my idea. I didn't think it would be a bad thing for—"

"I just got off the phone with Tim Berg over in South Dakota. He says that the boy's mother was in the sheriff's office three weeks ago." I noticed they were looking at me a little funny. "What?"

Dorothy spoke this time. "Walt, Cord seemed to intimate that his mother might've passed away."

I thought about it. "Since when?"

They looked at each other and then back to me as Nancy spoke in a low voice. "It sounded quite recent." She stepped in closer to my desk. "Walt, this boy shows all the classic symptoms of being a polygamy kid. I don't think there's anything wrong with him, psychologically speaking, but . . ."

"Well, Tim said the mother was from some compound over there, and as soon as he gets back to me we'll start getting some answers."

"What can it hurt?" Dorothy placed her fists on her hips and looked at me. "I need the help, and what else is he going to do, sit in one of your cells?"

I glanced at Nancy, who jumped in quickly. "It would take me a day or two to come up with a foster home for him, so if Dorothy's got a place . . . ?"

"He'll skip town like a Kansas City paperhanger."

Dorothy shook her head. "He won't."

Vic joined in the conversation, and I was glad of another sane voice in the room. "Who the hell says?"

"He does." Dorothy crossed her own arms. "I made him promise." We stood there looking at each other, the immovable object meeting the irresistible force. "He can stay here and work over at my place till we get him settled out."

Nancy joined Dorothy at the other side of my desk. "Walt, if it's true that his mother is dead or has run off, then he's lost his advocate within that group and they're probably not going to want him anymore."

Throwing my hat onto my desk, I sighed and sat in my chair. "All right, but if he bolts, I'm holding the two of you responsible." I glanced at the chief cook and used-to-be bottle washer of the Busy Bee. "And I'm going to want free lunch for a week."

Dorothy leaned in and looked down at me. "Oh, Walt, you know there's no such thing as a free lunch."

I guess after the Kansas City paperhanger remark, she thought I deserved it.

It was five after five when Tim called, and he was none too happy. "They say they never heard of the boy or the mother."

I leaned back in my chair and slipped a foot under my desk to keep from doing my usual sheriff backflip with a full twist. "Are you sure that's where she said she was from?"

"Yes, damn it."

I stared at the receiver for a moment. "You seem a little agitated, Tim."

There was silence on the phone, and then he spoke. "I damn well am."

"Mind if I ask why?"

"I don't like having guns pointed at me in my own county."

"What happened?"

He breathed a deep sigh, blowing some of the agitation through his teeth, and I could hear him easing himself into a chair. "I drove out that way, and mind you, this is the first time in a long while that I've been up in that Castle Rock territory near the South Fork of the Moreau except for that pipeline they got going through there." He swallowed. "It's a fort is what it is, Walt. I mean to tell you that they've got walls and fences up all over the place and gun towers—honest-to-God gun towers. Now they call 'em observation posts, but they're gun towers is what they are. I saw individuals up there with deer rifles, and I gotta tell you I am not happy about this happening in my county."

"Who did you talk to?"

"Some jaybird named Ronald Lynear. I get the feeling he's the grand imperial Pooh-Bah around the place—him and another fella by the name of Lockhart and some severe-looking individual by the name of Bidarte."

I leaned forward. "And they say they never heard of either of them?"

"Yeah, and I know that's bullshit, because I've still got the slip of paper she gave me with directions on how to get to the place."

"Did you get any ID from her?" I raised my head as Vic came in and sat in her usual chair, propping her usual boots up on my usual desk.

"Walt, these people don't carry any ID. I got a name from her, Sarah Tisdale. The funny thing is, there was a phone number down here at the bottom that I didn't pay any attention to 'cause it was out of state. Walt—it's Wyoming."

"307?"

"You bet."

"Give it to me."

"I already tried calling it, but there wasn't any answer and no answering machine, of course."

"Give it to me anyway." He read me the number, and I scribbled it down on the paper blotter on my desk, tore it off, and handed it to my undersheriff. "We'll get the reverse registry and find out where it is." Listening to the troubled man on the other end of the line, I dropped my pen and enjoyed the view as Vic left in search of the information I needed. "Tim . . . ?"

"Yeah."

He sighed again, and I waited, then asked, "What's really troubling you?"

"Walt, you know me; I'm for freedom, folks' rights to bear

arms and all. . . . I mean that Waco shit needed to be handled better, but it needed to be handled."

"Yep."

"Well, what's going on up there near Castle Rock is wrong. I was up there the first time about a year ago when we started getting complaints about abuse and Child Services wanted to know how many kids were up there and whether they were getting a proper education."

"Uh-huh."

"We found out about 'em because a few of 'em came in filing for welfare benefits, claiming that their husbands had run off and left when their damn husbands are sitting out there in the pickups waiting for 'em." There was another pause as he caught his breath. "Those kids aren't going anywhere but the school of hard knocks, and the funny thing is that the majority of 'em are young men about the same age as the one you've got. They have all this heavy equipment, I mean more than you'd need in a ranching or farming operation, but they'd sunk lines into the river for water and didn't have any irrigation rights—and you know as well as I do that there's more men died over ditches than bitches in this country."

I leaned back in my chair. "True."

"Well, the local ranchers got in an uproar, and we went up there with warrants and got in the place." There was another pause. "Walt, my grandfolks come up in the dirty thirties, hard times when you had to do whatever it took to survive. I've looked at the pictures and heard the stories, but I've never seen anything like this. It's one thing to read about this stuff in the news, but it's something else to come up against it face to face. People up there are just living in sheds—women and children. . . . Thirteen-year-old girls married to fifty-year-old men—I mean, they're not married in the legal sense—that's how they try and get away with the support checks. They marry these girls off to these men, *seal* 'em, they call it, in private ceremonies." There was another pause, and when he spoke again, there was a catch in his voice. "There was a little girl. . . . She didn't look right—birth defects. There was this one little girl that comes up to me. . . . Right. We're busting up these irrigation pipes they've got going in the river, and she pulls on my pant leg, wanting to know why it is we're taking away their water so that they can't water the cows that they're gonna milk to make enough money to have something to eat. I kneeled down and took her little hand, and Walt . . . she didn't have any fingernails."

"I don't know what to say, Tim."

"How's that boy, the one you found?"

"He says his name is Cord." Vic reentered and sat in her chair with a massive computer file, her index finger stuffed in the middle. "Normal, or appears to be. I had the school psychologist give him a going-over, and she seems to think that he's all right."

"Lucky you."

I fingered the brim of my hat, spinning it on the crown and thinking how the simple gesture was sometimes indicative of the job as a whole. "I'll keep you informed as to what's going on over here—and you'll do the same for me?"

"Sure will."

I hung up my phone and looked past the bruises that looked like crow's wings spread beneath the Terror's tarnished gold eyes. "There, but for the grace of God, go I."

She dropped the book onto my desk and opened it. "Trouble in rabbit-choker land?"

"That polygamy group up in the north of Tim's county; he doesn't know what to do about it."

"It's a cult; they're fucking cults. The fact that they're trying to cover this shit up under the auspices of actual religion only makes it that much worse."

"I thought you thought all religions were cults."

"Some are worse than others—I should know, I grew up Catholic." She heaved the book around, her finger pointing to a number about a third of the way down the page. "Surrey/Short Drop General Mercantile."

I read the exchange and picked up my phone. "A commercial number?"

"Surrey/Short Drop—they're in-county, and I don't even know where either of them are."

Surrey and Short Drop were tiny towns in the southeast corner of the county. Surrey had been named after a remittance man, born the fourth son of four. In the late eighteenth century, the first son of a British nobleman inherited the family fortune, the second went into the military, the third into the clergy, leaving the fourth to ride into Powder Junction every month for his remittance check so that he could drink himself to death on the high plains. Short Drop, which was a stone's throw away, was where a member of Butch Cassidy's Hole in the Wall gang had been caught and lynched—hence the name referring to a short drop on a long rope.

The other point of interest in the area was the infamous Teapot Dome of Teapot Dome scandal fame, named for a tiny rock formation on top of the U.S. Naval oil reserves, which had brought rightful disgrace upon the administration of Warren G. Harding in the twenties. The illegal sale of the Teapot Dome to Sinclair Oil had been the biggest national scandal in the country until a few guys back in the seventies had gotten caught burgling an office in a place called Watergate.

I dialed the number and waited, not particularly expecting anyone to answer. Imagine my surprise when someone did.

"Short Drop Merc."

The voice was older, female, and didn't sound like it would brook much nonsense.

"This is Sheriff Walt Longmire—"

"Well, it's about time."

I made a face for the benefit of nobody in particular. "Excuse me?"

"Is this the so-called sheriff of our county?"

"Well, yes it is—and who is this?"

She ignored my question and launched into a tirade. "Look, I talked to that moron you've got posted over in Powder Junction, and he said you were going to send somebody around to talk to those idiots over near East Spring Draw down near Sulphur Creek."

I remembered Double Tough mentioning something about disagreements in the area but that he wasn't sure how to proceed. "Yep, I'm kind of following up on that and was hoping you could give me a little more information."

"They threatened a bunch of people with a shotgun, and we're about to go out there and do a little threatening ourselves."

"Well, we wouldn't want that. I'll send a deputy to have a word, but for the time being I'd appreciate it if you would just avoid them."

The harrumph carried across the county. "That's going to be a little tough since they own twelve thousand acres around here."

"I'll speak with them myself, if need be. In the meantime, I was wondering if you'd ever heard of a young woman by the name of Sarah Tisdale?"

There was a long pause, and the woman's voice changed. "My daughter. You've heard from my daughter?"

3

Vic reached over and turned on the heater as I took the exit at Powder Junction and followed 192 southeast across the Powder River, leaving the sun as it lingered along the mountains to the west, and drove on toward Surrey/Short Drop. In the perversity of western geography, the poetic-sounding locale of Surrey had pretty much dropped off the map, but the town of Short Drop had, in a small-town way, thrived.

The rolling hills were a khaki brown even with the wet summer and shimmered bronze against the snowfields at the southern tip of the Bighorn Mountains, but everywhere you looked there were oil derricks rhythmically heaving the crude petroleum from the earth. I'd worked as a roughneck on an oil crew for an entire summer in my youth, part of my father's plan that I should see what a life without a proper education meant. Though only a half hour from the interstate highway, the suburbs of Short Drop might as well have been on the moon.

"No fucking way."

I glanced at my undersheriff's Technicolor eyes and felt another twinge of sympathy. "What?"

She gestured at the surrounding landscape. "Who the hell travels two-thirds of the way across the country and stops here thinking this is it, this is where I want to spend the rest of my life?" She shook her head. "No fucking way."

I glanced around at the stark shadows being thrown from the sharp angle of the sun, causing everything to suddenly glimmer the way only dying things can. "It's a lot like Nebraska down here."

"If that's supposed to recommend it, it doesn't." We drove along, and she remained unimpressed. "So, how come I haven't ever been down here?"

"Because you didn't receive the traditional hazing that all the other deputies get when they sign on."

She smirked. "As it should be."

The radio crackled, and the voice of one of the said deputies resounded through the tinny speaker. Static. "Sheriff, this is base, come in."

Vic pulled my mic from the dash and keyed the button. "What do you want?"

Static. "The kid's back over from working at the Busy Bee, and I was wondering if I had to lock him up or was it okay if I just let him sleep in the cell with the door open?"

"Is Dorothy still trying to get that spot above the garage behind her squared away for him?"

Vic asked the question, and Double Tough took a minute, probably asking the kid.

Static. "Yup, but he says it's not ready yet."

"Fine by me if the door is open."

Static. "And Ruby left Dog here; you want me to feed him?"

Vic spoke into the mic in a pretty good impersonation. "Yup, and when Saizarbitoria gets in you can head back to Powder Junction."

Static. "Roger that."

She flipped the mic up onto my dash and propped a boot against the transmission hump again. "He doesn't sound too happy about coming back down here, does he?"

We drove on, watching the grass sway in the wind like the waves of some lost ocean, the landscape remaining pretty much the same as it had for the last fifteen minutes. I looked at Vic again. "Let me guess. . . ."

"No fucking way."

I grunted. "My family settled here."

"No, your family settled about an hour north up against the mountains where it's pretty."

"Define pretty."

"Green with a variation in altitude."

Victoria Moretti and I had a running argument about what, exactly, constituted aesthetic beauty in the American West, and I couldn't help but point out that her view always included green grass and trees—or the American East.

I glanced around. "It has a more subtle beauty."

The response was nothing if not predictable.

We came over the rolling hills of the Pine Ridge and could see the ancient, still-leafy cottonwood that was supposedly over a hundred years old at the bottom of the valley. "There, a tree. I hope you're happy."

We pulled along the turnoff, and I dropped the three-quarter-ton into the town of Short Drop proper, where a wooden sign with burnt-in lettering proclaimed **SHORT DROP, THE PLACE WHERE "LAUGHING" SAM CAREY, THE LAST OF BUTCH CASSIDY'S HOLE IN THE WALL, TOOK A SHORT DROP ON A LONG ROPE.**

Along one of the gigantic limbs of the old tree hung a noose of thick hemp, swaying in the breeze, monument to a violent act over a century old. Vic slumped back in her seat. "Leave it to you assholes; you finally grow a tree tall enough, and you hang somebody from it."

I followed Main Street's dirt road and took a right onto Jackson as Vic gazed at Short Drop's country school whose teams had the likely nickname, "The Hangmen." "Why do they bother?"

I misunderstood. "Go to school?"

She pointed. "With signs—there are only four streets."

I nudged my truck across the red-dirt roadway and parked in front of one of the commercial buildings, the Short Drop Mercantile, and killed the engine. "This is it."

She leaned forward and craned her neck, looking back and forth at the Merc, a bar, and a trailer with a sign out front. "The library is a singlewide?"

"At least they've got one." I unbuckled my seat belt and cracked the door open. With the fading sun, the air was growing sharp, and I was glad that I'd brought my leather jacket. "C'mon."

There was a wooden walkway that connected the four buildings that made up downtown Short Drop, but the overhead porch reached only across the front of the mercantile and the bar, the only buildings of any historical repute. They were the old types with the false fronts, and the color scheme appeared to be shades of gray with white trim. The paint was peeling a little, but they were both in pretty good shape, and I have to admit that my trajectory swayed just a touch when I saw the **RAINIER BEER** sign in the next-door watering hole—again aptly named The Noose.

Vic joined me on the walkway, our boots ringing in the silence of the town like some Anthony Mann Western. She lingered for a moment, and as if on cue, a slight wind came up and powdered its way through town. Her voice was low, but I could still hear it: "No fucking way."

Old-fashioned lettering spiraled across the bottom of the windows, offering up quilting supplies, books, ammunition, and gunsmithing. I ignored the hand-scripted **CLOSED HAPPY TRAILS** sign, pushed open the door, and walked onto swaled and cupped pine flooring with no board less than a foot wide. The ceilings were high, at least twenty feet, tiled with pressed tin. Black fans with wooden propellers spun idly and track lighting spotted us as we entered the establishment.

Rows of bookshelves staggered against the wall to my right, sagging with the weight of antiquarian tomes and thumbed paperbacks that appeared to be organized in no particular order. There was a counter to my right with an old cash register and a few glass cases that held groceries—bread, canned goods, boxes of cereal, and stick candy that I hadn't seen since I was a kid. There was a long counter at a forty-five-degree angle with a few rifles on stands, some pistols in a case, and above that the better part of a wall full of ammunition. Myriad taxidermy heads were on the wall, some from far-flung reaches like Africa and South America; they would've made my big-game hunter friend Omar Rhoades proud.

My eyes focused on a massive water buffalo whose head was slightly turned and who looked out into the street as if he might pull the rest of himself from the wall and make a break for it.

"Sheriff?"

I turned to see a woman coming down from a mezzanine at the back of the main room. She was in her sixties and holding in her hands what appeared to be a Crock-Pot, using a set of dish towels as oven mitts as she came. Handsome with a good spread to her shoulders, light brown hair streaked with gray, and, partially hidden behind a pair of cat's-eye glasses, direct, blue eyes— almost cobalt. She glanced at my deputy, who had stalled out by the case of books to the right, and then at me.

"Expected you earlier."

I tipped my hat. "We got here as quick as we could." With a curt nod, she walked past me around the center counter, where she used a hip to try and slide open a large, iron-trimmed door. "Can I help you with that?"

Without waiting, I gripped the steel handle and pulled the door open, revealing a short hallway between the Merc and the bar next door.

Her voice echoed after her as she walked through. "Come along, and I'll buy you a beer."

Seeing no reason to loiter, I glanced at Vic, who shelved her book and followed with an eyebrow arched, as usual, like a cat's back.

The doorway from the Merc opened up to the left of the bar, and it appeared as if I was going to get my Rainier. I ducked under a large rattlesnake skin tacked to a board and continued around the coolers on one end of a bar made from old barn siding. The surface had been sealed with polyurethane, entombing what looked to be close to fifty more snake skins. "Lot of rattlers around this place?"

She set the Crock-Pot onto the flat surface, reached into the cooler, and placed two ice-cold, longneck bottles of Rainier beer in front of us. "Not anymore."

I glanced at the labels. "You know my flavor."

"Everybody in this county knows your flavor, Walt Longmire." She stuck a hand across the bar and winked. "Eleanor Tisdale. I used to be on the library board with your wife. Sorry for your loss."

"Thank you." I shook her hand and nudged one of the wooden stools out with my boot for my undersheriff. "My deputy, Victoria Moretti." They shook, and I asked, "You own both places?"

She nodded and adjusted her glasses that trailed a set of pearls around the back of her neck. "Run the library, too, but people also borrow books from the Mercantile." She was classic

Wyoming, that indiscriminate age between thirty and a hundred where the women find a comfort for themselves and just
settle in. "I keep the door closed to discourage drunken shopping."
She reached up with hands that had seen hard labor and effortlessly twisted the caps off, sliding the pair of Rainiers further our
way. "You found my daughter?"

Vic sat beside me, and I turned my eyes to the bartender.
"Well . . ."

"She's in trouble?"

I paused for a moment, took a sip, and tried to decide how I
was going to play this. "Possibly."

"That would follow. It was always her signature." She leaned
her elbows on the business side of the bar and sighed. "My husband was in the oil business."

"Was?"

"Dale died about three years ago. Light-plane crash down in
Mexico."

"Sorry to hear it."

She gestured away my condolences with a wave. "Not as
much as I was. Sold the majority of the family ranch to those
yahoos over at East Spring before he died." She thought about it.
"Sarah was a lot like him. Headstrong to the point of idiocy. He
once told her that he wasn't going to save the ranch for her if she
left, so in predictable Tisdale manner, she did and he didn't."

I nodded, not quite sure what to say to that. "When was the
last time you had contact with her?"

She stared at me as if I'd just joined hands with the point-of-
idiocy group myself and then laughed. "Seventeen years ago,
come August 6th." She crossed her arms and settled the cat's-eye
glasses on Vic and then back to me. "Sheriff, maybe you better
tell me what you are wanting."

"Um . . . Eleanor, how about you take a seat?" She looked

concerned but remained standing. "We had a young man show up in Durant this weekend; looked like a runaway, about fifteen years old. I tracked him back to Butte County, South Dakota, where the sheriff there informed me that a woman approximately the age of your daughter, who identified herself as Sarah Tisdale, had come into his office and reported that her son was missing."

The tension in the woman's back pulled her up a little straighter. "Son?"

"When I called him and told him I had custody of the boy, he drove up to where it is your daughter was supposedly living, but the people there said they'd never heard of her or the boy. Interestingly enough, the map she left with the sheriff had a phone number scribbled at the bottom—your phone number."

Eleanor Tisdale groped for a stool and pulled it underneath herself. "Do you have any photographs, anything that might . . . ?"

I fingered the Polaroid that we always take to keep track of lodgers from my shirt pocket and held it out to her. "This is the boy."

She read the single word written in red Magic Marker at the bottom border. "Cord?"

"That's his name." She took it gently and held it as if it might vanish. "We don't have any photographs of your daughter, and to be honest we don't know where she might be."

"Oh, my."

I lowered my head to get in her line of sight. "I take it he looks familiar?"

"The spitting image." She got up and punched NO SALE on the cash register at the end of the bar and walked back to us with a school photo of a pretty young girl with long, blond hair and deep, sapphire eyes. "Where is he now?"

I took the photo and studied it; the resemblance was, as they say, uncanny. "He's safe in Durant at a friend's. I didn't see any reason for him to be shuttled off to a foster home since he has a mother looking for him and relatives in-county."

"Have you heard any more from Sarah?"

"Unfortunately, no. I was kind of hoping you had."

She shook her head. "No. Nothing in seventeen years. Dale, when he was around, wouldn't even say her name; he used to refer to her as 'that ungrateful child.'" Her eyes unfocused for a moment and she began a familiar verse. "'Turn all her mother's pains and benefits . . .'"

She faltered, and I continued the Shakespeare for her. "'To laughter and contempt, that she may feel / How sharper than a serpent's tooth it is / To have a thankless child.'"

The cobalt eyes stayed distant and then focused on the photo in her trembling hands. "He's fifteen?"

"Yep." I watched as she continued to finger the photograph like a holy relic. "The math works out, doesn't it? How about we trade photos, and I'll get this one back to you after we find her?"

I was about to add more when the bar door swung open to the accompaniment of an attached jangling bell. The middle-aged man in the doorway was pale and painfully lean, with red hair and a sharp face half-hidden under the bill of a black John Deere ball cap. His clothes, an off-white nylon dress shirt and a powder blue blazer, were rumpled and hung off him like a bad hanger. Slung over his shoulder was an expensive, spacey-looking tactical shotgun with a small flashlight mounted underneath the barrel.

Eleanor's voice sounded behind me. "Can I help you?"

I leaned to my right to see around Vic, who gave him a quick look and immediately dismissed the odd character as Ichabod Double-Ought Buck. She sipped her beer. "What, were you born in a barn?" She placed the bottle back on the bar and murmured to herself. "Yeah, you probably were."

He didn't move for a moment, then half turned as if to leave—evidently he wasn't happy to see the greater portion of the off-duty Absaroka County Sheriff's Department seated at the bar. He stood there in profile and then cleared his throat as if he was about to make a speech, but it was a short one: "Mr. Lynear would like to talk to you."

Eleanor looked puzzled. "Who?"

He looked even more surprised at her response and took a step into the bar with a vexed look on his face, as if he shouldn't have to be bothered with repeating, let alone explaining, himself. "Mr. Roy Lynear, owner/operator of the East Spring Ranch, would like to talk to you."

I stood, tucked the photo of Sarah Tisdale into my shirt pocket, and took a step toward him. "And who are you?"

Perhaps hoping for a prompter, he looked back out the door again. "George."

"Are you quail hunting at this time of night?" He glanced at me, but his eyes returned to Eleanor; evidently his one-track mind was always in danger of derailment. I pointed at the shotgun on his back. "It's against the law to bring a gun into an establishment that serves liquor."

The eyes switched to Vic and then back to me, and his voice and manner changed, telling me a great deal about him. "She's wearing one in this Godless establishment and so are you."

I took another step, bringing myself within arm's reach of him. "She's my deputy, and maybe I should introduce myself. I'm Sheriff Walt Longmire—and your full name is?"

"George Joseph Lynear."

He stood there looking back and forth between us again with a kind of wildness in his eyes. I thought for a moment that he was going to do something stupid, but he didn't; instead, he took a step back onto the boardwalk. "There, are ya happy now?"

I reached over and closed the door in his face.

Vic barked a laugh as I spoke to him through the glass pane. "Go tell your family you can come back in here when you learn some manners." He stood there looking at me with a blistering hatred, then turned and walked off the boardwalk toward a large, decked-out one-ton dually parked perpendicular to mine.

I turned back to the proprietor. "Who's Roy Lynear?"

She shook her head. "I guess he's the one everybody's been having trouble with the last few weeks. Some of his men . . ."

She was interrupted again by the sound of the door behind me, and this time I turned with my hand resting on my Colt, just in case. The sack-of-bones trapshooter wasn't there, but in his place was another odd-looking individual who was a hell of a lot more impressive in both stature and dress. He was a tall, well-toned Hispanic man in black jeans and a dark suit jacket, his pork-chop sideburns sticking out almost as far as the brim of his black cattleman's hat.

He quickly slipped it off to reveal full locks of curling, dark hair. "*Hola*."

I stood there looking down at him. "Hey."

"I would like to apologize." He gestured with the hat. "My compadre learned his social graces from cows."

I nodded. "So, are you Roy Lynear?"

He laughed, obviously much amused by the thought. "Oh no, I simply work for Mr. Lynear." He extended his hand toward me. "I'm Tomás Bidarte. I am the poet lariat of Nuevo Leon."

"Lariat, not laureate?"

He smiled, and it was a dazzling display, revealing some creative dentistry with more than twenty-four karats. "My poetry is more for the cantina than the parlor."

I took the hand. "What do you do when you're not rhyming?"

We shook, and his grip was like cast iron. "Work for Mr. Lynear."

I looked around the vaquero toward the truck with its

running lights on, sitting in the half-light of the approaching night. "Well, it's an odd time to come visiting, especially armed. Is Roy out there, because I'm dying to meet him."

He continued smiling, studying me. "And I'm sure he's going to want to meet you too, Sheriff."

"Send him in."

Bidarte turned his matinee-idol profile toward the door and then back to me. "That, señor, might be a little easier said than done."

The man in the back of the brand-new King Ranch one-ton diesel was testing its rear suspension—he must've tipped the scales at an easy four hundred pounds. He was comfortably seated in what must've been a custom-built La-Z-Boy throne, complete with his sheepskin slippers prominently displayed on the foot extension. He wore an oversized, expensive-looking bathrobe draped over a snap-button shirt with a large turquoise bolo tie and a pair of TCU purple sweatpants. On his head was an honest-to-God sombrero.

"'The harvest has passed and the summer has ended, and we are not saved.'"

Vic and Eleanor had joined me at the edge of the wooden walkway, an advantage that made us the same height as Roy Lynear.

"Jeremiah, chapter eight, verse two."

He turned his head and looked at me. "You know the word of God, Sheriff?"

"I know entire sentences."

He continued to study me, unsure if I was the real deal or if I'd only stumbled upon a line of scripture, then gestured toward one of his massive legs. "Inconvenient gout; I apologize for having you come out here into the night like this, but my joints are hurting so bad I'm afraid I wouldn't make it up those steps."

I watched as John Deere in a ball cap stayed on the other side of the truck bed with the shotgun in his hands.

The massive man in the chair settled his eyes on me. "I suppose I should introduce myself—I'm Roy Lynear."

Vic was quick to respond. "We've heard a lot about you lately."

He studied my deputy, and I was pretty sure he was both attracted and annoyed. "Have you, now?" He glanced at the sullen one behind him and to the caballero who had propped an ornately inlaid, pointy-toed boot on the rear bumper of the chariot near the Texas plate. "From these two?"

To my surprise, the Hispanic fellow spoke freely. "You are the company you keep."

The giant man laughed until he wheezed. "Tomás Bidarte here is one of the great vaquero poets. He's in all the anthologies, aren't you, Tom?"

He tipped his hat. "There's no accounting for taste."

Lynear issued a command. "Give us one, Tom."

Bidarte slipped an elongated knife from the back pocket of his jeans and pushed a button, the stiletto blade leaping out into the running lights a good eight inches. He cleaned his fingernails as he spoke.

"Have more than you show,
Talk less than you know.
Lend less than you owe,
Ride more than you go."

The older man shook his head and kicked a slipper at the poet. "That wasn't one of your best."

"Well, Patrón, you get what you pay for."

Lynear gestured quickly and nodded at the man behind him. "One of my dim-witted sons, George." He hunched himself a little forward and looked past me. "Excuse me, Sheriff. Mrs. Tisdale?"

She took a step forward and crossed her arms. "That's me."

"We haven't met formally, but I understand there was an altercation about the exact location of some fence?"

She glanced at George, the one who had just been dismissed. "My men said that they were restringing barbed wire near Frenchy Basin when a group of yours came up and threatened them."

We all stood there listening to the crickets rubbing their legs together as Eleanor's words hung in the crisp night. I was having one of those this-could-be-happening-a-hundred-years-ago moments when Lynear turned his shoulders and glanced at his son. "That won't happen again." He returned his gaze on all of us. "That, I can promise you."

I looked back at him, his eyes sunk into the fat of his face. "You travel well armed."

"Oh . . ." He reached up and shifted back the brim of his enormous hat. "As you can see, we've spent a lot of time down on the border; Hudspeth County to be exact. Do you know the area, Sheriff?"

"Not particularly."

"'Whoever commits sin also commits lawlessness, and sin is lawlessness.'" He shook his head. "It's a war zone down on the border—Godforsaken country—and we've just gotten in the habit of being prepared." He pointed at my sidearm. "As are you."

I put a hand up on one of the building's support poles and thumbed the grain of the wood. "There's a difference between preparing and provoking, Mr. Lynear."

He smiled. "Are we provoking you, Sheriff?"

"It sounds like your men might've been provoking Mrs. Tisdale's men, and I'd just as soon not have a range war in the southern part of my county."

His eyes remained immobile as he continued to smile, and it wasn't an attractive expression on his wide face. "Your county."

"Till the next general election, the people of this county have elected me to uphold the laws they deem fit to enforce."

"What about the law of God, Sheriff?"

"Not particularly my jurisdiction, Mr. Lynear."

He actually chuckled. "Oh, that's all part of our jurisdiction, and beside that fact, I happen to own a portion of your county, Sheriff. Almost twelve thousand acres, and as far as I know this is still a free country."

I sighed, suddenly tired of the man and his jingo philosophies. "Abide by the laws of the county, state, and federal government, and we won't have any trouble, Mr. Lynear, but if you start anything down here with your neighbors you're going to see me again."

He raised a hand. "I'm a God-fearing man in search of peaceful solitude in which to raise my family—I want nothing of the world, and the world wants nothing of me." He nodded as if giving a benediction. "There is a day of reckoning coming, though, a day when all men must take a side and the freedoms of some may impinge on the heresy and Godlessness of others."

I let George come around the truck before I spoke, specifically to him. "You need to register this vehicle in Wyoming."

He looked at his father, back to me, and then gave the slightest of nods before yanking open the driver's-side door; Tomás Bidarte folded his knife and climbed in the bed with his benefactor.

Just before George had time to preheat the coil and fire up the diesel, Vic waved and delivered one of my lines: "Happy motoring."

Roy Lynear looked thoughtfully at us from the bed of the truck as they backed up and pulled away in a cloud of smoke, sans a hardy Hi-yo, Silver. We watched as the big Ford skimmed out of the town proper and then took to the county road, its taillights looking like afterburners headed south.

"That was one fucker from strange."

Eleanor Tisdale sighed. "Which one?"

"Pick."

It was close to midnight when we got back to Durant, and once again all the traffic lights were blinking. Across Main Street there was a newly hung large banner, orange with black trim, that advertised Friday's big game between the Durant Dogies, whom Vic continually referred to as Doggies, and the Worland Warriors in their epic tiff—and the retiring of one Walt Longmire's jersey and that of Henry Standing Bear, both dutifully displayed on either side of the banner.

"Sixty-nine—really?"

I shrugged and thought about how I hadn't promised Nancy that I would be there. "I'd forgotten my number."

"Gives me ideas." I didn't rise to the bait, so she continued. "I bet you were popular."

I shrugged again. "I did all right."

She smiled, reading the banner as we drove underneath. "I bet ol' number thirty-two did better."

I thought about the Bear and how I'd better make a call out to The Red Pony Bar and Grill if I didn't want to face this ignominy alone. "Henry did better than everybody. He still does."

"I still want a corsage in the orange and black of the Durant Doggies."

"Dogies."

"What the hell is a doggie, anyway?"

"A dogie is a motherless calf."

She studied the storefronts as we drove through town, her thoughts darkening like the windows. "How appropriate. Do you find it worrisome that Cord escaped from or was expulsed by a religious cult and now we have one setting up camp in our own county?"

I glanced at her. "Our county?"

"Yeah, well . . . I wasn't elected, but I'm de facto."

"I thought you were a Moretti."

"Ha ha." She poked my shoulder with an index finger. "Answer the question."

"Yes, I do." I watched the buildings go by and had to admit that I liked the county seat quiet like this. "And it's even more worrisome since Tim Berg says the head honcho up at that place in *his* county also goes by the name of Lynear."

She turned to look at me. "You're kidding."

"Nope, but we also don't know for sure that our Lynear's place is a cult."

"Uh-huh—that conversation had more Bible quotes than a revival meeting." She thought about it. "You think Cord's mother might be mixed up with this bunch rather than the one in South Dakota?"

"Not with Sarah coming into the Butte County Sheriff's Office and the pants Cord had on from Belle Fourche, but there has to be a connection explaining why Cord showed up here."

"Other than a grandmother in Short Drop who obviously didn't know that he exists?"

"Yep."

"Considering the newfound information, I think it was very politic of you to not bring up the familial connection between the interstate Lynears with Eleanor Tisdale." She readjusted, tucking one boot under the other leg. "So, it sounds like you're getting ready to have a wide-reaching conversation with young Cord."

"I am now that the county psychologist says I can."

"What are you going to do about Roy Lynear and his bunch?"

I sighed. "Not a lot I can do until they do something against the law."

"Like walking around shoving their guns in people's faces and cleaning their fingernails with illegal knives?" She mused on the supposed compound to the south. "Your worst nightmare come true."

"And Eleanor Tisdale's, since apparently her husband sold the place to them."

She nodded to herself and smiled. "So, when are we going to go poke around the East Spring Ranch?"

I really didn't have the right, but I was curious, especially with the probable connection with the compound in South Dakota. It was also possible that I just didn't like Roy Lynear and his gun-toting son; either way, it was important to know what was going on down there in one of the neglected corners of my county. "First thing in the morning."

"What do you make of the Spanish blade?"

I thought about the man. "Doesn't fit, does he?"

"One severe case of badass, if you ask me."

"Why is that?"

"He wasn't scared, Walt. Considerate, yes, but not scared at all. Anybody else in that situation would've been just a little bit intimidated, but he wasn't." She waited to make the next statement after I passed the sheriff's office and took a left on Fort. "You're taking me home?"

"I figured that's where you'd want to go."

"Where are you sleeping?"

"The amazingly affordable and surprisingly comfortable

Absaroka County Jail." I glanced at her. "I figure I better spell
Double Tough since he's been babysitting Cord all evening."

"Then what's he supposed to do?"

It was true that my deputy's house was in Powder Junction, a
forty-five-minute drive south. "Don't you think he'd like to go
home?"

"Not particularly, considering that Frymire's girlfriend is visiting."

I thought about it as I took a right onto Desmet. "Yeah, I guess
they share a house."

She nodded. "A run-down, two-bedroom rental by the creek,
from what I hear. What, you think we can all afford houses on
what the county pays us?" We drove along in one of those silences
only women can produce, a ponderous, heavy quiet. "For your
information, I'm aware that you arranged the financing for my
house behind my back."

I pulled up in front of the little gray craftsman with the red
door. "I have no idea what it is you are talking about."

"I saw the papers."

I sat there for a moment and then tried a reverse in the back-
field. "I may have signed something that said you were an employee
in good standing with the sheriff's department—in short, I lied."

She didn't laugh but sat there studying her hands. After a
moment she unsnapped her safety belt, nudged her knees up
onto the seat, and, slapping my hat into the back, she slid herself
across my lap. She grabbed the back of my hair and yanked it,
locking her mouth over mine, and I could feel the waves of heat
from her body pounding me like surf on a coastal rock.

I snuck in the front door of the sheriff's office like a teenager getting in after curfew and could hear Double Tough snoring on the
bench in the reception area. I gave a salute to the painting of

Andrew Carnegie, a relic from when our building had been the town library, and quietly climbed the stairs past the 8×10s of all the sheriffs in our county's history, sure their eyes were watching me as I passed.

My deputy had dragged out a few pillows and a blanket from the supplies. The noise that he made was horrific, and I figured it was probably for the best that he wasn't sleeping in the holding cells with Cord—the poor kid would be deaf by morning.

I also reminded myself that tomorrow was Tuesday and that I would need to call my old boss, Lucian Connally, at the Durant Home for Assisted Living and cancel chess night if I was going to the southern part of the county to loiter with intent.

All of these things were roiling in my mind as I kicked an empty Mountain Dew can that Double Tough had left on the floor.

I stood there quietly as his snoring stopped, and he spoke. "You're grounded."

I turned and looked at him, or rather at the lump of gray wool blanket that passed for him. "How's our charge?"

"Asleep." He shucked the blanket and blinked at me. "Chief, you're not going to believe what we did tonight."

"I'm afraid to ask."

"You know the old TV and VCR down in the jail?"

"Yep."

He smiled. "I was walking by and saw a box of tapes in that stuff that Ruby's sending off to the church. I was feeling bad because the kid is just sitting in the cell reading his Bible like he's in solitary confinement, so I thought, What the heck, I'll make popcorn in the microwave and we'll watch a movie."

"What did you watch?"

"Well, it's not like we had a lot to choose from; I mean it was church lady movies. . . ."

I leaned against the dispatcher's counter. "Maybe that was for the best."

"*My Friend Flicka*, the one from a million years ago."

"Set in Wyoming—Mary O'Hara wrote the book."

"Yeah, well they filmed it in Utah. . . . But that's not the point." He swung his legs down and gathered the covers over his shoulders like a serape. "Chief, I don't think that kid has ever watched TV or a movie before, I mean ever." He stood and leaned an elbow on the counter with me. "I've never seen anything like it. I about fell asleep every ten minutes, but that kid was glued to the screen; he laughed and cried like the stuff was happening to him right there in the chair."

"I guess it's possible that . . ."

"He watched it three times."

"I'm sorry."

"That's okay; after the first time I just started watching him." He leaned down and picked up the can I'd kicked, crushing it effortlessly in his hand and tossing it into Ruby's wire trash can. "I hope Ruby don't mind, but I gave the kid the tape. I tried to explain that they had these new things, DVDs, but he didn't care. . . . You'da thought I gave him the friggin' horse."

"Where is he now?"

"Back in holding."

I yawned. "I'll check on him, and then I'm going to hit the hay in the other holding cell." I pushed off. "Seeing as there's no room at the inn."

I checked my office on the pass by but didn't see Dog and assumed that he must've been in the back keeping an eye on the young man. I tried to remember what the first movie was that I might've seen but could come up with nothing. I'd grown up on a northern Wyoming ranch about as far from everything as was possible in what seemed like a different century, but I watched

TV and couldn't imagine the kind of lifestyle where young Cord had never seen one.

I turned the corner in the dark room, quietly slipped along the wall to where I could see into the holding cell, and was immediately greeted with a rumbling half bark.

"Shhh . . ." I moved over to the bars and noticed that Double Tough must've changed his mind and decided to close the door. I pulled on it gently but discovered that it was locked. I glanced around and then reached over and flipped on the light; the only occupant in the cell was Dog.

4

"How long do you think?"

Double Tough was as flapped as I'd ever seen his unflappable self. "An hour at the most."

I thought about it. "He's on foot. Couldn't have gotten very far; the question is—did he go south or east?"

"You go one way and I'll go the other, but the highway or surface roads? The little idiot's so uninformed that he could be walking along the center stripe of I-25." We were moving toward the doors now, passing the reception area where I'd found Double Tough asleep only minutes ago. "Do you want to call in more staff?"

"No, we'll . . ."

The phone on Ruby's desk rang, and the two of us looked at each other, my deputy the first to vote. "We could ignore it."

I sighed. "That's not the sheriffing thing to do." I strode back to the desk and snatched it up. "Absaroka County Sheriff's Department."

The line buzzed and then became clear. "Walt?"

"Yep?"

More buzzing, and then the voice again. "This is Wally Johnson down here on the Lazy D-W."

I recognized his voice—I had heard Wally many times at the

National Cattlemen's Association, where he served as counsel. "How can I help you, Wally?"

Buzzing. "I'm sorry, I'm on this damn cordless down at the barn. You're not going to believe this, but I've got a couple horse thieves down here."

I waited a few seconds and then attempted to establish some priorities. "Wally, is this something we could discuss tomorrow?"

His turn to pause. "You mean you want me to let them go?"

I thought about the location of Wally and Donna's ranch, just a little south of town on the secondary road. "You mean you've *got them* got them?"

"Yes."

I glanced over at Double Tough and marveled at our good fortune; five more seconds and we would've been out the door. "Is one of them a skinny kid, blond with blue eyes?"

"Yeah, says his name is Cord."

"Who is the other one?"

There was a brief scrambling and some conversation in the background, and then the rancher came back on the line. "Old fella, says his name is Orrin Porter Rockwell, though I kinda find that hard to believe."

I thought of the Book of Mormon in the young man's possession. "Orrin the Mormon."

"Excuse me, Walt? Darn this cordless."

"Nothing." I readjusted the little cradle on Ruby's phone against my shoulder. "You say you've got them there?"

"Yeah. Bruce Eldredge is staying with us on his way back to Cody and was coming home from a friend's house and said there were two idiots out in the north pasture running around trying to catch the horses by hand. Hell, Walt, that's rough stock. They're lucky one of those horses didn't kick their brains out."

"Can you hold them till I get there?"

"Sure. Donna's got a shotgun on them right now, but the kid came up to my truck and volunteered your number; said you were probably looking for him."

"And the other one?"

"He's a pretty old, hippie-looking fellow, and he's still winded from chasing those horses all over the damn place. . . . I thought he was going to have a heart attack." There was some talking in the background. "What?" More talking. "Yeah, yeah, that's probably true."

"Wally?"

The rancher came back on the line, but I could hear his hand cupping the receiver to his mouth in an attempt to keep this portion of the conversation between the two of us. "The boy says that it wasn't anything like *My Friend Flicka*." His voice dropped even lower. "Walt, I've only been around this kid for twenty minutes, but he's something strange on that movie; I think he's brought it up about twelve times, and he's carrying an old VHS tape of the film with him."

When we got to the Lazy D-W, the two outlaws were sitting in the calving shed adjoining the main barn, the place where cowboys stayed on call during the time in the early spring when the cow mothers did their duty. I'd seen all kinds of calving sheds in my life, some just dirt-floor lean-to shanties with a snubbing pole in the middle to heated buildings with entertainment centers and rows of comfortable sofas on which to sit back and while away the half-sleep hours through the nights when most heifers decide to thicken the herd.

The Lazy D-W was the latter and not the former, and through the glass panel in the breezeway door I could see our two would-be horse thieves watching *My Friend Flicka* in studious rapture.

I glanced at Wally and especially at Donna, still holding the shotgun.

There were rumors about Donna Johnson. In my experience you couldn't swing a dead trench coat without hitting all kinds of folks who claimed to have worked for the CIA, but I'd heard the rumors about Donna, and my suspicions that she had indeed been employed by that organization were based on the fact that she never talked about it.

Never.

She shrugged. "It was the only place we had a VCR."

I studied the old man seated next to Cord on the edge of one of the leather sofas; he was smallish with silver hair hanging past his shoulders that feathered into a dark brown, and with a beard that stretched to the third button of his old-fashioned tab-collar shirt. Around his neck was a scarf with a pattern that made it look almost like a prayer shawl.

He was the man who had waved at me on the street in Durant.

I glanced at the screen and could see Roddy McDowall on the back of a horse racing hell-bent for leather across the green hills of a cinematic Wyoming—read Utah. Rockwell was leaning forward with his wrists resting on his knees and his gnarled hands gripping imaginary reins.

You didn't see hands like that much anymore. The fingers were thick, and I could see where the knuckles, especially those of the fore- and middle fingers, had been broken numerous times. There was only one type of activity that would sustain that kind of mutation; so whatever type of hippie Orrin the Mormon was, he hadn't been a peace-loving man.

Pushing the door open, I stepped into the room with Double Tough covering the doorway.

Cord immediately stood and smiled at me. "Hi, Sheriff."

The older man ignored us completely and began imitating the movements of the horseman on the screen, exerting a body English in an attempt to keep young Roddy in the saddle.

Cord looked up at me as I watched the Orrin character. The boy glanced back at the man and then up to me again. "He's never seen the movie before."

I smiled. "You mean this movie?"

He started to speak but then stopped. "There are others?"

I stared at the young man's face just to make sure he wasn't pulling my leg. "Yep." I glanced back at Double Tough and watched as he put a thumb and forefinger at the corners of his mouth to keep from smiling as I turned back to the boy. "Thousands of them, probably millions."

He stood there, looking at me askance, and then gestured toward the television. "Like this?"

"Well, not exactly like this, although I think there are a couple of sequels to this one. . . ."

"What's a sequel?"

Behind me, Double Tough smothered a laugh.

"Um . . . Look, we'll talk about that later." I gestured toward the oblivious man with my chin. "You know this fellow?"

"Uh-huh."

"He kidnap you?"

"I . . . I guess."

I rested the web of my thumb on the hammer of my Colt. "He did or he didn't?"

"Well, he asked me to go with him, but I told him I'd rather stay, and then he said we ought to go. So, I did."

That probably wasn't going to hold up in court. "Where were you going?"

"He didn't say."

I shook my head. "Are you in the habit of following people just because they tell you to?"

We both turned when the man who called himself Orrin Porter Rockwell made a noise in his throat as the horse on the screen leapt into a corner fence and fell, tangled and kicking. Cord's eyes turned back to me. "Him I do."

"He's a friend of yours?"

"He's my bodyguard."

I tipped my hat back on my head and stared at the young man. "You have a bodyguard?"

He shrugged. "I guess; he looks after me."

"Where's he been for the last few weeks?"

"Looking for me."

I sighed and glanced past the boy to the man. "Well, I guess he found you." I took a few steps, placing myself directly in the man's line of sight.

He leaned to the side and then shifted over to where he could get a better view, completely ignoring me.

"Sir?"

His face stayed on the screen, so I reached around behind me and punched the button, turning off the set.

A cry escaped him again, and he was immediately on his feet with his hands between us, but it wasn't a threatening gesture; rather, the fingers were splayed with palms up in a beseeching manner. "Sir, please . . ." Like the boy, his eyes were the amazing thing about him, but whereas the young man's were like sapphires, his were a pale blue almost to the point of being white. Opals. "The horse is endangered."

I stood there looking at the irises, unable to help myself, at least until the smell got to me, forcing me to lean back a little. "He'll be fine; at least he has been the other twenty-seven times I've seen it." I turned and hit STOP, then EJECT, and pulled the tape out, returning it to the cardboard sleeve.

Rockwell's eyes followed my hands as if I were holding the Hope Diamond.

"Mr. Rockwell, I presume?"

"Yes, sir."

"Danite, Man of God, Son of Thunder?"

He actually smiled. "Yes. Do you know me, sir?"

"Only by reputation. I'm going to need you to come with us, Mr. Rockwell."

His grin faded. "Am I under arrest?"

"Not yet, but I'm working on it."

"I won't be arrested." I started to reach toward his shoulder, but he dipped and took a half step back. "I won't have hands laid upon me neither."

We stood there looking at each other, the age-old standoff between arrestor and arrestee, the moment where everybody both inside and outside the law had to commit. I smiled, pretty sure I could take him; anyway, I didn't think I wanted to expose the boy to a wrestling match, so instead I leaned down a little and gazed into the luminescent eyes as I brought the videotape up between us. "I'll let you watch the rest of *Flicka*."

"Orrin Porter Rockwell."

Double Tough's voice carried across the room to my ears, muffled under the blanket that covered my face. It was my turn on the wooden bench. "Find anything?"

I smiled as he continued to punch buttons on the keyboard of Ruby's computer like a monkey trying to find a way to fit the square pegs in round holes. "Well, yeah. . . ."

"Still having fun?"

I listened as he leaned back in the desk chair. "He's a murderer."

"I know. According to history, about a hundred people

and the attempted assassination of the governor of Missouri, for one."

I joined him at the computer, where there was a photo of a man who appeared to be a forty-year-old version of the one watching *My Friend Flicka* in the basement. Double Tough leaned back in his chair and pointed. "That's him; he's younger there, but that's him."

"Well, that would figure." I looked over his shoulder. "Since according to this, he's two hundred years old."

The similarity was uncanny and patently impossible.

"When I read the name in the book some warning bells went off, but not loud enough to really catch my attention; then when Cord referred to him the way he did, I started putting two and two together." I gestured with a hand, introducing Double Tough to one of the most intriguing and mythical historical figures of the American West. "Meet Orrin Porter Rockwell, Danite, Man of God, Son of Thunder, and the strong right arm of the prophets of the Church of Jesus Christ of Latter-day Saints, commonly known as the Mormons, Joseph Smith Jr., and Brigham Young."

"No shit."

"The Danites were kind of a Mormon vigilante arm that exacted what they called Blood Atonements, and he was one of the chieftains, but he was also a mountain man, a gunfighter, and even a deputy marshal at one point." I leaned in even further and read the description. " 'He was that most terrible instrument that can be handled by fanaticism; a powerful physical nature welded to a mind of very narrow perceptions, intense convictions, and changeless tenacity. In his build he was a gladiator; in his humor a Yankee lumberman; in his memory a Bourbon; in his vengeance an Indian. A strange mixture, only to be found on the American continent.' "

Double Tough straightened up and stretched his back. "He's also very fond of *My Friend Flicka*."

"Yep, a true devotee."

"And as Lucian would say, and I would second, crazy as a waltzin' pissant."

"That, too." I yawned. "I'll have Vic run his prints through the IAFIS and we'll find out which bin he escaped from; then we'll go from there."

"What about the kid?"

"I don't know. His grandmother wants him, but we've got to find the mother."

"Wouldn't that be South Dakota's job?"

I folded my hands into church and steeple, burying my nose in the front door. "Strictly speaking."

"No fucking way."

I raised my hat up and looked at my undersheriff, who, despite the landscape, appeared to be enjoying driving my truck, and then shifted around to glance at the Cheyenne Nation studying the ancient copy of the Book of Mormon in the backseat.

"Let me guess: these sublime surroundings do not meet with your picturesque approval."

I'd told Henry Standing Bear that our numbers were being retired at the high school this weekend, and the rambling conversation that ensued had included the jaunt to South Dakota, and the Bear had decided to come along.

Vic nodded. "What's the next town in the land that time forgot?"

I glanced around, getting a reading. "Beulah, at the state line."

"Does the scenery change a lot at the border?"

"Not particularly." I shook my head and looked at her, noticing how the two black eyes were transmuting to purple and yellow. "Haven't you ever driven this way?"

"Not sober." After a moment of smiling at herself and at Henry in the rearview mirror, she spoke again. "So what's in Beulah, other than a Shell station?"

"Ranch A."

"What the hell is Ranch A?"

I raised my hat up to block the full-on sunshine that slanted through the side window and thought about how the sleeping portion of the trip might be formally over. "A is for Annenberg."

She threw me a little tarnished gold over the purple and yellow. "Annenberg as in the Philadelphia Annenbergs?"

"Yep." I gestured to the right. "Just over those gently rolling hills is one of the most beautiful ranches in all of Wyoming—evidently the Annenbergs thought it was a nice place to stop." I placed my hat back over my face as the Bear finished the salvo.

"Maybe you need to get out more."

The Butte County Sheriff's Department is in Belle Fourche, South Dakota, and is right on the main drag of Route 85, but Tim Berg's house was off that beaten path. A beautiful Craftsman facing Hanson Park, the house was made such mostly due to the ministrations of his red-headed wife, Kate. It was all forest green and oiled wood with hanging baskets and multilayered flower beds that exploded from the rich South Dakota soil like vegetative fireworks.

As Vic parked the truck, Henry and I stepped over the painted curb, and I raised a hand to the woman in Bermuda shorts and a Sturgis tank top, who ignored me completely, wheeled a barrow around the corner of the house, and disappeared.

I allowed my hand to drop as Vic joined us on the manicured lawn. "Somebody you don't know?"

I shrugged and crossed the sidewalk, climbed the stairs, and knocked on the screen door. "Open up, it's the law."

From inside, a man's voice answered. "It's the law in here, too."

"Well then, let's have a convention."

"I've got beer."

The sheriff of Butte County was drinking a Grain Belt Nordeast at his kitchen table and watching a *Duck Dynasty* marathon on A&E on a tiny black-and-white television that looked like it got the same kind of reception as the one I used to have in my cabin back home before Cady had ordered DIRECTV. "Watching a family reunion, Tim?"

He reached out and turned off the reality show. "You know, Walt, even the women on this show have beards. Or maybe it's the reception." He shook hands with Henry and glanced up and saw Vic. He grinned broadly through the hair on his face, looking all the world like a happy hedgehog and not all that different from Orrin Porter Rockwell or the guys on TV. "Hey, good-lookin'!"

She peeled off his Minnesota Vikings ball cap and smooched his bald spot. "You in here drinking beer and watching must-see TV while your wife does all the work outside?"

"Kinda looks like it, don't it?" He quaffed the Grain Belt and resettled his hat. "You guys want a beer?"

"Nah, we're working." I pulled out a chair and sat, as the Bear and Vic did the same. "Anything more on the boy's mother?"

He nodded. "A few things; the folks in that compound up north still say they don't know who she is, but the librarian over here, Pat Engebretson, says what sounds like the same woman came in and was wanting to use the phone books to try and find a number—and that's the one that was scribbled on the bottom of that piece of paper you've got."

"It's her mother who hasn't seen her in seventeen years; she lives down in Short Drop in the southern part of Absaroka."

Tim nodded. "Well, Pat says that some young fellers showed up in a scours-colored Chevy pickup and hustled her out of there toot sweet."

I studied his beer and regretted my choice not to have one. "Any idea who they were?"

"Well, when I had my little confrontation with the kids up north, they were driving a pickup remarkably of that description."

Henry smiled, crossing his powerful arms across his chest. "Not showing a lot of reserve, are they?"

Tim took a paper towel from a holder on the table and wiped up the condensation from his beer that was staining the surface of the woven place mat. "Not their style."

"Anything else?"

"Yup, I was up north talking to some of the ranchers where they're running that Bakken pipeline . . ."

Vic interrupted. "The what?"

"Bakken shale oil pipeline from North Dakota; they're running it through here, around the Black Hills, and then over your way and down to the crude oil storage hub in central Oklahoma— move 200,000 barrels of oil a day. At least they will when they get it finished here in a few years. Anyway, I was talking to Dale Atta, who has a ranch north of here, and he said that he saw that same truck that day up on the ridge that separates his place from theirs; that it was still there when he got done really late that evening, but that it was gone the next morning."

"Where's the ranch?"

"I can show you easier than tell you." He pushed the beer away. "But first, I've got somebody I'd like you to meet." He stood and walked to the back door. "We can walk; it's not very far."

Henry, Vic, and I looked at each other and then followed Tim outside; Kate, having unloaded her barrow full of compost at the far corner by the fence, turned and wheeled past us.

Tim raised a hand. "I'm going to introduce 'em to Vann Ross."

She stopped, looked at all of us, and trundled on. "This will all end badly."

We watched her go and then turned to look at Tim, who stroked his beard. "She doesn't approve of this particular investigation."

I took a deep breath and shot it from my nose. "My wife and I had a few of those disagreements."

He looked at me, curious. "How did they end?"

"Badly."

Through a gate at the back, we entered what probably had been an alleyway but through disuse had evolved into an overgrown path that ran along the back of all the houses facing Hanson Park.

As we walked, I asked, "Who's Vann Ross?"

Tim smiled and continued on. "Oh, I better let Vann speak for himself."

At the end of the block, the street butted into a hillside and there was a fence like those on the other lots, perhaps not in as good a shape, but higher. From the angle in the alley, you could see that the structure was roughly of the same vintage as the Bergs' but had not weathered the years as well. Some of the windows were broken, and it looked as if they had been patched with sheets of cardboard. Large areas of shingles were missing from the roof, and the rusted gutters hung from the eaves.

I watched as Tim knocked on the gate. "Hey, Vann, it's Tim Berg and I've got some folks who would like to meet you."

There was no sound from inside.

Vic ventured an opinion. "Maybe he's not home."

Tim knocked again. "He's always home—hey, Vann!"

There was a noise, almost as if someone was banging away from inside an old iron bathtub, and then the sound of someone mumbling, at which point the gate nudged away from us with a metallic sound; it opened inward about four inches to reveal a very tanned and wrinkled elf in a faded pair of hibiscus-patterned, pink-and-baby-blue-colored Hawaiian shorts.

"Hello, Timothy, how are you?"

The sheriff nodded. "I'm good, Vann, and you?"

"Fine, just fine." Pulling the hair at his eyebrows, he looked past Tim toward Vic, the Cheyenne Nation, and me. "Who are your friends?"

"Just some folks who would like to see your handiwork."

Vann Ross glanced at us again but especially at Henry. "They're not from the government, are they?"

"No."

He seemed satisfied and opened the door just wide enough to allow us entry.

I have seen many strange things in my tenure as the sheriff of Absaroka County, my duty in Vietnam, and even my time spent in California, but nothing could've possibly prepared me for Vann Ross's backyard. There was junk piled against the outer perimeter and poles poked up through the rubble periodically to hold up what looked to be netted camouflage, the kind we used in the military to hide vehicles, aircraft, and other equipment from surveillance planes. All of this was pretty weird but paled in comparison to what took up most of the backyard: twelve perfectly formed and frighteningly realistic spaceships.

They were of different shapes and sizes but all made of what looked to be aircraft-grade aluminum, and there were hatchways and navigational bubbles that had been salvaged from other planes.

Henry and I looked at each other.

Vic mumbled. "Fuck me."

The spaceships looked like they had been constructed from old science-fiction drawings I'd seen on the covers of *Popular Mechanics* and *Astonishing Stories*, some elongated like futuristic cigars and others assembled into saucers that could have been poster children for the United States Air Force Blue Book.

Vann beamed in appreciation of our stunned faces, while Tim walked over to the nearest vehicle, which was named *The Dan*. "Looks like you're about to finish the last one."

The tiny and what I took to be at least eighty-year-old man stepped next to the sheriff and patted the riveted aluminum. "She's almost finalized." He smiled, revealing a set of perfect teeth. "I think she's my best one yet."

The Dan had the look of a mother ship and was about thirty feet long with large, tear-shaped observation windows that were most likely cannibalized from a PBY Catalina. I walked down the length of the thing, ducking under the circumference of a nearby saucer, and looked in the windows, where I could see rows of plastic seats with tubular handles sticking out to the sides.

"The seats are out of Subaru Brats; they had those in the beds of those little trucks. . . ."

"I remember." Still running a hand over his creation, I nodded. He pointed toward the aerodynamic stabilizers at the rear of the ship. "Of course, when it's finished I'll stand it up on its end for takeoff."

"Of course." I took the extra moment to get a good look at him and studied his face. He was definitely in his eighties, but the bone structure was fine. There was a small dimple at the end of his nose and curls of gray hair escaped from under a formless hat that might've been a Stetson Gun Club at some point. Evidently he spent a great deal of time out of doors, working in the reflection of the spaceships, because his skin was roasted like a coffee bean. "You did all of these yourself, Mr. Ross?"

He nodded, and his voice took on a fervent quality as he again plucked at his eyebrows. "I did; each one is named for one of the twelve tribes of Israel."

Henry joined us, and I glanced at Tim, but he was looking at the toes of his boots and smiling. "How long have you been at it?"

"Since 1957."

The Bear nodded his head solemnly. "Amazing."

I looked carefully up and down the thing, but for the life of me I couldn't see any air intakes or exhaust ports. "Where are the engines?"

He smiled at my naïveté. "It doesn't need them; it will ascend by divine power."

"Ahh."

He looked around. "I'm sorry to be so careful. I sometimes liberate parts from Ellsworth Air Force Base on the other side of Rapid City, and I'm afraid they've taken exception to my combing through their salvage yard over the years."

I fingered a seam. "I bet."

He noticed my interest. "I've used Ace Hardware heavy-duty gutter caulking to stand up to the rigors of interplanetary travel."

I concurred, sage-like. "A wise precaution." He seemed to want more, so I added, "My father used to say that extra dollar a tube is always worth it."

He fussed with his eyebrows yet again. "You see, Adam will return to Earth to take us away within the rapture and convey us to the twelve planets that have been reserved for us."

"Wow." I really wasn't sure of what else to say.

His eyes were drawn back to Henry. "Yes, and when the great battle arises between the races of black and white, he will return and those who are true believers will be taken with him."

The Bear looked at the elf. "That would be Adam, of Adam and Eve fame?"

"Yes." He patted Henry's arm. "You see, the Lamanites are going to help us overcome the Coloreds."

Henry and I looked at each other. "And have we got a time-line on that?"

He seemed a little disappointed that I'd asked and was giving his eyebrow hell. "It was supposed to be the millennium in 2000; there were a couple chances before that one, but it was the big one. Then in 2003 we were not struck by the planet Nibiru. . . ."

"Right." I nodded as Vic and Tim joined us.

"December 21st, 2012, didn't work out either, but I haven't lost hope."

Henry nodded in a comforting fashion. "One should always have faith."

Vic interrupted. "Vann, Tim here was telling me about your wonderful talent, the one with dogs?"

He turned back to me, nodding with a great deal of enthusiasm. "In my free time, I teach dogs how to talk. I use mental telepathy and can get them to say words like hello, squirrel, and hamburger."

"He's a relatively harmless old eccentric who keeps to himself and writes editorials to the newspaper as the One, Mighty and Strong, the Lion of Judah, and the King of Israel. He also calls in on local radio shows a lot."

Vic pursed her lips. "Hell, I'd tune in for that."

"You saw how tanned he is?"

We were walking back to Tim's house on the return route in the alleyway. "Yep, I figured he got it working on the saucers; did he do all the aluminum work, welding, and riveting himself?"

Henry piped up. "And caulking, do not forget the caulking."

Tim nodded his head and stuffed his hands into his jeans pockets. "He did—he's very popular around the neighborhood; you bring him anything and he can fix it. But did you see his tan?" Berg stopped and turned sideways to look at us. "Well, he wasn't always so popular around here. About twenty years ago the One, Mighty and Strong back there got a revelation from God saying the true believers were going to be taken to the City of Enoch on the North Star. Supposedly God tells Vann that they need to prepare for the journey by protecting themselves from getting burned on reentry into Earth's atmosphere, so they should get a good, all-over suntan."

Vic covered her face with a hand. "Have you ever noticed it's the people you don't want to see naked who are always taking their clothes off?"

"Uh-huh." Tim continued walking, and we followed. "As the story goes, Vann was married at the time to two women, Noemi and Big Wanda, and they had some kids—well, there they all were up on the roof of the house with no clothes on; caused quite a stir."

"I bet."

"They started praying up a storm for God to send 'em a flying saucer in the middle of the night, and when that didn't happen, Vann told 'em that he might've missed the landing spot and that they should all go over to the city park and wait for the spaceship." Tim stopped at his gate and undid the latch. "The old sheriff, Pete Anderson, said things must've gotten pretty busy over there 'cause Big Wanda claimed to have had sex with an extraterrestrial, which Vann interpreted as her being resurrected, whereupon he got another revelation that they should pass the resurrecting around by having sex first with one of his wives and then the other. Evidently, it was only when he got divine instructions to have sex with his dog that he started having his doubts."

Tim went inside as Vic turned to me and the Bear. "You know what I said about all the crazy people being in our county?"

"Yep."

"I take it all back."

We followed Tim through the gate—I stopped to make sure the latch was secured.

To my surprise, Kate was sitting under an umbrella at a round table with five glasses and a pitcher of iced tea. She and Tim were in conference as he pulled out a chair and sat.

". . . Because it's my job."

She shook her head as we joined them. "He's just a harmless old man, and I don't see why it is that you had to go down there and get him all wound up."

"We didn't wind him up; besides, he likes showing off his spaceships." He glanced at Vic. "Especially to pretty girls. You gotta admit it's much better than 'You wanna come up and see my etchings?' "

"Yeah, as lines go." Vic swirled her ice cubes with her tongue. "What's a Lamanite?"

The Cheyenne Nation poured himself a glass and handed me the pitcher. "Lamanites are American Indians, sworn enemy to the Nephites, both of which, according to the Book of Mormon, are descendants from the persecuted Jews of Jerusalem who migrated to America in 600 B.C."

I smiled and poured myself an iced tea. "So, you're Jewish?"

"Imagine my surprise." He squeezed a piece of lemon into

his tea and continued. "There was a war between the two tribes in 428 A.D. and we, the Lamanites, wiped out the Nephites. Then, about fourteen hundred years later, an angel by the name of Moroni, son of Mormon, a Nephite, reveals himself to Joseph Smith and gives him the golden plates to translate."

Vic leaned into me. "You know that part about Catholicism being crazy?"

"Yep."

"I take all that back, too."

The Bear set his glass on the table with a sense of finality. "And that is how Mormonism began."

Tim looked suspicious. "How come you know so much about Mormons?"

"I read the Book of Mormon in the truck from Durant to Belle Fourche."

Berg ran a hand through his beard. "That's a lot of reading."

"I am a quick study."

I interrupted the theological conference. "The visit with Vann Ross was all pretty entertaining, Tim, but I was just wondering why we went up there?"

"Well, I got to thinking about that bunch from north of town, especially when I saw that same scours-yellow truck heading down our street. Hell, Vann Ross's been around here since, like he said, in the fifties." He thought about it. "Except, I think there was a stint at a mental hospital in Lincoln, Nebraska. . . ."

Kate's voice was a little sharp. "Your point?"

"Well, I remember when we had to pick him up for the little fiasco in the park and did the paperwork. Hell, everybody around here called him Vann or Mr. Ross for so long I don't think anybody knew his last name."

Her voice grew even sharper. "Which is?"

Tim's eyes clicked to mine. "Lynear."

Vic was the first to react. "Oh, crap."

Tim nodded. "Yup."

"So he's related to the individuals you had the run-in with and the one we met in Short Drop?"

"His son is Roy, the one you were telling me about, and Roy's sons are George over in your county and Ronald in mine."

"Oh, boy." Vic coughed a laugh. "Okay, so we've got space cadet Vann Ross, the king of all loonies, living down the street, one crazy grandson living on a compound here in Butte County, and the son and another grandson who have taken up residence in our county, with a fifteen-year-old who's also a grandson, somehow tangled up in all of this?"

I sipped my iced tea. "Yep."

Henry pulled his dark hair back and captured it in the leather tie he kept in his shirt pocket for just such occasions. "Are all of them as . . . colorful, as Mr. Vann Ross Lynear?"

We all, with the exception of Kate, nodded.

"My question, then, would be what is the crime we are investigating?"

I thought about it. "Right now, I'm focusing on the missing mother, Sarah Tisdale."

Henry grunted. "Hhnh. And our next step would be?"

I turned to look at him and then Tim. "You say a rancher with a place adjacent saw members of the compound up there fooling around?"

"He did."

"Was it on his property or theirs?"

"Unfortunately, theirs."

I leaned back in my chair and listened to it creak in protest. "What are the chances of us getting a warrant?"

"In the greater flourishing of time."

"That's the problem with warrants, isn't it?" I turned and looked at both Vic and the Cheyenne Nation. "Do you know that we are at the geographic center of the entire United States?"

She glanced at Tim and Kate and then back to me. "You're not having the urge to build spaceships, are you?"

"Belle Fourche, South Dakota, is the geographic center of the United States."

Vic continued to look doubtful. "I thought that was Kansas."

"That's contiguous, but since 1959 . . ."

Tim, who was looking at me a little oddly, too, finished the statement. "Um, yup . . . when they included Alaska and Hawaii. There's a big visitors center down by the river."

"But the actual, geographic point is farther north, right?"

He nodded and sighed. "About twenty miles, actually."

Henry, getting with the plan, joined in. "I have always wanted to see that."

Tim leaned back and looked at the sun, well past its zenith. "We've got the rest of the afternoon to get up there."

I glanced at Kate and then back to him. "You're not going."

He immediately raised his short hairs. "All right now, Walt. Lookie here . . ."

"We're sightseeing, we got lost, and that's going to be a heck of a lot harder to sell if we're in the company of the county sheriff." I turned back to Vic. "Haven't you always wanted to see the geographic center of the United States?"

She started shaking her head no, then converted it into a nod and buried her face in her hands. "No fucking way."

5

The road to Dale Atta's place was straight up Route 85 and then onto Camp Creek Road. Tim had called ahead, and when we got to Atta's place the genial rancher had already drawn us a quick map and told us how to get to the outer hay fields where he had been working when he'd seen his neighbor's truck. He warned us that the road, or what there was of it, was pretty rough leading onto the ridge and that there was only one way up or down.

I navigated the furrows and tried to avoid the areas where there might be irrigation lines and a center pivot as we made our way along a rapidly flowing creek bed. Vic kept an eye out for the pickup in question.

"What the hell are scours?"

Henry was quicker to answer, even though his nose was still in the Book of Mormon. "Calf diarrhea."

"Oh, gross." We bumped along in four-wheel-drive low, so as to do the least amount of damage to the rancher's field. "So, I'm looking for a truck the color of butt butter?"

"You got it."

"Have I told you how disenchanted I'm becoming with the romantic vision of the American West?"

I gestured toward the limitless vista outside the windshield. "And here you are in the very heart of it."

I steered us across a bridge that had been made from an old freight car, a common practice in our part of the world, and pulled up to a number of strands of barbed wire with a steel sign affixed, which read **KEEP OUT, PRIVATE PROPERTY**, followed by **TRESPASSERS WILL BE PROSECUTED.**

I slowed the truck to a stop and looked at the shiners riding shotgun. "Feel like doing something unlawful?"

She cracked the passenger door open and climbed out. "Always, and all ways."

I was surprised that there was no padlock and watched as she pulled the lever, releasing the pole the fence was attached to and pulling it wide so that I could drive through as the Cheyenne Nation intoned from the back. "So, how did she get the black eyes?"

Vic's shiners had turned out to be not as bad as I'd thought, but there were still traces of a rainbow underneath her eyes. "The runaway ran over the top of her."

"And she did not shoot him?"

"She was unarmed at the time."

The Bear grunted. "Lucky kid."

I drove through the opening and then watched as she started to reattach the gate, stranding herself on the other side, but then realized her mistake and quickly stepped through, capturing the pole in the loop and leveraging it shut.

She climbed back in. "Don't say it."

The trail was rough with more than a few large boulders we had to ease over, but we finally got to the ridge, a desolate spot with only a few copses of Black Hill pines, stunted and bowed from the crippling wind.

I pulled the Bullet to the right, where there was a space between some of the ragged trees, and parked. The wind was blowing so hard that it was difficult to open the door, but once I did I snagged my field glasses from the pocket in the back of my seat. I cranked my hat down tight and stared off through the binoculars to the northwest, the direction from which the gusts seemed to be coming. I could see the fresh-turned earth where the Bakken pipeline Tim had mentioned had been bored along the surface of the land, cutting diagonally from northeast to southwest toward Wyoming. Deceivingly durable, the surface of the high plains held the marks of man almost as long as the land itself marked those same men.

Henry drifted toward the center of the ridge, and Vic joined me at the tailgate. "NFW."

"It is pretty desolate."

The Cheyenne Nation had walked toward a small wreath of rocks to the west so I followed a broken path and stopped before entering the bowl of soft earth. From this vantage point, I could see that Henry was staring at one of the towers that Tim had mentioned. It sat at the corner of another county road near the hillside leading to the ridge. There were a few trees in the area that were making believe they were green, and it was painted to blend in. "See anybody?"

"Yes, someone watching us with a pair of binoculars."

Henry, of course, didn't need binoculars, but I couldn't see any movement in the area, aside from a small cloud of dust on the far horizon.

I raised my own and adjusted the eyepieces enough to see an individual at one of the windows of the tower before he darted away. Then my eye was drawn to a vehicle racing down the powdery road, but still too far away to make identification. I handed the binoculars to Vic as she joined us. "Keep an eye on that, and let me know if it's who I think it is."

She raised the glasses. "How could they have found out about us so quickly?"

The Bear pointed toward the tower and then turned and approached the dirt bowl we'd walked past. I followed him and then his gaze. There were boot prints in the area, and tire tracks where you could see they had backed in.

His voice was low. "Why back into a place with a pickup unless you were unloading something?

A small line of powder on the lee side of a fist-sized clump of dirt stuck with a few stalks of buffalo grass caught my eye.

Vic's voice challenged the wind as she called over her shoulder. "Are scours a kind of muddy yellow?"

"Yep."

"It's them."

I sighed. "How long to get here and up the road we came in on?"

"At the rate they're going, ten minutes, tops."

Henry's eyes narrowed. "Not enough time to exhume what could be a body, even if we knew where to dig."

I walked over to my undersheriff. "Hey, have you got a lipstick on you?"

She lowered the binoculars and looked at me. "I do, but I don't think it's your shade."

"Gimme the top, would you?" She did, and I walked back and kneeled, gently pushed a little of the white powder into the elongated plastic top, and then smelled my finger.

"Quick lime?"

"Yes." I carefully put the makeshift container in my shirt pocket, started toward my truck, and called back to Henry. "C'mon, we better not let them catch us at this exact spot."

We set about the business of getting off the ridge, unable to hurry because of the boulders. We'd gotten to the last straight, but I was pretty sure we weren't going to make it. We arrived at the gate, and I could see them approaching from the access road on the other side. I figured they'd meet us on the bridge, if we gunned it.

When I got to the gate, I rolled to a stop and turned to Vic. "Undo the gate but don't bother with putting it back; just throw yourself into the bed as I drive through."

"Got it."

She was out like a Philly flash. The Bear climbed out, too.

"Where are you going?"

He grinned the wolf smile. "What, stay in here and miss all the fun?"

Henry shut the door behind him, and I watched as Vic popped the lever on the gate and threw it aside with enough force that I had no trouble driving through. I heard the two of them clambering into the bed as I got to the bridge, but the Chevy roared up the incline and halfway across before I could get that far. He slid to a stop about a foot from my bumper and leaned on the horn.

There were four of them, two in the cab and two standing in the bed. The ones there were holding Winchester carbines while the passenger displayed a revolver and threw me what he considered to be a dangerous smile. The driver was probably the oldest of the bunch at maybe eighteen, and he popped the clutch, jumping the two-wheel-drive half-ton forward in a threatening manner.

Evidently, they weren't intimidated by the stars on my doors or the light bar on top.

Advance party.

A pack.

I heard a clattering on the top of the cab and looked in the rearview mirror, and was treated to Victoria Moretti's legs spread in a shooting stance, Henry next to her, leaning against the roof. I turned my eyes back to the Chevy and sat there waiting, looking at them.

After a moment, the passenger, who had a mop of black hair falling over his face, leaned out the side and yelled, "Back up!"

I shook my head no.

There was a brief conference with the driver, who had the same hairdo as his passenger, only blond—must've been the style of the month. "We can make you!"

I didn't move, and the driver leapt the half-ton forward again, now only inches from the front of my truck. He revved the hopped-up engine, the exhaust brapping—no mufflers.

The problem with the younger generation is that they confuse horsepower and torque. Most people think horsepower, which can lead to higher top speeds, is the most important—but the thing that gets you there is torque. Neither one of us was likely to reach top speed on the limited length of the bridge, and I was reminded of Mark Twain's adage: thunder is impressive, thunder is loud, but it's lightning that gets the job done, even in one-mile-an-hour increments.

I pulled my transmission selector down and inched forward in granny gear, four-wheel low. He answered by unleashing the clutch on the half-ton and crunching into my rubber-padded, traffic-pushing grille guard.

I kept an even pressure on the accelerator, just enough to hold the three-quarter-ton in place. He was getting angrier as I held him steady, and he gunned probably four hundred horses forward, causing the rear end the Scours Express to emit blue smoke and kick its heels slightly sideways.

Mistake.

I waited until he'd reached the farthest point on the pivot and then nudged the broad nose of my 450-foot-pounds of torque forward.

He had two wheels pushing—I had four.

It was time the young men had a lesson in physics.

Slowly and achingly, I drove him back at an angle. He slammed on the brakes, but I already had him moving and there was little chance that, with my extra weight, I was going to be stopped.

The driver's-side rear wheel was the first to go off, and I have to admit that I found the looks on the faces of the boys who were standing pretty amusing. I kept the pressure on and watched as they leapt from the truck onto the surface of the bridge. The Chevrolet kept going backward.

There was a pretty heated conversation going on between the two in the cab, especially when the driver's-side front wheel also went over the edge. I kept pushing, and the Chevy looked as though it was just getting to the point where I thought it might go over and fall on its side into the shallow creek four feet below. The conversation had reached the screaming-teenager stage when the mouthy passenger started making moves to open the door and climb out.

It was then that I heard someone walking over the top of my truck and watched as a pair of moccasined feet stepped down onto the cowl and strode across the hood. The Cheyenne Nation placed a hand on the grille guard and then lightly leveraged himself onto the wide, wooden planks of the bridge.

I let off the accelerator and watched as he made it to the door of the tipping truck before the kid could get it open.

The two who had abandoned ship were standing a little ways away, still holding their weapons but unsure as to how to proceed. One started to take a step forward but then thought better of it.

The mouthy passenger made the mistake of shoving his pistol toward the Bear, but he simply snatched it out of the kid's hand and casually tossed it into the water. I could see the veins in the young man's neck as he screamed at Henry, but the Bear just stood there looking at him. After a moment, the teen had to pause to catch his breath, and Henry took the opportunity to say something, which caused the driver to join the high-volume vitriol.

The Cheyenne Nation turned to look at Vic and me, shrugged his shoulders, and then casually, almost dismissively, reached down and grabbed the rocker panel in both hands. I don't know how much weight it was or how much effort it took, but the Chevy rose in his grip, jerked once, and then gracefully tipped over the side, landing in the mud with a tremendous splash.

The near wheels were only a few feet from the bridge, and the dry side of the USS *C-10* was a couple of feet higher than the wooden surface. The two still in the truck were scrambling to get out the passenger-side window as Vic and I joined Henry in surveying the damage.

"I thought you were trying to save them."

He sighed. "Me, too."

The passenger's legs and feet were wet, but the driver was soaked as their truck bucked a few times and then died in its watery grave. The passenger, who on closer inspection might've been Hispanic, was, of course, the first to speak. "You're gonna have to pay for that!"

I glanced at the pair who had been in the bed and who were still standing at the far end of the bridge, and watched as Vic, with her sidearm hanging in her hand, turned to face them.

I swiveled my gaze back to the two U-boat commanders. "I doubt it."

The driver whined. "You pushed us off the bridge!"

I threw a thumb at the Cheyenne Nation. "Actually, he did."

The passenger was back at it. "Well, somebody's gonna have to . . ."

I held up a finger. "You know, back when I was doing my

initial training at the Law Enforcement Academy in Douglas, Wyoming, long before either one of you were born, one of the first things a crusty old instructor taught me about dealing with the public, and that would be you, is that we can argue as long as you'd like—and then I win."

They didn't seem to know what to say to that, so I continued.

"If you keep running your mouths, I'm going to haul the bunch of you down to Belle Fourche and throw you in jail for interfering with a law-enforcement official and his sworn duties, let alone brandishing weapons in an unlawful manner."

I could feel Vic looking at the side of my face; she loved it when I made up laws, and I could almost hear her wondering if there was a way to brandish weapons in a lawful manner.

I let the dust on that one settle before sticking my hand out. "Would you like some assistance in exiting the vehicle?"

The passenger spit in the distance between us. "We don't need no help from you."

I shrugged and gave the cadre of gunmen at the end of the bridge a hard look and then started back toward my truck with the Cheyenne Nation and my undersheriff in tow as the driver called after us. "Hey, could you give us a ride?"

I stopped and looked at Henry and Vic and then back to the kid. "Where?"

There wasn't much room with all four of them in the cab with us, but at least I'd made them give up all their weapons, which were now in the toolbox in the bed of the Bullet.

The Bear had his arms draped over the shoulders of the kids in the backseat, which included the driver of the pickup. The passenger who had brandished the pistol was seated between Vic and me, and I had to admit that I found it pretty humorous that the mouthy one, who seemed indifferent to all the trappings of authority, was completely buffaloed by my very attractive deputy. We'd been driving for ten minutes, and I wasn't sure he'd made eye contact with her yet.

She propped an elbow on the armrest and supported her chin in the web of her hand as she looked at him, and I could actually feel him crowding me in the seat in an attempt to put some distance between the two of them.

I cleared my throat and decided to throw the kid a lifeline. "So, what's your name?"

He cleared his throat. "Edmond." He glanced at Vic. "Eddy."

"Eddy what?" I asked, half expecting him to say Lynear.

"Lynear."

There was a chuckle from the back, but I wasn't quick enough in the rearview mirror to see who had thought that was funny.

"And what are the names of the rest of your Merry Men?"

"Well, that's my older brother, the one that was driving the truck before it went in the creek. His name is Edgar Lynear. . . ."

To my trained eye, they didn't look anything alike. "The two of you are brothers?"

He shrugged with one shoulder. "Well, more like half-brothers."

"I see."

He turned. "The other one in that corner is Merrill Lynear, and this one on this side is Joe."

Joe even went so far as to produce a hand on my shoulder, which I shook. "You're a Lynear, too?"

He nodded. Eddy stayed turned in the seat, and I could guess who he was looking at; evidently six-and-a-half-foot-tall Cheyenne warriors were safer to gaze upon than five-and-a-half-foot Italian deputies who filled out their uniform shirts in interesting ways.

"Are you a real Indian?"

Henry waited a moment and then replied, "Honest Injun." He extended a hand to him. "I am Henry Standing Bear, Bear Society, Dog Soldier Clan."

Eddy shook his hand. "Wow."

Joe asked the next question. "Are you under arrest, too?"

Vic laughed, and Henry's voice took on a gentle tone. "No, the sheriff is a friend of mine."

Eddy turned to look at me. "You're not the sheriff; we've met him and he's got a great big beard."

"I'm a different sheriff, from another county—another state." I paused a moment. "Didn't you guys read the emblems on my truck?"

There was no response, and a depressing thought crossed my mind. "You fellows mind if I ask you a question?" Nobody voiced an objection, so I continued. "It's a school day; how come none of you are in class?"

"We don't go to school no more."

I glanced around at them—they looked about Cord's age. "None of you?"

Eddy, obviously the spokesman of the group, shook his head. "Nope, we all graduated, and now we're the First Order, guaranteed seats in the Celestial Kingdom." He looked out the window and went into a now familiar autospeak. "We guard the perimeter of the Apostolic Church of the Lamb of God, keeping the faithful safe: the shepherd unto his sheep."

"Baaahh . . ."

He turned and for the first time made eye contact with Vic, the one emitting animal noises. "Are you an unbeliever?"

Vic sighed. "Don't fuck with me, kid. I'm a recovering Catholic, and we owned most of the known world when your bunch started promising people planets and wearing funny underwear."

Thankfully, Eddy interrupted the theological debate by raising his hand and pointing to a T in the road just beyond a plastic-
flowered cross, the kind that marks vehicle fatalities—I'd seen
enough of those, especially on the highways to the Rez, to last
me into eternity. At the other side of the turnoff there was a girl,
looking fragile and unprotected in a homemade prairie dress and
bonnet, who was sitting behind a card table with what looked to
be baked goods. "You take a right here."

Thinking it had been quite a while since I'd had some homemade baked goods, I slowed the truck. The kid must've misunderstood my change of speed. "Umm, you can just drop us off
here."

I looked down the rutted dirt road and could see that it
stretched to the horizon. "That's okay; I think I'd like to make
sure we get you all the way home."

"There'll be trouble."

I swiveled my head to look at him. "For whom?"

He glanced around at his buddies. "For us. They're not going
to be happy about us wrecking the truck, getting our guns taken
away, or bringing . . . you, to the inner circle."

Vic raised an eyebrow. "What, you're going to lose your
celestial folding chair and have to stand for all eternity?"

I didn't give him a chance to respond. "What happens if we
drop you off here?"

"We walk back, or we'll catch a ride if somebody comes
along."

"The gist being that you'll have your weapons and won't
have introduced us to the inner sanctum?"

Henry's voice rumbled from the back. "Two out of three."

Eddy nodded and then looked at his lap.

"On one condition." He looked at me. "If you answer a few
questions, then I'll let you out here, but you have to answer them

and you have to be truthful." I eased the truck to the side of the dirt road across from the baked goods table. "And I'll warn you that I'm an expert in knowing when people are lying to me."

He turned in the seat, glanced at the others, and then nodded. "Okay."

"Have any of you ever heard of a woman in your group by the name of Sarah Tisdale?"

No one said anything.

"A blonde woman with blue eyes, roughly thirty years of age?" I pulled the school picture that Eleanor had given me at the bar from my shirt pocket and held it up for them to see. "She would be about seventeen years older than this photo."

Still nothing.

I pulled the truck's gear selector down.

"Wait."

The voice had come from the back, and I turned and looked at one of the boys, the driver and Eddy's half-brother, Edgar. I held the photo out for him to see. "You know her?"

He glanced at the others, and Eddy was quick to speak. "Shut up."

I started turning the wheel to pull us back onto the road.

"Not Tisdale."

I stopped and turned to Edgar, after giving Eddy a strong look. "She may have another name?"

"Lynear."

I rested my face in a hand; of course, it had to be. I waited a moment and then opened the door and climbed out. "Edgar, why don't you and I take a walk?"

Walking around the back of the Bullet, I waved at the girl at the table, who looked to be may be ten. Henry and Vic had allowed Edgar to get out of the truck and now corralled the rest of the boys by the grille guard.

Steering the skinny youth to the side of the road a little away from both the Bullet and the girl, we pulled up at the floral cross, victims of our upbringings and unwilling to walk on the symbolic grave.

"Do you know where she is?"

"No, sir." He paused and looked over at the others. "She was cast out."

"From the Apostolic Church of the Lamb of God?"

"Yes, sir."

I brought my face up from the marker and turned to look at him. I still couldn't see any family resemblance between him and his half-brother. "When?"

He shrugged a shoulder. "About a month ago."

That would've coincided with her appearance at the Butte County Sheriff's Department when she'd been looking for her runaway child. "Why did she get kicked out?"

"Because of her son."

"Cord?"

"Yes, sir."

I studied the floral cross adorned with blue plastic lilies and chrysanthemums. "Was he kicked out, too?"

"Yes, sir."

"Why?"

"He was found wanting."

I was getting tired of the coded churchspeak. "What does that mean?"

"He wasn't selected as one of the three sons of the One, Mighty and Strong."

I sighed. "And who is that?"

"Roy Lynear."

I massaged the bridge of my nose, attempting to rid myself of the headache that was trying to grow roots there, and thought about the domineering and obese man I'd met the other night in the back of the fancy pickup. "So, Sarah Tisdale was married to Roy Lynear?"

"Yes, sir." He paused for a moment and then lowered his voice. "Cord is in line for the inheritance of the mantle of celestial supremacy in the Lord's true church but committed apostasy and turned away."

I knew there was a reason I liked the kid. Here he was attempting to get out of this loony bin, and his mother was excommunicated for looking for him.

What a world.

I studied the teen in front of me and thought about all the good that religion could do and all the bad. "Do you mind if I ask you another question?"

"Nope."

"If all of you are related, then why do none of you look alike?"

He glanced around, embarrassed. "We are lost boys—were kicked out of the communities in Hildale, Utah; Colorado City, Arizona; and Eldorado, Texas. Mr. Lynear adopted us and gave us a place to be."

Somehow that was a notch in Roy Lynear's favor, but I still wasn't convinced. My reveries were suspended as he looked down the road at a spiraling dust cloud that approached from the straight-as-an-arrow distance to the horizon.

"Oh, no."

I followed his gaze. "Somebody you know?" I walked the boy back to the truck and joined the small group at the grille guard.

Henry, never one to miss anything from near or far, was looking down the road and called out to me. "We have company."

"Hmmm." I thought I'd left the others as I walked across the dirt road to where the young woman sat in the chair by the card table, but when I got there, I noticed that Edgar had followed me.

I studied the array, which was indeed full of plastic bags of cookies, cakes, and an amazing assortment of pies.

The girl looked up at me from under the shade of the bonnet, where I could see her Mongoloid features. Her face looked like a full moon in a night sky; when she noticed the young man standing beside me, her voice was an excited croak: "Hello, Edgar!"

"Hi, sis."

She was already up and around the table when he closed his arms around her and ushered her back to her chair. "Have you been out here all day?"

She clutched his hand and answered, her voice breaking, "All . . . All day!"

When she turned to me, I could see that her lips were chapped, and when I glanced around I couldn't see a blanket, a cooler, a bottle of water, or anything with which the child might've been supplied.

"Would you like to buy some cookies?"

A tide of emotions attempted to draw me under as I was reminded of Melissa Little Bird, a young woman I knew, a victim of fetal alcohol syndrome and the daughter of Lonnie Little Bird, the chief of the Northern Cheyenne. "Yes, um . . . Yes, I would."

She recited the prices of the individual items in a long list and then smiled up at me, her rounded cheeks almost completely hiding her eyes.

I dug my wallet from my back pocket. "Are you thirsty?"

She thought about it and then looked at Edgar for approval.

The young man smiled and nodded. "You can answer for yourself."

She looked back at me. "Yes?"

I motioned to the Bear, who was still standing in the center of the road. "Hey, Henry? Could you grab me one of those pops from the little cooler under the backseat?"

He did as I asked, still keeping an eye on the approaching vehicle, and then tossed the Coke across the road to me. I stuffed my wallet under my arm and caught the can, tapped the top in order to disseminate the carbonation, and then gently pulled the tab and handed it to her.

She looked at the pop and then to Edgar.

The young man glanced away and then up to me. "We're not supposed to have soft drinks."

I motioned toward the can in the girl's hands, now noticing that she had no fingernails.

"I think in this case that you shouldn't worry about it."

He smiled and gestured for her to drink, which she did.

I have relished numerous beverages in my life, from the Rainier beer I discovered in my teens and still drank, the Tiger beer I slugged to support my sweat habit in Vietnam, to the Pappy Van Winkle's twenty-three-year-old Family Reserve I drank from the bottle hidden in the corner cabinet of my old boss, Lucian Connally, but I'm sure that I've never enjoyed a sip of anything as much as that girl enjoyed her first taste of Coca-Cola.

"It makes my nose tickle!"

Her brother and I smiled at her, but the young man's face sobered at the arrival of a late-model maroon Suburban with tinted windows. We both watched as the dust from the vehicle blew past us and down the road like an ill omen.

I watched as four men got out of the SUV and stood by the doors, their attention divided between Henry, who was still standing in the middle of the road in front of them, Vic, with the other boys at the side of my truck, and the three of us at the bake sale table.

The man who got out of the passenger side was tall, with a

dark suit and with hair in a reddish pompadour that swept up the sides of his head and around his enormous ears. The driver was darker, bigger, older, bearded, and heavyset, in a dress shirt with a straw cowboy hat that looked like white plastic. Out of season.

I stood there with my wallet in my hands and waited.

One of the other men was middle-aged, in a black polo shirt—he had exited from the driver's-side backseat and was careful to keep an eye on the Absaroka County undersheriff and Henry Standing Bear of the Bear Society, Dog Soldier Clan, still standing in the middle of the road.

The one with the hair and the one in the plastic hat ignored Henry and started toward me along with the fourth man who was also in a black polo shirt and chinos. Unless I was mistaken, he was the muscle.

The tall, red-headed man was the first to talk, and he did it slowly, as if it tired him to speak with mere mortals and so that, with our limited faculties, we would be able to understand and obey. "Hello, I'm Ronald Lynear. Is there some sort of trouble?"

I waited until they were next to me, keeping my head in my wallet, pretending to count out bills as I kept my attention on young Edgar and his sister. "Nope, just buying some baked goods."

Lynear glanced across the road at the stars on my doors, making a point of looking around the Cheyenne Nation, who now stood facing us with his muscled arms folded across his chest. Ronald put out his hand, feminine with long fingers and manicured nails, in an attempt to press down my wallet. "There's no need for that; I'm sure we'll be happy to make a donation to . . . the Absaroka County Sheriff's Department."

He left his hand on mine until I looked up at him. "No need."

He shot a look at the huge man beside him and stuffed both hands in his pants pockets. "This is my friend and spiritual advisor, Earl Gloss."

I glanced toward the Bear, still standing in the road with a slight smile on his face. "That's mine."

Ronald Lynear waved at Henry and then turned back to me. "He's Native American?"

"Northern Cheyenne, to be exact."

He nodded and called out. "We will look forward to Lamanite assistance in the apocalyptic wars to come with the dark-skinned children of Satan."

Henry's grin broadened and his voice, even though it was low, carried in the wind like a scythe. "I would not count on it."

Lynear's eyes hardened a little, but he disguised it by turning back to me. "Where, exactly, is Absaroka County; if you don't mind my asking, Sheriff?"

"Wyoming."

"Oh, and what brings you to our fair state?" He gestured toward the table and the two young people still standing in his presence. "Besides the baked goods?"

"I'm looking for a woman."

He didn't look surprised. "And how can I help you?"

"Her name is Sarah Tisdale, and I have reason to believe that she is a member of your group.

He turned to confer with the older man. "Earl, have we heard of this woman?"

Gloss was quick to speak up. "Not that I am aware of, Mr. Lynear."

I gave the two of them a nice, long stare. "Strange, because she made inquiries at the Butte County Sheriff's Office concerning her child, Cord. I don't suppose you've heard of that person either?"

Lynear turned again, and I was starting to get the impression that he was a pirate talking to the parrot on his shoulder. "Earl?"

The bearded man shook his head. "No, never heard of him."

I stared at Gloss. "Funny, I didn't say anything about it being a him."

He looked past me at Edgar, who still stood by his sister, now clutching the can of pop to her chest, both of them keeping their eyes to the ground. "Edgar, where have you been and where is your truck?"

I interrupted. "There's been an accident; no one was hurt, but their truck was dumped in a creek bed up near one of your gun towers."

It was his turn to pause and then emphasize, "Observation towers."

I glanced at Edgar, still studying the few sprigs of grass at his feet, and then turned back to Ronald Lynear. "And what is it you're observing?"

"The Lord rewards those who are prepared."

"I'm afraid I ran the boys off the bridge, but I'll be happy to pay for the damages. We were just giving them a ride home."

"I'm sure that also will be unnecessary, Sheriff."

I kept my eyes on him but spoke loudly enough for them all to hear. "I am an honest man, Mr. Lynear, and pay for my mistakes. Besides, we've got the room for the children, and I'd kind of like to get a look at your place."

"We're a private people, Sheriff—I'm sure you'll understand if we don't offer you an invitation." He gestured for Gloss to retrieve the children and, legally, there was little I could do, and he knew it.

The big guy bumping my shoulder as a parting shot smirked as he went around me, but then made a tactical mistake by pushing his luck just a touch too far. He shoved Edgar toward his so-called father and then reached down and viciously slapped the can of soda from the girl's hands. "We don't allow our children to drink such trash."

Henry said later that the man might've fared better if he'd had any idea what it was that was about to happen next. The Bear said he might've even been able to stay on his feet, but I doubt it. As it happened, when my clenched fist struck the side of his head and sent him reeling into the ditch, he slapped against the ground like a poleaxed steer.

The Cheyenne Nation, always aware of what I was going to do before I did it, had already stepped out to block the other back-seater, and I could see that Vic had unsnapped the safety strap on her 9mm and was looking eye to eye with one of the polo shirts before he turned to study me.

The scouring of wingtips grazed the inside of my lungs and the coolness overtook my face as my hands grew still. I faced the two remaining men with my knuckles resting on the card table and thought about how Edgar's sister had been sitting out here all day without supplies, and how she was likely to be left behind until there was nothing more to sell.

"I haven't bought my baked goods."

6

One of the best ways I have discovered to get back in the good graces of your staff is to show up with a couple of boxloads of desserts and deposit them in the communal area near Ruby's desk. I had done so and was now brooding in my office over a tepid cup of coffee that resided in my old-school Denver Broncos mug with the chip on the rim.

It was resting on a couple of magazines, and my forearm was lying flat on the desk with my chin propped on it as I slowly turned the mug by the handle and studied the chip, stained and grimy-looking from coffee residue.

"You could get a new one."

I continued staring at my sole piece of office drinkware. "I don't want a new one."

The Cheyenne Nation leaned in my doorway, drinking a mugful himself. "Then what do you want?" He noticed the magazines under my arm. "Do you mind if I ask why you have the 1972 January edition of *Playboy* magazine on your desk?"

"I'm thinking of taking up airbrushing." I waited a moment and then asked a favor. "Hey, do you think you could take Mr. Rockwell out for a walk long enough for me to talk to Cord about his mother?"

"Yes." He waited and watched me continue to contemplate

my mug awhile before asking, "Are you depressed because you missed chess with Lucian last night?"

"No."

"Are you depressed because the Durant Dogies are retiring your number?"

"No."

He nudged his sizable shoulder off the doorjamb and loitered. "Are you mad at yourself for that roundhouse punch that planted that farmer like seed corn?"

I thought about it. "I suppose."

"Some seeds need planting."

"It's not going to make that boy and his sister's lives any easier."

He sipped his coffee. "How do you know that? It's possible that now that he has been manhandled, he is less likely to man-handle."

"That's not how it works, and you know it."

He considered his own mug, which obviously belonged to Vic and read in bold script PHROM PHILLY AND PHUCKING PROUD OF IT. "You could arrest them."

"Tim Berg could arrest them."

"Yes."

I rose up and leaned back in my chair, hooking my foot under my desk again in an attempt to not imitate Buster Keaton. I listened to the geese honking and glanced out the window in time to see the tail end of a large V-pattern headed due south.

His smile lingered. "They are complex, those chambers of the human heart."

"Yep, they are." Henry stood there for a while, both of us saying nothing.

"You do realize that it is simply a myogenic muscular organ, right?"

I sighed and stood, leaving the copy of *Playboy* on my desk but folding and stuffing the gun magazine underneath in my back pocket. "I know it can carry a lot of weight."

The Bear followed as I walked out of my lair and into the Turkish bazaar that had become my sheriff's office. From somewhere, Ruby had procured paper plates and plastic utensils and even a triangular spatula that she was now using to divide up a pecan pie.

"How are the goods?"

The newly returned Saizarbitoria and Vic were sharing a bag of cookies and were seated on the bench beside the stairs; the Basquo was excited. "We should go back and buy more."

"I bought them out." I turned to Ruby. "Need I ask where our two lodgers are?"

She glanced at the old Seth Thomas on the wall above the stairwell. "Well, it's 8:43, and I'd say they are downstairs watching the 8:43 showing of *My Friend Flicka*."

"As opposed to the 7:13 or the 10:03 presentation?"

"Exactly."

When Henry, Vic, Sancho, and I arrived at the base of the steps, the pair was still transfixed by the television on the rolling cart. I thanked the lucky star on my chest that Frymire had been able to find a dual-deck player that accommodated both DVDs and VHS tapes. A lot of our certification and training classes were still on videotapes, which I tried hard not to think about. "How's the horse?"

We'd timed our entrance pretty well in that the end credit music was swelling, and the two looked over at us. Rockwell stood, the way he always did when Vic entered the room, to her unending puzzlement. "It is interesting that the story only changes in small ways each time the machine tells it."

"I think you'll find it's exactly the same."

The old man disagreed. "No; subtle but definitely different."

"Uh-huh." I made my way into the briefing room, pulled out one of the chairs, and sat. Vic and Santiago followed my lead, but Henry remained at the base of the steps.

Rockwell studied the Cheyenne Nation. "You have a savage with you."

I glanced over my shoulder. "Actually, he's the most civilized of all of us."

Henry made a show of waving at the crazy person.

"I was hoping that you might take a walk with him while I have a chat with Cord."

Rockwell, probably weighing his odds, studied the Bear. "Where would we be going?"

The Cheyenne Nation spoke from the stairs. "Just down the block."

The Man of God, Son of Thunder stood, gathered his coat from the chair beside him, and for the first time I noticed that he walked with a slight limp. "The cookies were delicious, but I could stand a real breakfast."

Henry glanced at me and then back to Rockwell. "Sure."

We all watched the unlikely pair do an exit dance at the foot of the stairs, with the Cheyenne Nation finally realizing the mountain man wasn't going to allow the savage to get behind him.

We watched the two of them ascend, and then I turned to look at the young man. He was as earnest as usual but looked a little tired from watching the quadruple-feature of *Flicka*. "How you doin', kiddo?"

"Good." He smiled. "I'm hungry, too. Can we get something else to eat?"

"Soon, but I'd like to talk a few minutes if that's okay?"

"Yes, sir."

I leaned back in one of the plastic chairs, form-fitted to fit no one's form. "I think I met some friends of yours over in South Dakota yesterday."

"Who?"

"Eddy, Edgar, Merrill, and Joe Lynear."

He smiled some more. "I do know them."

"I also met some other members of the church—elders, I guess you would call them." I waited a moment. "Any idea why it is that they would say they didn't know you?"

His eyes dropped, and, trying to get a read on what was going on in his mind, I studied him.

He spoke slowly. "When you are banished from the First Order, you lose your seat in the celestial realm and are deemed a traitor. If they've decided I don't exist, then that's the best I can hope for."

"What's the worst?"

"Death."

I glanced at Vic and Sancho. "They would try and kill you for leaving the Apostolic Church of the Lamb of God?"

"For testifying against it."

"Have you . . ." I had to choose my words carefully. "Known of them killing anyone?"

"I've never seen it, if that's what you mean, but people disappear, especially since things changed."

"People like you?"

He thought about that one. "My situation is different."

"How?"

"I'm the One."

"In what way?"

"Through lineage, I am the One of Three."

I sighed. "Three what?"

"The One, Mighty and Strong."

I could feel a headache coming on from all the cultspeak. "Who are the other two?"

"My brothers." He then added, "My half-brothers. George and Ronald."

I thought about how Eddy had referred to Edgar, and tried not to think about the tangled webs of ancestry within the Apostolic Church of the Lamb of God. "And are they still in the church?"

"Yes. You see, my father's teachings are different from those of the Church of Latter-day Saints; they believe through the proclamation of Joseph Smith Jr. in 1832 that there will be a leader of the church who will come to set the house of God in order, that he will be the One, Mighty and Strong. According to my father, the mistake they make is that it will be one man, when in reality it will be three."

"So you're the One, and your brothers George and Ronald go by the titles of Mighty and Strong?"

"Yes."

I rested my face in a hand and spoke through my fingers. "So, let me get this straight: your father is Roy Lynear?"

"Yes."

"And does he know where you are?"

"No, I don't think so."

I threw a thumb over my shoulder. "Then who sent your bodyguard, Mr. Rockwell, the Danite, Man of God, Son of Thunder?"

"I don't know."

I brought my face up to look at him. "Have you discussed this with Mr. Rockwell?"

"Yes, and he won't say."

"Well, I'll take that up with him. In the meantime, do you remember the conversation you had with Nancy Griffith, the school psychologist?"

"Yes, sir."

"Well, she told me that you said something about the possibility that your mother might be dead." He didn't say anything but looked at the blank screen on the television as if there might be some comfort there. "She mentioned that it might've been something that happened recently."

He cleared his throat, then blinked and nodded with a disconcerting certitude. "She's dead."

I let that one settle for a while before continuing. "I'm sorry to have to ask these questions, Cord, but how do you know?"

His eyes glanced off mine for an instant. "She hasn't come looking for me."

"She was in the Butte County Sheriff's Office a few weeks ago, asking for you."

He nodded and continued to stare at the screen.

I glanced back at Vic and Saizarbitoria, sitting on the edge of their seats. "If she was killed, who do you suppose killed her?"

He stammered. "I . . . I'm not sure."

"I think you are." I reached behind me and pulled the gun almanac from my back pocket. "Is this yours?" He nodded as I leafed through the dog-eared pages. "You've got a lot of high-powered weaponry circled—any idea who you might want to use them on?"

His eyes went back to the TV, blank as the screen. "I get angry sometimes."

"That's normal; everybody gets angry." I waited, but it didn't seem as if he was willing to come forward with anything more. "Cord, if someone has done something bad to your mother, then I'm in a position to do something about it."

We sat there in the silence for a while, and then he spoke again. "Those horses down at that ranch . . . They weren't friendly like Flicka."

I smiled at the change of subject. "No, those are loose range ponies and they don't have that much interaction with human beings."

His mouth moved, but no words came out for a moment. "Do . . . Do you think they can smell it?"

"Smell what?"

"The killing; do you think they can smell the killing on us?"

I was at a loss as to how to respond to that and discovered my hand had crept up to grip the lower part of my jaw. "What do you mean by killing?"

His eyes shifted to the floor, and but for the subject I could've sworn he was discussing the weather. "When we misbehaved one day, they took us out to one of the cattle ranches back in Texas, Mr. Lockhart's ranch."

"And who is Mr. Lockhart?"

"One of the elders of the church; he's tall like you but with bristly hair."

The man on the road with the black polo shirt and the crew cut.

"It was one of the places they took you if you were bad." The intake of breath rattled in his lungs like tin siding in a high wind. "There was a metal rack that held the cattle. . . ."

"A squeeze chute?"

His eyes rose to mine but then sank again, and his voice grew quiet and almost inaudible. "It held the cattle still with their heads sticking out." His cobalt eyes stared at the concrete floor. "They had a chain saw there, and they made us cut the heads off the cows." He swallowed, but his voice was dry like a rasp. "While they were still alive—said it would toughen us up."

I'd never met Bishop Goodman from the Church of Latter-day Saints and had never even darkened the doors of the church that

made its home in the now-defunct carpet store at the south corner of the Durant bypass that reconnected with the interstate
highway.

"He has an almost encyclopedic knowledge of the history of
the Mormon church and its teachings."

Henry Standing Bear and I were having lunch with the bishop
at the Busy Bee Café, and I was watching Cord through the sometimes swinging door as he washed dishes in the kitchen like a
madman. The madman we were discussing at present, Orrin
Porter Rockwell, was asleep on a bunk in my holding cell. "So,
he is a Mormon."

"More than that." Goodman glanced at the Bear. "When
your friend came walking into the church, I thought I was having a vision. Not only is he the living embodiment of the historical figure physically, his understanding of the church is absolutely
period as well."

"Meaning?"

The tall, thickset man with an unruly head of hair adjusted
his glasses and leaned forward. "The Mormon Church of Latter-
day Saints has gone through a number of reformations, including
disavowing polygamy in 1890 with the threat of excommunica-
tion, but he doesn't seem to be aware of any of these things. His
knowledge of the church seems to have had an arrested development and stops at around 1880. Also, his personal knowledge
of Joseph Smith, Brigham Young, and Ina Coolbrith . . . He
even told me of a personal conversation he'd had with the
explorer Richard Francis Burton when he was staying with
Bishop Lysander Dayton in a village near the City of Salt Lake,
and how, over the bishop's objections, he had sent for a bottle of
Valley Tan Whiskey. The two of them sat there all night, shot
for shot, and Rockwell advised the Ohioan to sleep with a
double-barreled twelve-gauge shotgun and to make a dry camp

miles from any campfire and to avoid the main trail because they were choked with White Indians. No offense, but you know . . ." He looked at Henry. "Individuals who passed themselves off as real Indians so that they could prey on travelers on the roads to California."

The Bear looked back at him. "None taken."

He straightened in his chair and shook his head. "The man is a veritable storehouse of historical knowledge."

I sipped my coffee. "Bishop Goodman, you don't really believe that . . ."

"No, of course not, but if the man's dementia has caused him to research the real Orrin Porter Rockwell to the point where he may be one of the world's foremost experts, then he needs desperately to write a biography of the man." He smiled. "If not an autobiography."

"Maybe you should write it."

"I might." He thought about it. "Any idea how long he's going to be around?"

I shrugged. "Oh, seventy-eight to ninety-seven months if the government has anything to say about it." The bishop looked confused. "Kidnapping of any sort is a column-one federal offense."

"Are you going to turn him in?"

"Not if he behaves himself; I mean he's obviously as nutty as a pecan log, but he seems to dote on Cord and the kid calls him his bodyguard, so I don't think he's any real danger."

Henry raised a hand to get Dorothy's attention and a possible refill. "What did you find out from the IAFIS?"

I glanced at the puzzled look on Goodman's face. "The Integrated Automated Fingerprint Identification System."

"Ah."

I looked back to the Bear and shrugged. "Nothing."

He looked surprised. "Really."

"I don't know why you're so amazed; it happens on the Rez all the time."

"Yes, but this is a white guy." He turned to Goodman. "No offense."

The bishop nodded, still preoccupied with the thought of cowriting a historical religious epic. "None taken."

We walked along the two blocks that were downtown Durant before the Cheyenne Nation broke the silence. "Is that the old jacket your parents bought you?"

I'd made a nod to the fact that the weather was cooling off and deigned to wear the thing. "Yep."

We walked on. "I was trying to remember if I ever saw your father in a church."

"You didn't."

"Ever?"

I shook my head. "Ever."

"Why?"

"He just didn't believe in organized religion." I thought about it. "I don't think he believed in much of organized anything."

"Your mother did."

"Yep."

He studied me. "What about you?"

"What about me?"

"This case appears to be concerning you, perhaps more than others, and I was just wondering if it has something to do with the religious aspect?"

"I don't know." I breathed a sigh. "I haven't been in a church since Martha died, you know that. I've been in more sweat lodges than churches in the last five years." He nodded but said nothing.

"Like anything else, I think organized religion, like most human endeavors, is good when it's doing good and I think it's bad when it's doing bad."

"And you think these people are bad?"

"I think the people in charge are, yes." The wind blew up Main, and I watched as the leaves trembled. "I've always been taught that religion is supposed to be a comfort to people, not a threat. I think these people have perverted something that's supposed to be holy and turned it into a weapon." I pulled in a lungful of the crisp air. "I think there's a hierarchy at work here and quite a bit of megalomaniacal madness. I mean, the patriarch is climbing on his roof naked and building spaceships in his backyard."

He smiled. "And you do not want them here?"

I stopped and looked at the cracks in the sidewalk and in my own logic. "No."

"Why?"

"Because I do not approve of their methods."

"Their methods or their beliefs?"

I stopped and turned to face him. "Well, one's kind of responsible for the other, now, isn't it?" He continued smiling, and I continued walking. "And stop grinning at me."

"So, what are you going to do?"

"Well, nobody's threatening Cord. . . ."

"Mostly because you haven't formally told his father, who is lodged in the southern part of your county, that you have him."

"That's the next step."

"So you are still concentrating on the missing woman?"

"Yep."

We walked along. "Speaking of missing women, have you heard from your daughter lately?"

"No." I stopped on the sidewalk and looked at him again. "Have you?"

"No."

We continued walking. "I think she's glad she bought that old tannery building; it's got plenty of room, and since there are going to be three of them . . ."

He stuffed his hands in his pockets as we started up the steps leading to the courthouse. "The baby is due in January, yes?"

"Yep."

"Lola."

"Lola." I paused for a moment. "I mean I don't know if she's told Michael. I think she wants it to be a surprise."

A funny look played across his face.

I broke eye contact with him and looked back down the main drag at the banner proclaiming the impending homecoming festivities. "I told you, it's something that Virgil said on the mountain."

"Live Virgil or dead Virgil?"

I raised an eyebrow at him. "I haven't decided yet." I glanced up at the Bighorns, at the new snow there. "He made some predictions about my life; about it not all being good."

"Whose is?"

"This sounded a little more dire." I watched the breeze pull at his hair—a wind that seemed to urge us southeast away from the mountains. "I guess I'm getting scary in my old age."

He climbed a few stairs and turned to look at me. "You are truly concerned?"

"I suppose."

"What would you like to do?"

I thought about it and shook my head. "Nothing. I mean there's nothing I can do besides call Cady and tell her I've got a bad feeling and she should stay at home and hide in the closet."

"I do not think she will do that."

"Me either."

"You put a great deal of stock in Indian prophecies?"

I grunted. "More and more these days."

He stepped back down and placed a hand on my shoulder. "Then I will make one—she will be fine."

I stared at him, wanting to believe. "You promise?"

"Yes; there are two things I know beyond any shadow of a doubt."

"And they are?"

He started back up the steps. "That the future is uncertain, and that it can change."

I followed after him. "And the other?"

"The most important thing about a rain dance."

"Which is?"

He called over his shoulder. "Timing."

"They have not delivered my fucking corsage yet."

The Bear looked at me as we stood in the doorway of her office. "She wants to go to the homecoming ceremony Friday night, and she wants a corsage."

"Black-and-orange, same as the Doggies."

"Dogies."

"Whatever."

"Rockwell?"

She logged off her computer and tipped her chair back. "Cousin Itt is back in the holding cell communing with a higher power between viewings of *My Friend Flicka*."

I pushed off. "I'm going to have a conversation with him and then make a run down to Short Drop and have a chat with Roy Lynear about his son and the possible whereabouts of Sarah."

Her interest was immediately piqued. "Can I go?"

"If you promise not to shoot anybody."

She smiled the wicked little smile she reserved for the more energetic aspects of our occupation. "Cross my hairs and hope to lie."

I was not in the least comforted and, leaving them to discuss the finer points of shooting people, started off for the holding area.

Rockwell was reading from the old Book of Mormon and was seated on the bunk with the cell door open, his graying hair hanging down to the edge of the mattress pad and cascading over it. He didn't move when I came in but continued to harken to the word.

"I see you got your book back."

Pulling off a pair of gold-rimmed reading glasses, he noted the page number and gently closed it. "It brings me comfort."

"It's probably worth a fortune with that inscription from Sara Rockwell."

He folded the glasses and placed them in his vest pocket. "My mother."

"Um." I paused. "Yep." I pulled up a chair. "That's actually something I'd like to talk to you about."

He set the book on the bunk beside him. "This is not the only time I have spent in a jailhouse, Sheriff Longmire."

"I know Orrin Porter Rockwell spent eight months in the Independence, Missouri, jail."

He nodded his head enthusiastically. "A horrid place with food unfit for dogs."

His performance was spot-on, and I started wondering if maybe we could get the old guy a job in some outdoor drama in Utah. "Rockwell was there because he attempted to murder Lilburn Boggs, the governor of Missouri."

He shook his head, and the pearly hair swayed back and forth. "Another act in which I had no part; the proof of said statement resides in the fact that the man survived. If it had been I, such would not have been the case." He leaned forward. "I will tell you my theories on who was party to the attempted assassination; it was none other than the storekeeper, Uhlinger, who accused me of stealing the pepperbox pistol that was found that night."

"Uh-huh."

"I would never have overcharged the weapon, which led to its being dropped upon firing. Another point being that with so many weapons at my disposal, why would I steal one from a local merchant who at first claimed that it had been stolen by Negro slaves and then by me?" He laughed. "Oh no, if you can find a suitable villain in the public's eye, which we Mormons were at that period in time, and I think Philip Uhlinger did, then you are free as a proverbial bird."

"Uh-huh."

"Have I told you about fishing from the second-story window of the Centennial jail with corn dodgers? I never caught a Missourian, but I had numerous vigorous nibbles!"

"Mr. Rockwell . . ." I sighed, long and loud so that he would be aware of my mood. "You'll excuse me for saying so, but I find it very hard to believe that you are approaching two hundred years old."

He smiled, and there was a twinkle in his opalescent eyes. "I don't look a day over a hundred and fifty, do I?" He sat forward. "My name is Orrin Porter Rockwell, and I was born June 28, 1813, in Belchertown, Hampshire County, Massachusetts, and was endowed in the Nauvoo Temple on January 5, 1846."

I pinched the bridge of my nose with thumb and forefinger. "So, that's your story and you're sticking to it?"

"It is a strange one, yes?"

I looked up at him. "Yep, it sure is."

"I will attempt to explain, Sheriff." He edged forward on the bunk and rested his elbows on his knees. "I was the subject of a direct prophecy by the prophet Joseph Smith."

"Which was?"

His face brightened. "As you mentioned, I had just spent eight months in a pestilential hellhole jail in Missouri. Filthy and starved beyond recognition, I made my way back to Nauvoo and arrived unannounced at a Christmas party at the great prophet's home." He stood, overcome with enthusiasm for his story. "I remember the soft and golden glow of the parlor oil lights as I stumbled into the room and the beaming face of the prophet. There were other men there, bodyguards to Joseph, who grabbed hold of me for fear that I might mean the great man harm." He laughed. "Perfectly reasonable when you consider my appearance, but Joseph stepped forward and placed his hands upon my head, telling me that as long as I kept the faith and never cut my hair, no bullet or blade would ever harm me."

"Like Samson."

"Exactly, but something must have happened in that moment when the prophet laid hands upon me in that my rate of aging crept to a standstill; as near as I can tell, within the span of the last two hundred years I have aged only forty!" I stared at him. "Eighty-five years old and as strong as the day is long—is that not miraculous?"

"That's one word for it."

His eyes sharpened under the bushy brows. "You do not believe me."

I spread my hands. "Well, you've got to admit that it's a pretty fantastic story."

"It is!"

"So, how do you explain the recorded death of one Orrin Porter Rockwell in 1878 due to natural causes, who was subsequently buried in a Salt Lake City cemetery?"

"It is a fundamental belief in our faith that no true believer shall be interred in the earth without a proper physical monument to indicate the site, but it is not I, sir—and it is the true Orrin Porter Rockwell who stands before you." He limped out the open door and half-crouched beside me. "The burial of the nameless man was a clever ruse by the church in an attempt to keep the populace from pestering the prophet into another use of his miraculous powers as he had with me."

I stared at him. "I see."

"You still do not believe?"

"No."

"What is it I can do to convince you?"

I sighed the way I always did when I'd reached the limits of my energies when dealing with crazy people. "To be honest, not a lot."

He casually reached under his herringbone-patterned vest into his inside coat pocket, past the vintage eyewear, and pulled out a Colt 1860 Army model with a shortened barrel, deftly turning it in his hand in a flash and holding it out to me, butt first. "Here, shoot me with this, if you like."

I sat there, looking at the black-powder pistol, more than a little concerned with the dexterity the old man had just displayed.

He thumped his chest with a broad hand, indicating a target for me. "I will not be harmed, I can assure you."

I took the big pistol and examined the beautiful gleaming finish of the museum piece. "Have you had this the entire time you've been here?"

He nodded. "Oh, yes. I never take the air unarmed." I

thumbed open the cylinder, taking in the rounds. "Honestly, you may fire upon me at will."

I rested the weapon in my lap and placed my face in my open hands. "Mr. Rockwell, do you have any other weapons on your person?"

I carefully placed the hog leg pistol along with a Navy-model .44, a Derringer, a wicked pair of brass knuckles, two knives of moderate length, and a frighteningly sharp Bowie knife with the initials OPR burnt into the hickory handle onto my desk.

Vic raised her head to look at me. "You didn't search him?"

"We never formally arrested him." I shook my head at myself. "It's my fault more than anybody's." I slumped into my chair and looked at both Saizarbitoria and her. "He still claims to be *the* Orrin Porter Rockwell of frontier repute." I gestured toward the assortment of weapons. "But faced with his personal armament here, I'm afraid it puts a new complexion on things."

Ruby joined Sancho in the doorway as Vic sat in my guest chair and placed her boots on the corner of my desk as always. "So we're putting Orrin the Mormon on the Evanston Express?"

I thought about the state psychiatric hospital in the southwestern part of Wyoming. "I hate it because he seems like a nice old guy."

Vic's voice was muffled as she spoke behind the fist at her mouth in an attempt to not burst out laughing. "He's a nice armed-to-the-teeth old guy."

Ruby volunteered, "And he's very helpful." We all turned to look at her, and she felt compelled to elaborate. "He takes out the trash, washes out the coffee mugs; he even raked the leaves on the lawn out beside the courthouse this morning."

Santiago folded his arms on his chest. "Not to change the

subject, Walt, but was there any mention of who it was that sent him?"

"No, I thought the first order of the day was to disarm him."

The Basquo's attitude was conciliatory. "How did he respond to having his weapons taken away?"

"Disappointed." I looked at all of them and then down at the cache on my desk. "Not that his weapons were gone, but more that he was disappointed that we would think of taking them. He told me about being a federal marshal back in the day and that he'd be happy to help us in our investigation."

Ruby took a step closer but shuddered as if the weapons might leap to action on their own. "Did you ask him about the Tisdale girl?"

"I did, and he wouldn't give me a straight answer."

"How did he take to getting arrested?"

It was quiet in the room.

Vic looked up. "Tell me you arrested him."

It was quieter in the room.

"Oh, Walt." She got up and started through the doorway as Ruby and Sancho made way for her.

"Where are you going?"

Her voice carried from the hallway: "To arrest the son of a bitch."

I looked up at my remaining staff. "I just couldn't do it; he's two hundred years old and he looked so depressed."

Santiago nodded and walked over to my desk. "They're loaded?"

"Yep."

He picked up the shortened Army Colt and carefully examined it. "Looks like the real deal to me."

"I think it is, too. We can check the thing for model numbers and manufacturer's impressions; I'm no expert, but I'd swear it's the genuine article."

He fingered the edge on the Bowie knife. "Forged steel with a Damascus finish—looks like it was honed from a barrel stave."

I nodded. "Common practice in the 1800s."

Vic returned to the doorway, a little flushed from the run. "So, nobody's going to be surprised that he's gone, right?"

7

"You wouldn't think that a manhunt for a gimpy two-hundred-year-old would be this difficult." We stood there on the street behind the sheriff's office and looked past Meadowlark Elementary toward the trees along Clear Creek that came from the Bighorn Mountains. Vic followed my gaze. "Maybe he'll meet up with Virgil White Buffalo and solve both of our problems."

"At least he's unarmed."

She snorted. "As far as we know."

It was the middle of the day, and it was unlikely that Rockwell, or whoever he was, had gotten far. "Any ideas?"

"In case you haven't noticed, I spend my days trying not to think like a nut job."

"Where is our Indian tracker when we need him?"

"I'm betting The Red Pony and then home." She paused. "Drats, huh?"

I thought about the situation and what the old man's intentions and motivations might be. "Where is Cord?"

"I assume still gainfully employed at the Busy Bee." She turned and looked at me. "Surely you don't think . . ."

I started across the courthouse parking lot toward the stairs leading down to Main Street. "It's why he's here."

She followed, quick-walking alongside me in an attempt to make up for her shorter stride. "So, we know why he's here?"

Staying to one side, I navigated the stairs. "Cord says he's his bodyguard. I just wish I knew who sent him."

My undersheriff jumped a few steps to confront me. "But this Rockwell character tried to kidnap him."

I barely stopped before bowling the two of us down the stairs. "True."

"And he was headed south, which kind of indicates Orson Welles in the three-quarter-ton."

"Roy Lynear, the father."

"Looking out for the son while we search for the Holy Ghost."

"I suppose, but his father is the one who kicked him out."

"Doesn't mean he doesn't want somebody to keep an eye on him."

"Well, Rockwell hasn't shown any interest in kidnapping Cord since being in contact with us. I guess he figures Cord is about as safe as he can be without being locked up."

She glanced over her shoulder. "Then why are we sprinting to the Busy Bee?"

"Because you never can tell." I moved past. "Let's get off these stairs; I'm having way too many serious conversations here."

When we got to the sidewalk, Saizarbitoria pulled up in his unit and reached across the bench seat to manually roll down the passenger-side window. "I want a new car."

Vic laughed. "Get in line."

"I'm not joking; there's a guy over in Story that's got a four-wheel-drive with cruise control and electric windows—I'll pay half." He lowered his head so that he could look up at me. "It's even white. Please?"

"Put in a requisition, and I'll see what I can do." I rested my forearms on the sill of his door. "Anything on the fugitive?"

"I put an APB out on him and figured I'd make the loop down by the church just in case he decided to go there."

"Good thinking."

"Ruby called the Ferg in, and he's on Route 16, started for the mountains to make sure he didn't head up that way." He threw a wrist over the steering wheel and glanced down through the heart of town. "He's ancient. Where the hell could he have gone off to?" He pulled the car from the curb, flipped on the lights and siren, and the few cars in the main drag cleared to allow him to pass.

"Way to sneak up on 'em, Sancho." She turned to look at me, the tarnished gold pupils dialed up to high, and planted a Browning tactical boot forward in a provocative manner. "Hey, Walt?"

"No, you can't have a new vehicle."

She started to punch my chest with the index finger that sometimes felt like a truncheon but then slowed the velocity until I could barely feel the tip of her finger as it rested there. "You know she's dead, right?"

I stared at her.

"The mother, Sarah Tisdale, the one you're hanging this whole investigation on. You know she's dead."

"Not necessarily."

"Missing persons after the first twenty-four—you know the percentages." She squared off in front of me, folded her arms, and looked at the sidewalk, which gave me a little relief from the metallurgy. "Three weeks and nobody's heard from her? I don't know who killed her, Walt, but she's dead as Kelsey's nuts."

"She could . . ."

"No, she couldn't." She stepped in close and looked up at me. "Stop it." She ran her fingers along the edges of my jacket lapels. "I know how you are and don't think I don't appreciate it." Her hand rested over my heart. "I sometimes think that's where your true strength lies, in that bullshit hope of yours, but I've also seen the aftermath when it doesn't work out and we all get to watch you crawl from the wreckage." She patted my heart and let her hand drop. "I'm just warning you that this is going to be one of those times."

I nodded and raised my head to find the boy standing on the sidewalk only about ten feet away. "Hi, Cord."

Vic turned and looked at him. "Jesus."

He dropped his head, and we watched as a brief exhale wracked his narrow chest. None of us moved, and then his face rose and he smiled the crooked smile. "Hi."

Vic traded the hand from me to him and held it there between them. "Kid, I'm sorry."

He nodded. "It's okay."

The skinny youth started to walk past us toward the steps as Vic glanced up at me in appeal. I cleared my throat and called out to him. "Hey, Cord, how would you like to go meet your grand-mother?"

He stopped and glanced back with a confused look on his face. "Huh?"

"Your father is Roy Lynear, and your mother is Sarah Tis-dale?" He looked at me blankly. "That's your mother's maiden name, the name she had before she married your father—Tisdale. Did she ever mention any relatives you might've had here in Absaroka County?"

His head dropped, and he nodded. "Yeah, but she never told me any names."

"But that's why you really came here, to look for them, right?" He stared at me for a moment and then nodded again. "Would you like to meet your grandmother?"

His eyes escaped for an instant but then came back to mine, and the color there was like fear. "Would she like to meet me?"

We weren't having much luck in locating Rockwell, so I took the opportunity of a trip south in hope of possibly finding him on the roadside as we had before. Figuring the kid could probably use some company in the backseat, I stole Dog back from Ruby; the only thing I was worried about now was that he was going to wear the brute's hair off petting him.

"So, do you have any idea where Mr. Rockwell might've gone?"

He shook his head at me in the rearview mirror.

"We don't want to hurt him; we may not even arrest him, but it would probably be a good idea if we knew where he was."

He looked at Dog, who looked back at him.

Vic, still evidently feeling a little embarrassed at having Cord overhear our conversation, was now half-turned in the seat in order to attempt to engage the youth in conversation. "So, what are you doing with all the money you're making washing dishes, Cord?"

I glanced at him in the rearview as he continued to pet Dog.

"Saving it."

"What for?"

"I don't know."

My undersheriff pulled a leg up and tucked it under her. "A car?"

"I don't drive."

"How are you ever going to get a girl if you don't have a car?"

He shrugged. "You have to have a car to have a girl?"

She smiled, exposing the lengthy canine tooth. "Doesn't hurt."

I interjected, "Especially if you've got a mustache and your name is Rudy."

She reached over and slapped my shoulder without looking. "You ever had a girlfriend?"

"One time, kinda."

"What's kinda mean?"

He looked embarrassed. "I made a necklace for this girl I knew, but she'd been promised to her uncle, who was one of the elders." He plucked a tuft of dog hair from the seat and let it float. "He was an old guy."

Vic glanced at me and then back to Cord. "That's fucked up, just so you know."

I thought the kid's head was going to explode. "You know you're going to hell, right? I mean it's okay—I'm going to hell, too."

Vic's voice took on a different tone as she continued to study him. "What makes you say that?"

"All my family is on the inside and they're going to heaven, so where does that leave me?"

"What if they're wrong?"

"I don't think that they can be wrong."

"Kid." She gestured between the two of us. "Our very livelihood depends on everybody being wrong sometimes, trust me." She leveled the eyes on him again. "So, what are you saving up for?"

He squirmed a little, obviously taken aback by Vic's unadulterated attention—I knew how he felt.

"I don't know; maybe a gun."

I thought about the magazine the kid had buried in the pump house and unconsciously let off the accelerator. I put my foot down again when Vic glanced at me. There was an uncomfortable silence as I drove south on the two-lane blacktop. "What do you need with a gun—you've got us."

He stopped petting Dog and glanced at me. "I won't always have you, so I'll need a gun."

My undersheriff readjusted herself, the irony of her squeaking gunbelt underlying her next statement. "Who you wanna shoot?"

He sat there under her interrogation. "Nobody in particular; I just want to be left alone."

"I get like that sometimes."

I laughed.

She ignored me. "Cord, there are people out there who are good at believing things and following orders, and then there's the rest of us, the ones who have urges and get mad about shit; the ones who ask questions. I'm one of those people, and I think I turned out all right." She pointed a loaded finger at me. "Shut the fuck up."

"I didn't say anything."

". . . Anyway." Her eyes softened as she studied him. "Just so you know; there's room for all of us."

I wanted to kiss her but just kept driving as the afternoon sun cast rays across the rolling hills in that horizontal light like clean windows.

Cord was leaning forward when we got to Short Drop, his eyes staying on the cottonwood from which the noose twisted in the breeze. "Did they hang somebody here?"

"A long time ago, or at least they think they did."

"They're not sure?"

I pulled the truck down the embankment and into the town proper. "Back in the day, saying you'd hung somebody was almost as good a reputation as actually having done it."

"I don't understand."

"This is cow country, and back in the late nineteenth century there was a lot of rustling, so if a town had a reputation of being hard on criminal activity, fewer operators were likely to go free-lance and rustle cattle."

His eyes were still on the noose as we drove by. "So they didn't really hang anybody."

I parked the truck in front of the Short Drop Mercantile. "I didn't say that."

Eleanor was standing on the boardwalk as we climbed out of my truck, and as tough as she was, I saw her sway just a tiny bit and then rest a hand on one of the support beams of the porch when she saw the boy.

I let Dog out, and he baptized a tumbleweed that had lodged itself against the steps. "Hey."

Vic brought Cord around the side of the truck with a hand on the young man's shoulder, and I watched as the breath caught in Eleanor Tisdale's throat. "Um . . . Howdy."

Cord glanced at me and then returned his eyes to her for only a second before dropping them to the gravel at his feet. "Hello, ma'am."

Gathering herself, she pushed off the post and stepped to-ward the edge of the porch. "How would you folks like to come up and have a soda to wash the dust out of your mouths?" She started in but then added, "You can bring that grizzly bear, if you want."

The beast and I followed Vic and Cord as they mounted the steps, and we followed the little troupe into the Merc, where, strangely enough, stacks of books stood all over the wide-planked oak floor in piles about three feet high. Eleanor tracked her way through the maze and stood amid the piles like some acolyte of literature. "I have a problem."

I nodded as I reached down and plucked a particularly vin-tage tome from the nearest stack. "I know—it's hard to borrow shelves."

"I go to these auctions and estate sales and the one thing I cannot resist is the books, so I'm thinning the herd and taking the excess over to the library."

I opened the volume to the title page and read: *"The Works of Hubert Howe Bancroft, Volume XXV, History of Nevada, Colorado, and Wyoming 1890."* I gently closed the heavy, leather-bound hardback and rested it against my chest. "Is this book for sale?"

She smiled at me with all the warmth of a Moroccan rug salesman. "Do you know what it's worth?"

"I do."

"Twenty-five dollars."

I studied the marbled edges of the pages. "That's not what it's worth."

"I wasn't negotiating a price; I was simply trying to see if you knew the value." She sighed deeply and picked up another from one of the towers near her. "I'm past the point of caring what things cost; I just want to know that beautiful and important objects are in the hands of people who will appreciate them." She thumbed open the book in her hands. *"Tensleep and No Rest,* Jack R. Gage, first printing and it's signed; do you know he was the governor of Wyoming for two years?"

"I do."

She thumbed the binding. "I guess he wasn't much of a governor, but he was a hell of a writer." She tossed the book to me, and I caught it. "Twelve dollars."

I stood there holding the two books and looking at the piles around us—they were like literary land mines just waiting to explode minds. "Um, is there any way I could get you to lock the front door and not sell any more books until I've had a chance to go through all of them?"

"I'm going to have the books out of here by Sunday afternoon. I'm closing the place and selling the merchandise—other than what goes to the library, of course." She glanced at Cord, who stood holding his own selection. "Did you find something of interest there, young man?"

His eyes came up slowly from the open pages. "There's a book?"

The proprietor's eyes shone. "Well, I'm not sure which book it is you're talking about."

He tipped the cover up so that we could see the familiar green hills, a boy, and a horse.

"Oh, *My Friend Flicka*. Is that a book you'd be interested in?"

He looked embarrassed. "I, um . . . I don't read that well."

Vic took the book from him and flipped a few pages back. "First edition, first printing, signed and dated."

The owner/operator turned back to look at me. "My mother was a friend of Mrs. O'Hara down in Laramie."

I looked around the stacks on the floor, estimating that there must've been close to two thousand volumes. "I repeat my request."

She spread her hands. "All gone come this weekend." She turned and walked toward the heavy door leading to the bar. "C'mon, the refreshments are this way."

We followed her into The Noose, and Eleanor scooped a few pops from the cooler at the bar-back and placed them on the counter.

"Mrs. Tisdale, we were thinking of making the run out toward the East Spring Ranch and taking a look around, and I was wondering if it would be possible for us to leave Cord and Dog here with you?"

She studied the young man now seated on the end barstool, his nose buried in the book, his finger tracing the lines as he read very slowly with his lips moving. "Hey, youngster."

His head swiveled, and he looked at her, smiling.

"You think you can tote books?"

He nodded enthusiastically. "Yes, ma'am."

I gestured to Vic, and we started toward the front door of the bar, but only after I paused at Eleanor Tisdale's side. "You do know what that book is worth, right?"

She smiled as she watched her grandson, his lips moving in time to the words. "I know what it's worth to him."

"You told her about *My Friend Flicka?*"

I drove south and east of the little hamlet, the road undulating with the rolling breaks of the Powder River country. "It might've come up."

She studied the stack that reposed on the seat between us, then picked up the heavier of the books and began studying the Bancroft. "It's like a history of the state?"

"*The* history of the state."

She leafed through the pages, marveling at the imprinted words on them, her fingers touching them like braille. "'Even the serpent, emblem at once of eternal life and voluntary evil, was not absent, taking up his residence in the underground inhabitation of the prairie dog, to escape the blistering heat of the sands, where he sometimes met that strange inmate, the owl, also hiding from the intense sunshine of the plains. So did this region abound with life in ages when the white man, to the knowledge of the red man, was not.'"

"Pretty good for a historian, huh?"

She silently watched the scenery, or, in her opinion, the lack thereof, pass by. "Why do you suppose she didn't mention closing the Merc when we were here before?"

"Seems sudden, doesn't it?" I admired the profile of her features at once refined and dangerously focused. "Maybe something to do with news of the daughter and the grandson."

"In what way?"

"Sometimes we spend our lives thinking we're doing something, when in reality all we're doing is waiting; maybe what Eleanor's been waiting for has arrived."

"Yeah, well . . . I wouldn't know anything about that mother/daughter relationship thing."

"Uh-huh."

She closed the book in her hands carefully and looked at the Roman numerals on the binding. "Twenty-five of them?"

"Yep."

"Think the ol' broad's got all of them?"

"Looks like."

"So, what are they worth?"

"Thousands."

"Let's go back and rob the place."

I smiled. "That would be against the law."

She settled in the seat and propped her boots onto the dash. "We've done enough for the law—look where that's got us."

"Where's that?"

She opened her arms and gestured to the landscape with dramatic flair. "Nowhere."

We'd taken a left just after another of the roadside fatality markers onto a gravel road with a ranch gate hewn from strapped-together logs with an archway that read **EAST SPRING RANCH**. It wasn't exactly the end of the earth, but you could send it a telegram from here, not that you'd get an answer.

I ignored the signs warning us that the land was posted and didn't welcome trespassers and continued down the road toward what looked like one of the towers we'd seen in South Dakota. Once we got to the structure, I could see that the distance in both directions was strung with a ten-foot chain-link fence with three strands of diagonal barbed wire on top.

We stepped out of the Bullet and, looking at the desolate landscape, I got the odd sensation that I was back in the military. A breeze was coming off the mountains, cool and putting a rub in the air that I could feel between my teeth. I sighed the way I always did when I got that feeling, walked over to the large gate seated on a pair of rolling casters, and noticed a small intercom with a plastic shield to protect it from the weather.

On closer inspection of the greenish wooden tower, I could make out a small security camera under the eaves. "We may or may not be on *Candid Camera*."

Vic walked to the fence and then across the dirt road. "Not motion activated, and it may not even be hooked up."

"How can you tell?"

"The unconnected wires hanging off the back." She returned to the gate and the intercom, flipping up the plastic cover and pushing one of the buttons. "Hello, have you found Jesus Christ as your personal savior? We're on a mission, and we hear you fuckers are up to some really heinous shit in His name." After a moment she turned to look at me with an eyebrow raised like a question mark. "I don't think it's working."

"Are there wires hanging out of the back of it, too?"

"No, but it doesn't make any noise, static, nothing—smart-ass."

I came over and looked at the intercom and then the three massive padlocks on the gate. "I guess they're serious about not wanting visitors."

"You bring your bolt cutters?"

"Unfortunately, no."

She looked past my shoulder toward the road, where a two-tone brown '71 Plymouth Satellite station wagon with its leaf

springs resting on its axles slowed at the turnoff. "Company."
The car stopped as the dust behind overtook it and blew our way,
partially concealing us. "Is that color scours?"

"No, more of an Autumn Bronze Poly, as I recall."

She glanced at me.

"I had one."

She continued to stare at me and then muttered to herself,
"Family man."

The driver, an aged, extremely heavyset, Hispanic-looking
woman in a powder blue prairie dress got out of the station
wagon, went over to the roadside grave marker, and straightened the plastic, floral wreath attached to a makeshift wooden
cross. Her hands were clasped at her waist and her head lowered.

Her ministrations continued for quite some time, and Vic
finally spoke. "She praying her way to heaven or what?"

I stepped past her toward the newcomer on the dirt road.
"Some people need it more than others."

Probably hearing our voices, the woman's head rose, and she
looked at us through the thin veil of dust. Maybe it was the dress,
maybe it was the surroundings, but I had the feeling that it was
an old stare—one from a different era, a different time.

I waited as she slowly made her way back to the vehicle and
climbed in, shifting the still-running car into gear and turning
where we were parked, effectively blocking the road. I raised a
hand and motioned for her to move. She paused, even going so
far as to look back up the road for traffic, which was absurd considering our environs, but then turned, looked at me, and finally
drove forward.

I walked over to her and strung a hand on the fender as I
stooped to look inside, Vic walking past me, taking a textbook
stance behind the woman's left shoulder.

Her bloated face was surrounded by straggles of dark hair,
gray at the roots, that had escaped from the bun high at the back

of her head, and I could barely see her dark eyes. Her voice was surprisingly high and decidedly Spanish. *"Sí?"*

I looked into the station wagon, the backseat covered with an abundance of bulk-food containers, drinks, and home supplies in franchise plastic bags, and finally allowed my eyes to rest on what looked to be two dozen bricks of 12-gauge, .30-06, .357 Mag, and .50 BMG ammunition on the seat beside her. "I didn't know Sam's Club in Casper sold ammo, especially .50."

Her hand dropped down and pulled the plastic back over the ammunition as if that might make it disappear. *"No hablo Inglés."*

The blue-black smoke of the aged engine bellied out from under the rocker panels, and I just hoped we could get a few answers before dying of asphyxiation. "Well, señora, that's going to make it hard for you to have a legal driver's license."

"Oh, I has license, Officer."

My undersheriff chimed in. "And evidently more English than at first supposed."

I smiled. "I'm a sheriff."

She repeated, "Sheriff."

I extended my hand, and she shook it with one that was swollen and moist. "I'm Walt Longmire." I gestured toward my partner in noncrime. "This is my undersheriff, Victoria Moretti. And you are?"

"Big Wanda."

"Wanda, do you mind if I have a look at that driver's license?"

She hesitated for a second, then reached down again, dragging a sizable purse onto the transmission hump, and snuck a hand in to pull out a turquoise wallet stuffed with bills. She thumbed through a number of cards, then pulled out a Texas license and handed it to me.

I studied it and then handed it back to her. "Ms. Bidarte." I thought about the tall, lean man I'd met at the bar and continued to smile, just so she'd know I wasn't rousting her. "Are you by any chance related to the poet Tomás Bidarte?"

She nodded with enthusiasm. "*Sí*, he my son."

"Well, you must be proud." I also remembered Sheriff Berg's remarks about the two women who had been married to the space jockey, Vann Ross—one of them having been named Big Wanda. "Well, I'm looking for Roy Lynear, and I understand he lives at this address?"

Her eyes, or what I could make of them, stayed steady. "He be my husband, but he not here."

That's one way of keeping it in the family. "Roy Lynear is your husband?"

"*Sí.*"

"I gather you were married before, then."

"*Sí.*"

I nodded as I thought about what Tim had said concerning how the women in polygamy cults would file for abandonment to receive social services funding. "This license is almost four years old, ma'am. If you are residing in Wyoming, you'll have to get a new one."

She said nothing but tucked the license back into the billfold and rested it in her lap.

"Your husband—he's not at the ranch?"

"No."

I glanced around as if I might spot the man. "Then where is he?"

"*Sur* Dakota."

I nodded. "Visiting family?"

"*Sí*. His father not good." She shifted her bulk and glanced at the clock in the dash of the old car for a long moment, and I would've bet that it wasn't working. "I got food in the car and need to go."

"Would you mind if we followed you in?"

She stared at the dash, and I could see the agitation in her growing. "You cannot. No."

"Then you won't mind answering a few more questions here, will you?" Her eyes roamed the interior of the car but could find no easy avenue of escape. "Do you mind turning your motor off?"

She shook her head with a quick motion, still trying to avoid my eyes. "If I kill motor, it no start again."

I glanced up at Vic, who had taken a step back to avoid the fumes. "Well, I'll try and be brief. Wanda, we're looking for a woman by the name of Sarah Tisdale. Do you know her?"

Her eyes shifted toward Vic and then refocused on the dash. "No."

"No, you don't know her or no, you'd rather not say?"

Her breath picked up. "No heard of her."

"How about Sarah Lynear?"

She paused for a second and then glanced back at Vic again, and I was beginning to wonder what the attraction was. "No."

"Well, that's odd, seeing as how she was also married to your husband." I kneeled down and rested my arm on the sill, pulled the photograph from my shirt pocket, and held it out to her. "You're both married to the same man and you've never heard of her?"

Wanda glanced at the photo for only an instant and then patted the steering wheel as if urging it to go. "She no married to my husband."

I continued to hold the photograph of the blonde woman out to her. "Maybe you should take a closer look."

Instead, she moved to tuck the wallet back into her purse, accidentally opening it more than she'd wanted, exposing the Pachmayr grip of an S&W revolver where her hand lingered.

Still holding the photo in front of her, I gently slipped my hand down on the elk grips of my Colt, unsnapping the safety strap, a motion that did not go unseen by Vic. As I spoke, my undersheriff slipped the Glock from her holster but let it hang at her side, unnoticeable to the woman unless she looked specifically backward. "Mrs. Lynear, I need you to remove your hand from your purse very slowly and place both of them on the steering wheel."

She didn't move.

"Mrs. Lynear, I need you to do that right now."

The beauty and the horror of a life in law enforcement is that you will, in your time, be stupefied at what people will do. I watched in that adrenaline rush of slow motion as Wanda withdrew her hand from the purse and reached up like a foregone conclusion. She threw the Satellite wagon into reverse and floored it.

I stumbled backward and Vic scrambled to the side, raising her 9mm and leveling it at the Plymouth as it tore backward down the dirt road toward the intersection. "Wait!"

She held the Glock steady but turned her head slightly to bark at me. "I'm shooting the radiator and/or the wheezing motor."

I stood and joined her, watching the retreating car. "I don't think that's going to be necessary." We watched as the majestic beast, still hanging low on its springs, rocketed backward across the macadam and slid off the other side with its prow in the air like an Autumn Bronze whale. "Thar-she-blows."

Vic kept her weapon out and followed me as the tires ground on the side of the roadway in an attempt to find traction, the front wheels of the wagon sawing left and right like an upended tortoise.

After a moment the motor groaned, and the rear tires caught traction, lumbering the Plymouth up onto the road as Vic and I scattered like chickens in an attempt to get out of the way.

We watched as the car wheezed up to a good forty miles an

hour and headed for the horizon. Vic joined me at the centerline and reholstered her weapon. "Are we about to engage in the slowest car chase in cinematic history?"

I sighed. "I believe so."

We caught up with the station wagon in about three minutes. I had my light bar on but had left the sirens silent so as not to scare the woman any more than she was already.

Vic adjusted her seat back and put my hat over her face. "How long before she runs out of gas?"

"Nebraska."

"Don't bother waking me up."

I tooled along behind the Plymouth, a confused rancher pulling his pickup to the side of the road and looking at me with a puzzled expression on his face as we passed him. From underneath my hat, Vic's voice rose. "So, this would be classified as a low-speed chase?"

"Any slower and we're walking." I studied the road ahead and figured the station wagon would be crossing over into Campbell County before too long. I could call Sandy Sandberg and get him or the Highway Patrol to set up a roadblock and become the laughing stock of the entire Wyoming law enforcement community, or we could go to Nebraska.

There was a smallish knoll on a dividing ridge where the road took a slight S-curve, which was possibly the only creative feature between here and Scottsbluff. Periodically, Big Wanda would look into her rearview mirror and stare at me. What was she thinking I was going to do, shoot her? Granted, she had a weapon, but I doubted she'd intended to use it.

I kept my eyes in her rearview mirror, I was that close, and could see her still looking at me as we approached the curve—

the only one, I was certain, between here and the Great Plains. I honked my horn and pointed ahead, in an attempt to get her to stop; Vic pushed my hat away and sat up.

"Did she break down?"

I honked again, but Big Wanda wasn't watching the road; instead, paying no attention to what was coming up, her head leaning to the side, she continued to look at me through the rear-view mirror as her right front wheel went off the road. I watched as she snapped around and yanked the steering wheel to the left, which would've been fine on any other portion of these hundred miles of road, but not this one.

The left front of the vehicle dipped into the gravel, and she sawed the thing to the right again, but the powder was thick and the slope at the side of the road steep and we watched as the big Plymouth rose up on two wheels. There was that second when I thought she was going to make it, but then the thing started over like a lazy dog into the slowest roll I've ever seen. It only went over onto its top, and then slid the rest of the way down the hillside into a slight depression at the bottom of the barrow ditch.

I pulled my truck over and parked it above the station wagon. Vic was already out of the other side and joined me as we picked our way down the clumps of dry grass and withered sagebrush on the hillside. The Plymouth sputtered a few more times as the carburetor attempted to pump gas skyward, and then miraculously smoothed out and continued to idle. "She's going to need some help getting out of there."

Vic still held her sidearm at the ready. "You do it."

I gestured for her to take the passenger side as I took a few steps around the back, looking at all the groceries that were now lying on the headliner. "Mrs. Lynear?"

There was no answer over the sound of the motor.

Vic had made pretty good progress on the far side, crouching so as to not reveal too much of herself but getting close enough to see the woman. She paused and aimed the 9mm toward the car, taking a moment to raise her other hand and mimic an out-stretched thumb and forefinger gesture that could only mean *gun*.

With a sigh, I pulled the .45 from my holster and called out again, raising my voice so she would be sure to hear me over the idling car—evidently the vehicle preferred upside down. "Wanda, you're not in any real trouble yet. If you'll just toss that pistol out the window, I'm sure we'd all feel a lot better!"

No response, but Vic continued forward.

It was about that time that the snub-nosed revolver fell from the driver's-side window.

When I rushed forward, I could see Big Wanda clearly chok-ing to death hanging from the seat of the Plymouth, her face purple and even more bloated. I grabbed the door handle, but the window rail was lodged in the dirt. Her hand reached out to me, and she grabbed my arm as I drove a hand in my back pocket to yank out my old Case knife. I reached up past her shoulder to get at the belt, but she must've misinterpreted my intentions and evi-dently thought I was trying to cut her throat because she began slapping at my hands. I forced myself in the window in an attempt to get a better angle on the webbing but still avoid her neck. She continued to choke and beat at me as I pushed her arms aside, reached past her head, and slit the belt, her entire three hundred pounds falling—on me.

She coughed, choked, and gasped a few breaths, and it was all I could do to catch mine in that a particularly large breast cov-ered half my face. Her eyes turned to mine and she whispered, *"Lo lamento . . . Lo siento, por favor."*

Vic had opened the other door and some of the groceries slid out onto the ground. She reached across the car with a smile on her face, shoved the gear selector into park, and switched off the ignition, the big Satellite giving up the ghost with a shudder, an elongated wheeze, and finally a hiss. Pulling the keys from the ignition, Vic tossed them near my face. "I guess she really didn't want to kill the motor."

8

"Have I told you lately how much I hate mauve?"

"Not lately, no." We were in our usual spot in the Durant Memorial Hospital lobby, waiting for the medical musketeers Isaac Bloomfield, his understudy David "Boy Wonder" Nickerson, and Bill McDermott. I listened to the clock ticking and took in the carpet and matching walls. "It's probably supposed to be soothing."

"Like a bowel movement."

"Better than scours."

She stood and walked across to the hallway leading past the receptionist desk where Ruby's granddaughter, Janine Reynolds, was filling out paperwork and trying to stay awake.

I was having the same problem and was even thinking about stretching out on the sofa for a few winks when my undersheriff returned with hands on hips and looked down at me over her still-multicolored eyes. "We didn't lean on her that badly."

"No, we didn't."

"She kept looking at me when we were asking her about Sarah out on the road; did you notice that?"

"I did."

She reached down and took the photo from my shirt pocket, her familiarity with my person and clothes breeding indifference.

She studied the photograph. "I don't look anything like this woman."

"No."

"So why was she looking at me?"

"I don't know." I studied the question. "You had a gun, she had a gun. . . ."

"You had a gun, but she hardly looked at you."

"Maybe it's a cultural thing—she wasn't used to seeing a policewoman."

She snorted. "A Mexican in Texas? She's probably on a first-name basis with the entire law-enforcement community."

I pleaded exhaustion and slumped deeper into the worn sofa molded into the shape of sorrowful anxiety. "I don't know and I'm dead tired."

"How are we supposed to inform them that we've got her—hang a note on the razor wire?" It was quiet again, and I could feel the tension in her body as she sat on the sofa next to me. Two minutes later, she was sound asleep.

Clear conscience.

I must've nodded off, too, but uneasy and half awake, I listen to my parents arguing about religion. My mother, a devout Methodist, is seated at the breakfast table with my father. She looks the way she always does in my dreams, backlit, the sunshine in the kitchen window striking the sides of her pupils, making her blue eyes that much more transparent, like her blue willow china, overwashed, but never broken. She is like that, more beautiful with each passing year. We are all surprised by it, but for her it is her life and she accepts it; nothing astonishing, just a honing of her appearance. Never a small woman, she has retained her tall figure and her face remains unwrinkled, the hollow of her cheeks and the sculpting of her brows defining the strongest of her features—those eyes.

She rests her coffee cup in the saucer, and the only sound in the warm, springtime room that Sunday morning is the click of ceramic against ceramic.

My father whispers, but his voice carries to the stairs where I sit in my pajamas. "You force him to continue going and he'll hate you for it." There is a silence, and I strain to hear their voices. "He's of an age where he needs to make decisions like this for himself."

"He's too young to be making decisions like this for himself."

"Older than you think."

I tuck my naked heels against my rear and wait on the wooden steps my father had made in the house he had built.

"He'll grow to hate you for it."

The tick of the china again, indicative of a poise neither he nor I have. "He doesn't hate."

"Resent, then."

A silence. "You're sure this isn't a theological difference. . . ."

"I don't have a theology."

"Oh . . . Yes, you do."

My head snapped back at the sound of somebody swallowing and awakened to find Saizarbitoria standing over me while sipping coffee from a Styrofoam cup.

"Hey, boss."

I yawned, careful not to jostle Vic's still-sleeping head on my shoulder. "Hey."

"You were talking in your sleep."

"I say anything interesting?"

"Something about blue willow."

He sipped his coffee again, and I glanced at the clock, still dragging its hands around the wee hours of the night. "What are you doing here this late?"

"News from the rabbit-choker state."

"Yep?"

"Tim Berg said to tell you that some guy named Vann Ross Lynear died."

That was a bit of a shock, even if he was approaching a hundred years old. "That's a surprise."

"Fell off his roof without any clothes on."

Vic's voice sounded against my shoulder and then she snuggled in deeper. "That's not a surprise."

I glanced at her and then back up to my deputy. "Anything suspicious?"

"You mean other than he fell off a roof without any clothes on?" He glanced down at me. "He didn't say, but he intimated that you shouldn't return to Belle Fourche anytime soon, that there's a warrant for your arrest." He finished his coffee. "You roughing up the church folk over in the Black Hills, boss?"

"It was a misunderstanding about soda pop."

He glanced toward the reception area where Janine had succumbed and now rested her head on her folded arms. "Remind me to not get in your way at the water cooler."

I thought about what Wanda had said before things had gotten interesting down at the entrance to East Spring Ranch. "Does Tim know that Roy Lynear and his bunch were in South Dakota yesterday?"

"Not that I am aware."

"Would you like to make him aware?"

He looked around for a trash can. "Not at two in the morning."

"Any sign of Orrin Porter Rockwell?"

"Faded into the pages of history so far."

"Cord?"

He had found the trash and chucked his cup. "Locked up in protective custody with Dog, a copy of *My Friend Flicka* lying on his sleeping chest."

"How was the coffee?"

His eyes narrowed, the muscles in his jaw bulging like the hocks on a horse. "Wretched. I wouldn't recommend it."

Wanda, as I'd suspected, would be fine. She'd sustained a little damage to her shoulder and throat, but other than that she'd only had a mild concussion and would be held overnight for observation purposes.

I was restless and didn't feel like going home or to the office; it was past the middle of the night, and I was driving around town like a teenager. Staring at the blinking red light, I sat there at Fort and Main and thought about my life. I guessed that's what people did at three in the morning—thought about their lives. Parents—gone; wife—gone; and a freshly married daughter who might as well have been gone, too.

Five o'clock in Philadelphia; too early to call.

I missed Dog.

There was an ambient light in the cab now, and I was starting to think I was having a visitation when I noticed it was the headlights of an eighteen-wheeler in my rearview; he was probably intimidated by the stars and bars into not honking his horn at the crazy sheriff who had been sitting at the blinking stoplight for the last three minutes.

I was startled by a knock and looked out to see a man standing in the road in an IGA ball cap.

Rolling down the window, I placed an elbow on the door. "Howdy."

He looked a little uncertain. "Hi?" He glanced back at his truck, idling behind us, and the vacant streets of the county seat. "Is there some kind of trouble?"

I rubbed my face with my other hand. "In my line of work—pretty much all the time."

He didn't seem too sure as to how to answer. "Oh."

I looked across the street at Wilcox Abstract, housed in a building that had been driven into twice by drivers not paying attention to where their cars were going. "Do you think the biggest troubles in life are a result of doing or not doing things?"

He edged back just a bit. "I really wouldn't know."

"Me either."

He swallowed. "Hey, Sheriff?"

"Yep?"

"Did you know that there's somebody in the back of your truck?"

I opened my door, stepped out into the street, and unsnapped the safety strap from my Colt: the tonneau cover was unfastened from the left corner. "You're sure?"

The trucker nodded. "Yeah, there was this hand sticking out, trying to get that cover shut."

I resnapped the safety strap on my sidearm and spoke in a loud voice. "Mr. Rockwell?"

A muffled reply came from under the tonneau. "Yes, sir."

"Would you like to come out now?"

"Not particularly."

"I'd prefer you did."

His hand appeared at the corner, and he pushed the cover back further, smiled at me, then turned to the truck driver. "Damn your eyes, sir, as an informer."

The trucker looked at me. "I should be going."

He looked both ways to make sure he wasn't going to get run over, which might have been a trifle cautious in that it was pretty desolate in Durant at three in the morning. Rockwell and I watched as he backed up the big truck and drove around us, took a left, and headed out of town.

The old man marveled at the size of the thing as it passed.

"My Lord, big as a house. . . ." Pushing himself up the rest of the way, his long hair and beard looking more unkempt than usual, he turned to look at me. "You, sir, drive a great deal."

"How long have you been in there?"

"Since this afternoon."

I undid the rest of the snaps, lowered the tailgate, and reached a hand up to help him down to street level. "I'd imagine you're hungry."

He looked at me. "You are one big son of a gun, are you not?" He straightened his pants out and gave a shiver. "A little cold and thirsty, mostly, but I could eat."

I thought about taking him back to the jail, but in all honesty I didn't want to awaken Cord. I gestured toward the passenger side. "Climb in."

He went around the truck as I shut the door behind me and put on my seat belt. When I looked up, he was still standing by the door. I hit the button and stared at him. "Is there a problem?"

He glanced at me and then at the door handle. "Don't know how."

We had to find out what booby hatch he'd escaped from. "Just pull sideways on that black thing.

He did as I requested, and the truck door bumped open. He slid in and climbed up on the seat. "Amazing, truly amazing."

"You drove in the truck on the way back from the Lazy D-W, where you tried to steal the horses."

He shook his head. "We only intended to borrow them." He pulled the door closed behind him but not strongly enough for it to latch. "And at that time I never operated the mechanism."

I sighed. "Well, you're going to have to open it again and close it harder."

He stared at the inside of the door.

"It's the lever toward the front; pull it and push out."

He finally got the door secured, and I drove us over to the Maverik at the on-ramp to I-25. "You'll like this place—it's owned by Mormons." I got out and reminded him, "Lever on the front."

I introduced Orrin Porter Rockwell to the wonders of the frozen burrito, microwave oven, and root beer, in that order. We now stood at the cash register, where I slid a fifty across the counter to the pimpled kid working the late shift. "Sorry, all I've got."

Rockwell reached across and laid a few fingers on the bill, studying it. "Ulysses S. Grant on the denomination of the Union?"

"For quite some time now."

The kid took the bill, studied the portrait of the eighteenth president of the United States, and then the old man. "Friend of yours, pops?"

"He was a drunkard."

The kid used a marker to identify the bill as genuine. "I wouldn't know."

Rockwell got the door shut this time and was happily munching on his burrito as I stared at him. "So, you were in the truck when the woman crashed her car?"

"Which woman was that?"

"Wanda Bidarte Lynear."

He stared at the dash, and I could tell he was choosing his words carefully. "I don't know her." He thought about it. "Sounds Spanish." Turning, he focused the pale eyes on me and threw a thumb toward the back of my truck. "Nice and warm back there, under the tarp, but not as nice as this."

"Uh-huh." I continued to watch him eat. "How about Vann Ross Lynear; have you ever heard of him?"

"No, sir."

"How about Roy Lynear?"

He continued eating as I watched, but he paused if for only a second and then shook his head. "Don't know him either."

I reached over and pinched Rockwell's arm.

"Ouch." He looked at me. "And why, may I ask, is it you did that?"

"Just to make sure you're actually here—I've been having a little trouble with that lately."

He paused and then nodded knowingly. "Visions?"

I thought about Henry Standing Bear and smiled. "That's what a friend of mine has been calling them."

"Perhaps you are the One; you certainly seem to have the size for it."

I stared at him. "Excuse me?"

"The One, Mighty and Strong."

I laughed. "I'm not a Mormon; I'm barely a Methodist."

He went back to eating his burrito. "Pity."

I continued to watch him for a while longer and then pulled the truck into reverse, backed out of the convenience store lot, and took the on-ramp to I-25 South. "Well, let's go introduce you to Roy Lynear then."

"Oil?"

The rippling effect of the Powder River set the keynote for the topography of the southern part of my county, where the Bighorn Mountains relaxed their grip and allowed the hills to subside into prairie.

The area had been the source of one of the largest oil holdings in the United States, but that time had passed and now the Teapot Dome reserves were only a testing ground, leased out to numerous oil companies for the development of experimental methods.

I followed Rockwell's eyes to one of the pump jacks in the distance beside the front gate of the East Spring Ranch. "Yep."

The nodding donkeys kept time to the geothermal beat, but it was unlikely that they were pumping much oil. The entire area had been put up for sale by the federal government, but there hadn't been any takers; the other major naval oil reserve in Elk Hills, California, however, had fetched over three and a half billion—the largest privatization of federal property in history.

The Teapot, on the other hand, was pretty much empty.

Standing outside the chain-link fence, I tossed the station wagon's keychain in my hand and thought about what a bad idea this was.

I caught the keys and looked at the fob—a plastic, prism-like portrait of Jesus that fluctuated as I tipped the thing back and forth. First, it was the Messiah appearing thoughtful and prophetic with His eyes down, and next He was looking to his Father with blood trailing across his face from the crown of thorns on his head—it was the kind of kitschy macabre stuff that was sold in trinket shops in Mexico.

Flipping through the keys, I found three short ones that were similar—all of them marked Master Lock.

Rockwell, who stood beside me, studied the fence and then the chintzy fob in my hand. "I did not think the Methodists, even with their many faults, were given to brazen idolatry."

I tipped the holographic image back and forth for his entertainment. "Not mine." Reaching up, I undid the highest lock, then the middle one, then the bottom, and pushed the gate sideways on the casters.

There were no sirens, no lights, nothing.

We climbed back in the Bullet—Rockwell didn't have as much trouble this time. I pulled forward, then got out and closed the gate but left it unlocked just in case we had to make a hasty retreat. I climbed back in and turned to stare down the freshly graded red-scoria road that led into the dark. I was now at the portion of this particular exercise in stupidity where I was going to have to make up my mind as to what, exactly, I was doing.

I figured I had about three hours before the sun came up. Evidently, I had been thinking pretty hard, because Rockwell heard it. "What are we doing here?"

"That's a really good question." I laughed and glanced at him. "Officially, we're here to notify one man that his wife—and another man that his mother—has been in a car accident."

"This Wanda Bidarte Lynear?"

"Yep."

He looked down the darkened plain. "Am I correct to assume that there is something clandestine about our arrival?"

"Boy howdy."

"Oh, good. I used to specialize in such activities." He nodded his head and smiled, and I shook my own.

I pulled the three-quarter-ton down into gear. There was a glow on the horizon to our right so maybe we didn't have that three hours I had been assuming. A worn track led east, but the main road veered left, and I figured it was best to see where it led. About a half mile north we came to a draw that went to the right where there was a newly built road toward an old ranch house and barn with a few cottonwoods surrounding it. There were a bunch of outbuildings and a number of Quonset huts and prefabricated steel buildings that were popular in our area because they were inexpensive and could be quickly assembled.

I figured the ranch house and barn were from the twenties, but the rest of the place was most decidedly recent.

The only lights evident were a dusk-to-dawn arc light in the common area between the house and barn and a block of illumination cast from the open door of one of the very large steel buildings. It looked like there was movement in that area, and shadows appeared to be passing back and forth inside.

I wondered what it was that they could possibly be doing under the cover of night as I pulled the Bullet to the right alongside an old post-and-pole fence that protected myriad wash lines with an abundance of women's and children's clothing hanging from clothespins; it looked, from the assortment of items, as though there must've been close to a dozen women and thirty children in residence.

I cracked open the door and looked at Rockwell. "You might want to stay in the truck; I'm not sure what kind of reception we're going to get."

He snorted, and this time had no trouble finding the door handle.

I walked toward the entrance of the metal building. The bonnet on a 357 Peterbilt truck was tipped forward and at least a half-dozen men were working on what appeared to be a massive, portable drilling rig.

I recognized two of the men right off—George, Roy Lynear's son, and Tomás Bidarte, the other man I'd met at The Noose bar. I was surprised to see how adept the Hispanic poet appeared to be at working on the big diesel.

I didn't see the father but figured he was there somewhere.

Orrin Porter Rockwell joined me in the doorway, and it wasn't long before another one of the men, one I didn't know, nudged George, who raised his head, jumped down from the running board of the truck, and advanced with a torque wrench in one hand.

"What are you doing here?" He looked to the left and smacked the two-foot tool in the palm of his other greasy hand. "And how did you get in?"

I waited a moment and then didn't respond, at least not in the way he wanted. "Mr. Bidarte?"

At the sound of my voice, Tomás raised his head. It was easy to see the similarity between him and his mother, weight notwithstanding; it was the look, the same look she had given the grave decorations at the front gate. There was something about the lack of movement, an old-world stillness that carried no intention, just a waiting quality that was slightly unnerving. "Yes?"

"Mr. Bidarte." I turned to George. "Is Roy Lynear here, also?"

"What's it to you if he is?"

I wondered if anybody who had ever met George had anything but the urge to punch his teeth down his throat. "I need to speak to your father."

He smirked, which appeared to be his signature expression. "What's it like to need?"

A sonorous voice carried from our right. "Who is it, George?"

"That sheriff." He gave Rockwell the once-over. "And some hobo."

Rockwell looked at me, and I was glad that I'd disarmed him.

"It's Sheriff Longmire, Mr. Lynear."

After a second, the elder spoke again. "Well, come around here, Sheriff."

I walked past George, careful to get the point of my shoulder as close to his chin as I could as I passed, and walked around two banks of rolling tool cases plastered with stickers, almost all of them in Spanish. Rockwell followed me, but the old guy seemed to be unable to take his eyes off of Bidarte, who remained on the running board of the dismantled truck.

Roy Lynear was seated in another of his custom-built La-Z-Boy chairs that usually were meant to accommodate two, if not one and a half, but at present was filled to capacity with the great man himself. He was enthroned in a space that was like a miniature living room with a vintage Navajo rug spread out underneath the faux-leather chair. Lynear had what looked to be a motor manual for the drilling rig open in his lap and, of all things, a diet soda resting on his knee. "Hello, Sheriff." He closed the book. "A surprise visit in the middle of the night?" He glanced past me at Rockwell.

"You don't appear to be sleeping, so I'm guessing I'm not disturbing your rest."

He waved at the drilling rig. "The water here is putrid, so we're digging a new well. I can assure you that all the proper paperwork has been filed and the appropriate permits are in order."

"I have no doubt." I looked back at the derrick and the 550-horsepower Caterpillar engine and accoutrements. "That'll dig a heck of a well."

"We've found it best, living in the areas that we are forced to live in because of our religious beliefs, to be self-supportive. The cost of contracting these types of activities is financially prohibitive." He gestured toward the book. "With our limited funding, we are forced to buy the equipment we can and make do."

I studied the Peterbilt. "I worked for a summer as a roughneck—granted that was quite a while ago—but that looks impressive."

"Looks can be deceiving." Lynear laughed and gestured toward the book again. "Especially since it won't run." He set the motor manual on a side table that I was sure had been placed there explicitly for that purpose. "Now, who is your friend?"

It felt silly saying it, but until we found out just who the crazy man was, I was forced to use the name he'd provided. "Well, this is, umm . . . Orrin Porter Rockwell."

The fat man, in a state of fascination, hefted himself forward in the cushioned chair and peered at the man beside me. "And a damn fine resemblance." An embarrassing moment passed, and then he turned back to me. "I was unaware that your department was in the habit of traveling with a troupe of reenactors."

I ignored the statement and got down to one of the reasons I was there. "I was sorry to hear of the passing of your father."

He shrugged. "The man was quite old, and I think there comes an age where you shouldn't be climbing around on your third-story roof." He narrowed an eye at me. "I understand you met my son Ronald and a few of his people, including Mr. Lockhart and Mr. Gloss, in South Dakota."

"I did."

"I also understand that there's currently a warrant for your arrest."

"I heard that, too." I took a step forward and was aware that the men who had been working on the truck had all joined George at the edge of the rug behind us and that Rockwell had turned to face them. "And, I'm afraid I've got some bad news, Mr. Lynear."

"And that would be?"

"Do you have a wife by the name of Wanda?"

"Big Wanda is one of ours, yes."

"But not a wife?"

"Mine, no."

I waited a moment before continuing. "She identified herself as a wife of yours."

He shook his head. "No. Wanda and I were never officially married, but I'm assuming you have news of her? We were afraid since she seems to have gone missing."

"Who would be her relative or next of kin?"

"This is all sounding rather serious." He looked past me to the men. "Tomás here—whom you've met—he's her son."

I turned and looked at him. "Mr. Bidarte, your mother has been in a traffic accident."

His eyes stayed steady on me. "How?"

I moved toward him. "Would you like to step outside, sir?"

George stepped forward. "You'll tell us what happened, and you'll tell us here and right now."

I ignored him and spoke to Tomás. "Mr. Bidarte?"

His head had dropped, but his eyes stayed with mine. "*Sí*, you can tell me."

"We were at the front gate of the ranch when Ms. Bidarte pulled up, I'm assuming from getting groceries in Casper. We spoke briefly about a missing woman, Sarah Tisdale, and I asked Ms. Bidarte for some ID. I noticed she was carrying an unlicensed pistol in her purse and before we could do anything she put the car in reverse and drove away. She went off the road and rolled the station wagon at a slow rate of speed. She's okay, but we've got her up at Durant Memorial for observation."

Bidarte took a deep breath and studied his boots. "I see."

"This is just the kind of harassment that we had to put up with in Texas, and now an innocent woman is hurt." George leaned over, effectively blocking my view of Bidarte as some of the other men crowded in. "Where is her car?"

I stepped forward and placed a hand on George's chest, pushing him out of the way and speaking to Tomás. "I'm really sorry, but I need to ask you some questions that are of a personal nature. Are you sure you wouldn't like to step outside?"

George slapped my hand away. "You talk to him here, where we can all hear what it is you've got to say. The last one of us that talked to you . . ."

"That's it." I stepped in and watched his mouth freeze in an open position as my nose stopped about two inches from his forehead. "You utter one more word in this conversation, and I will consider it an obstruction and place you under arrest—not one word."

I turned back and took Bidarte by the arm, leading him toward the opening where we would be out of earshot, if not sight. Rockwell followed me and then turned to look at the group, George Lynear in the front, his face as red as a blister.

In the half-light of the open doorway, I could see Tomás's eyes shining. I tried to reassure him. "She's fine."

It took a while for him to reply. "Yes."

"Is there any reason you can think of as to why your mother would have run from us like she did?"

He swallowed and scrubbed his eyes with the balls of his thumbs, his face growing stony. "She is a simple woman from the provinces. She had been abused by some *soldado* back in Mexico when she was a girl and my brother was killed by some security men from PEMEX; it's possible that she . . . That when she saw the uniforms . . ."

I nodded. "That might've been a mitigating factor, but what seemed to set her off was my mentioning Sarah Tisdale." He said nothing. "She reacted as if she knew the name and possibly the woman."

His jaw clinched, and I knew we were done.

I watched as he crossed his arms over his chest and then spoke softly to him. "I'm sure you'll want to come up to Durant and see about your mother."

"Certainly."

I walked him back into the shop and something strange happened—Rockwell extended his hand, and Bidarte, who paused for only a moment, shook it. He then reapproached the big truck, not speaking to any of the men, climbed back onto the running board, and submerged himself in the work.

I took the extra steps into the group and turned to look at Roy Lynear. "I noticed the number of children's clothes on the wash lines, Mr. Lynear. I trust that if those children are not going to the public schools here in Absaroka County, they'll be registered with Child Services so that county officials can see to their needs?"

He sighed. "I suppose that's a final and parting shot?"

I hitched a hand up onto my sidearm. "I wouldn't say final."

Rockwell followed me as I turned to go, and it might've been the look that he gave George Lynear that caused the loudmouth to break the rules I'd laid down.

"I still wanna know where our car is and how you got in here."

I could've ignored him, I could've let it go, but I didn't. Instead, I grabbed his nearest hand and drew his arm up into a reverse wristlock that placed him firmly against the facing of the shop opening, his chin pressed against the tin, forcing him to look skyward. I snapped the cuffs on him and yanked him next to me. "You're under arrest."

The others stood there looking at us but made no move to stop me, and that's when I noticed they weren't even looking at me but at Orrin Porter Rockwell. I glanced at the old man and could now see he casually held a .38 revolver at his side.

I walked George over to where I could see his father, fished the religious fob and ring of keys from my pocket, and tossed them onto his lap. "Wanda's keys, one of which is missing as the car has been impounded for evidence; you can come and get the groceries." I hefted his son's arm, so that he had to stand on tiptoe. "And this you can pick up anytime after the judge sets bail."

With George's cuff chained to the D-ring on the floor of the Bullet, I drove us out of the compound and up the canyon road until we got to the flat above. A glimmer of light was starting to cast a pinkish glow across the horizon to the east and the high spots of the rolling hills were just starting to blush with the growing day.

Still in a huff, I turned to look at Rockwell. "What are you, the Houdini of guns?"

He looked at me blankly.

"Give me that pistol."

He looked unhappy about it but pulled the .38 from his inside coat pocket and handed it to me. "Careful, it's loaded."

I popped the lid on the center console and thumbed the cylinder open, dropping the shells inside; afterward, I tossed the side-arm in there and closed the lid. "Where did you get it?"

He nodded his hairy head toward the bed of my truck. "Out of the box in the back of your conveyance; there are shotguns, rifles, and all sort of armaments back there."

I'd forgotten about the weapons I'd taken from the youth of South Dakota. "Jesus."

Rockwell nodded. "He works in mysterious ways, does He not?"

When we got to the main gate, I undid the clasps, pushed it open, and drove through. Thinking about what I'd just done, and not being particularly proud of it, I sat there with my hands gripped on·the wheel. In a fit of remorse, I opened the suicide door, reached in, and uncuffed George.

I pulled him from the truck and stood there looking at him, his eyes growing wide with the thought of what might happen next.

I let him think for a few seconds, watching sweat trickle down from his hairline, then walked him back to the gate, and placed him on the other side. I closed it, the chain-link still rattling as he stood there staring at me.

He wiped the sweat from his face and took no time in locking the three massive padlocks. I replaced the cuffs in the holder on my belt. He took a step back—I suppose just to make absolutely sure that he was out of reach, the signature smirk returning. "You come around here again, and I'll be waiting."

I sighed and pulled my jacket back to reveal my .45.

He stood there for a moment, his eyes opening even wider, and then started backing up, finally turning and running down the road.

I yelled after him, "When you get back, tell them you escaped—they'll be impressed."

9

"They say that as you get older, you need more sleep."

I felt myself coming back as if from death. I was trying to climb out of a hole, but something large and feathery kept landing on my chest and pushing me deeper into the earth. Catching my breath, I'm pretty sure I snorted and then spoke through my hat. "Actually, you need less, which might explain the end result." I pulled my hat from my face. "I thought I locked that door."

"It doesn't have a doorknob. How could you lock it?"

She had a point.

Rolling over, I lay there on my side on the stack of blankets and pillow I'd liberated from the jail. "What time is it?"

"Daytime." She sat in my guest chair with a stack of papers under one arm and two mugs in her hands. She looked down at me, and it looked like the multicolor bruises under her eyes were just about gone. "Why didn't you sleep in the jail—the kid goes to work at five."

"There was no room at the inn." I coughed again, half expecting feathers to fly out of my mouth. "I don't know, all his stuff is in there. It felt like trespassing."

She handed a mug down to me. "Here, mother's milk." I sat up and hunched against one of my bookcases, taking the coffee as she smiled. "So, the staff is dying to know how you single-handedly captured public enemy number old."

I mainlined the caffeine and tried to clear my mind, buying time with clever repartee. "Huh?"

She nodded her head toward the holding cells, and I noticed she was wearing a ball cap, which was trouble as it indicated a bad hair day. "Cousin Itt."

"Oh . . . Yep."

She sipped from her mug and pulled the papers from under her arm. "Where did you find him?"

I told her she was never going to believe me if I told her and then did.

"Get the fuck out of here."

I raised a hand. "As God is my witness."

"He was in the truck all afternoon, even when we were down in Short Drop?"

"Twice."

She settled in the chair with the papers in her lap, crossed her legs, and bobbed a tactical boot about a foot from my head. I wondered if she was going to kick me. "You went back?"

I sipped my coffee. "I did."

"Alone." She looked out the window, and I was pretty sure she was going to kick me now. "In the middle of the night."

I gestured with my mug toward the holding cells. "With Cousin Itt."

"You took him with you?"

I yawned, even though it was probably a bad move. "It seemed like a good idea at the time."

The tarnished gold focused on me, and I was pretty sure it was the same look pythons give you just before they crush you to death and eat you. "And?"

"Roy Lynear claims Wanda is one of theirs but not his wife; however, it turns out she is Tomás Bidarte's mother."

She pursed her lips, and I had to fight to concentrate. "The guy with the knife we met at the bar?"

"Yep." I sipped my coffee some more. "How 'bout you run a check on Tomás with the Mexican authorities; he made mention of a brother being killed by PEMEX security, and that struck me as being a little strange."

She continued to study me doubtfully. "Mexican authorities—isn't that an oxymoron?"

"Oxymoron is a little south of Mexico City, isn't it?" I smiled for the first time this morning. "How's your Spanish?"

She yelled over her shoulder. "Sancho, translation!"

I drank my coffee as if my life depended on it, which it did. "That bad, huh?"

She reached down, scooping up the sheaf of papers and handing them to me. "Anything else?"

I stared at them, a complete dossier from the NCIS on the entire Bidarte family. "Did I already ask you to do this?"

She shook her head. "I ran the SOP on Wanda and the rest of the family popped up, kind of like Ancestry.com for criminals." She sipped her coffee. "They got a lot of little leaves in that family."

I thumbed through the pages and looked up at her. "Do I have to pay a quarter for the audio presentation?"

She set her mug on the corner of my desk and held out a hand.

It was a habit she'd adopted in getting me to read reports that only worked when I had pocket change. "I think I liked you better when you weren't making house payments." I handed her back the papers and then struggled to get two bits out of my jeans, finally depositing the quarter in her open palm.

She poked the change into her shirt pocket—I was pretty sure I'd paid for a third of a living room by now. "The earliest mention of the family is a Philippe Bidarte who was a big deal in the Mexico oil business in the twenties till he climbed in bed with a lot of the big American oil interests. With all the revolutions, Mexico was changing governments every twenty minutes, but the one thing all the revolutionaries could agree on was getting the gringos the fuck out of Mexico. Philippe, on the losing end of one of these wars, found himself guarding the ex–el presidente, some old one-armed fart by the name of Álvaro Obregón. Anyway, the jefe has a price on his head, and Philippe makes a lateral career move, whereupon he and his men shoot the old guy, asleep in his tent, dead."

"Oh, my." I sipped the last of my coffee and rolled my hand to prompt the history lesson.

"Bidarte Sr. and his men, mostly family, are seen to be viable muscle in certain quarters unimpeded by such a useless appendage as a conscience. They hire out as a kind of private army through the decades, and then in the eighties, they become the strong arm for the most powerful drug cartel, Familia Escobar in Chihuahua."

"Where the dogs come from."

She stared at me. "Did you wake up on the funny side of your pile of blankets or what?"

"So Tomás and his mother are connected to the drug trade?"

"No."

"No?"

"No. Eduardo and Wanda shipped Tomás, their baby boy, off to—get this—Universidad de Salamanca in Spain."

She glanced at the file to freshen her memory. "There's a vacant time period for Tomás after college where there are reports of his involvement with the Basque terrorist group, something called the Euskadi Ta Askatasuna, or ETA for short, but about twenty years ago Tomás's father, Eduardo, splits from the Escobar family because he sees what drugs are doing to an otherwise virtuous business like the Mexican mafia; he walks away and joins the Church of the Little Lambsy-Divey or whatever it's called."

"The Apostolic Church of the Lamb of God."

"Whatever."

I looked in my empty cup. "I thought all the mafiosos, no matter what their nationality, frowned on that—it's the in-for-life kind of thing."

"Evidently Eduardo had the juice to do it for six months, and move to los Estados Unidos; Hudspeth County, Texas, to be exact."

"Six months; why do I not like the sound of that?"

"Because the sheriff down there said the story goes that they filled him so full of holes you could've used him for a colander."

"Hmm."

"Wait, it gets better. Our man Tomás Bidarte shows up in northern Mexico like the Shadow, and suddenly Escobar personnel start disappearing wholesale, by the carload, by the houseload—until every single member of the family is dead: men, women, and children. Now there's nothing to connect Bidarte to any of this, but in good old Mexican tradition, enough people are paid enough bribes to get Tomás thrown into Penal del Altiplano, the worst prison in all of Mexico, for what turns out to be twelve years. Just as a side note, the life span of the average prisoner in that place is only five."

"He got out?"

"Yes, and reestablished his ties with the Apoplectic Church of Sheepskin, which had a compound on both sides of the Rio Grande near a little town called Bosque. Whenever they got in trouble for the polygamy thing in the U.S., they would run over to the Mexican side, and whenever they got in trouble with the Mexicans, they would come back."

"Who did you talk to in Texas?"

"The new sheriff, a guy by the name of Crutchley."

I hoisted myself off the floor and stretched my back in an

attempt to get it somewhat in line, and noticed Santiago standing in the doorway of my office. "What are you looking at?"

His grin displayed the trademark dimple in his right cheek. "Jeez, I've seen buffalo get up more gracefully than that."

I ambled to my chair and sat down. "Just wait, your day is coming."

He leaned against the facing. "Somebody need a translator?"

"Do you want Crutchley's number?" Vic laid the papers on my desk, pointing at a number she'd scrawled in the margin, including her signature period she added to everything; it looked like somebody had stabbed the sheet of paper with an ice pick. I dialed and glanced up at her and Sancho. "Bidarte—that doesn't sound Spanish."

Without looking at him, Vic snapped a finger and pointed at Saizarbitoria's face, and he responded. "Basque, it means 'Between the Ways.'"

"He's Basque?"

"Vasco," Santiago nodded. "At least part; Basque heritage makes up about twenty percent of the bloodlines in Mexico."

She looked up at Sancho. "Dismissed."

He didn't move.

The phone rang twice and then a female voice with enough twang to string a mandolin answered. "Hudspeth County Sheriff's Department."

"Hey, I'm looking for Michael Crutchley. This is Sheriff Walt Longmire of Absaroka County, Wyoming. Who's this?"

"Buffy, his wife. I think I talked to an eye-talian woman from your department this morning about those cuckoos down near Bosque." There was a pause as she rearranged the phone against her ear. "I'm sorry, but our damned dispatcher/receptionist is pregnant again and out of the office."

I hit the speakerphone and rested the receiver back in the cradle. "Sorry about that."

"Nowhere near as sorry as I am—I married into Team Crutchley for better or worse but not for lunch." None of us were quite sure what to say to that and listened as she talked to someone in the background. "Maybe he doesn't want to talk to you— maybe he wants to talk to me."

We could hear a man speaking: "Buffy, gimme the phone, God-damnit." More jostling. "Hey, Sheriff, I apologize for my wife; she thinks she's funny." There was a pause, and I assumed he was walking into his office with the phone. "How can I help you?"

"I believe you had a conversation with my undersheriff about the Apostolic Church of the Lamb of God folks who were down in the southern part of your county?"

"Yeah, they used to be here, up until about a year ago."

"What happened?"

"Oh, back taxes, but from what I remember they got paid in full here a couple of months ago. And there were some problems with the Department of Child Services, who got all over 'em about not having some of their adolescent boys properly educated. They claimed they had a school for them, but these teenagers couldn't even tell you the capital of Texas."

"Hmm."

"It's Austin, by the way."

I grunted. "Thanks."

"Bosque's in the southern part of the county; I've got a shoestring budget and 4,572 square miles of sidewinders, sand, sagebrush, and sons-a-bitches trying to make it to the promised land. I guess you don't have those problems with the Canadians up there?"

"They would have to go through Montana first." I waited a moment. "That's north of us."

He grunted back. "Thanks."

"What's the story on Eduardo Bidarte?"

"Ancient history, like I told your deputy. He's about twenty years dead; the cartel over in Chihuahua decided to use him for target practice, and by the time they were finished their marksmanship got really good."

"I understand there was some wholesale retribution?"

"It's common knowledge that the son, Tomás, killed everything that crawled, walked, or flew with the name Escobar."

"No proof, though?"

Crutchley laughed. "It's Mexico; proof doesn't enter into it."

"Any drug ties to the ACLG church?"

"Nope. I've got drug problems on every point of the compass, but I didn't with the Mormons." He waited a moment, and when I didn't say anything, he asked, "What's the problem up there, Sheriff?"

"For now, just a traffic accident."

"Name?"

"Wanda Bidarte, lately Lynear."

"Big Wanda?"

I stared at the tiny red light on my phone. "You know her?"

"She was Eduardo's wife and Tomás's mother and was pretty much involved with every charity in the county. She even started going to the Catholic Church up here in San Marcos; thought she was going to revert, but I think they put the clamps on her." He sighed. "Traffic stop, you say?"

"Yep. We had her pulled over and she tried to make a run for it."

"Jesus." A pause. "She was jumpy that way."

"Meaning?"

"Uniforms made her nervous; I think I remember a story about her being kidnapped and raped by soldiers when she was young. I believe her daddy tracked 'em down and killed them, killed everybody they knew. So, I guess it runs on both sides."

"Rough justice."

"Yeah. Find anything in the car?"

"Just groceries, a gun, and a dozen bricks of ammo. Why do you ask?"

"Well, in south Texas it's always about drugs or oil."

"I thought you said they were drug-free?"

"Far as I know, but things change." Another pause. "So, that's it?"

"No, I've also got a found Lost Boy and a missing woman."

"Names?"

"The runaway boy's name is Cord, and the mother's name is Sarah Lynear, formerly Tisdale."

"Well, the Lynear part doesn't help since that's what just about everybody in that group goes by."

"Blonde woman about thirty years of age. I've got a photo of her, but it's an old one."

"If you want to scan it and e-mail it, I'll have one of my people run down to Bosque and ask around." There was a pause. "Did you say her maiden name was Tisdale?"

"I did."

"She have family? An oil man by the name of Dale Tisdale who died in a plane crash down here a few years back?"

I remembered the story Eleanor had told us about her husband and found that bit of information to be of interest. "That would've been this woman's father. Was there any connection between the ACLG and him?"

"Not that I'm aware of, but the accident happened right across the border. I'll ask around about that, too."

"I'd appreciate it." I examined the cuff on my sleeve—threadbare; might need a new shirt one of these days. "Can you tell me anything about Roy?"

"Lynear? He's a piece of work; kind of thought of himself as the king of Texas, at least down there in his shirttail end of it.

He's charismatic in a way, but I guess you need to be if you're going to be the leader of a cult." He paused. "I'm not an overly religious person, but the few times we were down there, I noticed that they didn't even have a church. There were all these Quonset huts they were living in, and the whole place was set up like a military bunker." He paused again. "You see him stand up yet?"

"Excuse me?"

"He lived down here for twenty years, and I don't think anybody ever saw him standing on his own two feet." There was another even longer pause. "Anyway, I guess they're your problem now, huh?"

I nodded and then remembered I was talking on the phone. "Yep; if you could check on those few things we talked about and get back to me, that'd be great."

"Consider it done. Adiós."

I hit the conference button and looked up at Vic and Sancho, the Basquo the first to speak. "That means good-bye."

I nodded. "Thanks." I sat forward. "There were some words she said: 'Lo lamento . . . Lo siento, por favor'?"

The Basquo grinned. "The literal translation of lo siento is 'I feel it,' but the meaning is generally 'I'm sorry,' especially in conjunction with lo lamento, which is the more traditional form, and por favor is, of course, please."

I glanced out my window at the cloudless day. "So, I'm sorry and please."

"Yeah."

I thought about what Crutchley had said about drugs and oil and asked Sancho, "You checked the entire vehicle?"

"Yeah."

"And?"

"Like you said, the gun, all that ammo, and groceries."

"Anything else?"

He thought about it. "There were some spare car parts, a rear-end differential, and some bearings, but that was about it." We were silent for a moment, and he grinned. "So, we have the historic Western figure back in custody?"

I smiled. "We do."

"I brought Mr. Rockwell some hot tea; he seems to like tea." The Basquo smiled back. "He's quite taken with you—says he hasn't been arrested in a hundred and fifty years, but he'll put up with it from Sheriff Longmire."

Vic turned to look at me, the faded to yellow bruises providing nothing if not emphasis. "Well, at least this time you arrested him." She continued to study my face. "You did arrest him, right?"

I didn't say anything.

"Oh, for Christ's sake." She stood and stalked from my office, headed for the holding cells.

Sancho sat in her seat. "I hope he's back there, for your sake." I guess he noticed the concern on my face. "Don't worry; he was back there a few minutes ago. Anyway, if we lose him we'll just back your truck up to the jail and unload him again."

"Boy howdy."

"By the way, they called, and the Bidarte fellow is coming up to check on his mother and get the groceries; I guess they're getting hungry down at East Spring Ranch." He continued to watch me. "Did you know that's the exact station wagon that was on *The Brady Bunch?*"

I stared at him.

"It was a TV show."

I then stared at my desk.

"Something about that car bothering you?"

"One of the sons, George, seemed more concerned about the Plymouth than Wanda."

"So, he's a prick?"

I nodded. "Oh, yeah, but more than that."

"Do you want me to get all Border Patrol on the Satellite? That's something I've always wanted to do."

"Tear a car down to its nuts and bolts?"

"Yes." He continued to study me. "You're thinking about it, if for no other reason than it'll piss off this Lynear bunch?"

I leaned back in my chair, hooking a boot underneath the corner of my desk as I always did. "Yep."

Vic reentered, standing in the doorway. "He's arrested. Officially." Her eyes flicked between us like a cat's tail. "What are we discussing now?"

Saizarbitoria volunteered. "Going Border Patrol on that station wagon."

"Just to piss 'em off?"

Everybody knew my methods. "Yep."

She started to smile, the canine tooth, just a little longer than the others, growing more evident as she smiled more broadly. "I am all about pissing people off."

"Take it down to Ray's Sinclair; if you find anything, call me."

Sancho grinned, got up from my guest chair, and joined Vic in the hallway. "What are you going to do?"

I pulled my hat down over my face.

My nap lasted forty-seven minutes before Ruby knocked on my door and told me Tomás Bidarte was here to visit his mother. I pulled my hat from my face and wrestled myself from the chair.

The Basque/Mexican poet/mechanic was standing in the reception area, alone, and I took the time to study him. Older than I'd thought in my first couple of meetings with him, he looked more like a poet than a killer. Everything about him was elongated, stretched, but still balanced—maybe more of a bull-fighter than a poet—like a poised steel spring.

"You're by yourself?"

He kept looking at the ground, and I noticed he'd made a gesture to the cooler weather by donning a black leather jacket. "No, there are more men in the truck outside."

"Would you like to load the groceries or visit your mother first?"

He pulled at the corners of his mouth with a thumb and fore-finger, and I was amazed at the length of them, like a concert pia-nist. "First, I would like to see my mother."

I walked him out to the office parking lot, watched as he spoke briefly with three men in the front of another, relatively new, flatbed pickup that I hadn't seen. There was what appeared to be a brief argument, and then Tomás joined me. I stood beside the door and watched the three men, George Lynear being the one on the far passenger side. He leaned forward and watched me for a moment and then leaned back in his seat in a huff.

I thought about walking over and looking for the shotgun he'd carried the other night but decided that there wasn't reason-able suspicion—yet. I opened my door and looked through the window at Tomás, still standing there. "It's unlocked."

His face rose, and he stared at me. "*Qué?*"

"The truck—it's unlocked."

He nodded and pulled the door open, climbing in and closing it behind him.

"Trouble?"

He looked at me. "What?"

I smiled the warmest smile I could summon up. "Trouble with your *compadres*?"

"They are not my friends."

I sat there for a moment and then started the Bullet, backing it out and pulling past the sullen crew. "I don't think they're mine either."

We drove the three blocks in silence, and I parked in my OFFI-CIAL VEHICLES spot beside the Emergency Room. "I think my truck knows the way here so well I could just drape the reins over the steering wheel and go to sleep."

"You see a lot of people hurt?"

I turned my head and looked at him. "Not particularly; generally it's me." He said nothing more. "How about you?"

"My father was in a business that required a great deal of violence, but he walked away from all of that; unfortunately, it did not walk away from him." He sat back in the truck seat, and it seemed as if he wanted to talk. "My mother, in an attempt to insulate me from the family business, sent me to school." He stared at the dash of my truck, not seeing it at all. "After college and before all of this, I returned home and became involved in my father's business. I believe it might be one of the reasons he walked away from all of it—an attempt to save my mother and me." He laughed. "I was younger then and impressionable, before I learned the ways of the world."

He stopped talking, and I was compelled to ask, "And what are those?"

His eyes shifted and looked at me, surprised I didn't know the answer. "They all involve money."

"Well, I guess in some circles it's pretty important. . . ."

"It is everything. The only thing that can possibly compare would be power, but the only true path to power is through money." He glanced around the vehicle. "This truck, your badge, gun, and the oaths you have sworn—they are all simply for the protection of the status quo of power and wealth, the muscle for what is and what must be. Anything else is delusional."

It was silent in the cab, and I didn't want to argue with the man, but his philosophies were heading down a dark road and I thought I should redirect them. "I guess I disagree."

A hard smile crept to the corner of his mouth as he slipped the stiletto from his back pocket and flipped it open. "Which part?"

"All of it."

He held the beautiful but worn cutlery out for me to see. "This knife, it is clumsy, unbalanced, and useless except for show—but it is the knife I carried in prison and I am partial to it. . . ." His dark eyes turned to mine. "I know you have done a background check on me, Sheriff. It would have only been prudent." He looked at the knife again. "It is a horrible throwing knife, but I had plenty of time to practice—we do the best we can with what we have." He laughed. "Perhaps we are all delusional."

"Well, you wouldn't be the first one to say that."

"You will argue the primacy of love or family?"

I sighed. "Fortunately, my jurisdiction doesn't include those."

"But for you, they are truths?"

"Yes."

The smile grew more rigid. "They will fall away—love, family. . . . Without the support of money and power even they will fall away." He rubbed a long, flat hand across his knee, as if polishing it. "You have family?"

"Yep."

"Children?"

"A daughter and a grandchild on the way."

"Wife?"

"Passed seven years ago, cancer."

"I am sorry." He looked at me with those dark eyes for a while longer and then unfastened his safety belt.

"What about your family, Mr. Bidarte?"

He sat there, looking through the windshield of my truck

toward the entrance of the Emergency Room. "I have only her left."

Isaac Bloomfield met us at the double swinging doors past the mauve waiting room. I looked around for the other two medical musketeers, but evidently the doc had decided to give them the afternoon off.

Isaac studied Tomás through his thick-lens glasses. "She's right in here."

We followed as he made an immediate left and down the hall to room 22. Big Wanda was propped against a team of pillows and was reading from a Gideon Bible that she'd procured from the nightstand. She looked up, and her cheeks bunched back in a joyous smile when she saw her son. "Tomasito!"

He hurried to the bed and embraced her but then quickly stepped back and looked at us. "I would like a moment with her alone, please?"

"Sure." I escorted Bloomfield out the door into the hallway and past the unoccupied nurse's station where the wall clock ticked loudly and the coffee pot was always on. I snagged a Styrofoam cup from the stack and poured myself one. "Doc?"

"No, thanks." He waited a moment and then added, "You look tired."

I brought my coffee over to the counter and rested my elbows on the plastic wood-grain surface. "In answer to your observation, I'm operating on about two and a half hours' sleep."

We both straightened as Tomás came through the doors. "I am ready to go."

"That was quick." I gulped what passed for coffee at Durant Memorial and tossed the cup in the trash. "All right."

"I will be taking my mother with me."

I glanced at Isaac, who spoke in a conciliatory tone. "I'm afraid you'll have to allow for the twenty-four hours that's customary with cases of concussion, even mild concussion."

Bidarte folded his arms, and I listened to the leather of his jacket crinkle like the skin on a snake. "All right, if it's really necessary." He turned to me. "But I will need the vehicle she was driving."

We all listened to the clock above the nurse's station as it ticked, or at least I did. "Um . . . That might prove to be difficult, too."

I'd explained that the car had been impounded and that it would take longer to get it.

Tomás supervised the loading of the groceries while George sat in the truck, the job obviously beneath him. I promised Bidarte that I'd check on the station wagon while they ran some errands in Gillette—told him that I would leave word with Ruby as to how he should proceed and gave him one of my cards.

He'd left without saying good-bye.

I drove over to Ray's Sinclair, which had been Ray's Shell, Ray's Texaco, and Ray's Red Crown before that. It was an old-style, two-bay filling station, the office with a wall of glass block on the side. The bathroom key was attached to an exhaust manifold, and as far as I knew, no one had ever bought one of the withering candy bars from the glass case upon which the cash register sat. No one came to Ray's for the ambiance; they came for Fred Ray, automobile mechanic extraordinaire.

I walked through the office and underneath the shark-like looks of a familiar '69 Mustang GT convertible that was on a lift in one of the bays. Ray was loosening the drain plug on the oil pan of the 428 Super Cobra Jet engine.

I reached up and placed a hand on one of the original bias-ply tires. "So you're the one that keeps this thing in shape for Barbara Thomas, huh?"

The mechanic smiled at me through the grease smudged on his chin and upper lip. "Do you believe this thing has only seventeen thousand miles on it?" He rolled over an oil-catching container and unscrewed the plug the rest of the way, catching it in his well-trained hand before the golden liquid could carry it into the barrel. He brought his fingers up, rubbing a little of the viscosity between his fingers. "She lets that nephew of hers drive it, with her in the passenger seat, about a hundred miles a year and then sends it in here to get the oil changed and to keep it serviced. Hell, the biggest problem is keeping the battery charged."

"Why doesn't she just give it to Mike?"

Ray laughed. "She's afraid he's going to hurt himself in it. Can you believe that? I mean, he's what, fifty years old?" He shook his head and placed the drain plug on the top of the barrel. "She thinks he's seventeen. . . ." He glanced up at the mammoth engine in the small car. "Hell, maybe he would kill himself driving it. I know I would." He wiped his hands on a red cotton rag. "You looking for the demolition derby?"

"Yep."

"Next stall over."

I nodded and walked through the doorway into the chaos of the garage, pieces of Plymouth Satellite scattered everywhere. "Boy howdy."

Saizarbitoria's head appeared with an inside door panel in his hands. "There is nothing in this car except car."

I nodded and walked over to where the backseat sat with some cardboard boxes, and squatted down. "Where's Vic?"

"Under here." Her voice echoed off the concrete floor, and she rolled a creeper from underneath the Plymouth with a trouble light in her hand and a black grease smudge on her nose, looking completely at ease. "I want that Mustang."

"I bet you do; everybody in the county wants that Mustang." I studied her—she had a rag tied around her head in the front like Rosie the Riveter, and she was wearing a pair of coveralls she must've borrowed from Ray—she looked hot, as she always did.

"You're enjoying this, right?"

"Among my Uncle Alphonse's numerous, nefarious enterprises, he had a chop shop on Christian Street where I used to do lube jobs."

"I bet you did."

She smiled and disappeared under the car again. "I was very good at it."

"I bet you were." I caught the Basquo's eye as he stood with his fists on his hips. "Anything at all?"

He sighed. "Nothing."

I nodded and fingered the flap on the largest cardboard box beside me. "Well, we need to put it all back together as fast as we can, since I promised Tomás that we'd let him drive it back to East Spring later this afternoon."

Vic's head reappeared like a snapping turtle. "You're kidding."

"Nope." I flipped the flap open and looked inside. "I'm sure we can get Ray to help us put it back together." Reaching into the box, I moved some of the newspaper that surrounded a metal housing. "What's this?"

Saizarbitoria peered over the top of the station wagon. "That's that differential yoke I was talking about—the one we found in the spare-tire well. I didn't look at it closely, but it's huge and weighs a ton, so I don't think it goes on the Plymouth."

With both hands, I ripped the cardboard and looked at the massive piece, then turned it over. From this angle, it looked like nothing that could possibly go on any automobile, but especially this one.

Vic rolled the rest of the way out from under the Plymouth. "What is that thing, anyway?"

I looked more closely at the piece of industrial equipment. "This is a polycrystalline diamond Hughes tricone drilling bit."

10

Before Howard Robard Hughes Jr. became a business magnate, engineer, aviator, film producer, philanthropist, Jane Russell's bra inventor, and all-around loony, he was the nineteen-year-old inheritor of 75 percent of Howard Robard Hughes Sr.'s empire. Like most billionaires, Howard Hughes was not a self-made man; the backbone of his fortune was built upon the development of the modern oil drilling bit already patented by the family company, Hughes Tool, in 1909. Being a pretty shrewd Texas oilman, H. H. Sr. had made the lucrative decision to lease the bits rather than sell them after he commercialized them.

I'm not sure if Junior ever came to Wyoming, even though Paramount offered to sell him *Shane,* the film they'd made in Jackson Hole, because it was so far over budget. Hughes turned down the opportunity even though he hadn't seen it. Rumor had it that Paramount had settled on the loss and was going to turn the movie out to pasture as just another oater when Howard finally viewed the rough cut of the film. He offered to buy it outright, Paramount reconsidered, and the rest, as they say, is cinematic history.

If Hughes never made it to Wyoming, however, his daddy's invention did; I'd seen it the summer I spent roughnecking after my senior year in high school, which was another part of my father's campaign to teach me the value of higher education. All the lessons had taken, and I'd spent the next four years as an English major at the University of Southern California in an attempt to never return to the oilfields; so far, it had worked.

The two-cone roller bit—and, more important, its descendant, the three-cone roller bit—looked like the mouth of one of Frank Herbert's giant sand worms in *Dune*, and with the addition of diamonds it appeared to have gone gangsta.

Double Tough spelled it out for Vic and me, his Appalachian drawl fitting the description. "One hundred seventy thousand dollars if it's a penny."

I studied the toothy-looking piece of heavy equipment that had taken two of us to lift onto the desk of the Absaroka County Sheriff's Office Substation in Powder Junction—our version of the French Foreign Legion and possibly the most depressing place in the world. I glanced up at a massive, yellowed map of the area so old that the interstate highway didn't even appear on it. I noticed a cot in the back room through the open door and assumed this was where Double Tough was sleeping while Frymire had his fiancée in town. "Do you guys ever think about fixing this place up a little?"

He ignored me, rolled one of the teeth in the device, and picked a thick fingernail at one of the diamonds. "Polycrystalline, but they're diamonds nonetheless. Hell, I only seen one of these one other time and that was down in Bolivia."

I sipped coffee from the cracked Hole in the Wall Bar mug. "I'll kick in some county money if you want to get a rug or something."

Vic's voice rose behind me. "Look who's talking about home décor."

Double Tough's shoulder muscles rolled as he took the device and turned it over, looking at the manufacture marks from under the bill of his ball cap. "Hughes Christensen, that's the real deal."

"The Cadillac of drill bits?"

He glanced up at Vic, standing by the desk. "More like a damn Lamborghini."

She smiled. "Did you know they made tractors before they made cars?"

"No shit." His eyes shone as he visually caressed the bit. "The Chinese are makin' a bunch of cheap stuff, but that right there is the real deal." He whistled through his teeth. "Directional drilling and antiwhirl technology; that ol' boy'll go just about anywhere you want to point it."

I set the mug on the corner of his desk. "Water?"

His eyes came up. "Yeah, but it'd be like plowin' yer field with that Lambo." He smiled. "The car, not the tractor." He studied the shaft of the beast. "It's got a lease mark here. I've still got some connections in the biz and I can give 'em a call to try and find out who it was leased to."

"Why not call Hughes Christensen?"

He shrugged. "Well, I don't want to get anybody in trouble. . . ."

I glanced up at Vic, standing by the desk with her arms folded as she reached over, picked up the receiver, and handed it to him. "Fuck it—get 'em in trouble."

The ex-roughneck shrugged and began dialing.

I walked over to the window in the door and looked through the sun-faded, peeling decal of our star, past the weather-beaten station wagon at the playground across the street. We hadn't planned to be looking out the window at a public school from every office we had, but that's how it had panned out.

Vic joined me at the door as Double Tough spoke on the phone. "Why would they have something like this, and why would it be hidden the way it was?"

"I don't know."

She paused to pick up the box that the bit had been in, partially crushed and filled with Mexican newspapers. The side read MISSION TORTILLA ROUNDS, RESTAURANT STYLE, IRVING, TEXAS. "Do you think they had it and forgot about it?"

Tapping the lid of the box with a forefinger, I laughed. "If you had a one-hundred-seventy-thousand-dollar piece of equipment" . . .

She finished the statement for me as she looked at the vehicle belonging to the Apostolic Church of the Lamb of God. ". . . in the spare-tire well of that piece-of-shit *Brady Bunch* station wagon, no, I wouldn't forget about it. I'm betting that's why they are more interested in the car than in Big Wanda." She pulled one of the wadded newspapers from the box and stretched it flat. "Ciudad Juárez, they've got a sale on tire-tread sandals." She glanced around and when it became apparent that I wasn't paying any attention to her, she nudged me with an elbow. "Hey."

"Yep?"

"Thanks for not sending me down here—I think I might've slit my wrists."

I looked through the dirt on the window and realized the majority was on the inside. "I liked it when Lucian sent me down here, but you're welcome."

"What're you thinking about?"

"I'm wondering how the Apostolic Church of the Lamb of God is all of a sudden paying off hundreds of thousands of back taxes up and down the Great Plains." I let out a long, slow exhale. "Something is going on with these people."

"Ya think?"

I did think and turned and looked at Double Tough as he hung up the phone.

"They're going to call me back, and I have to admit that it was fun telling them this had to do with a criminal investigation and they better do it pronto."

I nodded. "They say they're drilling a new water well over at East Spring Ranch—is there any reason why they would use a bit like this for that kind of application?"

He considered. "Well, it's a rock bit; I guess if you were bound and determined to drill a water well in one spot you might use it if you ran into a lot of rock."

"Like down here in the southern part of the county?"

"I guess."

I studied him. "You don't sound convinced."

"I'm not; why not just move the well? Anyway . . ." He gestured toward the Diamond Jim Brady of bits. "It'd be overkill to use a piece of equipment like this."

"So what would you use it for?"

"I told you: oil, gas, something worth big money."

I thought back to the detailed description I'd given him at the beginning of the conversation. "Could you drill oil or gas with the kind of rig I described seeing down at East Spring, the one on the back of the Peterbilt?"

"Not here, no way." He shook his head, and I watched as his mind sank into the ground, plummeting through the strata he knew so well. "It's all tapped out, at least the stuff that's easy to get to. You'd have to drill almost twelve thousand feet before you got to the Niobrara shale, Shannon and Sussex formation above that; you're talking about a ten-thousand-foot vertical well with possibly a five-thousand-foot lateral section, and setting up the equipment to sell the oil, you're looking at a good ten million dollars just to get started." He sat on the corner of the desk and placed a hand lovingly on the bit. "Do your friends over in East Spring Ranch have that kind of money?"

"I don't think so."

"Anyway, they'd have to permit that kind of activity through the Oil and Gas Conservation Commission, especially if they were God-fearing and law-abiding."

"Well, the jury is still out on at least one of those."

Vic joined us in staring at the bit. "What would you do with the oil?"

Double Tough laughed. "Tanker trucks or, better yet, a pipeline."

"Have you seen any activity like that down here?"

"No, but I haven't been looking."

"But you say there isn't enough oil to bother with?"

He shook his head. "Not on an industrial scale."

I glanced back out the window—a familiar pickup filled to the gills with men had pulled in behind the station wagon. "Right now I have to go return some rightful belongings."

I started toward the door but watched as he rolled the bit over on the table with a loud *thunk*. "That include this?"

"Not unless they ask for it."

The phone rang, and he reached for the receiver. "What're you gonna do?"

Vic tossed the box to the floor and followed as I turned the knob and pushed open the door. "Go fishing."

Roy Lynear was seated on his throne atop the Super Duty and was holding a somber sort of court. "Hello, Sheriff."

"Mr. Lynear."

He leaned forward, and I watched as Lockhart, the guy with the crew cut, got out of the driver's side and stood by the door. Another man stood at the front corner of the bed and looked at Vic and me; it was only after a moment that I noticed the swollen eye and recognized him as the guy I'd punched in South Dakota. "My driver is Mr. Tom Lockhart, and I believe you're acquainted with Mr. Earl Gloss?"

I studied him for a moment and then looked back at the

driver, the grip of a semiautomatic just visible under a navy Windbreaker. I returned my eyes to Lynear. "I was hoping to see Mr. Bidarte; I was hoping he was doing better."

The big man glanced back at Gloss, who immediately started for the station wagon. "I think he's thrown himself into his work at the ranch; some men respond that way." He tried to keep my attention, but I watched as the man with the swollen face walked to the back of the car and tried the rear door, which was locked.

I thought about tossing the keys to Vic, but she'd stepped to my left to keep an eye on Lockhart. I started toward the station wagon and watched as Gloss's eyes widened and he glanced at his boss, then to me again, before reaching toward the small of his back. "Just so you know; I won't have hands laid on me again."

I paid no attention and kept coming, watching out of the corner of my eye as Vic countered to face the other man. "Really."

I was putting my hand in my jacket pocket when Gloss slipped a late-model, expensive-looking .45 from his waistband and pointed it toward me. "Don't come any closer."

I wasn't too concerned, seeing as how I could tell it wasn't cocked. Granted, any capable marksman could pull the hammer back if there was a round in the chamber, but I got the feeling from Gloss that he was not a member of that group, at least not with a uniformed, armed officer bearing down on him.

He raised the pistol a little higher, directing it toward my face. "I'm not telling you again."

Sometimes, you can slap a sidearm out of a shooter's hand; it's a roll of the dice because sometimes you can't and then they shoot you. But I was feeling full of piss and vinegar and took the chance. Gloss's pistol flew through the air and into the soft dirt on the far bank of the barrow ditch between the road and the school parking lot.

Standing close to him, I dangled the keys between us and then bent over to unlock the tailgate of the old station wagon.

Gloss glanced at his gun, a good twenty feet away. "You had no right to do that."

I turned the key, the rear window whirring down with a herniated whine, and then lowered the door. "Just for the record, I had every right. Just because you can carry a sidearm, doesn't mean you can brandish and threaten a sworn officer." I tossed him the keys and then stepped back.

He glanced at Lynear for a moment and then reached in, immediately opening the spare well where the drill bit had been. He pulled out of the station wagon and quickly shook his head.

"Lose something?"

"I just don't like driving without a spare."

I addressed Lynear, coolly watching from the mountaintop of his mobile throne. It was easy to see who was the brains of the outfit: "Did you ever get your drill rig running?"

His head canted to one side. "Unfortunately, we're still working on it."

"I received a call from the county assessor's office about the logistics of your water well, and they wanted someone to run down with a GPS and get the exact location of the drill site."

He didn't smile. "Is that so?"

I went ahead and smiled—I'm friendly that way. "I volunteered for the job."

"I'm sure you did."

I gestured toward Vic, still facing the driver. "We'll be there tomorrow—if you can make arrangements for someone to meet us at the gate around noon."

"I'll see what I can do."

"If not, I'll just run through it."

Lynear nodded, and I got the feeling we'd made progress in

clarifying our relationship, but our stare-down was interrupted by Gloss having moved from the station wagon and going for his pistol at the far side of the ditch. "I wouldn't do that if I were you."

He stopped at the sound of my voice. "That's my gun."

"Yep, it is, and we have another law here in Wyoming concerning unauthorized firearms brought onto school property—it comes with a mandatory sentence—and that weapon, now, is most certainly on school property."

He glanced at the autoloader, gleaming in the dirt like an unobtainable treasure. "Well, what am I supposed to do?"

"I guess decide if that pistol is worth five to seven years in Rawlins—it's a nice enough town, but I'm not sure if the accommodations at the maximum security prison are all that great."

Vic, still standing off the driver, volunteered in a loud voice, "Fish sticks and Tater Tots on Fridays." I think she even winked at Lockhart.

Lynear's voice intoned from the truck, "Earl, I think it's time we were going."

Gloss circled around, careful to go to the front of the wagon in order to avoid me, then threw open the door of the Plymouth and climbed in. "I want my gun back."

"Just as soon as I check the serial numbers and you show me a Wyoming or Texas permit for carrying it."

He slammed the door and probably would've headed out in a tire-squealing, fishtailing, thunder-roading display if the tired Satellite's ignition hadn't given out with a terminal and diminutive click.

I glanced at Lynear. "You guys have any jumper cables?"

Back in my office, Vic examined Gloss's Wilson Combat Supergrade Classic, jacking the slide mechanism over and over and spitting shiny .45 dumdum rounds onto my desk with a determined ferocity. "It would've hurt if he'd shot you, you know?"

"Right."

She held up one of the pursed, open-tip rounds. "These hurt worse than normal, you know that, right?"

"Right."

She was pissed, but she kept her voice low so that no one else in the outside office could hear her. "You're a moron; you know that too, right?"

"Right."

"If that shitbird had shot you then I would've had to shoot everybody, which doesn't really concern me, but after that I would've had to lift your two-hundred-and-sixty-pound—"

"I'm down to two-forty-five."

She shot an index finger at me. "Shut the fuck up."

"Right."

"—ass off the roadway and load you into your unit, drive at the speed of light in hopes that you would not leak all your precious bodily fluids out onto the floor mats and die." She leaned back in my guest chair, her eyes like twin black holes with surrounding solar flares, swallowing everything, and all I could think was how ferociously gorgeous she looked—thoughts that if were voiced would, most likely, put my life in jeopardy again.

I eased back in my chair. "Can I talk now?"

"No, you cannot talk until you show some semblance of being able to behave like a rational, reasonable law-enforcement professional."

I considered. "I'm not going to be able to talk for the rest of my life?"

"No."

I glanced out my window and honestly reflected on my actions earlier. "I'm sorry."

She yanked herself forward and hissed. "Don't say that, don't even say that, because all that's gonna do is piss me off even more. And you wanna know why? Because you don't mean it. You walk around with this ten-foot-tall and bulletproof attitude, which, I might add, you should've gotten over during that last little jaunt in the mountains."

"That's how I lost the fifteen pounds."

"Shut. The. Fuck. Up." She was really angry now and stood, still holding the confiscated .45. "There are a lot of people around here who kind of depend on you, you know." She paced and then stopped, taking a deep breath and running her fingers through her hair. "A lot of people, and if you're not going to think of yourself then maybe you should think about them." She scratched the end of her nose with the barrel of the semiauto.

Being a fast learner, I said nothing.

With very little warning, she tossed the Wilson onto my desk, where it struck my leather blotter with a resounding thud and slid toward me. "That is a five-thousand-dollar sidearm—what the hell is Farmer Green Jeans doing with a gun like that?"

I raised my hand.

She dismissed me with a flapping of her own. "Talk."

"I don't know."

She turned to look down at me. "You used your opportunity to talk for that?"

I shrugged and studied her and gestured toward the pistol on my desk. "At the risk of you loading the aforementioned weapon and shooting me—are you all right?"

She turned very slowly. "What is that supposed to mean?"

I put my hand on the .45 and slid it out of her reach.

"I just want to be clear about this." She thumped a forefinger at her chest. "I'm dressing you down and you're asking what's wrong with me?"

"You just . . . You just seem a little on edge."

She walked over and closed my office door the rest of the way and then came back and sat in front of me on my desk, near me and the pistol. "Fuck. You. Again. I am trying to have a serious conversation about your recent juvenile actions and you're trying to use that hackneyed old chauvinistic tactic of blaming all this on my emotions?"

I raised my hand again.

She raised a tactical boot and planted it firmly between my legs, grabbed the front of my shirt, and pulled me in close, forcing me to grab the arms of my chair for balance. "I am in complete control of my emotions."

As they go, it was the Mount Vesuvius of kisses—shocking, overpowering, molten, and leaving nothing but paralyzed ash in its wake. I thought for a moment I was going to suffocate when she released the fistful of my shirt like the ripcord on a parachute.

Her face hovered there, and I continued to breathe her breath, feeling the warmth of it on my jaw and neck. "Any more questions about my emotions?"

"Nope."

She pushed with the foot, and I felt my boot dislodge; it was only then that I realized that my chair was flipping backward. I scrambled to grab the edge of my desk, Vic, or anything, but she'd already stood and stepped away and I crashed backward onto the carpet-covered but still unforgiving hardwood floor.

I lay there, attempting to focus my eyes and get the air back in my lungs as she walked over and stood above me, her hair framing her face like anything but a halo. The back of my head hurt, and I squeezed my eyelids together in an attempt to purge the ache that was starting at the back of my head.

She leaned over at the waist to inspect me crawling from the wreckage and whispered in a sultry voice, "I didn't call on you, teacher's pet."

Boy howdy.

Reaching a hand up, I was able to graze my fingers across her muscular calf as she turned and marched away. My eyes closed again for what I thought was only a moment and when I opened them she was gone and a different head, panting with a different sort of breath and with a worried look on his long face, was hanging over me. Unsure, he slathered a lick on the side of my head with a tongue as wide as a paperback, correct in the belief that a good kiss made everything better—well, almost everything.

I reached up and grabbed his ruff and massaged his ear. "How you doin', rascal?"

He wagged and disappeared as I noticed someone standing in my doorway.

"Walt?"

I tried my best to sound casual. "Yep."

"I heard a crash."

"That would've been me." Ruby walked in, and I noticed she was wearing a pair of her sporty, reflective running shoes; funny the things you noticed from this perspective. "What's up?"

"Saizarbitoria wants to talk to you, and Double Tough is on line one—something about a leased piece of drilling equipment?"

"Could you hand me my phone and tell the Basquo where I am?"

"Sure."

She rested the whole thing on my chest, picked up the receiver, and handed it to me, a finger poised to punch the button. "Do you mind if I ask what you're doing?"

"Nope, I don't mind at all."

We both waited.

Finally, she pushed the button and then smeared a thumb over my lips. "You might want to get rid of the lipstick—it doesn't become you."

I watched as she stood and disappeared out my door. "Do we have any aspirin?" Readjusting the receiver in the crook of my neck, I thought about getting up, but I wasn't really that uncomfortable, so I just spoke. "What've you got for me, Tough?"

"Hey, Chief. Hughes Christensen got back to me, and let me tell you that's the fastest that's ever happened."

"What'd they say?"

"It's stolen."

"Well, fancy that."

There was a rustling of paper as he read from his notes. "The original leasing was through PEMEX, the Mexican government-owned petroleum company?"

"The big dog, huh?"

"Big to the tune of four hundred and fifteen billion in assets."

I whistled. "How did they even notice it was missing?"

"They didn't; it was subleased to a private contractor." I noticed a few cracks as I stared at the ceiling in my office and listened to him. "That's the way these big operations work; they order up a bunch of this stuff if they get even an inkling that they might need it, because, unlike the rest of us, they don't wait on anything."

"I see."

"But then they got all this equipment lying around that they're not using and start thinking about recouping their losses. Well, the small operators are desperately in need of the equipment, but the big companies have it all tied up, so they have to go to 'em with their hats in their hands and then the big boys overcharge 'em to get back some of the lease money they lost."

"Who was the subcontractor?"

"An even bigger Brazilian company called Petrobras, but then they subleased the bit to a company called . . ."

"No offense, Tough, and I really appreciate your efforts, but—"

He laughed. "Seventeen more leases."

"You're kidding."

"I want a raise."

"I offered you a rug."

"The final operator was a . . ." He read from the paper. "DT Enterprises."

"Never heard of them."

"Me neither, but there are a ton of these little wildcat operations down there; it's like the Wild West."

"And you are telling me this because?"

"These operators are not the best bookkeepers, because it is sometimes not beneficial to these operators to have the best books kept."

"I'll buy you a lamp to go with the rug."

"You're going to have to do better than that; you're gonna have to find somebody else to work down here."

I was mildly shocked. "Are you quitting on me?"

"Nope, but Frymire is; he dropped off a letter for you this afternoon. I guess him and the fiancée are movin' down to Colorado. He says he can stick around for another week if you need 'im."

"Do we need him?"

"Well, things are heatin' up around here, but I figure I can handle it."

"Any more contact with the East Spring bunch?"

"Nope, after you helped 'em get that piece-of-shit Plymouth goin' they just headed on down the road."

"What did you do with the bit?"

"I got it locked up in the back of the Suburban with my dirty laundry on top of it."

"Sounds safe."

"I wouldn't touch it, unless I had to."

As I thought about some of the things Sheriff Crutchley had said, I spotted one of the .45 dumdum rounds that must've rolled off the top of my desk. I picked it up and held it in front of my face. Neville Bertie-Clay, the British army officer who had worked at the Dum Dum Arsenal near Calcutta, had developed the hollow or soft point bullet that to this day carried the arsenal's name. The things should've been called Bertie-Berties.

"Walt?"

"Yep?"

"Anything else?"

The British had used the ammunition in the venerable .303 against Asians and Africans because it had sufficient enough stopping power to deter a determined charge. The Hague Convention of 1899 had found the dumdum too cruel for use against fellow European countries, but some police departments still authorize them because they mostly do not pass through intended targets and continue on into innocent bystanders.

"Sheriff?"

I'd seen what they could do in Vietnam, and the fistfuls of flesh they removed. "Yep. Hey, where is DT Enterprises licensed?"

There was a pause. "Mexico."

"Where in Mexico?"

There was more paper rustling on his end. "Chihuahua."

"Where the dogs come from."

"I guess."

"See what you can dig up on them."

"Roger that. Anything else?"

"Start taking applications down there, would you?"

He laughed. "Yeah, okay. Why don't you just send Vic? I've got my cot set up in the back."

"I don't think that would work out, but don't worry, I'm going to call in some reinforcements."

He chuckled on the other end. "Smoke signals or war drums?"

Double Tough knew my methods. "I'll let you know." I hung up the phone and moved it off my chest, crossed my arms, and tried to think, once again, about my dwindling staff, but DT Enterprises kept getting in the way. Why did that sound familiar? Was it something somebody with Lynear had said? I didn't think so—maybe it wasn't the Enterprises part.

DT.

Sancho came in and sat on the corner of my desk with a sheaf of papers under his arm, one hand cupped around some aspirin, and a glass of water in the other. "You sleeping down there tonight?"

Dog followed him in and sat by my desk. "Just me and my faithful companion."

"Sit up and take your medicine. Ruby's orders."

I took the four aspirin and the glass from him and leaned against the bookcase where I'd started the day. "Thanks." I swallowed. "Everybody gone?"

"Cord is still working over at the Busy Bee, and Mr. Rockwell is reading about himself in his cell." He studied my quizzical look. "Ruby went over to the library and picked up all the books they had on Orrin Porter Rockwell and gave them to him."

"How's he doing?"

"He's been awfully depressed since Vic arrested him, but I think he appreciated the books." He smiled, and I couldn't help but think how handsome that face would be on a sheriff's election poster. "Bishop Goodman came by, and they talked for about four hours."

I laughed. "Our bishop may be fianchettoed."

"Huh?"

"A chess move where the bishop can form a long, diagonal defense of a castled king. Anyway, I think the good bishop wants to write a book about Orrin Porter Rockwell, and the prisoner in question might be a shortcut in the research department."

"He seems to know an awful lot about him."

"That he does. Any word on who he really is?"

"I tried to get his fingerprints, but he resisted, so I took them off of a glass of water."

I glanced at the one in my hand. "Remind me to never get on your bad side."

He pulled the papers from his underarm and looked at them. "It makes for some interesting reading."

I studied the Basquo's face. "Oh, now, why don't I like the sound of that?"

"Well, you know we're limited to service personnel and criminals on the fingerprint bank. . . ."

"Right."

"Well, I got nothing."

"So he's clean?"

"Not exactly." He flipped one of the pages over and handed it down to me as Dog settled in and stretched out, figuring we were here for the long haul.

There was an enlarged, washed-out, mimeographed two-by-two photo, not unlike the one that had accompanied Saizarbitoria's résumé from the Wyoming State Prison in Rawlins back when he'd been attempting to flee working in corrections. The man in the photo was trim, young, and straining with wiry muscle. There was an intensity in the light, opal-like eyes that was hard to miss and still in evidence. His hair was so close-cropped to the side of his head that his ears looked like he was cleared for takeoff—ears I thought I'd seen somewhere before on someone else.

The official form from Ellsworth Air Force Base was a military identification for the year 1957 but stated that all information was classified.

"Intelligence."

"Maybe, maybe not." He tapped the papers in his hand. "I had a friend at the National Personnel Records Center who found this in the files that said he was on loan to Civil Air Transport, under the auspices of the American Airdale Corporation. . . . Get it? Air, Dale . . . ?"

"No."

"You will. Two years later Civil Air Transport and American Airdale changed their name to the much storied Air America."

I knocked the receiver off the phone. "CIA?"

"Spooky as the night is long." He laughed. "Up to '62 he flew direct and indirect support for CIA Ops Ambidextrous, Hotfoot, and White Star, and then trained the Royal Laotian armed forces. After that he was involved with something called Project 404 as an air attaché to the U.S. embassy in Vientiane, and then he provided logistical support to the Royal Lao and Hmong armies under the command of General Vang Pao."

I'm sure what the Basquo had discovered was pretty important, but I was getting a little tired of all the dramatics. "C'mon, CIA?"

"Wait, there's more." His eyes returned to the paper. "He was shot down in '64 while making what they called a *hard rice* support run in the mountains dropping off weapons to tribal leaders who were opposed to the North Vietnamese. He was listed MIA, but by the end of the war in '73 he was listed as a war casualty. Okay, so jump-cut to this VISTA volunteer working in Vietnam who happens to see this white guy with a beard and long hair working on a prison road crew in '75 and goes over to him and asks him his name."

"Yep?"

"The guy looks up slow and has some trouble getting his voice and remembering how to speak English before telling the kid his nickname, *Airdale.*"

"I don't get it."

"From Short Drop, Wyoming."

I stared at him.

"Dale *Airdale* Tisdale."

DT Enterprises.

11

Henry sipped his beer and leaned back in Ruby's chair. "The woman who owns the mercantile, his wife, Eleanor, says he died in a plane crash in Mexico?"

I glanced back at him. "Yep, but he supposedly died crashing a plane in North Vietnam, too. It seems to me he's made a habit of crashing and dying all over the globe."

The Bear, the Basquo, and I had been surprised to find a few Rainiers in the commissary icebox and were sitting in the dispatcher's area at the front of the office like truants.

Sancho sat on the bench by the steps and turned the copy of Tisdale's faded, black-and-white head shot in his hands, then stretched an arm out and forced Henry and me to stare it in the eye. "Tell me that's not him."

The thing looked like a photo of a ghost. The eyes were the same, but the identifying feature was the ears—ears exactly like his grandson's. "So what was he doing flying around Mexico?"

"You tell me."

The Bear added. "And dead, no less."

I thought about it. "If he's Sarah Tisdale's father, then he had to be back here in Wyoming for at least a night."

Saizarbitoria sipped his Rainier. "Uh-huh."

"You thinking what I'm thinking?"

He looked at the can. "That this is the shittiest tasting beer ever?"

"That's not what I'm thinking." The Cheyenne Nation chuckled, and I took a long swig out of my own can, just to make a point. "That he was still on the Company payroll down in Mexico."

Sancho belched and made a face. "Lawyers, guns, and money?"

"I guess I need to talk to Eleanor Tisdale, not that I'm looking forward to it."

The Basquo nodded his head, knocked on the bench as if it were a door, and broke into a faux, flowery announcer voice. "Mrs. Tisdale, we're sorry to report that we think your daughter's dead, but guess who we have behind door number two?" I sighed, and he continued. "You guys know anybody at the CIA?"

Henry and I glanced at each other, and then I pulled out my pocket watch. "As a matter of fact, we do."

Wally was surprised to see me at eight o'clock at night at the door of the main house at the Lazy D-W but maybe even more surprised to see the Cheyenne Nation. The patrician-looking silver-haired man led us into their den, where Donna sat with a wine glass of sparkling water at her side.

I noticed that she casually flipped the top sheet of a prodigious stack of papers to keep the Bear and me from seeing the title. "Are those your memoirs?"

She laughed. "Something like that." She and her husband made eye contact for a moment, and then Wally gave us a brief nod and left.

Looking at all the stacks of books, photos, plaques, and awards that the woman had accumulated over the years, my eyes wandered around the crowded room—Donna with presidents Nixon, Kennedy, and Johnson; Donna with ex-senators; Donna with movie stars. I pointed toward the one of Donna and LBJ standing together. "Relation?"

She smiled. "Nope, but he gave me the best advice I ever got about public life."

"And what was that?"

"You know, Walt—never turn down the opportunity of a free meal or a chance to go to the bathroom."

There was another photograph near where Henry sat of Donna in a parka and a man in army fatigues and an Airborne cap. The Bear reached over and tapped the glass protecting the black-and-white photo of the two, who were seated with a snow-capped mountain in the background. "Is that Larry Thorne?"

"The man who brought modern skiing into the United States Army despite the United States Army. Sure is." Donna smiled and pulled her chair closer, plucking the frame from the wall, turning it over, and handing it to Henry. "Recovery mission; the bodies from a military transport that crashed on an Iranian glacier in '63. There was bad weather, and I radioed him to see if he wanted to wait on the operation. The weather got worse and transmission got sketchy, but I finally got through and Larry asked me if we wanted them to put the bodies back—they'd already gone up and gotten them."

The Bear carefully returned the photo to the wall. "He was the only white man that ever outran me."

"Fort Bragg?"

Henry nodded. "Twice our age, and he could run all of us into the ground." The Bear glanced back at the photo, the man's features looking like they'd been carved from soapstone. "There were rumors that he was a Nazi."

Donna laughed. "He was from Finland." Johnson settled back into her chair and stared at her lap. "Lauri Torni. He fought against the Soviets when they invaded Finland; then when the

Germans invaded Russia, the Finns went after what they'd lost to the Russians." She looked up at us. "The friend of a friend is a friend, the friend of an enemy . . ." She didn't have to finish the proverb. "Anyway, after the war, 'Wild Bill' Donavan, who knew what Torni was worth, got him and shipped him off to North Carolina as a citizen and second lieutenant with a new name, Larry Thorne." She smiled at the Cheyenne Nation. "And that's probably where you met him."

Henry grinned at the thought of the man and then stiffened. "He was the first Study and Observations Group personnel to be listed as MIA."

It was the first time I'd heard the Bear use the proper name of his old outfit, SOG; evidently he was feeling comfortable with the reclusive ranch woman.

"Hey, Donna?"

She turned to look at me.

"I've never asked you what it was you did with the government, and to be honest, I really don't want to know—but it's getting late, I don't want to keep you till tomorrow, and I've got a situation on my hands that I need some help with."

She adjusted her glasses, looking for the entire world like some Harvard don. "Does this concern the *My Friend Flicka* boy and that man?"

"As a matter of fact, it does."

She nodded, and I could see her weighing the options. "How can I help?"

I explained the situation, indicating that my only interest was in finding out what was going on in my county concerning the boy, a missing woman, and a bad feeling I had about the whole Apostolic Church of the Lamb of God.

She glanced at a fancy computer monitor and the stacks of papers she'd casually covered up, and all I could think was that these might not be the first things Donna Johnson had been responsible for covering up. "Why don't you show me what you've got?"

I reached in my jacket and pulled out the folded papers that Saizarbitoria had given me—the Basquo had pleaded with us to take him, but I'd told him that if Donna had to kill us after giving us the information we'd requested, it might be better if he went home to his wife and child.

Johnson took them, stared at the photo first, and then flipped through the pages. "Who collated this information?"

"My deputy, Saizarbitoria."

Donna studied the papers, her eyes sliding over them like fingers sweeping keys on a piano. "He's very capable, this young man."

I nodded and compressed my lips. "Does that mean you have to kill us?"

Donna smiled. "Not yet." She looked at me. "If I do this for you, you mustn't let anyone know that I've done it—anyone at all. I'm very serious."

I kept my eyes locked on hers, just to demonstrate the severity of the promise. "Agreed."

She glanced at the Bear, who crossed his heart. "Honest Injun."

She smiled and gave a definitive nod of her head. "Well, it will take a little time, so why don't you gentlemen adjourn to the kitchen for a few moments—have you eaten?"

"Antelope ravioli; I made it myself."

Sitting around the counter in the kitchen of the Lazy D-W, I had to admit that the impromptu meal was one of the finest I'd ever eaten. "Wally, thanks. You really didn't have to feed us."

"Oh, I don't mind; it gives me something to do. Gardening is over, and things get a little boring this far out from town."

I studied him, enjoying the camaraderie of being in his kitchen. Donna's family had had the ranch for as long as there had been a county, and as near as I could remember, they had both known my late wife. A lot of men would've had a problem being Donna's husband on a lot of counts, but Wally seemed to wear the mantle easily. "Nonetheless, it's kind of you to take us in on such short notice."

Henry scraped the remains of the ravioli from his plate and licked his fork clean. "This was delicious. I could not have done better myself—antelope is tricky."

I sipped the fancy beer that Wally had poured out of a growler and smiled at him. "That was a supreme compliment."

He sipped his wine and studied the Bear and then me. "I assume that all this has to do with that young man Cord?"

I was surprised he remembered his name, but then they probably didn't get that many horse thieves around these parts. "Tucked in and sleeping at the jail."

"Is he still fixated on *My Friend Flicka*?"

"He and his friend were watching it again when we left."

He nodded. "The crazy one that thinks he's Orrin Porter Rockwell?"

"Yep."

"It's an interesting life you lead, Walt."

"I meet a lot of people." I set my stylish Royal Pint glass down. "So is your wife . . ." I glanced around, just to impress on him and the Cheyenne Nation that I could be covert, too. "Is she really writing a book?"

"God help us." He rested an elbow on the cherry counter. "For the last ten years."

The Bear interrupted. "Tell her not to feel bad. I cannot type either."

He laughed. "It's the Company censors; the last time she turned in six hundred and five pages, they returned two hundred and two."

"Ouch."

"But she's decided to attack the problem from a different angle."

"How so?"

"She's writing it as a spy thriller."

"Fiction?"

"Yes. She's just changing all the names to protect the not-so-innocent. Most of the fact-checkers at Quantico are so young they won't have any idea what Donna's writing about, but it should send a shiver through the intelligence community."

A voice sounded from behind us. "Are you telling all my secrets, hon?"

He tipped the bottle of Domaine de la Solitude and poured her a glass. "Just the ones I know, dear."

Donna sat on the stool beside him—the file on Dale "Airdale" Tisdale that she put on the counter had grown. "I have no secrets from you."

"Of course not, dear." He turned to look at me. "The benefits of marrying a spy are that you always know that they're not telling the truth."

Donna made pointed eye contact with Henry and me. "I was not a spy, I was an administrator, a facilitator who made phone calls and got things done."

I sipped my fancy beer. "Donna, as long as you don't break the speed limit too much or write bad checks here in the county, I don't care what you did—and I hope your book is a best seller." I pointed at the stack of papers. "Is that the international man of mystery?"

She placed a steady hand on the pile and looked at me. "Are you sure you really want to see this?"

I waited a second before replying. "Why do you say that?"

She looked pained. "Walt, there are things that are better not known—I mean, isn't it enough that you know who he is and that he's just a crazy old guy now?"

I glanced around as if the answer was obvious. "No."

She nodded. "Whenever a field agent is involved with an operation, he's given a new name, history, everything. These cover stories are called Legends, and the problem is that after an extended period of activity and a bunch of Legends, some individuals exhibit marked psychological aberrations—they become the Legend so well that they forget who they are, like an actor who becomes the role forever. Robert Littell wrote a really good book about one of them—fiction, of course." She smiled.

"And that's what happened to Tisdale?"

Donna picked up the papers and handed them to me. "One of the things."

I took them, folded them, and placed them in the inside pocket of my jacket, which was hanging on the back of my stool. "He thinks he's Orrin Porter Rockwell; what were you guys trying to do, infiltrate the Mormon Tabernacle Choir?"

She laughed. "Dale Tisdale really was CIA, unlike all these jaybirds around here who say they were—just once, I'd like to get one of the fake ones crossways with me so I could show them what the real CIA is capable of."

Henry read by the overhead map light as I drove. "So, he hadn't lost his mind when he was in Mexico, which is a shame because I think I lost mine in Cabo one time." The Cheyenne Nation studied the papers. "Sometimes it is a gradual process; I think that is what Donna was trying to intimate to us."

I steered the Bullet south on I-25 through the chilling night and glanced past Henry toward the invisible mountains, taking comfort in knowing they were there and that I was not climbing them. "Why would the CIA send someone like that back into duty?"

"Possibly because they did not know how much of a psychological break he had sustained in Southeast Asia?"

I gave the Bear the horse eye. "Kind of hard to miss a guy with a beard and hair down to his ass who claims to be a historical Western figure."

He sighed. "As I said, it would appear that the Orrin Porter Rockwell manifestation of his character is relatively recent—say, when he was arrested by the federal authorities in Mexico. It would appear that the CIA claimed that the entire operation was rogue and they hung Tisdale out to dry."

"For the second time at least." I shook my head. "Remind me to never work for the CIA."

"It is possible that some of it was a rogue undertaking; Tisdale conceived the idea and named it Operation Milkshake. Evidently, because of his specific skill set, he was put in charge of this operation in Mexico that involved the appropriation of crude oil." He stopped reading and gazed through the dark windshield. "I recall a while back the Justice Department found out American refineries had been buying massive quantities of stolen oil from the Mexican government." He turned to look at me. "The bandits and drug gangs tap into pipelines out in these remote areas and some of them were even building their own pipelines to siphon off hundreds of millions of dollars' worth of oil a year."

"So Operation Milkshake was not a penny-ante operation."

"No, and it would appear that a portion of the American government wanted to get in on the action." His eyes dropped. "There were a number of subsequent investigations, indictments, and arrests—one of whom was Tisdale." He shifted in his seat. "Operation Milkshake . . . That sounds strangely familiar; where does that come from?"

"Albert Fall, the secretary of the Interior under Harding, was convicted of taking bribes for oil rights on public lands, namely from the Teapot Dome Naval Oil Reserves just a little south of here. In a congressional hearing, the senator from New Mexico was famous for having made a statement about the process of directional oil drilling—'If you have a milkshake and I have a milkshake and my straw reaches across the room, I'll end up drinking your milkshake.'"

"What a typically white venture."

I ignored the remark and continued. "Tisdale appears to be something of an expert in history and would know that statement."

"Whatever happened to Fall?"

"Died penniless in El Paso." I took the off-ramp at Powder Junction. "Do the papers indicate where all this Mormon stuff comes from?"

The Bear synopsized. "After an unfortunate incident with a Cessna Bonanza, the U.S. government denied his existence and reported him dead. The Mexican government, left with an unidentified prisoner, dumped him in Penal del Altiplano where he shared a cell with newfound Mormon Tomás Bidarte."

I turned and looked at him. "You're kidding."

Henry shrugged. "Evidently, Dale Tisdale converted to the point where he actually thought of himself as Orrin Porter Rockwell; as a Caucasian finding himself in the environs of a maximum security prison in Mexico, it might have been a survival instinct and the only way he made it through."

"So he and Bidarte were locked up together; I thought there was something that passed between them when they shook hands down at East Spring." I stopped at the sign at the bottom of the interstate ramp alongside the rest stop. "How did he get out?"

The Cheyenne Nation nodded. "As you have surmised, with Bidarte's help, they bribed their way to freedom by selling Tisdale's land holdings in East Spring Ranch to Roy Lynear."

"Well, I'll be damned." I made the left through the underpass and stopped at the next sign where the Short Drop road crossed Old Highway 87. A Powder River Fire District truck approached from the south with its siren and lights going but made a left before getting to us.

"He was picked up in Utah by the Highway Patrol while kneeling by a roadside cross; he was then incarcerated in a psychiatric ward for observation, but once he admitted to having lived in Wyoming, they shipped him off to Evanston."

"Why didn't they contact his family?"

"At that point he claimed to have no living relatives and asserted to be *the* Orrin Porter Rockwell, and before anyone could ascertain just who he was, he escaped."

"So he lived the Legend."

"It would appear so."

We sat there in the darkness at the four-way stop in Powder Junction, Wyoming, the caution light intermittently flashing and giving me the feeling it was a metaphor. I listened as the siren from the volunteer fire truck stopped—it didn't sound all that far away. "Then why is he here now, protecting his grandson? Who contacted him? Who knew he was still alive? Bidarte?"

"The answer to that question does not appear to be in the file." The big Cheyenne Indian looked at me with a sad smile. "What about the daughter?"

I sat there, idling. "Unavailable for comment, and not very popular with her parents."

He nodded, the yellow light flickering its warmth on the reflective surface of his dark eyes. "Now everything leads to Mexico, Operation Milkshake, and the Apostolic Church of the Lamb of God."

"Agreed."

Another truck pulled up across the road and sat there, obviously waiting for me to go first, so I reached down and flicked the lever, throwing my brights at him so that he'd know it was okay to proceed. "Double Tough says the Teapot Dome Reserves are tapped out and that the federal government tried to sell the place off to private developers but nobody bit."

"Then why are they here?"

I blinked my lights at the truck again; obviously he'd noticed the stars and bars on my vehicle and figured it was a trick. "According to Vic this is the end of the world, and maybe they're what they say they are, religious zealots looking for a place to be left alone; wouldn't be the first time that type has turned up on the high plains."

The Bear completed my thought. "The drill bit, the weapons, and . . ."

"And what?"

"One of these things is not like the others. Tom Lockhart, Tomás Bidarte, the man Gloss—some of these individuals do not seem to fit the religious modus operandi."

I flipped on my light bar for an instant, just to give the guy in the truck an official assurance he could go ahead. "Anyway, I just want to know what's happened to Sarah Tisdale."

"So, when we get through at the substation, we are continuing on to Short Drop?"

"You read my mind." I watched as the truck lurched from across the road and pulled alongside us. The driver rolled his window down, and I recognized him—Powder Junction's mayor. "Brian, what's the matter with you. Are you drunk?"

Kinnison, who was usually smiling, looked very serious for a change and perplexed. "What?"

"Why were you just sitting there?"

"I thought you might want to get by—Walt, the sheriff's sub-station is on fire."

The Powder River Fire District truck was pouring water onto the Quonset hut with four different high-powered hoses, but with the flames rippling through the broken windows, it looked to me as if the building was well on its way to melting.

I forced my way through the volunteer firemen—Double Tough's Suburban was parked a little ways away in the lot, and I remembered how he had said he was sleeping in the back of the office to give Frymire and his fiancée a little privacy. I turned back to the inferno. "I've got a man in there."

The fire chief, a fellow by the name of Gilbert, wearing full gear with the rubber coat and leather helmet with face shield, threw a hand on my chest. "We checked; there's nobody in there, Sheriff."

"How about the back room?" The look on his face told me he wasn't sure, and I started pushing past him, the cool coming over my face along with the stillness in my hands. "One of my deputies—he was sleeping in the back."

He grabbed hold of me. "Walt, you can't go in there." Another man joined him, but my momentum carried all of us forward through the pools of water reflecting fire at our feet; it was like the world was in flames, but I'd seen fire up on the mountain and was unafraid. "Walt, if he's in there, he's dead."

I shrugged them off and continued toward the closed front door. "Not this guy."

Gilbert made a last grab, dragging my jacket down my arm. "Walt, there are chemicals from the bus barn that this building lodges up against—that whole back area is going to go up any minute." His last grasp had turned me just a little. "You can't go in there!"

I stared at him for an instant and then yanked my arm completely free, sending him falling backward toward a group of men holding one of the hoses.

My boots slipped on the puddled asphalt, but I got my footing back and, feeling the intensity of the heat on my face, lurched toward the door and pulled my gloves out of my coat pockets. Holding one of my gloved hands up to protect my face as I planted a staggering shoulder into the door, I exploded it inward, the glass with the Absaroka County Sheriff's Department seal shattering as my hand struck the middle of the pane, the shards cascading out like a broken spider's web.

The flames rushed toward me as I tripped, like something alive in pursuit of the fresh, cool oxygen of the night. It was lucky that I'd fallen, because there was a ceiling of black smoke about waist high with flames licking at the corrugated steel of the perimeter, all of them making for the door I just came through. The desk and chairs to my left were on fire, along with the stacks of newspapers that had concerned me earlier. To my right, the decrepit sofa burned, the smoldering edges of the carpet remnant were curling upward into flames, and the paint was peeling off the walls in burning strips that slid toward the floor,

Suddenly, something with the force of a buffalo pushed me forward, smashing my face against the glass and flattening me against the door on the floor. Whatever it was it stayed there, and it took every measure of strength I had to press up onto my hands and knees. It was only when my hat skidded forward toward the inner doorway and I felt the rivulets of water falling down the sides of my face that I realized the pressure was from the hoses Gilbert and the volunteer firemen were directing on me to keep me from becoming barbeque.

It shot around me, making a prismatic outline of my bulk in a mist that evaporated instantaneously. I staggered up only to be knocked down again by the hundreds of gallons that were propelling me forward. My hand hit the soaked surface of the sodden carpet, and I crouched, deciding that, between the fire and the high-pressure water, I damn well better stay low.

I watched as my hat hit the door where I had seen Double Tough's cot and I felt the heat just above the top of my head even as the water attempted to beat back the carnivorous flames, and heaving my shoulders forward, I drove with my knees, which made me feel like I was back at USC pushing blocking sleds; I tried to breathe through the fingers of my glove, but the water poured off me like a forking river and I felt like I might drown before I got there.

Widening my eyes and trying to keep my bearings along with my balance, I stared ahead. The door was closed and the brim of my hat, lodged under its edge, was slapping up and down like some seabird attempting to take flight. I reached out and pulled it back toward me, figuring a little dripping beaver-fur protection was better than no protection at all.

There was a whooshing sound above me to my right and the quad sheet map came floating through the smoke to land on top of me. I could see the ink on the thing blackened from the heat tracing a straight line toward the door.

Using both hands, I pushed myself up from the carpet and the inch-deep puddle and skimmed forward into the wall beside the back door; the plywood the map had been mounted on was on my back, deflecting the two blasting jets of water up into the rounded top of the corrugated ceiling, driving the smoke long enough for me to partially stand.

Some idiot voice in the back of my head told me to feel the door before opening it, but I barked back at it, fully tasting the smoke, ash, and moisture in my spoken words. "I know there's a fire behind the damn thing—there's fire everywhere."

I reached down with my saturated gloved hand and watched the water drain from my grip, the knob not turning. Who knew why—possibly because the boards were warped from the heat, possibly because Double Tough was afraid of monsters; it didn't matter, nothing mattered except getting through the door and getting him out of there.

I knew what was going to happen when I shouldered the thing open, so I bumped the cheap, two-panel door, just to get prepared, figuring I'd blow through and fall onto the concrete floor as the flames came out.

I put everything I had into the crouching bull rush and felt my feet come right off the ground as the pressure from inside the superheated room escaped, carrying the two neatly halved portions of the door and my hunched body backward into the main office. The sound stuffed my ears and stayed there as I lay on the soaked rug for a moment trying to clear my head.

My hat was bumping against my face, and I caught it with one hand before it could attempt a repeat performance and run away with the force of the water. I jammed it on again, dumping a good gallon onto my face in the process, and then half-crawled, half-slithered toward the door, the pressurized jet stream still hitting me as I hand and kneed it across the floor.

The doorway was glowing, and I was sure the flames were ingesting the old wood and then vomiting the coats of leaded paint that made up the lean-to, not to mention the unknown horrors in the fifty-five-gallon drums in the bus barn at the other side of the exterior wall.

No one could be alive in there.

No one. Not even Double Tough.

I pitched forward again, but the smoke was like a shroud and hung even lower than before, instantly gritting my eyes, nose, and mouth. I shifted the wet glove in front of my face again and breathed as shallowly as I could, coughed, and tried to get the stuff out of some passage or another but only succeeded in clearing my ears, the only sensory organ I didn't particularly need.

I remembered that the cot was against the center of the back wall, and I started crawling in that direction. The blasts of water were still prodding me forward, now hitting me in the ass, and all I could think of was how I was going to knock the damn hoses out of the volunteer firemen's hands when and if I got out of there.

I could feel the leg of the low-slung cot and was amazed the aluminum hadn't melted in the heat. I felt for the mattress and found the sopping blankets, my hand bumping against something that felt like a shoulder. I grabbed hold of it but couldn't get a grip, so I gathered all the covers, yanked them toward me, and felt the fabric tear.

Going for broke, I shot both arms over the top and clamped them down like hooks. The cot collapsed, and a two-hundred-pound man slapped against my chest, and I fell backward. "Damn it to hell."

I closed my mouth and just pulled his lifeless body along with me back toward the door. We were only a few leg-drags in that direction when I heard a cracking noise and saw part of the shed roof disengage and fall, taking a third of the joists with it, the sudden rush of air momentarily pulling the flames and smoke toward the other side, at which point I could see that the rafters on my side were in no better shape.

Grabbing the wet bundle that was Double Tough, I prepared for a mad dash through the doorway, into the hose streams and the parking lot. This hope was hammered as I watched the top beam disconnect from the back of the Quonset hut and slam down diagonally in front of me in a cascade of sparks, flame, burning wood, and tar paper.

I scrambled backward until my shoulders lodged against the skillet-hot ridged surface of one corner; I was trapped like a rat and yelling like a madman.

Double Tough was lying across my legs. The side of his head was badly burned, and I wasn't even sure that the eye was still there. He wasn't breathing, and all I could do was pull his body next to me and try to think fast.

I wasn't sure what was still on the other side, but it had to be better than this.

I hoisted the two of us, shrugging Double Tough's body against my chest again in a modified fireman's carry, and prepared for the hunched dash to freedom. All I could think was that I couldn't stop—no matter what happened, keep going.

I had pulled some of the soaked blankets over me for a little protection, but I couldn't see because they covered my head. Suddenly it felt like the wall behind me was giving way. I half-expected the remainder of the ceiling to come crashing down and tottered forward still in hopes of finding a way out. About then two great weights slammed onto my shoulders, and the only thing I could think was that the roof had finally let go and the sixteen-inch centered rafters had landed on either side of my neck.

I struggled to pull free, but I could feel myself losing my balance and I fell backward, crashing into the exterior wall. The grip on my shoulders didn't let up—something was dragging me. I held on to Double Tough's body as I shot backward, but the smoke was invading the blankets at this height, my brain started to fog, and the grip on my shoulders felt like talons digging into my flesh.

This must have been what it was like to die—a giant messenger of the dead swooping down and carrying me along that hanging road to the camp beyond. The talons had to be from some giant owl, the only bird that eagles steered clear of.

His claws sunk deeper, and I felt the circulation cut off from my arms. I hit the hard ground and just lay there with the weight of the wet bedding and Double Tough's body on top of me, trying to summon enough energy for another go. Not dead yet.

Suddenly, his body disappeared. I lifted my arms and tried to get hold of him, but there was nothing there. I flopped to my side and tried to pull the blankets off of me, but it was as if I were glued to them. Slowly I backpedaled out from under and finally slid my head clear.

I rolled over on my back and breathed, staring at the star-filled night and feeling the cold just starting to sink its teeth in. I felt around, but still couldn't find his body anywhere nearby. It would appear that the giant owl, having given up on taking both of us, had dropped me and continued onto the camp of the dead with him alone. The hanging road was there, the thick strip of the Milky Way draped like a hammock from horizon to horizon in icy clarity.

I allowed my head to drop back onto the parking lot pavement and then rolled it the other way, finally seeing what had plucked my deputy and me from the burning building.

The giant owl was beating on Double Tough's chest. I watched as my deputy's head bounced against the asphalt. I reached out but couldn't get to him. I yelled and shouted for the thing to go away, slapped my hand on the ground in an attempt to get his attention, but it ignored me and went back to tearing at Double Tough's chest in some sort of ceremonial rite.

I raised my voice but could only croak out a warning that if I got my hands around the big owl's neck he was going to rue the day he had decided to make birdseed out of us.

Finally the owl swiveled its head, shuddered, and took notice of me. I tried to sit up, but it pinned me to the ground. I coughed and choked up some of the soot from my throat and spat it to the side, then turned to grab hold of him in return.

The big bird fell to the side, seemingly as exhausted as I was. I still held on to the legs of the thing but then slowly realized that they were arms. It shook me loose and reached up to pull away its own wet, protective blanket that hung over its head, revealing Henry's smudged and dirty face.

He sat there looking at me as I sank back to the pavement, but only for a moment, then turned and looked toward the fire, the wetness in his eyes reflecting the flames as they consumed the rest of the Absaroka County Sheriff's Substation.

I said something, but he wouldn't look at me.

Feeling the weight of my head as it slipped sideways, I could see another set of eyes looking at me from a short distance away.

Double Tough.

I dragged myself across the asphalt through a couple of puddles and began to shake from the cold. My hand reached his face, the scorched glove touching his chin, but he didn't blink.

12

I sat on the tailgate of my truck, sipped at a Styrofoam cup of coffee, and pulled the dry blanket a little closer around me, attempting to quell the constant shivering.

I watched as the Powder River Fire District volunteers recoiled their hoses and gathered their gear to beat a tired retreat back to the firehouse and their beds. The EMTs had loaded Double Tough into their van and had left.

Henry's voice sounded distant. "One of the neighbors from across the street says he saw the light from inside but just thought it was the reflection from a wood-burning stove; the next time he looked, he said, the entire building was going up."

I lowered the cup and looked at the pool of illumination from the dusk-to-dawn light on the other side of the parking lot, the halogen spilling onto the faded red Suburban, pink and unearthly. The truck sat there like some bashful ingénue at center stage, backed against a copse of fledgling aspens leaning in like a parted curtain.

I remembered how much better the thing had run after Double Tough had taken it under his mechanical wing; how numerous times when I had made the drive down to deliver paychecks, I would find his hillbilly ass under the hood of the thirty-year-old unit, reveling in the big-block, carbureted, dual-exhausted monstrosity.

"There were some other individuals at the periphery behind the sawhorses. I interviewed them, but none of them appeared to have seen anything."

I remember Double Tough telling me he was from someplace back East, some hollow in the middle of the Appalachian mountains; about how he'd gotten a degree in geology or mineralogy or something. I thought about how I'd wished I'd listened more closely to his story.

"Walter."

I stared at the truck and thought about what a dinosaur it was, and how it was a lot like him—unsophisticated, honest, and durable.

"There is nothing more you could have done."

I stood, dumping the rest of the coffee from the cup and tossing the container into a bucket that served as a trash receptacle, and, pulling the blanket up higher, squished my way toward the large SUV with the Cheyenne Nation in tow.

"I heard you yelling, punched through the wall, grabbed you by your shoulders, and pulled you out. He probably did not know what happened, Walt."

The sun would be up in a few hours—the dawn of a new day. From the flats of the Powder River country, a gaseous ball of hydrogen billions of degrees in heat would brighten the mountains behind me. I would meet that day with a serious degree of heat myself, a smoldering little ember that would become the size of a man, I'd say—most certainly more than one—which I would tinder until I could find just the right fuel.

"Walter?"

I fumed like the fuse on a bundle of dynamite and looked at my best friend in the world, the man who had just saved my life again.

The Bear stared into my face and didn't like what he found

there, but knowing me as he did, he didn't say anything, just kept pace.

I took the last few steps and stopped at the corner of the official vehicle of the Absaroka County Sheriff's Department, my department, and stared through the back window of the Suburban. Double Tough's clothes were piled in the back, and it looked as if nothing had been disturbed.

I hitched the old army blanket higher to cover my neck, turned, the tail end of the thing flaring with my effort, and walked toward the crumpled husk of the substation with the Bear trailing after me. He moved a little to the right in an attempt to see the side of my face with those dark eyes of his, seemingly darker than before, his eyes always growing deeper and more liquid as these crucial, emotional moments became a part of his soul.

At what used to be the front door, I looked straight at him to assure him that I wasn't just wandering, sidestepped in, and went over to the scorched empty key rack. I stepped on something and stooped to pick up a set of keys that were under a couple of inches of dirty water. They were on a funny ring I'd never noticed before from some second- or maybe third-tier amusement park with an image of a giant character who looked a little like Bozo, leaning on a structure that read **CAMDEN PARK—AT THE SIGN OF THE HAPPY CLOWN**.

There was something else, too, that I noticed as I bent over—the vague scent of kerosene.

I turned around and started back toward the Suburban. I flipped to the second key and attempted to get it somewhere in the vicinity of the keyhole that unlocked the tailgate. My hands continued to shake, and the damn thing fell. I started to lean down, but the Cheyenne Nation was quicker, as usual, even catching them before they struck the pavement.

He stood and slipped in front of me, and I listened to the

unctuous whir of the window descending. He reached inside, pulled the latch, flipping down the tailgate, and glanced back at me, standing there quaking. "You need to get out of those clothes."

I pointed a quivering hand at the dirty laundry and willed my finger to stop shaking—if it didn't, I silently swore, I was going to bite it off. It must've heard me and grew steady.

Henry sighed and pushed the clothing that smelled like my deputy aside till there was nothing but the ribbed surface of the Chevrolet's floor. He turned to look at me and then walked around the vehicle, systematically unlocking and opening each door, looking inside and then closing it.

He finished his investigation, had circled the vehicle, and, leaning against the quarter-panel, stopped beside me. "Nothing."

I nodded, still staring at the back of the beat-up truck. "Inside the substation, did you smell kerosene?"

"Yes."

When I extended my hand, he'd already pulled his cell phone from his shirt pocket and handed it to me with Verne Selby's number punched in and ringing. I held the device to my ear and waited through five rings before Verne's wife, Rebecca, answered their phone.

She whispered. "He—hello?"

"Rebecca, it's Walt. I need to speak with Verne."

There was a rustling of sheets, and her voice rose. "Walter, do you know what time it is?"

"As a matter of fact, I don't and I don't mean to be rude, but gimme Verne."

I heard her talk to the judge, and after a moment I heard his voice. "Hello?"

"I need a warrant."

He cleared his throat. "Now?"

"Now."

"I can get the paperwork going in the morning. . . ."

"Right now. I'm going into East Spring Ranch down near Short Drop with or without a warrant—you can back me up with some paperwork or I can just go in there on my own. I'm in Powder Junction right now, and either way I'm headed south in a few minutes."

I could almost see him nodding into the receiver. "I'll fax it to the sheriff's substation."

I took a breath, staring at the powdery paint of Double Tough's unit but refusing to look at the burned-out corpse of a structure across the parking lot. "Send it to the town hall instead."

"We are waiting?"

"We are not." We were standing at the counter of the Powder Junction Town Hall with Brian Kinnison, in anticipation of the warrant, when the Bear sabotaged me by handing me his cell phone again.

I looked at him, but he gestured for me to talk and walked away.

"What the fuck are you doing?"

I sighed. "I'm going in there and none too friendly."

"Then what?"

"I'm going to find out what's going on, and I'm going to get who did this."

I could hear her struggling to get her boots on. "You need help."

"I've got help."

"I'll be there in twenty minutes."

"I'll be gone in five." I walked over to Henry and handed the phone to him. "Here." Vic was still yelling on the other end. I returned to the counter just as Brian was pulling the papers out of the fax machine. He put them on the flat surface and looked at me.

"You're sure these people did this?"

"Yep, I am."

"You want me to alert the militia?"

I half-smiled, in spite of myself. "I didn't know you had a militia."

He glanced at the clock on the wall and smiled back. "Seems like a good time to start one up."

I stuffed the warrant in the inside pocket of my jacket, which wafted the smell of a dead campfire, sat my water-mauled hat on my head a little straighter, and started out the door. Henry was waiting for me as I hit Powder Junction's one-block board-walk, and I could see he was thinking. I stepped up even with him and asked. "Why the substation? Why not just take the bit? They had to know this was going to start a war."

"Yes."

"But why him? I was the one pushing; I'm the one most likely to go after them." I patted the papers in my pocket. "This guarantees it."

"Yes."

"They thought they could steamroll us out here in the mid-dle of nowhere and get away with it?" I stuck an index finger toward him. "Don't say yes."

He grunted. "I am hoping that is not the case."

I gestured to the tiny street. "Because he was closer?"

The Bear shrugged. "We are only forty minutes away."

"Twenty, according to Vic."

He nodded. "We should be going; I think I can keep you from shooting people, but I am not sure I can dissuade her."

I climbed in on the driver's side and pulled the door closed behind me as the Bear slung himself in. I watched as he reached over, pulled the Remington Wingmaster from the brace that held it against the dash and transmission hump, and jacked the breech of the twelve-gauge like a sidekick in some bullshit TV show where they did such things a dozen times. The unspent shell went flying into the back, unlike on TV, and I looked at him. "We might need that round."

He smiled, and a line settled alongside the upturned corner of his mouth as he popped the lid on the center console—he knew all my caches and clichés—and pulled out an extra box of shells. "What other weapons do we have?"

I started the Bullet and pulled the gear selector down into drive. "Steadfast resolution." I turned and looked at him, not as if he would take the option, but it had to be said. "If you want out, now would be the time."

He actually laughed as he reloaded the round. "I try never to miss an episode of *Steadfast Resolution*—it is my favorite program."

The Cheyenne Nation was the first to notice that the lights were on at the Short Drop Merc.

I slowed my truck from its sonic speed and pulled to the side of the road just past the turnoff into the pint-sized town. I leaned forward; it seemed as though almost every light in the place was on, especially in the bar, and a few vehicles were parked out front, including a decked-out Ford King Ranch pickup.

The Bear shook his head. "You do not think . . . ?"

"Yes, I do." I threw the Bullet into reverse, scorching the scoria surface of Route 192 with two black strips of Michelin rubber about ninety feet long. I locked it up and spun the wheel, bouncing the three-quarter-ton over the edge of the pavement and down the slight grade leading into town past the signature hemp noose that swung from the cottonwood.

I kept my brights on as I slid up to the boardwalk hitching post alongside the other vehicles, my headlights directed into the front windows, a copious cloud of dry, ochre-colored dust drifting past us and blowing against the structure like an angry orange smell.

"I take it we are not counting on the element of surprise?"

I threw my door open. "Nope."

His hand caught mine as I started to exit. "Does not make sense; remember that."

I looked at him, said nothing, and then nodded.

We mounted the steps, and I didn't bother with the knob, instead choosing to enter the room boot first. The door bounced off the wall and started back, but I caught it with one hand and stood there holding it.

I noticed my hands had stopped shaking for good.

The only person in the room that I did not want to shoot was standing behind the bar with her hands on her hips, keeping enough collateral damage distance between her and what appeared to be her unwanted patrons—smart woman, that Eleanor Tisdale.

There were three men at the bar and two more playing pool at the table to my left.

I noticed the Cheyenne Nation drifting in the door behind me like casual death, the shotgun trailing behind his leg completely unnoticeable.

"Well, howdy, Sheriff. You look like you could use a drink."

I looked at the three, especially at the one with the mouth whom I recognized as Ronald, Roy Lynear's oldest son, the one from over in South Dakota. Behind him were Lockhart and the younger strong arm whose acquaintance I'd made from a distance in Butte County.

Gloss and Bidarte were at the pool table, and the Bear had already taken a few steps in that direction. Having cased and set the room, I started toward Ronald and Lockhart and watched as the muscle slid in front of them. I guess they thought they had numbers on their side, but maybe they had never seen an episode of *Steadfast Resolution*, let alone the season finale.

Lockhart was the unstated leader, I was sure of that, but he lingered and made no move to engage me. I hit the younger one a good, solid roundhouse to the side of his head, which sent him into the bar where he made the mistake of trying to catch himself; I took that opportunity to uppercut him and send him back, dragging along a few glasses and more than a few beer bottles with him as he fell.

The favored son and Lockhart didn't move and stayed there, not lifting a hand from the edge. Ronald Lynear's eyes widened as I pulled up over him, my nose about an inch or two higher than the top of his head.

His face turned upward as I made a show of breathing in his scent. He appeared to be paralyzed but finally eased out the words in a smoother voice than I would've thought him capable of in such a situation. "Do you mind if I ask what you're doing, Sheriff?"

I breathed in deeply. "They say that guilt has a specific odor, one you can smell from a mile away."

He waited a moment and then asked, "And what is it that one of us might be guilty of?"

Still sniffing like a bloodhound, I leaned a little to the side. "The willful destruction of county property."

"You don't say?"

I brought my face around to his. "I do." Leaving him, I stepped over the fallen man and gave Lockhart the once-over. "You see, the sheriff's substation . . ." I glanced back at Lynear and then settled my eyes on Lockhart again. "The county property in question was burned with a chemical accelerant, probably kerosene." I bent down to the glass-jawed guy, slid a Wilson Combat/Tactical .40 from his inside-the-pants holster, and propelled it across the gray hardwood floor where it lodged under Henry's uplifted boot with a solid thunk.

Nobody moved.

I sniffed the younger man's head and then lifted an arm, attaching one end of my handcuffs to his wrist. "Guilt is a lot like kerosene; the scent stays longer than you might suspect." I dragged the cuffed individual along by the arm like an after-thought, turned toward Gloss and Bidarte, and took a few steps into the center of the room.

Gloss put the butt of his pool cue on the floor, his hand tight-ening around the shaft of it, and glanced at Henry and then at me. "You stay the hell away."

The Bear and I looked at each other, and he was the first to speak. "That sounded remarkably like an admission of guilt."

"Yep, it did." I cocked my head. "You wouldn't be armed again, would you, Mr. Gloss?" I gestured with the unconscious man's arm. "I mean, not like your friend here, who I'm betting is going to be spending a few weeks in my jail in violation of the carry laws of the state of Wyoming." I stepped to one side of the table, and they countered by moving to the other. "Do you have another weapon on you, by any chance? I took the last one you had, which means if you didn't acquire a different one, you would have to find some other way of doing your dirty work, some-thing like an accelerant—say, kerosene?"

He glanced at Henry and then at me and the holstered .45 on my hip.

His eyes came back up to mine, and I could see the panic-driven thought that was there. I reached down and drew back my jacket and unsnapped the safety strap from my Colt. "It doesn't take much to carry one of these things—forty ounces of milled steel and eight rounds." I pointed toward his shirttail, hanging past his waist. "Whatever you've maybe got there probably carries more, but caliber, rate of fire, that doesn't really matter—doesn't mean anything really. All that matters is being willing—willing to pull it, willing to fire it, willing to kill." I took another step, still dragging the now half-conscious man along with me. "It's one thing to set a place on fire with a man sleeping inside, but it's another when a man is standing right in front of you, ready and willing."

Bidarte sidestepped slightly to the left but carefully raised his hands, keeping them where Henry and I could see them. "I don't know what this is all about, Sheriff, but we've been here, playing pool all night." He gestured toward Eleanor and kept moving sideways. "The lady, she can tell you. . . ."

"That's far enough; I'm not that bad a shot."

He smiled but stopped.

I glanced at the proprietor, and she shrugged with a sad humping of her shoulders. "They came in here around six, all of them." She looked away. "I wish I could tell you something different, but I can't."

I looked over to Henry and remembered what he said before we'd entered—it does not make sense, remember that. When I turned back, I could see Gloss had dropped his hand and was starting to raise it toward the underside of his shirttail. There were about six feet between me and him, which was the range in which most sidearm fatalities took place. "You shouldn't miss from that distance, but then again, neither should I."

Gloss started to shift his weight. "Look, I don't know what you're talking about. . . ." He glanced to my right, where Lockhart was watching him.

I heard a noise behind me—the Cheyenne Nation must've stooped to pick up the pistol—but I was pretty sure it was the shotgun that he was aiming in Gloss's direction.

I cleared my throat. "Now, in these types of situations, if

you're properly trained, the next step would be to distract the assailant just long enough for the primary target to pull his weapon, but I've nullified that possibility by having backup, right Henry?"

"You bet your lily-white ass."

I gestured toward Gloss's waist. "I'll tell you what, if you want to get it out of your pants and ready to go, that's fine by me."

His lips moved, but it took a few seconds for him to come up with something to add. "Look, um, is this some kind of joke?"

My turn not to say anything.

He shook his head, stared at the long green of the felt, and looked at the ceiling. "I want a lawyer."

"Place your weapon on the table—thumb and forefinger only."

He made a show of doing exactly that and carefully placed another high-priced, carbon-steel .45 with some kind of fancy finish on the flat surface.

I reached across and picked it up.

"You want to smell me now?"

It was the wrong thing to say at the exact wrong time, and I made that clear by bringing the butt of the semiautomatic up and popping it into his nose. Blood blew from his nostrils, and his hands went up to his face. Bidarte actually laughed until I looked at him; then he gently placed his hands on the pool table in a position that didn't look unfamiliar to him.

I glanced at the others. "Anybody else want to join the conversation?"

There were no takers, so I unhandcuffed myself, walked around the table, and yanked Gloss's hand away from his face so that I could handcuff him to the other probable felon.

Bleeding profusely, he attempted to staunch the flow with his other hand, but the blood was spouting onto the front of his shirt and his voice was muffled and nasal. "We haven't done anything."

I gestured with the confiscated pistol. "Oh, you've done all kinds of stuff—it's just a question of whether you've done this *one* thing, and if you have, are you going to be sorry."

Vic, never one to miss a party, arrived a few minutes later, and we loaded Gloss and his pal into the back of her unit. My undersheriff glanced in the cage with a smile, noticing the man's nose, still bleeding through the bar towel that Eleanor had provided. "Jesus, what'd you hit him with, a two-by-four?"

I handed her Gloss's other gun. "Here, for the collection."

She studied the weapon. "Another Wilson; you sure this guy's name is Gloss?"

"No, I'm not, but I figure you'll be able to tell me by morning."

She whistled as she studied the sidearm. "A .38 Super, Combat Carry Competition—three grand, at least."

"Yep, the boys seem to have money."

"Must be the bake sales."

"Uh-huh."

She glanced at them again. "Can we keep their guns?"

"Sure, we'll have a sale of our own."

She nodded. "So what's Double Tough's condition?"

I stared at her.

She stared back at me.

Of course, Henry hadn't told her over the phone. I took a breath, just to clear the pipes before trusting the words. "He's gone."

Her mouth dropped open just a little bit and hung there. We didn't get many fatalities in the department; as a matter of fact, this would be the only one—and on my watch.

She sat there with all that training and experience she'd culled from the Philadelphia Police Department stamping down on her emotions, but I'd had a lot of experience with unquenchable fire lately. The tarnished gold eyes sharpened like a straight razor as she turned to regard them. "Oh, you fuckers."

"Book 'em, run 'em—I want to know everything."

After a moment, she turned and nodded at the dash. She took a deep breath, reached down, and started the engine. "You will."

I looked at the group. "Call the Ferg in to help."

Her beautiful jaw stiffened. "There's a problem with help."

"What's that?"

"Witnesses."

I stepped back as she laid her own strip up Main, fishtailing sideways as she sped through the intersection at 192 and shot up onto the highway about as fast as her old unit could travel.

I turned and started to walk up the steps almost into the owner/operator of The Noose. "They were here all night, Walt."

I stood there three steps down and looked her in the eye. "When did they get here?"

"Early—six, maybe six-thirty."

I sighed.

"Not what you wanted to hear."

"No." I stared past her at the lights illuminating the Merc proper. "Looks like you've gotten rid of the majority of your books."

She adjusted her glasses and smiled. "Most of them went to the library, but I've got a stack for you in the back."

I didn't move. "I find it strange how suddenly you've decided to give up the ghost and close your business."

She didn't say anything for a moment, but I could see the incredulity growing in her eyes. "You don't believe me?"

I scrubbed my eyes with the heels of my hands. "I don't know who to believe." Forcing her to move back, I started up the remainder of the steps. She moved, but just enough to force me to brush by her, her voice sharp with righteous indignity. "So we're no longer friends."

I stopped and stood there. "It's dangerous being my friend; you might not want the job."

Henry was behind the bar with the shotgun lying on the surface; he was drinking what looked to be orange juice.

"Like a day without sunshine?"

He slipped a look at Ronald Lynear and Tom Lockhart at the other side of the bar. "Fights germs."

Lynear was the first to speak. "We're going to get them out as soon as you set bail."

I nodded. "That should be in a few weeks."

"Then I'm filing a wrongful arrest and harassment charge against your department."

Lockhart placed a hand on his arm and then slid a piece of paper toward me. "Take a look at this." It was an ATM slip from the small branch bank across the street, dated yesterday, with a withdrawal of two hundred dollars—the time, six thirty-two. "What's that look like to you?"

"It's an ATM slip for what looks like two hundred dollars, but since I have a career in law enforcement, I'm not sure how to count the number of zeros."

He attempted to control himself. "You see the time?"

"Yep, they teach us how to do that at the academy over in Douglas; they say it's important."

"We grabbed some cash when we got to town and came straight over and started drinking and playing pool." He gestured behind me where Eleanor stood by the door. "You've got a reliable witness who tells you the same thing." He shook his head at me as if I were some child in need of reprimand. "You haven't got a leg to stand on."

Shooting a glance at Ronald, I reached over and stole the Bear's juice. "I'm curious, Reverend, what it is you're doing in a den of iniquity like this?"

He smiled. "I'm not drinking, but I thought I'd join in the celebration."

"And what is it you're celebrating?"

He made a face, as if it were obvious. "Our new water well."

I turned and looked at them. "And how were you able to drill that well without the benefit of your Hughes polycrystalline three-cone bit?"

He looked at me with an expression as blank as the biblical nonshifting desert sands. "Our what?"

"The industrial one-hundred-seventy-thousand-dollar bit we found in the back of Big Wanda's Plymouth that she ran off the road to try to keep us from finding."

The sands remained still. "We used the one that was attached to the Peterbilt that you saw the other night. Tomás fixed it. I'm sure I don't know what other drill it is you're talking about."

"Maybe you don't." I set the glass down and squared off with Lockhart. "But I bet he does."

A long moment passed, and Lockhart placed a hand on Lynear's shoulder and spoke to the confused man. "Ronald, why don't you head back to the ranch; I'm sure your father is wondering what's happened." He slapped him gently. "Go on, we'll be along in no time."

The man of religion glanced at all of us and then quietly departed, excusing himself as he passed Eleanor, still standing at the entrance.

Lockhart stood there for a moment more and then started toward the door. "Could I get you to step outside with me for a moment, Sheriff?"

I stared at him, at Eleanor, and then back to Henry. I pushed off the bar and followed him out the door.

It was cool, but the rays of the sun were just starting to rise over the plains with a diffused, yellowish-gray glow. I turned to Lockhart, leaning against one of the support poles.

Lynear was just backing out in an older Buick with a crumpled fender that had been touched over with gray primer on the passenger side. We both watched as he pulled out and drove away.

"I'm a professional; I want you to know that."

I turned and looked at him, folding my arms over my chest. "I do. It's a professional *what* that I'm trying to figure out."

"Sheriff, how much money do you make a year—forty, fifty thousand?"

"I don't know; like I said, they stopped teaching us remedial math at the academy."

He nodded. "But you can tell me what time it is, right?" He turned and looked at the rising sun, and I watched him shiver. "Well, how about I tell you what time it really is?" His face returned to mine. "Time to look the other way."

I said nothing.

"How old are you, Sheriff? Closing in on retirement with a half-finished house would be my guess, with children, a daughter, maybe? Newly married and expecting your first grandchild? A professional herself, possibly a lawyer in a large eastern city, an associate with hopes of making partner. . . ."

I cut him off. "I get it, you know all about me—I sure hope there's more to this conversation than that."

"I hope so, too, Sheriff, I hope so, too." He shivered a little more, and I had to admit that I was enjoying his discomfort.

"What if I told you that I'd like to make a donation to the Walt Longmire reelection campaign?"

"I've already been reelected."

"Oh, this money would be disassociated from any political responsibilities; you could use it for whatever you wanted, finishing your house, a gift for your daughter, college for the grandchild. Anything you'd like, it doesn't matter. A lot of money, Sheriff. Like Senator Everett McKinley Dirksen used to say: a billion here, a billion there, and pretty soon you're talking serious money."

I dropped my head and spoke into my folded arms. "So, we're talking about serious money, then."

"Very serious."

I raised my head slowly and stared at him. "Mr. Lockhart, are you trying to bribe me?"

He smiled. "Hasn't it ever been tried before?"

"Nope, generally people are smarter than that." I tilted my head and looked at him. "They don't know, do they?"

"Who know what?"

I gestured toward the departed car and the general direction of East Spring Ranch. "Your religious friends, they don't know about whatever it is that you're doing that's going to result in serious money."

"That's really not the point here, is it?" He shivered some more, looking in the bar and longing for the warmth inside. "So, am I to take that response as a no to my offer?"

"That was an offer, was it?"

"Yes, it was and still is. Just for looking the other way. Nobody gets hurt."

"Nobody gets hurt." I probed the grain of the boardwalk with the toe of my boot. "And that's why you killed Double Tough, because he had a working knowledge of whatever it is you're doing?"

A look of exasperation flitted across his face. "Why would we kill your deputy?"

"For a Hughes polycrystalline three-yoke bit."

His response was swift and a little angry. "Sheriff, if I wanted, I could have a truckload of them within twenty-four hours." He pushed off the pole and stood in front of me. "I didn't kill your deputy—it makes no sense. I have to admit that I didn't know about you before, but now that I do I can see that you would be a formidable adversary." He took a breath. "I'm a businessman, beyond all the things you think I am or the things you think I do—I am in business. Now, you tell me, is it good business for me to take you on?"

I said nothing.

"Why would we want a war with you?"

I still said nothing.

"Well, there's your answer." He gestured toward the bar. "Do you mind if I collect Tomás? It's been a long evening."

I gestured with a nod and watched as he went to the door, opened it, and called inside. Lockhart started for the truck and a moment later was followed by Bidarte and the Cheyenne Nation.

As Bidarte passed, I stuck out an arm and stopped him, leaned in, and sniffed him. He stared at me for a moment, then stepped onto the gravel, and, standing by the door of the truck, he studied me as Henry and I leaned on either side of the wooden pole.

Lockhart pulled his keys from his pressed khakis and hit the button to unlock the doors on a black half-ton, then stepped off the boardwalk and opened the driver's side. A thought occurred to him, and he spoke again. "By the way, I have to ask—did you smell kerosene on Gloss?"

I studied the horizon, where that first glimmer was simmering under the streaked sky. "No."

I saw a flash of movement to my left but before either the Bear or I could react, there was a loud thunk in the post between us. I turned my head slowly and could see Bidarte's blade buried in the coarse grain of the wood just at head height, still vibrating from the impact.

Henry and I stared past the foot-long stiletto at each other's faces. The Cheyenne Nation reached up and plucked the knife from the post, expertly nudging the tang and folding it back before tossing it to the tall Basque. "If you were aiming for the post, that was a good throw."

Bidarte tucked the knife into his back pocket. "Oh yes, señor. I was."

I ignored him and studied the horizon.

Looking at the sun for a moment, Lockhart followed my eye, and patted the top of the cab as an afterthought. "Concerning Mr. Gloss and the kerosene, it would've been easier to lie."

I kept my eyes on the rising sun as the two of them climbed in the truck and backed into a sweeping arch that gave them a clear trajectory up the embankment and south onto 192.

"No, it wouldn't."

13

"I think Dog sleeps with you more than I do." She had elected to pass up her usual seat on the guest chair in my office and sat on the floor near me.

I had slept on it again, as there wasn't any room anywhere else. The hard wood, barely covered with a thin pad and thread-bare carpeting, was killing my back, but at least I had had company. I reached over and scratched the belly of the beast that happened to be sleeping with his paws in the air, which displayed his more personal attributes. "He's very faithful."

Looking nowhere near as tired as I felt, she sat with her back against the bookcase. "So am I, and look what it gets me."

"Were you up all night?"

She shuffled the papers in her lap. "Yes."

I peeled the blanket back and started to stretch; my back ached but not nearly as much as my left knee, which had been worrying me since my adventures on the mountain last May. I rolled over and looked at her, still equipped with the bad-hair-day cap from last night. "You wear it better than I do."

She glanced at me and then reached down and, giving me a nonverbal critique on the current state of my hair, handed me my hat. "I was just booking and researching scumbags, you were having the gunfight at the O.K. Corral, I am to understand." She kept looking at me and grinned. "As your undersheriff, it is my duty to inform you that you are looking more and more like an unmade bed."

I propped myself up on one elbow and placed my smoky, water-stained hat on my head. "Better?"

"An unmade bed at, say, Bob's Flophouse by the river."

I yawned. "Right."

"The kind you rent an hour at a time?"

"Got it."

She nodded as if she'd finished a report. "I have news."

I pointed at the stack of papers. "It looks like."

"More important than this crap."

I struggled my way into a sitting position, which disturbed Dog, who also rose, licked my face, then gingerly stepped over Vic, and, likely in search of a second or third breakfast, disappeared out the door. "What could be more important than this?"

"Like Lazarus risen from the grave . . . Double Tough is alive."

I turned and stared at her. I'd been thinking about nothing else as I'd drifted in and out of sleep all morning, half-convincing myself that what had happened last night hadn't, but it just wouldn't wash. "If this is a joke, it's not funny."

She shook her head. "They hit him with the defibrillator in the EMT van and the fucker popped back to life—I swear to God." She turned and sat Indian-style. "They say that Henry breathing for him all that time must've kept him going long enough for them to bring him back with a couple thousand volts. I told him he probably had a disease from all the places that the Bear's mouth had been."

I could feel the swelling of heat behind my eyes and a ballooning in my chest as I sat there—almost as if coming back from the dead myself. "He can talk?"

"No, at least not yet." The emotion was about to overwhelm her, too, but she laughed and wiped a bit of moisture from the corner of one eye—I had the feeling she wasn't telling me everything. "I mean, he's half covered with second- and third-degree burns, and he's going to lose the eye—but he's alive."

I felt a tear streak down the side of my face and watched as she half-sobbed another laugh.

"Uh oh, the waterbed has sprung a leak." She put her hand on my face and continued smiling, even as the tears were now streaking her own. "He squeezed my hand, you know, when I told him about getting cooties from Henry. I mean he's screwed up; nobody goes through something like that without sustaining some kind of brain damage and with him how can you tell, but he squeezed my hand when I was joking with him."

"Billings?"

She looked at her wristwatch. "No, Denver. They're taking off with him in about an hour if you want to go up to the airport and see him off."

"I do." I pushed the blanket away and slowly stood. "That's two out of his nine lives that we know about."

She glanced back toward the reception/dispatcher area. "Everybody wanted to wake you up and tell you, but Ruby wouldn't let us. So I waited till you turned over."

"I don't think I turned over."

"I don't care." She smiled fully, crinkling her eyes and showing that canine tooth to full advantage, wiped the tears from her face with the back of her hand, and took her customary seat. "You got the good news; you want the bad news now or when we head to the airport?"

"Now." I again pointed at the stack of papers. "This stuff?"

She shook her head. "The elusive Orrin the Mormon is once again at large."

"Junior or Senior; please don't say both."

"Cousin Itt."

I slumped into my chair. "This is getting embarrassing."

There was more than a little accusation in the next statement. "It's because we're running the place like a revolving door; the kid is in and out going to work, and the two of them are endlessly watching *My Friend Fucking Flicka*, so you turn your back for an instant and he takes French leave."

"I'm sorry."

She sighed. "I mean he's relatively harmless, or as harmless as you can be when armed like a commando, but it's starting to insult the credibility and professionalism of the department; I think it reflects badly when schizophrenic derelicts and arrested peoples are using the jail like the Kum & Go."

I smiled. "Agreed."

"We looked for him in the beds of all the trucks."

"Good thinking."

Her face came up, and the smile had returned. "Double Tough's alive."

I laughed. "Yep."

She came around the desk and roosted in front of me, but this time I kept a hand on the edge, determined not to have a repeat of the Flying Wallendas. She leaned forward and put her arms around my shoulders, pulling me in. Despite all common sense, I found my own arms rising up and folding around her in a return embrace and thought about what this might lead to if we had been at my cabin. Her lips tickled my ear as she whispered, "I'm not sure if I'm happier that he's alive or that I don't have to watch what you were going to do to yourself."

I pulled back and placed my forehead against hers. "Thank you."

She softly head-butted me and then leaned back a respectable distance, placing her hands on the stack of papers that she had placed on the desk. "Speaking of people trying to get out of jail . . ."

"They didn't escape, too, did they?"

"No, they're doing it the old-fashioned way, with lawyers—makes Orrin the Mormon's technique seem honest and forthright." She stood and looked down at me. "You want some coffee? I want some coffee."

I nodded my head as she went out, calling after her, "Big lawyers?"

The answer ricocheted off the hallway walls. "Shephard, Baldwin, Coveny, and Spencer over in Jackson."

"Gary Spencer?"

After a moment she came back in with two mugs. "The big dog hisself."

"Well, hell."

She sat the coffees on my desk and thumbed through the papers. "They're suing the county, the department, and mostly you for unlawful arrest, excessive force, harassment . . . all of which is supported by your actions in South Dakota and in the bar last night." She picked up her new Philadelphia Flyers cup—the hockey season had just started—and sipped her coffee. "You've got to stop hitting people."

I sipped my own and thought about my actions as of late. "There was only one or two . . ."

"Three, including the chopping and channeling you did to Gloss's nose—twice."

I tried not to look her in the eye. "That second time was an accident."

"Tell it to the judge." She set her mug down and continued perusing the papers. "They've pretty much called you everything but a Baptist and say you sleep with your dog—which I wouldn't have believed until I came in here this morning."

"How long?"

"We might hold them till the end of the day, but then they're going to post and walk."

I sipped some more coffee. "Can Verne stall on setting bail?"

She shook her head. "Nope, he heard the name Gary Spencer and folded like a card table at a bake sale in a high wind."

"They've got a lot of money."

"I know; I've seen their armaments."

"No, I mean a lot of money."

"More than you can make at a bake sale?"

"Enough to try and buy me off last night."

"I've bought you off before." She shrugged and picked up her mug again, winking over the lip. "Cheap." She continued studying me. "A lot a lot?"

"Yep."

"What, are they printing hundreds down there at East Spring Ranch?"

"Maybe." I sighed and sipped some more; apparently it was helping. "They also seemed to know an awful lot about me."

"Who?"

"Lockhart."

She raised an eyebrow. "The quiet man?"

"Up until last night; he got real talkative on the porch of The Noose."

"He probably thought you were going to hang him."

I pulled the ATM slip from my shirt pocket and handed it to her. "He made a convincing argument that he and his group had nothing to do with setting fire to the sheriff's substation."

"Just this? 'Cause this can mean that just one of them was there."

"No, Eleanor says they were there the whole evening."

"Then it was somebody else from the group; I mean, how many of them are there down there in that nest?"

"That's a good question." I reached over to my coatrack, pulled my jacket on, and slipped the warrant from the inside pocket. "I think I'll find out."

She continued sipping her coffee, and I watched the wheels turn as she watched my wheels turn. "What are you thinking about?"

"What you said, about the number of people down there." I unfurled the fax like a Biblical scroll. "Have you ever seen any women or children in the compound down at East Spring?"

"Personally, I've only gotten as close as the Mexican Grand Prix at the front gate." She thought about it. "We saw some over in Butte County—the rat patrol and the girl at the table—but not here." She thought some more and ventured. "So far, Big Wanda is it."

I nodded and came around the desk with her following. "There were clothes out on the line at the house and toys in the yard, but I didn't see any women or children."

"It was in the middle of the night when you went back there."

"Maybe that's it." Waiting at her office door while she grabbed her own coat, I rolled the warrant up and stuffed it back into my jacket. "But maybe not."

"Something else."

I stopped and looked at her. "What?"

"They're expanding their operation. I put out a query and got contacted by the sheriff departments of both Garden County, Nebraska, and Hodgeman County, Kansas."

I thought about it. "Why in the world would they need all these compounds stretched across the Rocky Mountain West down to Oklahoma?"

She shrugged and passed me in the doorway. "I guess that bake sale business is good."

Saizarbitoria and Henry were sipping coffee in the dispatcher/reception area as Ruby talked on the phone. The Bear looked a little tired, and I told him so.

"Not as bad as you do."

I nodded. "I guess you kept my deputy alive long enough for them to jump-start him."

The Cheyenne Nation smiled. "Yes."

"We're going up to the airport to see him off—you want to come?"

"I need to call The Red Pony to make sure somebody can cover for me."

I sometimes forgot about the Bear's going concern, his bar out by the Rez. "We'll tell him you send your love."

He continued to smile and shook his head in mock sorrow. "Please tell Double Tough that I do not think it is going to work out between us, but that we will always have Powder Junction."

"Lunch at the Bee for a planning meeting?"

"Yes."

I started down the steps. "See both of you in a half hour."

"Walt?"

Ruby's voice froze me two steps down. "Yep?"

"Dottie over at the courthouse says a platoon of lawyers just hit the beachhead at Verne's office, led by Gary Spencer himself."

Vic looked up at me. "Change of plan?"

I glanced at the Basquo and the Bear. "Change of plan. Meet us in Powder Junction in an hour."

The phone rang and Ruby stared at it, then at me. "And if I should be confronted with the posse of lawyers and the second greatest legal mind of our time?"

I shrugged. "Get an autograph; just make sure it's not on a subpoena."

He looked like hell. They had him so bandaged up it was almost impossible to tell who he was, but the one eye looked directly at me as they rolled him on a gurney under the slowly rotating blades of the helicopter. "How you doin', troop?"

The bandages pulled at one side.

"So you want me to find you a co-deputy down in Powder Junction, blonde, about five-seven?"

He actually nodded.

"I'll handle the interviews myself."

Vic punched my arm as the engine kicked in, and they loaded him into the elaborate confines of the medical chopper, locking the gurney to the floor. We both joined him until they were ready to take off and were grinning like possums. I leaned my face down next to his, just so I could speak and have him hear me. "I know you're hurting, but I've got to find out—did you see or hear anything last night?"

His voice was ragged and breathy. "Quiet." Maybe I was doing nothing but assuring myself that he could still speak, but his words became stronger. "Stopped a few milk trucks trying to avoid the scales and bunch of kids earlier, gave a warning, speeding, gave drunk ride home, read a little, went to bed, nine. . . ." He tried to move an arm, but they had him pretty well trussed up. "Next thing, woke up in van."

I smiled and placed my mouth next to his ear again and spoke over the roaring of the helicopter. "Good thing; if you'd awakened with Henry's mouth on you, you might've suffered irreparable psychological damage."

The EMTs pushed us away, and I took Vic's arm and ushered the both of us back to my truck, parked at a safe distance. I hung on to my hat as the blast of the engine lifted the thing skyward and it hovered there for a moment before pivoting and climbing in a direct line along the mountains, headed south.

She shielded her eyes out past the bill of her cap and watched the flight-for-life get up to speed at about a hundred and fifty feet. "What'd he say?"

"Nothing special, a few traffic stops on some milk trucks, some kids, a drunk, and home and cot by nine."

"What did you expect? They're CIA, this is what they do."

I turned and looked at her. "Are they CIA?"

She walked around the front of my truck. "C'mon, if you've got a quarter, I'll give you the audiobook version on the way to Powder Junction."

I took the bypass and jumped on the highway in an attempt to avoid the county courthouse and the litigious dangers that lurked there. Ruby's voice sounded from my radio.

Static. "Walt?"

Vic started to reach for the mic, but I raised my hand and stopped her. "Wait."

Static. "Walt, it's Ruby."

Vic studied me. "What?"

"Wait."

Static. "Walt?"

I boosted my speed up to a hundred and hit the light bar. "Have you ever known Ruby to not use impeccable radio procedure?"

Vic looked at the two-way. "They're there."

"Yep."

Static. "Walt, if you can hear me, make a stop somewhere and call in." There were some voices in the background and then Ruby again, this time a little sharp. "He doesn't have a cell phone."

The radio went dead, and Vic settled in with her papers still in her lap as I pulled out past an eighteen-wheel tanker and shot by, easing back into the right lane. "Are you going to hit the siren?"

"They'll hear it at the courthouse."

"My, aren't you crafty."

"What've you got?"

She pulled her lipstick container from her shirt pocket. "The sample powder we took on the ridge in South Dakota did turn out to be quick lime."

"So, if they killed her and buried her there, they moved her?"

She looked at the papers in her lap. "Yeah, I mean if this stuff was on the surface . . . But where?"

I reached over and tapped the stack. "What else have you got?"

"Nothing."

I glanced at her. "Nothing?"

"Yeah, but it's the pattern of nothing that's interesting. All of these guys have state or federal connections, assorted former jobs with the State Department, various think tanks. . . ."

"I refuse to believe that Gloss was a part of any think tank."

"Energy. He was involved with the oil industry in Oklahoma, then overseas in Iraq, Iran. . . . Even had a few fingers in Venezuela, Bolivia, and, of course, Mexico."

"What about Lockhart?"

"He was the one in State and even served on a few influential Pentagon policy panels, but then he jumped ship and started working for a Texas-based corporate intelligence agency called the Boggs Institute that bills itself as a shadow CIA—which to me sounds like shadow bullshit. They engaged him as a chief geopolitical strategist, and I guess he was quite an asset for them with little ol' clients like the Department of Justice, Homeland Security, and the Marines."

"My Marines?"

"Your Marines; I thought you'd enjoy that. Anyway, it was all milk and honey until those intelligence leaks a few years back when the Boggs Institute was exposed as just a bunch of money-grubbing assholes." She read from one of the sheets. "'With a geographical determinism that a lot of people mistook for predictive powers.'"

"What Henry Kissinger used to refer to as geopolitics?"

She nodded as she continued reading. "'The supposed amoral, dispassionate concern with national interests like mineral and energy access.'"

"What happened to this marriage made in hell?"

"Some of Lockhart's e-mails got leaked—a bunch of connections to a lot of CEOs of some really big corporations."

I thought about it. "Seems like that would just add to his worth."

"Not these leaked e-mails, which also included handy information for high-powered business travelers in search of brothels in Eastern Europe and Asia that specialized in child prostitution."

She glanced at me, but I didn't say anything.

"The Boggs Institute dropped him like a hot Mr. Potato Head, but he got picked up by a consortium of import/export businesses that dealt with consumer goods."

My hands tightened on the steering wheel. "Has the ring of legitimacy."

"Until they started expanding into tanker ships and crude oil; they reported more than a few shipments light, and Lockhart was called on the carpet before the Securities and Exchange Commission and put on notice. He supposedly retired shortly after that."

"Free to pursue his other sordid interests?"

She sighed. "There's also a little more on Gloss, but it doesn't seem like enough."

"What did you find?"

"The only criminal activity on the guy is a censorship by the Texas Gas and Oil Conservation Commission concerning some work he was doing in Mexico. I guess he was subpoenaed and gave sealed testimony to the Texans before they gave him the boot and told him he could never do business in the Lone Star State again."

"Must've been something pretty bad."

"For Texans to not want to do business with you? No shit." She shuffled through the stack and then threw it onto the floor in the back—she was left holding only a single sheet of paper. "There's information on all these guys, but just enough, never too much. I mean a shitbird like Gloss without a record? It just doesn't make sense." She placed an elbow on the sill and lodged a boot on my dash, something she always did when thinking troubling thoughts. "The connecting points are the government and the petroleum industry; all of them have ties with one or both of these things."

I shook my head. "But why here? I mean you can tell me they got religion, but . . ."

"It's gotta be oil, Walt."

"Double Tough says there's no oil around here, at least nothing worth drilling for."

"Have you checked that with anybody else?"

"Hell, he said they can't give the Teapot Dome away." I eyed her with a sad little pit growing in the center of my stomach as the whirr of the tires on the pavement and the continued roar of the engine were the only sound. "What, exactly, is that supposed to mean?"

"I'm just sayin'. . . ."

"Double Tough was a project foreman for an entire coal-bed methane operation down here, so I would assume that he's intimate with the geology of the entire area."

"Or?"

I stared at her and then returned my eyes to the road. "Look, I know we're in the suspicion business, but . . ."

"You said a lot of money, Walt—a lot of money." She looked at the sheet of paper in her lap. "He was in the energy industry."

"So, we're just going to arrest everybody in southern Absaroka County who's worked in the energy industry? We better expand the jail."

"He's ex-military, too."

She read from the paper. "Even had a few fingers in Venezuela and Bolivia. Sound familiar?" She studied the side of my face. "He never put any of that in his application or job history, nothing."

"You're saying he's in on it? So, what, he set fire to himself?"

"I knew this was how you were going to react, and I wasn't even sure I was going to tell you until I had more to go on." She turned her face and looked south, and we listened to the ten cylinders, pulling us along at a hundred miles an hour. "When's the last time you heard from Frymire?"

I looked at the back of her head, a little confused by the turn of conversation. "The last time I dropped off checks—about two weeks ago."

"Nothing since?"

"No."

"Don't you find it funny that nobody's heard from him except Double Tough, and the word from him is that Chuck is hitting the road with the fiancée that no one has met and moving it all, lock-stock-and-star to an undisclosed location in Colorado?"

I took a deep breath and then snorted at the thought. "Look, we've both been going without sleep, but that's just crazy."

"Maybe." She unlodged her boot and turned in the seat to look at me. "I hope I'm wrong; I'm praying that I'm wrong, but

I'd feel a lot better if we made a run over to the house they rent and talked to Frymire. How 'bout you?"

I didn't say anything and kept driving.

Saizarbitoria's unit was parked in the lot beside the Suburban, and he and Henry, drinking coffee in cups from the Sinclair station by the highway, were standing, studying the debris inside the burned-out husk of the Quonset hut.

As we pulled up, the Basquo came to my window. "Hey, boss, has Ruby been trying to get hold of you?"

"Yep, you?"

"Yeah, I answered and then some pompous asshole got on and wanted to know where you were."

"What'd you say?"

"Started beating the mic on the dash and telling them that they were breaking up and that I'd call back when I got in range."

"Now I know all your secrets.

"You bet." He looked around at the wreckage, pulled a hand up, and cinched it on his Beretta in reaction. "Somebody definitely set that fire; you can see from the scoring on the char that it burned hottest at the beginning."

I took his coffee and had a sip myself. "Where did you learn such things?"

"Frymire—remember? He was the fire investigation guy over in Sheridan."

I could feel my undersheriff's eyes boring into the back of my head.

The Cheyenne Nation's voice was low. "What is the plan, assuming we have one?"

"These guys don't like the heat, so they're going to call in the lawyers and piss on the fire—I can't have that." They both nodded, and I looked at Victoria Moretti, who was studying us with her Browning tactical boot back on my dash. "But first I need to make a quick stop."

None of us knew where the house was, and we couldn't call into the office without alerting the gaggle of lawyers to our whereabouts, so the Cheyenne Nation had a brainstorm and looked in the phone book.

The house was down by the Middle Fork of the Powder River, set back in some Russian olive trees and red willow. Two-story and large for the area, it probably had been built as a ranch headquarters seventy-five years ago, but as the town had crowded in, the ranch had up and left. The clapboard was covered in a black spray of mold where the overgrown trees rested on the surface. Overall, the impression was one of decay; just the kind of place where two bachelors might live.

"It's the House of Usher."

There was a late-model Chevrolet parked in the driveway with plates that read FRY, which lead us to believe that there was no reason to call first; the only disturbing thing was that the driver's-side door hung open. I parked in front of the bridge at the edge of the high grass. "They need a lawn mower."

We got out and walked to the driveway. Vic went to the overloaded mailbox and pulled out a handful of assorted mail. "What they need is a wrecking ball."

Henry looked at the windows, empty except for the Rebel flag hanging in the front. Still holding the shotgun, he took a few more steps forward and made his stand at the end of the driveway.

Vic sifted through the mail, dividing it into two groups as I joined her at the box. "Anything?"

"The usual crap, but there are handwritten letters to Chuck

from an address in Sheridan in a spirally script with little hearts dotting the i's."

"So the fiancée exists?"

"Apparently."

"Anything else?"

She stuffed the lot back into the mailbox. "I swear it's only guys that get the Victoria's Secret catalog."

Saizarbitoria joined us. "Would someone mind explaining to me what it is that we're supposed to be doing?"

Vic growled. "Social call."

The Basquo looked at the Cheyenne Nation still standing at the end of the driveway with the scatter gun. "You bet."

We all joined the Bear like the Bighorn Mountain Mod Squad. "Reservation warrant?"

Henry was referring to the old method of planting somebody at the back door to yell "Come in" as you banged on the front. "No, we'll just knock, and if nobody answers we go in."

My undersheriff frowned as she checked her Glock. "Inadmissible; we find a body in there then we need this to be by the book."

Sancho interrupted. "A body?"

I glanced at Henry, knowing well his habit of squirreling away ammunition. "Do you still have some of those extra shells in your pockets?"

"I do."

Saizarbitoria wasn't going to let it go. "What body?"

"Didn't Frymire say something about needing more twelve-gauge ammo?"

The Bear nodded. "I believe he did."

"Whose body?"

Henry turned and regarded the young man. "What body, whose body—is life really worth so many questions? Let us just go down there and shoot or be shot, shall we?" We watched as he blithely flipped the shotgun onto his shoulder as if it were a parasol in a fancy dress competition and paraded down the grass strip between the two gravel tracks in his worn moccasins as if it were a garden path—Sunday in the Park with Bear.

The Basquo glanced at me and pulled out his own sidearm as we started after the Cheyenne Nation. "How did we win?"

I shook my head. "I'm not so sure we have." I paused at the vehicle and peered inside, but there was nothing out of the ordinary; no blood, not even keys.

Pushing the door shut, I looked at the house; the storm door which had the glass busted out was open along with the main door—even more disturbing.

The front porch was a little rickety, and more than a few boards gave way as I took the point position. I stuck to my plan and knocked, loud and clear. I waited, but there was no answer— Henry reached over and gently pushed it the rest of the way open to reveal a living room.

There was a large, flat-screen television on a stand in front of the curtained front window with a number of devices attached to it with cables and what looked like plastic guns. Vic moved past me and knelt down to look at the stack of cartridge covers. "Looks like the boys are gamers."

Henry fanned out to the entryway that appeared as if it led to an abbreviated dining room as Saizarbitoria and his Beretta moved past into the kitchen.

I started getting the feeling that I should have my sidearm out, too.

Vic stood and looked around at the art held against the walls with thumbtacks; a few wildlife prints, posters from movies I'd never seen, and a silhouette target with the majority of his eleven-point heart shot out. She shook her head. "Men."

I backtracked into the entry and followed the Bear as he stood looking up the steps to what I assumed were the bedrooms. I kept my voice low. "Anything?"

He shook his head as Vic, also speaking quietly, joined me. "If, and I repeat if, there is no one here, why was Double Tough sleeping at the substation?"

"Maybe Frymire went to Sheridan and didn't tell him. I don't know."

Sancho had taken the basement, and Henry nodded toward the stairs and started up with us following. There was a landing at the top with one of those pull-down attic accesses, doors on either side, both of which were closed, and a window that over-looked the backyard. We split the duty as we got to the top, the Bear taking one door and Vic and I taking the other. The door was stuck to the old paint on the molding, but I bumped it open and found a mattress and box springs on the floor, the sheets and pillows looking like they got a regular workout. In an attempt at interior décor, there were a few Wyoming Game & Fish posters on the wall, and a large Turkish rug on the floor that looked out of place. The closet door hung open and clothes and an assort-ment of hiking and hunting boots were spilling out onto the floor.

As a token to amour, a small lamp with a pair of red panties hung over the shade was sitting on a cardboard set of drawers; it was still on and cast a pinkish glow on the cracked wall. Vic walked into the room and paused to read the label on the linge-rie. "Victoria's Secret. Of course."

I turned to look at the Bear, whose girth blocked most of the other doorway, his face turned toward the ceiling. Vic joined me in returning to the landing behind him, and I moved to his side as he took a step into the room. He slowly raised his hand and finally an index finger, touching one of the stained cracks in the ceiling. He picked at the crack until a chip fell away and something seeped from the plaster.

He withdrew his hand and rubbed the thick substance between his thumb and forefinger and his dark hair pivoted to reveal the powerful face as he held his fingers out for me to smell.

No mistake about it.

I watched as a drop fell onto the narrow-pinewood floor, the drip sounding like the beginning of a soft rain.

This room was also empty, with the exception of two folding chairs, a sleeping bag, and what appeared to be a broken transistor radio.

Stepping around Vic and back onto the landing, I reached up and pulled the short cord, lowering the folding stairs, and flipped the bottom section down, placing the spring-loaded rails on the scuffed, worn floor. I put a foot on one of the treads to test if it would hold my weight and then gripped the rails and started up.

It was dark in the attic, but there was a string hanging within arm's reach, so I pulled it, immediately illuminating the rafters with no insulation.

I backed down the steps and looked at the two of them. "Dead raccoon."

Vic smiled. "Natural causes?"

I glanced at Henry, but he was no longer paying attention.

"I'd wash my hands if I were you."

Vic started down the steps, and I spoke in a low voice. "I hope you're ashamed of yourself."

She stopped and turned as Henry continued downward. "Look, it was a perfectly reasonable line of inquiry, all right?"

"I was just joking."

She turned and started off again. "Wasn't funny."

There was a scream from downstairs, and I was pretty sure it wasn't the Cheyenne Nation. Vic leapt down the steps Glock-first, and I even found my hand on my sidearm as I half-leapt, half-tumbled down the steps after her. There was a young woman standing in the entryway with a pizza box on the floor at her feet and the Bear with a hand out in an attempt to quiet her. She screamed again when she saw us but then placed a hand on her chest and leaned against the wall in an attempt to catch her breath.

Vic holstered her weapon and looked back at me. "The fiancée."

Figuring it was my party by default and that I should welcome her to it, I stepped past Vic and Henry, and stuck out a hand of my own. "I'm really sorry about this; I'm Walt Longmire, Chuck's boss."

Her hand stayed on her chest, and she breathed deeply, finally pulling some of the blondish-brown hair away from her face. "Grace Salinas."

I smiled. "Hi, Grace." I looked down at the box leaking pepperoni and melted cheese. "Sorry about the pizza."

"Oh, it was some promotion they were supposed to be having over at the Sinclair station. They called and said we'd won a free pizza and that we could come over and pick it up, but when I got there, I had to pay for it. Not much of a promotion." She smiled back but then looked concerned. "You're here about the shooting?"

Vic and the Bear glanced at me, and I continued to look at her. "Shooting . . ."

"This morning—the raccoon?"

"The dead one in the attic?"

"I told him not to shoot it, but it was keeping us up at night. He killed it this morning—I figured you were here because of that."

"Not precisely, but is Chuck around?"

She glanced in the living room as if he should have been there. "He's here somewhere; I just ran out to get the pizza." She stooped and began scooping the pie back in the box. "If he went back to bed . . ."

"I don't think so; we were just up there."

She stooped for the box and started past us toward the kitchen. "Well, he's got to be around here somewhere."

Saizarbitoria was standing in front of the closed back door next to a table and chair; he leaned on the facing and smiled a stiff smile. The young woman considered him and then turned back to me. "Boy, the gang's all here. Really, is there something wrong?"

Sancho widened his eyes in the brief instant we had before she turned back and looked at him. I, in turn, made strong eye contact with Vic.

"Excuse me, Grace?"

Her eyes returned to me. "Yes?"

"How about you accompany my undersheriff back out front for a moment—I've got some things I need to discuss with Sancho."

"Sure." She studied me for a while and then started off as Vic followed her out. "I just can't figure where he got to."

The Basquo waited until he was sure she was gone and then stepped back, opening the door behind him enough so that I could see Frymire, in a pair of boots and a bathrobe, lying in the backyard with a shovel still in his hands.

14

Saizarbitoria, the low man on the totem pole, drew the duty, and I sent him to wait with Grace in her car until the Ferg and the Powder River EMTs arrived. Ferg would drive the distraught young woman home to Sheridan, and Sancho would stay with Frymire.

The rest of us were kneeling beside my deputy's body and trying to piece together what had happened. "He shot the raccoon, went down to dig a hole in the backyard, and somebody caught him out there?"

The Cheyenne Nation carefully lifted the flannel bathrobe, saturated with blood. "With a knife, a very large one, in the hands of someone who knows how to use it." He released the robe, and we watched as it settled back against the dead man's body. "Between the second and third ribs, up and to the side—professional."

I thought about the conversation I had had with Lockhart on the boardwalk in front of The Noose, and about professionalism, but mostly I thought about Bidarte and the knife that he'd stuck in the pole between Henry and me.

The Bear looked toward the stream, where the assailant would've most likely set up observation. "He waited, watched the house, called, and when she went out for the pizza, he went in."

Vic continued for him. "And when he wasn't in the house, caught him digging a hole in the backyard. But why was the door of his truck left open, the front door, the back door . . . and why take the chance and leave her alive?"

I nodded toward the house. "She was supposed to find him."

Henry sighed. "And call you."

I watched as Vic's jaw set, the way it always did before the storm. "This was a delaying tactic?"

I stood. "They're counting on this slowing us down enough so that they can clean up and get out of here or at the least get the lawyers between them and us."

"They didn't have a reason to kill Double Tough, but they had one to kill Frymire?" She stood. "What makes you think they're not already done and gone?"

I pointed at Frymire's body. "This."

"So, now what?"

The Cheyenne Nation also stood. "We go after them."

The elongated canine tooth trapped part of her lower lip as she smiled at both of us. "Now we're talking."

We piled in my truck, and Vic flipped up the center console in order to sit in the middle to allow the Bear to have her coveted shotgun seat. She stared at the dash as Henry slammed the door behind him, lodging the butt of the shotgun between his feet.

"Something?"

She nodded. "Yeah."

"You're not suspecting one of us now, are you?"

She stared at the dash, still distracted. I waited for a moment and then started the truck, spinning around on the other side of the bridge and flipping on my lights and siren as her hand came up. "Why try and kill Double Tough?"

I rocketed down Powder Junction's main street, a smattering

of traffic darting for the curbs so that I could pass. "We're not on that again, are we?"

She made a sound and threatened me with the hand as I waited, glancing at Henry, the two of us at a loss.

"Something he said."

"Who?"

"Double Tough. What'd he say about last night?"

I made the turn onto 192 and headed southeast. "Nothing important—he said he didn't see or hear anything."

"Before that, he said something about a traffic stop." We were just passing the burnt wreckage when she slapped me in the chest. "Stop!"

I hit the brakes. "What?"

She gestured toward the ex-station. "Pull in here—pull in!"

I did as she said and watched as she crawled over Henry, yanked the door open, and ran toward what was left of the structure.

The Bear turned to look at me. "What is this all about?"

We watched as she passed the building and continued on toward the Suburban, still parked where we'd left it early this morning. Henry clutched the open door as I spun the wheel and pulled across the parking lot to follow her. When we got to the SUV, she had the passenger-side door open and had dived onto the front seat, her legs sticking straight out of the open door.

The Cheyenne Nation glanced at me as we got out. "It must be something important."

We stood there as she extricated herself from the Suburban with Double Tough's duty clipboard in her hands, pulling the forms free of the clip and throwing them into the open cab.

"Vic?"

She ignored me and opened the inside of the clip where the white copies were usually deposited to be filed. She stood there

looking at the top one, finally turning it around and handing it
to me.

The form was a standard ticket written out as a warning to
one of the kids Double Tough had mentioned stopping yesterday
evening—he was driving an early-seventies C-10 pickup with
South Dakota plates, and his name was Edmond Lynear.

I raised my eyes to hers. "Eddy Lynear, late of Butte County,
South Dakota?" I thought about it. "The kids." I studied the form.
"What the hell were they doing over here last night?"

She shook her head. "I don't know, but they were here in that
diarrhea-colored truck and somebody got in there and took that
bit. Either you were wrong about Lockhart being unconcerned
about the damn thing or someone else was interested.

When we reached the entrance to East Spring Ranch, the scours-
colored truck was sitting on the other side of the gate with a gaggle of heavily rearmed teenagers in the bed, on the hood, and in
the cab.

I pulled my truck to the side of the road, still a little ways
away from the gate, and left the engine running. I shut off the
sirens but allowed the blue lights to continue racing across the
blockade like an accusation.

Eddy Lynear was, of course, the first one to speak. "That's as
far as you go."

Stepping from my truck, I watched as Henry, having left
the shotgun behind, slid out the other side. Vic, who evidently
had decided to hold back until this particular group of the
youth of America made their move, remained in the Bullet and
watched.

Henry joined me, and we walked toward the fence as I pulled
the paper from my pocket and held it up for them all to see. "This

is a warrant for admission to this property, and I will now ask you to move this vehicle and unlock this gate to grant us entry."

Eddy, who was holding some sort of tactical shotgun with a folding stock and built-in light, called down from the top of the cab, "We were told to kill you if you try and enter."

I looked up at the kid. "Hey, Eddy, why don't you climb down here and talk to us?"

The other four were now making menacing noises with their weapons like they were starring in an episode of *Steadfast Resolution*, beside the fact that these modern automatic armaments haven't had to be cocked since well before they were all born.

I rolled up the warrant, for all the good it was doing me, and put it away. The light from the shotgun was bright, and I raised my hand to block the beam. "Before you do something stupid, how about we talk?" My only concern at this point was that they might accidently discharge one of their exotic toys, and I knew from experience that accidentally dead was still dead. "I bet I can guess who it is that gave you these weapons."

He didn't say anything.

"I'm betting it was that character Tom Lockhart, wasn't it?"

He still didn't say anything.

"I bet he also filled your head up with a bunch of hooey about him being some kind of big wheel with the CIA, didn't he?"

You could see the doubt beginning to chip away at the others, but Eddy was still standing tall before the man and wasn't giving ground. "He says you're dirty."

"What?"

"He says you're planning on getting rid of us, that this is Armageddon." He motioned with the barrel. "I'm not kidding, Sheriff. If you try to get past us, I'll kill you."

I shook my head. "All right. First off, I'm here to tell you that Tom Lockhart is not CIA, FBI, Homeland Security, FEMA,

NASA, the Absaroka County Dog Catcher, or any of the other things he's been telling you. He's just a loudmouth with a checkered past—pretty much a never-was. Now I don't know if he got you guys to go after my deputy Double Tough and get the drill bit out of the Suburban. I don't know if you guys are the ones who set fire to the sheriff's substation as a diversion or what, but the important thing for you to know is that my deputy is still alive. I'd like to think that you didn't mean to hurt him or that you didn't even know that he was asleep in the back room."

The kid poked the shotgun at us with a little more enthusiasm. "Shut up."

"The point being that you haven't done anything that you're going to have to spend the rest of your life in an eight-by-eight cell paying for—unlike your buddy Tom Lockhart and his friends in there."

Eddy's face was red as he screamed down at me. "Shut up!"

"He gave you the guns and told you that was just the beginning, didn't he? Said he'd cut you guys in on the deal? Well, I've got news for you—he's just a money-grubbing lowlife who's tricking all of you into doing his fighting for him."

Eddy jacked the breech of the tactical shotgun.

Both Henry and I watched the spent unfired shell bounce off the sheet metal of the cab and land at our feet. The Bear looked at me, neither of us all that concerned with Eddy Lynear.

At that point I heard a roar from behind us and figured Vic must've accidentally stepped on the accelerator in trying to get out of the truck, but I should've known better. The engine racing had been a warning, kind of like when a bull snorts, paws the ground, and bellows. When Henry and I turned to look at her, she had already reached up and pulled the selector in my truck down into gear.

More readily able to tell the difference between a potential and absolute threat than I ever could, the Cheyenne Nation pushed me to the side with all his considerable strength and then leapt backward as the three-quarter-ton charged forward into the giant gate. The Bullet slapped the gate backward and in turn broadsided the truck on the other side.

The young men, not unaccustomed to vehicular assault, leapt from their vehicle, leaving Eddy as the only occupant. Vic pushed the aged Chevrolet down the road sideways, Eddy dropped the shotgun in an attempt to stay on the top the truck, and Henry and I stood at the center of the road as Vic continued to push the entire mess like an icebreaker.

"When do you think she will stop?"

"When she finds a cliff to push him off of." I stooped and picked up the shotgun, noticing that it, too, was a Wilson. "Fancy. They must have a dealership."

Vic finally took her foot off the accelerator as she deposited the Chevy into the roadside ditch like some botched Macy's Thanksgiving Day float.

One of the kids loped next to me, the others fell in, and pretty soon we looked like some lost platoon in search of transport. I reached down and took an elongated weapon from him. "You mind if I take a look at that, Edgar?"

He smiled. "Nope. I don't even know where the safety is, and it weighs a ton."

"It doesn't have a safety."

"Oh." He cantered along. "It was the last one, and nobody wanted it—I mean, it's a bolt action."

"Uh-huh." I held the exotic weapon up and looked at the barrel as we neared the two-truck pileup. "Fifty-cal BMG."

He looked puzzled as we arrived at the Bullet, where the window was still rolled down. "What's a BMG?"

Vic threw open the door, climbed out of my damaged vehicle,

glanced at us momentarily as she slammed the door with more than a note of finality, and straightened her ball cap. "Big Motherfucking Gun."

I clarified for the kid. "Browning Machine Gun."

Lynear looked at the weapon with renewed respect. "It's a machine gun?"

I studied the body of the thing, dark and dangerous. "It's an antimaterial sniper rifle."

"Sniper, huh?"

"Yep."

"What's antimaterial mean?"

The Cheyenne Nation offered as he came around the other side of the Chevy, "It shoots through walls."

"Wow."

Eddy Lynear was trying to climb out of the bed of the C-10 where he'd been deposited when the vehicle ditched, and Henry lowered the tailgate to make it easier on him as I surveyed the damage to the Bullet, now steaming and draining vehicular fluids onto the roadway.

Eddy was holding his head, where a substantial cut was bleeding through his fingers. "You wrecked my truck again."

I surveyed the damage to the trucks and to Lynear. "Doesn't look like it did mine any good either." I patted the tailgate and had him sit, laying the shotgun and the big .50 in the bed to keep company with the cases and extra ammunition that Lockhart must've left.

Vic was in the process of taking the weapons away from the rest of them as Henry appeared at my side with a confiscated ArmaLite and the first-aid kit from the Bullet.

I attempted to peel Eddy's hand away as the other teenagers gathered round, incapable of ignoring gore. "Let me see."

Vic was depositing the rest of the automatic weapons in the

bed of the Bullet and Eddy, being a male, was drawn to her. His next statement probably had to do more with the braggadocio of having his posse nearby than good sense. "I'd rather she did it."

"Oh, you don't want that." I sopped up some of the blood and laid the skin flap back over his forehead. "She's more likely to use it as an excuse to put you out of your misery."

"Or ours." My undersheriff studied my handiwork as I patched the young man up. "You're going to have a great scar."

I sealed the wound with some gauze and tape. "So, you guys were the ones that set fire to the substation?"

He said nothing until Vic reached up and slapped him in the back of the head. "Hey, that hurts."

"Talk, you little shit."

He sighed. "We overheard them and thought if we got the bit back that Lockhart would let us in on the deal. We didn't know anyone was in there. Honest."

"What deal?"

He shrugged, and the sullen look returned to his face as he glanced around at his friends. "We don't know."

"Eddy, playtime is over." I leaned on the side of the Chevy next to the Cheyenne Nation. "And I need some information."

He glanced at his buddies again. "We're not telling you anything."

"Well, then I'm going to arrest you."

Edgar Lynear was the first to ask from the other side of the truck bed, "We're not already arrested?"

"Not yet, but if I do it goes on your permanent record."

"What's a permanent record?"

I turned and looked at Henry. "Doesn't seem to carry the weight it used to."

He sighed. "No, it does not."

I glanced back to the wounded young man. "How old are you, Eddy?"

"Seventeen."

Vic breathed a response. "Jesus . . ."

Eddy considered her. "You know, you shouldn't blaspheme like that."

"Kiss my ass, Opie."

The others laughed as I waved a hand in front of his face to get his attention back on me. "I need some answers or people are going to get hurt."

He gestured toward his wound with a bloody hand. "I'm already hurt."

Vic reached up and smacked the side of his head. "Not near enough."

"Oww . . ."

"I mean really hurt." I straightened and looked to the left. "I know the main ranch headquarters is up this road, but that's not where Lockhart and his men are working, is it?"

He remained silent until Vic slapped him again. "Oww . . ."

I looked at her, and she shrugged. "I'm Italian, and I have brothers; I know how this works."

"Is it the road to the right up here?"

Vic raised her hand again, and the kid winced. "Yeah, to the right. I don't know what's there; they never let us go out that way."

I nodded, looked at the two-track that departed from the main road a good quarter of a mile farther, and then redirected my attention to the weapons I had confiscated. I reached in and plucked out one of the plastic cases, opened it, and looked at the rounds inside, each one as long as a cigar.

Edgar was next to me again. "What do the blue tips mean?"

I pulled one out and studied the deceptive pastel point at the business end of the .50 round. "Incendiary."

"What's that mean?"

The Cheyenne Nation's voice intoned beside me. "It blows things up."

"You think locking up their shoes with the guns will keep them there?"

"I can hope. Anyway, I didn't figure you wanted to volunteer for babysitting duty." We'd triangulated a route that would have us traipsing through the sagebrush and over uneven ground but would intercept the road by angling to the right.

"Are there snakes out here?"

"It's Wyoming; there are snakes everywhere. If you see one, shoot it with your ray gun." Vic had taken a spacey-looking desert tan FN carbine and was aiming it at the horizon. "And if you don't watch where you're going, you're going to step on one."

She turned back to look at me. "You're just jealous because mine weighs less than an anvil. Why did you decide to pack that thing, anyway?"

Loaded with the McMillan TAC-50 and thirty rounds of ammunition I'd dumped in a canvas satchel, I was bringing up the rear. "If these guys are as well armed as I think they are, I'd just as soon do my fighting from a couple of football fields away."

Henry glanced back from point, my shotgun hanging from his shoulder and the ArmaLite A4 carbine with two thirty-round magazines in his hand. "More like a couple of miles."

I called out to him, "If they'd had a flintlock rifle, would you have taken it?"

He walked on. "I like this weapon; it and I have spent a great deal of quality time together."

"Quality of life?"

"For me; perhaps not for others."

There was a chill, but maybe it was the cool of the late night.

I thought about the idiocy of what I was doing, pitting the three of us against who knew how many. The proper thing to do would've been to call in the Highway Patrol and as many fellow sheriffs and deputies as I could draw on short notice from the surrounding counties, but here I was lugging Ma Deuce across the high plains in a remake of *They Came to Cordura*.

Short notice was still too long, and these characters were too powerful to let slip away; after Double Tough, I thought I couldn't allow it, but after Frymire, I knew I couldn't.

It was possible that Lockhart and the others had already vacated to sunnier pastures, but I figured they were concerned with removing anything that might incriminate them. If I opened the conflict to a wider arena, the more opportunities there would be that they might slip through. Maybe I just wanted to mess things up for them myself—get my licks in before anybody else showed up.

I figured that Gloss, the others, the lawyers, and possibly the National Guard couldn't be too far behind, but I wanted to make sure that none of the nastier players got away and certainly not scot-free.

I stumbled over a berm of loose dirt and noticed that we'd gotten to the road.

Henry was crouched down, running his hands over the hard-packed earth. "Heavy equipment and a lot of it."

I nodded and sat the butt end of the TAC-50 on the road and sloughed off the satchel full of brass. "I wish we had a truck."

"People in hell want ice water." Vic propped the FN on her hip and glanced around. "I wish we had air support."

The Cheyenne Nation continued to look down the dirt road, where it rounded off at the flats and disappeared into a small valley. His face pivoted to the mountains and the morning star, likely thinking the same thing I was, that out here on the flat was a bad place to be without food, water, or much of anything else besides guns. He gestured toward the big rifle I carried, and, more important, the Nightforce NXS 8-32×56 Mil-Dot telescopic sight.

"Something?"

He nodded and pointed down the dusty road, stretching like the hypotenuse of an extended triangle that disappeared at the vanishing point.

I brought the burley rifle up and adjusted the optics till a man vaulted into clear view, a lean bundle of muscle with dark hair who sat in a lawn chair with an umbrella and a cooler behind a Jeep Rubicon, an autoloader rifle lying across his lap.

Lowering the .50, I handed it to Henry and watched as he scoped the individual almost a mile away.

"How the hell did you see him?"

He sighed and handed the weapon back to me. "Cheyenne radar."

Then he lifted the binoculars that I hadn't seen hanging at his chest and handed them to Vic. "And these."

"Advance guard."

"Yes."

I glanced around at the infinite space, at the sagebrush and the moon shadows of the few large rocks studding the landscape. "Too long to go around him; any ideas?"

The Bear nodded. "Yes. Shoot him."

"He might just be some roughneck they've got working for them."

"All the more reason."

I looked down at the howitzer in my hands. "Too much noise."

Vic handed me the FN before taking off her duty belt and

uniform shirt. Underneath she was wearing a white wife-beater T-shirt which highlighted portions of her anatomy. She ripped the front to show a little more cleavage and, adjusting her attributes, she flipped me her cap. She shook her head, and her exquisite face was haloed with her hair—presto, instant print model.

She tucked the Glock in the back of her jeans and started off with a swagger. "Watch and learn, fuckers."

I had every intention.

A few yards down the road, she latched a hand onto her hip and turned to look back at us, en vogue. "Not that I'm a sore loser, but if he should happen to shoot me, take his head off."

We watched as she continued walking down the middle of the road in a heart-jarring strut.

I looked at Henry, now standing beside me. "Why didn't I think of that?"

"You do not have the legs for it."

We moved in a little closer and then set the TAC-50 up on a flat rock the size of a toppled refrigerator; I pulled the bolt action, replaced the incendiary round with a regular one, and handed the blue-tip to the Cheyenne Nation. "Don't lose that; I've only got twelve of them."

He raised an eyebrow and dropped the .50 in his shirt pocket.

I brought the bolt forward and set the round, lowered my face to the scope as he sat on the edge of the rust-colored, lichen-covered rock, and raised the night-vision binoculars. "Twenty bucks says she takes him without a shot."

He snorted. "No bet."

Through the crosshairs I watched as the makeshift sentry stood at her approach, still holding the FN, not unlike Vic's except this one was olive drab. I also noticed he had an auto-loader with silencer stuffed in a holster. "Six hundred and thirty yards?"

"Six twenty-five."

I adjusted the scope and watched the winds blowing dust across the roadway in different directions at different distances.

"Strong latitudinal wind at about four hundred yards."

"I can see that."

Vic held her hands up in mock surrender as the man cradled the Spec-Ops rifle in his hands. She stopped at a respectful distance, and I could even see her jaw muscles through the scope as she spoke. He said something back, and she cocked a leg in a provocative manner, her hands going to her hips. He smiled broadly, pushing his ball cap up onto his head, turned, and balanced the rifle on the top of the spare of the Jeep. Cracking open the cooler, he fished out a bottle of water for her. The smile was even broader when he turned but quickly faded when confronted with the 9mm in his face.

"Does it work every time?"

She tucked her uniform shirt back into her jeans. "Not with homosexuals."

I had unbolted the spare from the Wrangler and had handcuffed the dark-haired guy to it and to the chair. He still watched Vic with considerable interest. "Please tell me she's really a deputy."

I looked back at the Botticelli-Venus-with-a-Badge, now buckling her duty belt, reholstering the Glock, and stuffing his pistol with the silencer in her own jeans. "She is."

"I was just sitting here thinking that this job wasn't bad, and the only thing I needed was . . ."

I looked at the Minnesota plates on the Jeep. "Who are you?"

"Name's Chet Carlson." He started to extend his hand for a shake and then remembered his situation. "Had a buddy get hold of me; said there was a welding job in Wyoming. When I got here, they had enough welders, so I took this."

"Did you know it was illegal?"

"No." He thought about it. "Does it matter?"

"Probably not." I looked down the road less traveled. "Did they tell you to kill anybody that came in?"

He shrugged. "They said stop anybody, and they weren't real particular about how I was supposed to do it." He glanced at Henry Standing Bear, holding the TAC-50. "I think I'm glad it didn't come to that; I don't think that .223 or .40 of mine would hold up against that antiaircraft weapon."

"Military?"

"Afghanistan, two tours."

"Lockhart hire you?"

"He did. Said it was a government job, real hush-hush, but when I got here I could see that that was bullshit, but I stayed. Gotta eat, man."

My eyes returned to the road. "Down there, what are they doing?"

He made a face and then looked at Henry and Vic, who had both drawn near. "Oil. Black gold. Texas tea. They got that Mexican with 'em, and he's a damned oil magnet; if he can't find it, it ain't there."

"I thought this area was pumped out."

He shook his head. "Not with the new technologies with horizontal drilling and fracking; at a hundred dollars a barrel, they're pulling quite a bit out down there, but it's just a sideline. I heard one of 'em, that Lockhart guy, he said this is just the tip of the iceberg and that something really big was coming."

"What's that?"

"He didn't say."

I sighed. "We need the keys to your Jeep."

He reached across with his free hand and pulled them from his jeans, then tossed them to me. "Here."

"We're taking some water. Here's a couple for you."

"Take all you want, just make sure you tell them where you left me."

I smiled. "Don't worry, we won't forget about you."

"That's not what worries me." He looked down the road this time. "You go down there, and they're going to kill your ass."

I tossed the keys in my hand as I took the .50 from Henry. "My ass takes a lot of killing, but thanks for the vote of confidence."

The top was down on the Rubicon—only a man from Minnesota would think this was top-down weather—and we didn't bother with trying to put it up; in my experience it took twelve men, a boy, and a week to do the job. There was just enough light to drive without the headlights, so I did.

Henry stood in the back periodically checking the horizon with the binoculars with his arms draped over the padded roll bar.

"Anything?"

"Just the unfurling and pastoral beauty that is Wyoming."

I glanced at Vic. "Forever West?"

"No fucking way."

The slope gradually led to a shallow valley that headed south, so I followed the wide dirt road and tried not to look off the edge that dropped into a tributary of Salt Creek.

Despite Vic's remarks, it was beautiful country, even the tang of turned earth where they had graded the road couldn't spoil the environs. There were pillars of rock ahead, and what looked like another canyon that dropped off farther into the narrow aperture to the west like sentinels into an ancient sea—a place from which humidity had departed forever. The moon was setting, pulling at tides that were no longer here, but you could feel the buoyancy of its light as it struck the rocks.

I noticed a batch of sage and tumbleweeds to my right and slowed. It looked like the entrance to a road that they had cut and then abandoned, but it was worth an investigation. I slowed the Jeep and pulled up to the somewhat hidden fork. Henry climbed out with the ArmaLite and looked at the brush alongside the road. Carefully, he reached down and took hold of one of the branches and pulled it; the rest of the vegetation pivoted along with its brethren, evidently wired together.

He looked back and motioned for me to drive through, which I did, and then pulled to the side. He walked over and made a cutting gesture at his throat, and I shut off the engine.

His head was cocked as if he were listening to something. I glanced at Vic, and we both climbed out and followed the Bear down the road toward the sound of heavy equipment. The noise echoed off the rock walls of the steep canyon, and it must've been an undertaking to put the road in. Evidently, they had thought it would be worth it.

We turned a sharp corner and suddenly, far below, there was a city.

The usual lights and illumination that generally accompanied a drilling operation were not there, and the entire drilling rig and outlying buildings were painted a flat desert tan. It was an operation, a big one, and in spite of the camouflage pattern, I was still amazed that no one had noticed it.

"How the hell do you keep something like this from being seen?"

The Cheyenne Nation started to speak but then looked up.

I followed his eyes—there were no stars and no setting moon. I allowed mine to adjust to the darkness and could see what was blocking the sky: a mesh of guide wires running across the distance of the canyon interlaced with gillie material—more than a mile of it.

"Holy crap." Vic stepped forward, looking at the gigantic canopy. "I'm impressed."

I made a noise in my throat. "But how do you get the oil out of here?"

The Bear's hand came up and pointed at a number of polished aluminum shapes parked against the base of the drilling rig, looking incongruous amid the military paint scheme.

I took his binoculars and could see the milk trucks being filled with the last tankers full of oil. "I'll be damned." I passed the binoculars to Vic and stood there, taking in the magnitude of the operation, unsure of what to do next.

She surveyed the entire scene. "I don't get it, though. They can't be making enough money to support all of this long term—what's the next step?"

"I don't know."

Henry's voice sounded from the darkness. "It looks to me like they are breaking things down and loading up just a few more tankers. I am betting they will be out of here by morning—just leave behind a skeleton crew to dynamite the canyon and nobody but us will be the wiser."

Vic nodded her head. "Smart."

I nodded. "Very smart."

The Bear remained silent for a moment and shook his head. "Not so smart."

We turned and looked at him as he pointed at the road on which we stood. "Only one way out."

15

The milk truck driver wasn't sure what to make of the shapely woman standing in front of the Jeep with the hood up near where the first sentry had been positioned, but he knew what to make of the .45 Colt I poked through the driver's-side window into his left ear.

As I cuffed him to the Jeep's spare along with Carlson, I started having second thoughts and figured maybe we should find something larger to pin them to. I turned to Henry. "Do we need the Jeep anymore?"

"For speedy egress possibly."

"If I cuff both of these guys to the spare they could just pick it up and walk off with it."

Vic looked around as she closed the hood on the Rubicon. "Where the hell would they go?"

She had a point.

I turned back and looked at the two of them, the one from Minnesota, the other from Louisiana. "You guys aren't that stupid, are you?"

They looked at each other and then back to me, their faces blank—and I was not reassured.

"Look, there isn't much out here that can eat you, but what can eat you is the distance, okay? If the two of you go on walk-about in the dark you're likely to get hurt or, more important, get lost and then you'll just be two corpses handcuffed to a spare tire—another great mystery of the high plains. Got me?"

They looked around again.

I was still not reassured.

I threw a thumb toward my undersheriff. "Or I will let her shoot you."

They seemed to get that last part.

I joined the squad back on the road, sighed deeply, and thought what a nice cool morning it was if you weren't up to the types of things we were up to. "I'm pretty sure I'm the only one who knows how to drive this thing." I studied the length of the milk truck and made some calculations.

The Bear stiffened and shook his head. "You are also the better shot."

I glanced at the eighteen-wheeler. "It's a tanker; I think you'll hit it."

He nodded reluctantly. "So, what is going to happen?"

"On Highway 1 in Vietnam, I saw a tracer round hit an oil truck."

Vic leaned forward into my line of thought. "And?"

"Well, it was aircraft fuel, not crude. . . ." They both stared at me. "And it was more than one tracer, probably a bunch of them." They continued to stare at me. "But it blew like a sailor on a three-day drunk."

The Bear's voice rumbled. "How many Claymores?"

Since Vietnam and our association with Claymore directional mines, Henry and I had developed our own private method of determining a demolition scale. "Eight."

His eyes quickly traveled from Vic's to mine. "Eight?"

"Maybe seven, but that was high-octane with lots of tracers."

He raised an eyebrow, the closest thing the Cheyenne Nation did to a guffaw. "The concussion will collapse the canyon."

"It's crude oil—won't be anywhere near that bad."

Vic stretched a hand out and placed it on my arm. "How about we simply jackknife the trailer on the road?"

"We'll fall into the creek. I think I'd rather blow it up and have them have to put it out, and I want a lot of smoke and noise." I reached over and tapped the extended barrel of the TAC-50. "One blue-point from this should do that." Henry still looked worried. "I don't want anyone killed—just want to plug the bottle until we can get the weight of the law to swing to our side."

Our attention was drawn to two individuals carrying a spare tire between them. I guess they were that stupid.

"Hey, where do you two idiots think you're going?"

The Cajun was the first to answer. "I was looking to see if there was another lawn chair in the Jeep?"

The Minnesotan was next, and his tone was a little indignant as he pointed toward the cooler. "We're out of water and figured we'd get a drink. Is that okay?"

My undersheriff made an exasperated sound, yanked the silenced S&W she'd taken from Carlson, and fired a round into the cooler. The two men might as well have been statues: still life, roughnecks with spare. "No, it's not all right. You are under arrest, and you need to sit down. Now."

They did, and quick.

The Cheyenne Nation continued to look at me. "Shoot one of them in the foot."

"Don't encourage her."

He glanced at the Kenworth, still patiently idling in the roadway, pointed in the wrong direction. "Why you?"

"I told you . . ."

"Tell me." Vic joined him in the interrogation, her eyes as angry as one of those snakes she so disliked. "Why you?"

I thought about it. "It's my stupid idea, and if anybody's going to get killed doing it, I'd just as soon it not be either of you." I set the muscles in my jaw. "Also, I want Lockhart."

The Cheyenne Nation shook his head. "That I can do better."

"I want him alive."

"Why?"

"Because we're better than they are."

He snorted. "I suppose we are about to find out if that is true."

Vic still didn't look convinced. "But if they start shooting, we shoot back, right?"

"I don't think they're that stupid."

"Well, you didn't think those morons were that stupid either. Let's do the math, shall we?" She counted off on her fingers. "Desperate + guns = stupid."

"I'm betting that the majority of the guys down there are just hired hands, brought in and told to keep their mouths shut."

Her lips stiffened. "Maybe, but then there's Frymire."

I added. "And then there's Bidarte."

In all actuality, the Kenworth had an eight-ball suicide knob and an automatic transmission, but I didn't see any reason to share that information with the rest of the crew. I had to drive the fully loaded tanker down to the T in the road before being able to turn it around but reassured myself by seeing that the blockaded youths were still hanging around the disabled vehicles.

I pulled the chain and sounded my horn as I turned, watching as they waved.

I throttled up the big tanker and started back down the road, pulling up and stopping to get Henry. He stepped onto the running board and shouted to be heard above the diesel engine. "We could still call in the Highway Patrol and the Natrona County Sheriff's Department."

I nodded. "We will, but first I want those hornets in a bottle."

"You will be in the front of the tanker when it explodes—you will be trapped with them in that bottle."

"I'm hoping to be out of the truck and a little ways down the road when the truck explodes."

"Signal?"

I smiled. "Me running for my life from this damn truck."

"Perhaps something more specific?"

I thought about it and remembered being told by a Special Forces colonel that in these situations a two-part signal was best so as to not inadvertently tip the shot. "I'll push my hat up and scratch the back of my neck."

He nodded. "They will see you coming and wonder why the truck has turned around."

"I'm counting on that."

"They will shoot you."

"Not until they know what's going on."

The eyebrow again. "Maybe, brother, maybe."

"Lockhart will want to parlay."

"And Bidarte?"

Indicating that I was ready to go, I shrugged and put my hands on the wheel. "If he comes near me with that knife of his, you have my permission to shoot his arm off."

Vic swung the Jeep out onto the road and pulled in front of the truck as he finally grunted a laugh. "Deal."

I watched as she turned her classic profile to look at us. "Keep an eye on her, Henry." He turned his head to regard my undersheriff. "Does she seem a little emotional to you lately?"

"She is worried about you."

I batted my eyelashes at him. "Aren't you worried about me?"

A full laugh. "No. I have this McMillan TAC-50." He stuck his hand out and waited as I gripped him back. "Pax?"

I nodded into the glint in his eyes, perfectly confident that if things went completely wrong, it would be me and not the Cheyenne Nation that screwed the pooch. "Pax."

The Kenworth was an older model but rode nicely on the hard-pack and in no time we were at the cutoff to the canyon. Vic pulled past as Henry jumped out, pulling the brush away. I flipped off the headlights so that they wouldn't reflect from the rock walls of the canyon, unconcerned with the noise of the engine since the machinery associated with the clandestine rig would mask that until the last moment.

It was quite possible that I wouldn't have to detonate the tanker; that parking it in the middle of the one-lane road and stuffing the keys in my pocket or tossing them into Sulphur Creek far below would be enough. I was hoping that was the case, but it was also possible that Lockhart and Bidarte and a few of the others were desperate enough to avoid prison that they would rather kill some no-name sheriff than serve time or worse. Lockhart, I was sure, would try and negotiate, but Bidarte, looking at a lifelong jolt in Rawlins at the least, was another matter.

I took a certain comfort in watching the Jeep swing around. Henry walked up and stood on my running board with the .50 in his hand. I inched my way down the incline toward the only major curve in the road and a pavilion of sharp-edged rocks that would provide good cover and a magnificent shooting position.

I pulled alongside the boulders, and he stepped off the running board with the McMillan and the canvas bag of ammo. I watched as he picked the exact spot I would've, another rock like the one before, although this one looked more like a chest freezer, that was angled a little downward with a protective shield of rubble in front. He began setting up the bipod for the big, magazine-fed bolt action, and I watched as he loaded the weapon with the blue-tip incendiary rounds. I guess he figured that an incendiary would take Bidarte's arm off as well as a regular one.

Vic appeared in the window with the binoculars around her neck, her disparagement in full bloom. I looked at her and noticed that her hair was longer and even had a few butterscotch streaks leftover from the summer. "Do you dye your hair?"

She shook her head at me. "That's what you're thinking about right now?"

"I guess."

She folded her arms on the sill and averted her gaze. "Yes, I dye my hair in hopes that you might someday notice."

"I notice your hair and the rest of you to the point of distraction."

The tarnished gold eyes came back to mine and stayed there. "So, where are we?"

"What?"

"You and me, where are we?"

I waited a moment before making the next statement. "You want to talk about that now?"

"You brought it up."

I smiled and fiddled with the eight-ball on the steering wheel. "I'm trying, kiddo. You once said that you didn't want hearth and home and to do like you said and take one day at a time. I'm attempting to adjust to that, but it's hard for an old dog to learn new tricks."

"Yeah, well, that may have changed." She sighed. "I'm thinking that I love you and don't want to share you with the rest of the populace."

I stared at her, and it was like the world had stopped on its axis. "Are you proposing to me?"

"No, dumb ass. I'm trying to get you to propose to me." She looked down the length of the Kenworth's hood in the direction of the rock cornice and the disappearing road. "Get as far away from this damn thing as you can before playing with your hat and neck, okay?"

"I am always careful when playing with my neck."

"Sure you are." She watched Henry make the last adjustments on the McMillan and arrange the rounds within easy reach like not-so-small soldiers standing at attention. He rolled over on the rock to look at us with a downturned palm to the chest and a fist.

I turned back to my undersheriff, thinking about the things she'd just said. "You spotting?"

"I am; you got a problem with that?"

"Don't shoot until I say so."

Her lips kicked sideways, and she studied the suicide knob on the steering wheel of the Kenworth. "They shoot you—I'm having the Bear unload into every flammable piece of equipment down there and then I'm shooting every single motherfucker that tries to crawl out of this burning hole." She turned back to look at me, and I could feel the warmth of her breath on my ear. "So for the sake of population density and your future relationship, don't get killed."

"I promise to do my levelheaded best."

She reached over and grabbed my chin, pulling my mouth toward hers. "You never had a levelheaded day in your life." She tasted like bottled water, sweat, and the slight tang of metal that was probably the uncertainty in both our mouths; she tasted good. She raked her nails across my jaw as she released me, and I was pretty sure there were fire trails there, marking my flesh. "Do not confuse that with a good-bye kiss." She stepped off the running board, and I watched as she swung the desert tan FN carbine onto her shoulder. She blew me a kiss with a smile at the end of it. "Hit the road, Jack."

I let off the air brakes and inched forward, getting a feel for the narrow road and making sure I didn't strike the rocks where my team was set up, which might cause an avalanche. The Kenworth was now in the line of sight from the rig below, but with all the activity it would probably take a while for them to notice me.

I thought about what Vic had said and had to admit that it made a lot of sense. There was the difference in our ages, but obviously she was okay with that. There would be talk, but there was always talk in a small town. Here I was just getting used to the terms of our relationship, when all of a sudden she wasn't. Perverseness of human behavior. Boy howdy.

I made the turn and started down the long straightaway, maybe an eighth of a mile. Still moving slowly, I glanced over the side into the drop-off that lead to Sulphur Creek, aware that if I made a mistake in my trajectory I would likely roll over and go into the shallow drink.

I guess I was going to have to reassess my relationship with Vic and go back to my old way of thinking. I would really have to finish my cabin. It was a shame she'd just bought a house, but even with the market the way it was, she could sell it or maybe we could keep the little house in town for when Cady visited. Things were changing on that front with her married now and expecting my first grandchild. What would Cady think? She'd been bold enough to ask me about the relationship between Vic and me this summer, but I'd told her in a polite way that it wasn't any of her business. I guess now it was.

The creek was a long way down, and I figured I better start paying attention to the job at hand when suddenly I felt as though somebody was staring at me. Feeling the adrenaline rush through my nervous system like a body blow, my hands jerked in surprise along with the rest of me as the hairy figure standing on the running board tapped on the passenger-side window.

Orrin Porter Rockwell.

I hit the brakes and watched as he almost fell off but then recovered and smiled at me with a grisly grin showing a missing tooth. He'd looked better—dried blood plastered his forehead and his hair stuck to one side of his face and beard. I caught my breath, slowed the truck, and punched the button that lowered the window. There wasn't enough room on his side to open the door. "What the hell are you doing here?"

He scrambled through, finally settling in the seat beside me. "Howdy."

"And where the hell did you come from?"

He laughed. "I apologize for my appearance, but I'm afraid when your lady friend had her accident I was knocked unconscious."

"You were in the back of my truck again?"

"I was, yes." He breathed heavily from his exertions and then shut his mouth sharply, as if the missing tooth was paining him. "I told the children to stay with the vehicles and started off in the direction they indicated. Fortunately, you came down the road in this majestic conveyance, and I couldn't resist the temptation of jumping on board."

I glanced down the road, aware that it was only a question of time before the men working below noticed a stainless-steel eighteen-wheeler sitting idling in the roadway. I also thought about the crosshairs of the Nightforce NXS 8-32×56 Mil-Dot telescopic sight that was now trained on the ass end of the tanker we sat in. "You have to get out of here."

He looked around and then asked with genuine curiosity. "Where is it I should go?"

His point was well taken; it was too far back up the road to safety, and he wasn't likely to receive any warmer a welcome than me if I sent him ahead. "Never mind." I released the brakes again and began the slow roll down the narrow road, my mind scattering thoughts like pea gravel as I tried to figure out what to do with him.

The activity on the rig had blown into a full frenzy, and it looked like they were finished filling the next tanker, which was pulling forward. I allowed the transmission to shift into a higher gear and hoped that I could get to the bottom of the incline before they pulled onto the road, which would result in, appropriately, a full-blown Mexican standoff. "Well, Mr. Rockwell, it appears that you are along for the ride."

He looked forward with an expression of deep anticipation. "I wouldn't have it any other way, Sheriff."

The driver of the other truck was the one to notice me first and tooted his air horns in confused concern. I in turn tugged mine to announce my arrival to any and all in a long, sustained blast echoing off the canyon walls.

There looked to be about forty to fifty men on and around the rig, but there might've been more in the few surrounding tin buildings to my right. All faces were turned toward us as I applied a steady pressure to the brakes and stopped dead in the road at the throat of the canyon where no one could pass. I listened as the air brakes locked like a vault, then switched off the diesel and tossed the keys over my shoulder.

I turned to Rockwell and spoke in a gentle and assured tone, thinking about how I wished that there had been another time for this, but that I needed to be sure that the man held some sort of mental stability in the coming moments. "We don't have a lot of time, and I need you to listen to me." He nodded his head. "These men up here are pretty bad, and I'm going to have a word with them. I would tell you to stay in the truck, but that isn't an option. Now listen to me and listen closely—I think you know you had a life before this one, before you were MIA and before prison. You had a name—Tisdale, Dale Tisdale, Dale 'Airdale' Tisdale." He seemed to be considering my words. "You had a wife—still have a wife—by the name of Eleanor."

He stared at me and then his head dropped just a bit. "I seem to remember something about that."

I studied him, hoping that I was doing the right thing in revealing this information now. I wasn't sure how he was going to react, but I figured I'd rather have him have his epiphany here in the truck rather than out there with all those guns pointing at us. "That's not all; you have a daughter, the young woman I'm trying to find—her name is Sarah."

He didn't move. "Hmm." Finally his hand came up and rested on the dash, almost as if seeking support. "My daughter."

"Yep."

He mulled on it, and I glanced out the windshield where a large group of men were watching us and slowly starting to move our way. "When I was in prison in Missouri . . ."

"That wasn't Missouri, Dale. It was Mexico."

He nodded his head. "The man I made an acquaintance with . . . The man is here."

I watched as the crowd drew nearer and concluded that we were almost out of time. "Bidarte, he's the one that you were in prison with all those years."

"He said he would help me find my daughter."

"And the boy, Cord? He's your grandson."

"I see." He studied me for a few moments, scratching at the blood flaking from his beard. "Sheriff?"

"Yep."

He continued to stare at me with the opal eyes. "You are behaving very strangely."

I nodded and pushed open my door; that's what I got for trying to be the only sane person in the world.

The men had streamed toward the base of the incline but parted as a few that I recognized from before who were holding rifles appeared from the small building to my right.

I jumped down from the running board and walked around

to the front of the Kenworth, forward enough, I hoped, that the Cheyenne Nation and Vic would be able to see me and, more important, my hat and neck.

A semicircle of men stood looking at me and my uniform. I searched their faces for somebody I might know, someone from in-county, but none of them looked familiar. Somewhere in the distance, someone shut off the generator that was making the majority of the racket and the other diesel truck shut down as well. Far from silent, it was a lot less noisy than it had been moments ago.

My voice sounded loud, even to me. "I'm looking for Tom Lockhart."

Nobody said anything as Rockwell/Tisdale joined me, but they continued to train the automatic rifles on the two of us.

"This is an illegal drilling operation, and I'm here to tell all of you that you're under arrest."

"Oh, I doubt that." Lockhart appeared from behind the crowd and approached with Bidarte trailing behind. The faux-CIA man was wearing a hooded tactical jacket, a battle dress uniform, and combat boots, all in black, effectively dressed for the role of a lifetime. "I'm not even sure we're in your county."

"Above 43"30' N latitude; and yes, you are in my county."

He pulled up a few yards away. "Well, if we are, then we are certainly beyond the scope of your jurisdiction." He turned and looked at the group, some of them looking at each other and then at me and my star. "You men can go back to work; we're running out of time here. . . ."

"You've run out of time." I spoke in what my father used to call my field voice so that they could all hear me. "You men know there's something fishy about this operation, but it's possible that Mr. Lockhart here has suckered you into thinking that he works for the government—well, he doesn't and he and his friend Mr.

Bidarte are responsible for the death of an Absaroka County sheriff's deputy."

Lockhart laughed. "That's bullshit."

I threw a thumb over my shoulder. "Now, at the top of this canyon, I've got detachments from the Absaroka County Sheriff's Department—"

Lockhart was shouting now. "This is a United States government project, fully sanctioned by the Department of Homeland Security and a number of other agencies. . . ."

I raised my voice over his. "This man has no connection with the federal or any other government other than some polo shirts with embroidered patches on them. When all that honest-to-God law-enforcement personnel come barreling down that road, they're going to take him and his bunch and lock them up. Now it's possible that none of you will face prosecution, but he and his buddies with the rifles will. It's up to you to decide how you want to play this, but my advice is to put your tools down, raise your hands, and get over to the side out of the line of fire."

The workers were now talking among themselves, and you could see that there were at least some concerns.

Lockhart raised his voice again, gesturing toward Rockwell. "And is that one of your deputies, Sheriff, or a derelict?"

Rockwell's voice rose above mine in a righteous indignation. "My name is Orrin Porter Rockwell!"

Lockhart smiled. "*The* Orrin Porter Rockwell, the Destroying Angel and Danite, Man of God, Son of Thunder?" Lockhart continued, turning to look at the group as he spoke. "The bodyguard of Joseph Smith and Brigham Young, frontier legend, marksman, and man of iron nerve?"

Rockwell was studying him now, aware that he might be being made the butt of a joke. "Some would say, sir."

Great. I stuck a hand out to silence the crazy man. "Orrin, you might want to let me talk here."

"But I was to understand that you died in 1878, Mr. Rockwell."

He looked at the crowd of them the way a bear would look at a baiting. "I was fortunate enough to receive the blessings of the Prophet Joseph Smith, saying that as long as I did not cut my hair I would be harmed by neither shot nor blade."

"That means you would be two hundred years old?"

Rockwell's eyes narrowed like train tunnels. "When the Prophet touched me, it imbued me with a spirit unlike any other living man and retarded the aging process so that I now stand here before you."

Some of the roughnecks were drifting off and going back to work, assured that the sheriff and the fruitcake weren't really a threat to the operation. Lockhart stepped in a little closer, with Bidarte and a few of the gunmen flanking him. "Thank you, Mr. Rockwell; you were most invaluable."

I watched as Rockwell's eyes moved past Lockhart to Bidarte. There was a change in his expression as he looked at the man, a softening that was unsettling. "Tomás, you can tell them."

Bidarte dropped his face a little and then raised it to look at the man he'd shared a cell with those many years. "Orrin."

Rockwell seemed disappointed, glancing first at him and then at Lockhart. "What are you doing working for this man?"

"It's a job, my friend. Just a job."

Lockhart spoke to me as the remainder of the workers siphoned off and began going about the business of dismantling the rig. "Sheriff, how about you and your friend here join me in the office and we can discuss what it is we need to do next?"

I shook my head at him. "How about you put your guns down and we stop playing games?"

Rockwell interrupted again. "I don't understand, Tomás."

"It's just a job, Orrin, like looking for your daughter. I will explain to you later. I promise."

"My daughter?" Rockwell stepped toward him as I reached out a hand. "You know where she is?"

"I do." Bidarte threw a hand around Rockwell's shoulders and pulled him in close. "I will take you to her."

I surged forward, but the barrels of three automatic rifles pushed against me, holding me in place.

I saw Orrin's shoulders slope and his body grow stiff, convulsing as Tomás Bidarte slipped the length of that deadly blade into him. Rockwell slumped, and I watched as the larger man supported his body and wrenched the knife up and sideways, a strike reminiscent of what he had done to Frymire. Tisdale went up on the toes of his boots in an attempt to ease the pressure, half-turned in Bidarte's arms, the opal eyes draining like twin moons in his face as he looked at me, his mouth hanging open as he tried to speak.

We all stood there, the gunmen providing a visual insulation to the killing of a man.

With my aborted movement, my face was only inches from Lockhart's, and I watched as a smile garroted his face before dropping into the easy speak of a boardroom deal maker. "You and I both know there's no army of sheriffs and deputies up there." He stepped in even closer. "This operation is chicken feed in comparison with what it is we're going to make. . . ."

"From the Bakken pipeline."

He stared at me.

"Which is why you're setting up other fake religious compounds in Garden County, Nebraska, and Hodgeman County, Kansas—you're planning on doing the exact same thing that you did in Mexico, siphoning off a percentage of the two hundred thousand barrels of crude oil a day that's going to be coming down from the Bakken shale development in North Dakota when it comes through all four of your compounds. Only this time, it'll be American oil."

He didn't say anything for a moment but then quickly shifted into damage control. "Sheriff, let's be reasonable and go in the office and discuss this like rational men."

I stared at Dale Tisdale and the saturated, dark dirt underneath him. "Reasonable rational men."

Lockhart glanced around at the armaments at his disposal, and most specifically at Bidarte, still standing at his shoulder, and whispered. "We can do this the easy way or we can do this the hard way."

"Well . . ." I reached up, casually tipping my hat back. "I guess we'll do it the hard way." I then tried to relax as I scratched the back of my neck.

16

It was as if the world inhaled.

You could feel it before you heard it, the rush of oxygen that pulled all of us up the hill toward the tanker truck. I was staring at the dust around my boots as it skipped along the ground in an undertow just before the sound and fury that was thousands of gallons of crude oil exploding with the ferocity of more Claymores than I'd imagined.

Knowing full well what was coming, I'd covered my ears in an attempt to have some semblance of hearing after the thing went. We'd all flown down the hill with the compressed heat of the explosion singeing our clothes and skin.

The three unfortunates, including Lockhart, who had been facing the tanker when it blew, were lying on the ground on their backs, with me on top of them.

It had ruptured in the rear where the incendiary had entered, causing the truck to split open along the top with massive clouds of billowing black smoke filling the canyon with eye-watering efficiency.

I rolled to the side and flexed my jaws in an attempt to equalize the pressure in my head but immediately regretted the taste of oil in my mouth. The stuff was everywhere, floating in the air like little droplets of death.

Pushing up on one elbow, I could see that the truck itself was still intact, but the rear end of the tanker was twisted and blown open like a beer can, roiling black billows of smoke and orange-tinged flames.

I watched as a fresh explosion jetted from the tank as another surge of oxygen must've been sucked in. The worst was over, but it would likely continue to belch fire and smoke into the limited air supply of the canyon. I looked up and could see now that the camouflage canopy was actually holding the slick of smoke and was slowly working its way down the face—before long nobody would be able to see or breathe anything if the cover didn't burn away.

As if on cue, a few pieces of the camo started flaming and floating like space debris, and I was just as glad to have on my cowboy hat, which provided me with a little more protection than the ball caps everyone else was wearing.

One of the riflemen was dragging himself to his feet and rubbing his eyes, the autoloading rifle hanging from his chest in a military harness. I reached over and disconnected the harness as his hands fumbled over mine. I gave him a quick elbow to the bridge of his nose and watched as he collapsed at my boots.

I moved a little unsteadily, grabbing all the remaining automatic rifles and tossing them indiscriminately into the creek.

One of the mercenaries started to argue and clutched his weapon, but I introduced him to the butt end of his stock and then propelled it after its brethren.

Rockwell was still lying on the ground and was attempting to crawl—but both Lockhart and Bidarte were gone.

I looked in the direction of the rig, where men were running everywhere, some of them attempting to protect the flammables, others trying to set up a pumping unit and hoses to put out the flaming tanker.

I finally caught a glimpse of Bidarte's leather jacket as he pushed through the men on the rig to continue toward the pinched end at the rear of the canyon. He paused for only an instant to stare me down. I wasn't sure if he was saying good-bye or memorizing my face with those dead man's eyes. We both froze like that for a moment, but I was sure he understood what my look to him meant.

My attention was drawn back to Rockwell as he raised a hand and touched my leg; when I looked back, Tomás Bidarte was gone.

Crouching beside Tisdale, I lifted his head toward me and lowered my face to his, amazed that he still had the energy to move. "Hang on, we'll get you out of here."

His bloody hand came up again and fell against my arm. "My daughter."

I nodded. "I'll find her, Orrin, I'll find her. You just hang on. . . ."

He shook his head sadly, air escaping from his lungs in bubbles like pink gum. "No." He smiled, just slightly, the missing tooth looking like a keyhole in his face. "Dale . . . My name is Dale."

His eyes remained the same, but his head relaxed to the side and I knew he was no longer there. I thought about a man who had been forgotten, forgotten by his wife, his child, and his country. I thought about a man who had been so many men that he no longer knew the man he was. Maybe he'd rediscovered himself here at the end. Somehow, in a pool of blood, Dale Tisdale had risen to the top like cream to reclaim himself; at least that's what I wanted to think.

The weight in my chest was enough to pull me over, so I lowered him to the ground and crouched there, thinking about Bidarte, and the look on his face as he'd seen me see him.

I continued to look around for Lockhart, but he was nowhere.

My eyes were drawn past the rig and the crowds of men racing back and forth toward the darkness at the back of the canyon.

The rock walls pinched together, towering overhead to a height of a hundred feet where the drainage of Sulphur Creek had chiseled through the rising bedrock of the Bighorn Mountains. It was dark in the constricted throat of the canyon, with only starlight peeking from underneath the backside of the canopy they had constructed.

The stars held the black sky in the arch of the Hanging Road, the thickest part of the Milky Way that the Northern Cheyenne and Crow said was the trail map to the Camp of the Dead. It was possible that the Old Ones were with me as the stars reflected from the murky water—starlight up, starlight down.

There was an abbreviated ledge to the right, but it petered out to a pile of rubble that slid into the dark creek.

Studying the ripples carefully in the reflection of the universe, I gently stepped into the cold and felt for the bottom as the water rose to midthigh.

I breathed a quick gasp, thankful that the level was no higher, and pulled the .45 from my holster, holding it high enough so that if I hit a deep spot I wouldn't submerge my one and only sidearm.

The bottom was sandy, and the current, though slow, was steady. I leaned forward and made progress as the channel grew narrower, the rock cliffs becoming sheerer. There was a break in the wall to my right, providing a wonderful spot that you might want to use if you wanted to cut someone's throat as they approached.

I slowed and countered by slipping to the left and keeping the Colt pointed at the darkness of the alcove. I waited a moment for my eyes to adjust to the gloom and could almost see the outline of somebody there. I waited a second and then realized it must've been a shadow before redirecting the possibility of my fire toward the oncoming creek.

It was then that he charged from the rock and slammed into me with the additional force of having launched from above. It felt like someone was trying to beat me to death with a rock, hammering the side of my head and shoulder. I took the first two hits and then bull-rushed the man against the canyon wall as pieces of debris fell down on us from the triangular slabs that projected upward like miniature pyramids.

I felt the air go out of him and decided that short of just blowing his brains out, slamming him against the other side of the canyon wall might be an option, so I did.

Whatever air was left in his lungs from the first impact most certainly left his body in the next, but with a lucky swing the rock made better contact and I felt my neck muscles give way along with my knees as I fell forward.

Expecting the knife to begin carving at my guts any minute, I pushed off and up, swinging the .45 but missing him as he ducked. I fell backward, and he continued to pummel me with the rock as I rolled to the side, trying to protect my head and bring up my sidearm.

I felt the big Colt 1911, a mechanical device that had stood the test of time by remaining cutting edge for more than a hundred years, fly from my hand as the most primitive weapon from the eons slammed against my arm. I drove my hand after the thing, but the rock grazed the side of my face, and I decided I'd better deal with first things first.

As he lifted the rock for one last skull-crushing blow, I drew my waterlogged legs underneath me and thought about a high school line coach who had said, "I don't care how big they are, boys; they can't do anything if you get 'em up off the ground." I pushed across the tiny channel and carried him out of the water against the rocks with as much force as I could muster, feeling not only the air go out from him but also the structural integrity of his rib cage give way.

I heard the softball-sized rock drop into the water as I held him and stood there, the weight of the two of us driving my boots into the deep sand at the edge of the creek. Breathing heavily, I wiped some of the blood from my face, pushed back, and looked at him still hanging slightly above me.

Lockhart.

He was breathing in sync with the popping sounds in his chest and the soft gurgle of his exhale.

I sank a little deeper and wasn't sure what to do with him before we both disappeared underneath the cloudy water. I reached behind him and unrolled the tucked hood of his tactical jacket, reversed the thing, and hung it over the top of the rock, effectively hanging him up like a side of beef.

I snapped the buttons on the front of the jacket so that he wouldn't slip out and drown in the three feet of water. "This time"—I gasped, trying to catch at least part of my breath—"you don't walk."

I started pulling one of my legs from the muck, lost my balance, and reached across to the other side with one hand, at least giving myself a fighting chance of working the boot free. Turned as I was, I could feel my left foot coming loose with a sickening vacuum. I eased it back down in order to attempt to lift the boot with my toe. I figured that if Bidarte got out of the other side of the canyon he would be on foot—a trail I would only be able to follow if I had shoes.

The boot came loose slowly, and I lifted it clear and took a step further down the creek to where my .45 had fallen into the water. Careful to not overstep, I searched the bottom with my hands, running them along the smooth surface of the sand, but feeling nothing. I worked my way forward, my face only inches from the surface of the water as my teeth began to chatter. I bit down hard in response, figuring I still had a ways to go and that the nearest weapon, other than the rock, was my own.

My hand brushed against something, and I pulled it out of the mud.

Lockhart's tactical boot.

At least I wasn't the only one.

I tossed it behind me, took another step forward, and became aware that there was more light on the surface of the water in front of me. Raising my head and wiping some more of the blood away, I could see that the canyon had opened into a small, rectangular pool.

And someone was standing in that pool of water and light.

Backlit as he was, I could see the outline of his hat and the drape of his leather jacket as his lean body turned slightly to the side, like a snake, relaxed but ready to strike; his left arm dropped down along his side, curved like a long fang.

The water reflected like some alternative universe, and I watched as he planted a leg forward, maybe twenty feet away: perfect throwing distance. "Sheriff."

With my chin only a few inches from the surface, I watched the water drip from the brim of my hat. I tried to think of a more compromising position but couldn't come up with one.

He didn't move. "You are looking for something?"

I lied, since it was the only option open to me. "I think I might've found it."

He adjusted his head, and I was sure he was looking at

Lockhart, still hanging from the rock but now making a few noises. "I heard the sound of the fight and thought I would come back to see who had won."

"Pick off the winner?"

"Señor Lockhart is in possession of some information that I might not like to be made public."

I continued to breathe heavily. "Like Dale Tisdale?"

He waited a moment and then moved his leg to indicate the water, the eddies of his movement rippling across the surface and lapping against me. "As I recall, your weapon is one of those old .45s."

Trying not to move my hands but desperate to feel steel somewhere, I stretched my fingers out underneath the surface. "Yep."

"My experience with ancient firearms is limited, but I think they still fire, even if submerged."

I stretched my fingers a little more and thought I felt something at the farthest reach of the third finger of my right hand. "I've heard that, too."

"But it also might blow up in your face."

I nudged my fingers a little and could feel the trigger guard as I carefully pulled it toward me. "It might."

"Or you could miss."

Gently turning it, I could feel the grip in my fingers. "I could."

"It will most certainly jam, so you will only get one chance." He gestured ever so slightly with his back arm, and I could hear the lethal click of the foot-long stiletto opening. "Whereas I am armed and ready."

Lifting gently, I slipped my finger in the trigger of the cocked and locked weapon. "I figured."

"Sometimes the knife is better."

"Maybe." I thumbed the safety on the submerged Colt. "But you could miss."

He laughed softly. "I could, and you would not be the first to bet his life on that." He still didn't move and, except for the voice, he might've just melted like the reflections and disappeared into the night. "I don't want to kill you, Sheriff, but I will not return to prison."

"Ours are a lot nicer than yours."

He laughed again.

"Color TV and Ping-Pong tables; with your hand-eye coordination, you could be a champion in no time."

"As appealing as that might be, I think I will pass."

I had the Colt in my hand now, safety off and ready for fire—but would it? When I brought the thing up, it would still be filled with water or plugged up with mud and would most likely blow up in my face, not shoot his. My choices were to fire it and take what happened, or throw the thing at him in hopes that it might upset his aim. I was battered and bloody, but I still liked my chances in hand-to-hand, especially if he'd already thrown the knife.

Eyes. Throat. With the weight of my horsehide jacket, I figured his targets were limited, but . . .

As if reading my mind, he spoke. "Why take the chance, Sheriff?"

I stiffened my muscles, ignoring the body-numbing cold of the water but allowing the coolness to come into my face and the steadiness into my hands, thinking about a young man lying in the backyard of a rented house in Powder Junction. "Frymire."

He nodded, and his black hat reflected in the water with the movement. "That was his name?"

"It was."

"Unfortunate." He remained maddeningly calm. "I didn't really want to kill him, but Señor Lockhart said it would slow you down."

"It did."

"But not enough."

"No."

"A shame. I appreciate the care you took of my mother; I will always be indebted to you for that. I have already retrieved her from your town and made arrangements for her transportation and comfort." He shook his head, the hat again dancing on the water. "This will all disappear, we will all disappear—you will disappear."

"I don't suppose, in the spirit of fair play, you'd let me stand, disassemble, blow the water out of my gun, and let me reassemble and reload it?"

"No."

I took a deep breath, just like I always did before exhaling into the steadiness of a shot. "I didn't think so."

I moved forward and aimed the Colt and about ten gallons of water to boot. I watched his arm extend toward me, anticipating the bite of the stiletto somewhere in the explosion of water, but the effort drove me to the side as I fired, the shot detonating out of the sidearm in my hand, my adrenaline so pumped that I couldn't even feel the thing firing.

At least in that split second, that's what I thought was happening.

The blast of the extended fire was faster than my .45 could cycle, and as I stumbled against the rocks I heard the knife go by me like a deadly hummingbird. I fell forward as Bidarte was lifted up and backward, the numerous rounds entering his body, jerking his arms and legs like some frightening, akimbo tango dancer.

I watched as he splashed into the pool like a depth charge and then floated there in the silence.

I stared at the slide mechanism of the Colt, lodged back and jammed, just as I'd thought it would be as I pushed off the rocks. I started to turn to see who was behind me when another round shattered the silence of the canyon by bouncing off the rock walls and striking the surface of the water with a vicious *spak*.

I ducked as another round followed that one, shooting by and skipping across the water, and then another.

She was standing in the creek in a two-handed shooting stance, the barrel of her Glock still extended toward Bidarte's floating body. Her voice was labored and rough. "Die, fucker." I watched as she lowered the semiautomatic, her arm bumping into something as she stopped and looked down to where the six-inch handle of the knife stuck out from her abdomen, slightly below the ribcage on her left side. "Oh, shit. . . ."

I got to her before she fell, took the Glock, and stuffed it in my jacket pocket. I leaned her back, careful to avoid the gleaming black handle protruding from her body, and supported her head with my shoulder.

Her eyes wobbled a little but found mine. "Is he dead?"

I didn't even bother to glance back. "Seven times over as near as I can count, and maybe three more for good measure."

"The fucker is Dracula; he's lucky I didn't run a stake through his heart."

I studied the knife in her and winced as the blood began spreading onto her uniform shirt. "Speaking of, how do you feel?"

"That is the Academy Award of stupid questions; I feel like I've been stabbed, you dumb ass. . . ." Her head rolled up on my shoulder, and she looked at the handle, rising and falling with her breath. "Is that close to the same spot where I got shot back in Philly?"

"A little to the center."

Her head relaxed against my chest. "Fuck me; he couldn't have stuck me in the boob or something?"

"I don't know how he missed."

She snickered and then let out a slow, liquid exhale. "At the risk of sounding melodramatic, I'm cold."

I could feel the surge of concern blooming into full-blown panic as I looked at the switchblade sticking from her like a pump handle. "I don't think I better take it out; I'm not sure what organs he got, and I'm afraid you'll bleed more."

Her eyes widened just a little. "Don't touch it."

Henry appeared from the shadows of the canyon, the sudden silence of the area disturbed by his movements. "Okay, but we need to get you out of here."

The Bear leaned forward, placing two fingers under her jaw. "Shock?"

"I think."

Her eyes flashed between the two of us, but her words were slow. "She's fine and stop talking about me like I'm already dead."

Henry left his fingers at her throat and then raised his eyes to look at mine.

I started lifting her.

Her head moved. "Wait."

"We've got to get moving."

The Bear watched silently as the panic I was feeling pro-gressed geometrically as Vic swallowed with difficulty and then had a little trouble catching her breath. "Just a second." Her hand came up and grazed the knife handle as she reached for my face. She grimaced and then smiled with half her mouth—that little upturn of the corner that drove me crazy. "I want to look at you."

"You can look at me as we're getting you to the hospital." Her hand stayed on my face and her fingers were cold, and all I could hope was that it was the water causing the coolness in her extremities, the water, just the water.

"You think about my offer?"

I focused my eyes on hers, willing her to be there with me now, disregarding every other thing in the world from my mind and hers in an attempt to hold on. "It's all I've been thinking about, and it almost got me killed."

She continued to grin the half smile, but it was fading. "I'm the one who saved you."

"Yes, you did."

The tarnished gold with the harlequin flecks seemed to dance in her sockets. "I'm quite a catch, huh?"

I shook my head and began lifting like a deep-sea salvage operation before the tears in my eyes robbed me of the strength. "Boy howdy."

EPILOGUE

I hate funerals, and it seemed like today I had a passel to go to; the only good thing was that I had company inside the perimeter of the POLICE LINE—DO NOT CROSS tape that surrounded us.

Henry studied me as I drove Vic's beat-up unit, a large manila envelope and a small white box lying on the center console between us. "Any word from South Dakota?"

I nodded. "Tim Berg says they raided the compound in Butte County and took the few women and children left there into protective custody. They confiscated the equipment and foreclosed on the property after the payments on the back taxes fell through."

"Same story in Nebraska and Kansas?"

I parked, and Henry and I got out of the vehicle. Pushing off the speed limit sign, I walked toward the two-lane blacktop and the roadside marker. "All the assets have been frozen, and without money the whole thing is shutting down."

"What about the Lynear family?"

I studied the tiny cross with the plastic white and maroon chrysanthemums, daisies, and blue lilies. The ever prevalent Wyoming wind kicked at the horizontal piece of wood of the makeshift cross, causing it to gesture with a will that almost seemed its own. "There are enough charges to put the whole bunch away, but chances are they'll all end up back in Texas where they started; without the money from the oil scams, I'm betting that that won't last long either."

"But that is Sheriff Crutchley's problem."

I chewed on the inside of my lip and watched as the wind caught one of the plastic flowers and sent it tumbling toward us. "I'm afraid so."

"And the adopted boys?"

I stooped and caught the blue plastic lily between my fingers. "Will be farmed out to foster homes."

He moved up beside me and stood there, his rough-out boots near my knee. "Kind of a mess, hmm?"

Henry Standing Bear and I watched as the Division of Criminal Investigation techs carefully removed the body of Sarah Tisdale from under the roadside marker at the entrance of East Spring Ranch where her remains had been reburied. Edgar Lynear had tried to convey that to me the best he could in our conversation in Butte County, and Wanda Bidarte Lynear's performance on the side of the road had raised my suspicions, but it had been Dale Tisdale's remark about never laying a body to rest in the Apostolic Church of the Lamb of God that had sealed the deal.

It had taken me an awfully long time to find that ungrateful child, but I finally had.

My voice sounded a little sharp as I spoke. "Most certainly a mess, but there's nothing I can do about that."

He said nothing for a while but then spoke gently. "There are no other bodies?"

I studied the plastic flower in my hands and twirled it by the stem. "No, thank goodness."

The Cheyenne Nation stood there beside me, his hair loose with the breeze, and we listened to the sound of the shovels. "I think goodness had very little to do with it."

I carried the flower toward the crowd at the edge of the

police tape, looking through the half-dozen people that were curious about DCI's undertakings, finally spotting the older woman with her arm over the young man, both of them seated on the tailgate of an International pickup.

Saizarbitoria caught the tape and lifted it, allowing us escape from the sad scene. "Ruby called and wanted to know if it would be okay to release Frymire's personal effects to his family."

I nodded my head. "Sure."

"They're planning on having the services next Thursday."

"All right." We both stood there having so much to say with the limited resource of language to say it. I finally came up with something we could address. "Any word on Double Tough?"

"He lost the eye."

I nodded some more and stuffed the blue flower in my coat pocket.

"Supposedly they want to ship him back to Durant Memorial on Monday."

"Do you mind going and getting him?"

He made a face and then smiled. "Don't you think they're going to want to send an ambulance?"

"I do. I also know Double Tough well enough to know that he'd rather ride with one of us."

I moved on to Eleanor and Cord, still seated on the tailgate a little away from the tiny crowd. When I got there, they were talking between themselves in low voices, and I waited a few steps away until the owner/operator of the Short Drop Mercantile looked up.

"Sheriff."

"Hey." I waited, and the boy finally lifted his face to look at me, his eyes red-rimmed. "How are you doing, young man?"

He didn't say anything, letting his gaze drop back to my legs.

Eleanor pulled him in closer. "I was telling him how you said his grandfather was very brave in confronting those men."

"I couldn't have done it without him." I adjusted my hat so it blocked the sun from my eyes. "Still closing the Mercantile?"

She watched the boy closely and then turned her face to look at me. "Now that I've got help, I thought I'd try and keep it open."

I smiled. "Can I talk to you privately for a moment, Mrs. Tisdale?"

She glanced at her grandson and watched as Henry sidled onto the tailgate on the other side of the youth. "Hey, Cord, did I ever tell you about the time I punched the sheriff here in grade school and loosened one of his teeth?"

He glanced at the Bear as I led Eleanor a few steps away, downwind, where the breeze would carry our words to Nebraska where no one would care what we said. She pulled up and stopped, gathering the cloth jacket she wore a little tighter around her shoulders, the pearl strand that held her glasses bumping against her exposed neck.

I took a deep breath, aware that now might not be the best time to bring up the subject but also aware that there might not be another chance. I gently placed a hand on her arm and led her even further away, finally stopping where the entrance road to the ranch tapered off into a culvert. "You sent him."

She turned and looked at me. "What?"

"Dale Tisdale . . . Orrin Porter Rockwell, your husband— you're the one who sent him looking for her, and that's how he accidentally discovered your grandson."

Her lips tensed, and we stood there looking at the DCI technicians as they brought evidence bags to the site. She took another step forward but then turned slightly to the side, and I could see her face again. "We didn't even know he existed, but after Dale sold East Spring to that bunch I figured the least he could do was find his daughter."

"He did more than that."

"Yes, he did." She gathered her fingers together and clutched them to her mouth, speaking through a fist. "I didn't know who else to call. I knew that Dale had connections to those people, and I thought he was the only one that could find out what had happened to Sarah." She turned the rest of the way and spoke to me, face to face. "Do you know what it's like to have someone like that in your family?"

"No, I don't."

"It's a living, breathing hell. You never know if they're alive or dead, if what they're telling you is the truth. Finally, I just gave up and decided to live my life the way I saw fit." She stepped backward, and her eyes were fierce. "Who are you to judge me?"

"I'm not—I'm just trying to find out what happened and why."

The fire in her eyes smoldered and then dampened as she glanced back toward the truck, where the Cheyenne Nation continued his animated storytelling by smacking a fist into his open palm.

"I killed him."

I stepped around her and down the slope a bit to face her at eye level, as it seemed we were always finding ourselves. "He made choices; sometimes they were good ones and sometimes they were bad, but he made them himself. He was possibly the most abstract individual I've ever met, but he was committed."

Rubbing a hand over my face, I could feel the resistance of a couple of days of beard growth. "I sometimes think that it's not our enemies that we resent in life, but rather friends we have who stood quietly by and did nothing. You couldn't say that about Dale—he threw himself into the fray over and over again." Her head dropped, and I brought up a hand to raise her chin. "I think it was the last great adventure of his life; an opportunity for redemption. . . ." I glanced past her shoulder toward the truck, then returned my eyes to hers. "And then he got to meet his grandson."

I looked out toward the open country beyond the collapsed chain-link fence. "A friend of mine called those made-up people that Dale became Legends. . . . I think he got caught up in that so much that he wasn't enough for himself, but in the end I think that he rose to the occasion and became bigger than all those imaginary selves, bigger than Orrin Porter Rockwell. Dale Tisdale finally became legendary—big enough so that he could die as himself."

She wiped her eyes with the back of her hand and then studied me. "It's a good thing you hold political office."

I smiled back at her. "It wasn't meant to be a speech."

"I'm glad of that." She stuck her hand out to me. "Friends again?"

I took her hand and put the blue plastic lily in it. "I'm not giving back the twenty-fifth volume of Bancroft's *Works*, but I thought maybe I should remind you that Bishop Goodman has the Rockwell Book of Mormon."

"I'll get it back."

I turned her around and placed my arm over her shoulder, tacking her through the wind and back toward Cord. "I bet you will."

Henry studied me as I drove Vic's unit, glancing periodically at the large manila envelope lying on the center console between us, and the small white box. "What about Lockhart, Gloss, and that bunch?"

I set the cruise control as I took the on-ramp to I-25, discovered it didn't work, and kept my foot on the accelerator. "It's an interstate jurisdiction, so the FBI field office in Casper is in charge."

He continued to study me. "The Department of Justice."

"Yep."

"The Department of Justice, clients of the Boggs Institute that employed Mr. Lockhart?"

"The same." I glanced around at the clutter that accompanied Vic's vehicle and thought about how the thing appeared to be more of a rolling nest than a police unit.

"Kind of a mess, hmm?"

My voice sounded a little sharp as I spoke. "Most certainly a mess, but there's nothing I can do about that either."

He didn't say anything more to me as we drove the forty miles back to Durant, but he looked at me questioningly as I took the early exit and jumped on old Highway 87 and turned south. After a few miles, I pulled over to the side of the road under the Lazy D-W ranch gate.

I slid the heavy envelope from the loose piles of refuse on the console and handed it to him, motioning for him to place it in the large rural-delivery mailbox.

He stared at the name on the envelope and then his eyes came back to mine. "What is this?"

"What's it to you?"

"I simply do not wish to be party to mail fraud."

I looked down the road. "Oh, it's not fraudulent."

He felt the heft of the thing. "This is the file on both Lockhart and Gloss?"

"Maybe."

He smiled the close-lipped smile that was his trademark, the one with no warmth in it. "You are sacrificing them to Donna Johnson?"

I shrugged. "You live by the trench coat, you die by the trench coat." I sighed, adjusted my hat, and lodged my chin in the web of my hand. "Donna Johnson can make their lives miserable." I turned my head to look back at him. "I think they deserve that."

He reached out, opened the mailbox door, and deposited the

envelope inside. He closed it, even going so far as to raise the flag.

I dropped Henry off at the office where he could grab his '59 Thunderbird for the last ride of the season. He said he wanted to accompany me over to Durant Memorial, but that he had a full Indian uprising out at The Red Pony and that if he didn't get out there and relieve the bartender who was covering, he would likely find the place burned to the ground.

"Please don't mention buildings burning to the ground."

He leaned on the door of the Baltic Blue convertible he called Lola, the gloom of evening reflecting the available light off the T-bird's glossy flanks. "Sorry." His face hardened a little with the next statement. "Does it bother you that Big Wanda is gone?"

I thought about it. "Not so much; Tomás told me that he had had her taken away."

"And the body of Tomás?"

I stared through the windshield and looked south, over the rolling foothills of the Bighorn Mountains to the plains of the Powder River country, my perspective down low among the sagebrush and the buffalo grass, racing across the ground until in my mind's eye I could see the tall man, his blood pouring into Sulphur Creek like an offering.

"You mean the lack thereof?"

"Yes."

The Division of Criminal Investigation had combed the area, but they didn't know it as well as I did—and they didn't have an Indian scout. "I was thinking about taking a drive down to Sulphur Creek in the morning and looking for a sign."

"What time?"

"Early." I leaned slightly out the window of the SUV and

turned my head, listening to the distant roar of the high school football game at the southern end of town. When I glanced back at Henry, I noticed his face had been drawn in that direction, too.

"Worland . . ." He thought for a moment. "Warriors?"

I nodded. "Go, Dogs."

He murmured back. "Go, Dogs."

"They're retiring our numbers at halftime."

A puzzled look spread across the Cheyenne Nation's face. "I hardly remember my number."

"Then you won't miss it."

"No, I would imagine not."

"Thirty-two."

He nodded his head and smiled. "Ahh . . . Yes."

We listened as the band played the Durant Dogies' fight song, and there was more cheering. "Do you think things were simpler back then?"

The Bear stared at the macadam surface of the parking lot. "No."

"No?"

"No." He fished the keys from the pocket of his jeans and drew open the door of the concours vintage automobile. He settled himself in and hit the starter on the motor of the big square Bird.

He said something more, and the rest of his answer hung there in the slight breeze. I watched in the side-view mirror as both the stately beasts made the right on Fort and the left on Main and headed out toward the Rez. Listening to the sounds drifting up from Hepp Field, I was drawn back to those days when the only thing I had to concern myself with was making sure that our star quarterback, Jerry Pilch, didn't get flattened.

Henry Standing Bear was right.

I pulled the old unit into gear and drove over to Durant

Memorial. Isaac Bloomfield was drinking coffee and leafing list-lessly through a five-month-old copy of *Wyoming Wildlife* at the reception area.

"How come you're not at the game, Doc?"

"Not my idea of a game. Anyway, I'll be here when the breaks, sprains, strains, and bruises show up." He studied me and the small white box in my hands. "I want to tell you how sorry I am."

I nodded but didn't say anything.

"I suppose it's an occupational hazard, but you hate to see something like this happen."

My head nodded of its own volition.

"You're going to want to see him before they take his body away?"

I nodded some more and watched as he closed the wrinkled magazine and brought the Styrofoam cup of coffee with him. We pushed our way through the double swinging doors of the Emergency Room's inner sanctum and made our way toward room 31, the makeshift morgue.

Isaac opened the door and ushered me inside but then closed it after me; he knew my practices.

You think you'd get used to it, but you don't; the lifeless form of an animal not unlike yourself. There is, appropriately enough, an otherworldly stillness to the dead and especially when it is someone young.

I placed a hand on the bare shoulder, feeling the coolness of the flesh, another reminder that the spirit that was here was now gone. I had hired the young man from a good family over in Sher-idan, and he had been a fine officer. Next Thursday they would put his body in a grave, another casualty in the war I'd been fighting for almost my whole life.

All for a few gallons of crude oil.

As the saying goes, a cynic is the man who knows the price

of everything and the value of nothing. Toy soldiers like Gloss and Lockhart would never understand the value of a single human life in comparison with their strident beliefs in geopolitical positioning. They had never been forged in the fire of battle where you learn that the only thing left in those stark and startling moments and the reason you fought in the first place was for the man next to you, your brother in arms.

I wished that I could take Gloss and Lockhart with me when I made what would feel like a long drive to the next county on Thursday, so that I could introduce them both to Chuck Frymire's family and let them look into the bereaved eyes of the young man's mother and father and fiancée, in order to see for once where that value lies.

When I came out, Isaac was flipping through some papers on a clipboard. He looked up at me, seeing me for the loosely stacked mess I was, watching for cracks, fissures, and faults. "You still look tired."

"You mean for the last thirty years?"

A sad smile crept across his lips. "Would you like to read the report?"

"I'll give you a quarter if you read it to me."

He stared, unsure. "Excuse me?"

"Sorry, private joke."

His eyes dropped to the clipboard, and he read, "'Single, thrusting action wound with a circular defect surrounded with a margin of abrasion with the predictable langer or cleavage lines. . . .'" He paused, and his brows collided together on his face. "It was a very long knife."

"You still have it?"

"I do."

I started past him toward the room across the hall. "I'm going to need it."

The old-world eyes went back to the sheet of paper and then he flipped the copy over, reading again, " 'Muscle and tissue were cut at an oblique angle with the resulting gaping injury with the muscles retracting and eversion at the skin edges; damage to the abdominal viscera and exsanguinations resulting in an internal hemorrhage.' " He slipped the clipboard under his arm and picked up his cup of coffee as I looked back at him. " 'Complications in association with peritonitis, sepsis infection along with damage to the uterus.' "

I withheld comment.

He sipped his coffee. "She's in remarkable shape, especially considering her condition."

My hand paused on the handle of the door. "You just said she was in remarkable shape."

"She is." He sipped his coffee some more. "For a woman who was seven weeks' pregnant."

I stood there, looking at him. "Was?"

"Was." He pulled the cup away from his face and scrutinized me. "I thought you knew."

"Um . . ." I could feel the dryness in my mouth as I tried to speak. "Kind of."

He waited a moment and then rephrased his statement. "You didn't know."

I took a breath, in hopes that I wouldn't pass out. "No."

He glanced at the door I was about to go through. "I don't suppose you'd care to return to the blissful state of ignorance in which you were as of a minute ago?"

I leaned against the doorjamb, still feeling more than a little weak in my knees. "So that she can tell me herself."

The doc nodded. "Yes."

"What if she doesn't?"

"It's very possible that she's unaware, in which case I will inform her, but either way it's between the two of you, and I am removed from the equation, which I desire most greatly."

I gathered my strength and smiled at him as I carefully pushed open the door, finally remembering to mumble some words. "You bet."

It was dark except for the light coming from the dusk-to-dawns in the parking lot outside. In an attempt to keep the room from being too stuffy, Isaac must've raised the window a few inches to let in a little fresh air, a practice of his that drove the nurses crazy.

She was asleep and breathing steadily, the IV at her side set on a steady drip.

I stood there in the middle of the room and listened to the vague sounds of the football game drifting through the space at the bottom of the window.

I looked at her and rubbed my hand over my face; finally, I lifted the guest chair from against the wall and quietly placed it beside the bed. My legs carried me around and seated me before I collapsed.

Her cheek made a small movement, and she swallowed.

I was as quiet as I'd been in the jungles of Vietnam.

She settled against her pillow, and I studied her.

My God, she was beautiful.

I don't know how long I sat there watching her. I could feel myself nodding off and even went so far as to rest my elbow on the bed, cupping my chin in my hand and studying her some more.

The noise from the ball game reached a distant crescendo and then subsided—the Dogies must be putting a pasting on the Warriors. I thought about what Henry Standing Bear had said when I asked if he thought that those early times in our youth had been simpler. He'd said no, but then had added—but we were.

The crowd roared again, and I opened the white cardboard box and carefully removed the dyed chrysanthemums, tied together with ribbons. I breathed in the scent of her along with that of the black-and-orange corsage that I carefully placed on the pillow beside her head.